CHAPTER 1

In amongst a sea of events and names that have been forgotten, there are a number of episodes that float with striking buoyancy to the surface. There is no sensible order to them, nor connection between them. He keeps his eye on the ground below him, strange since once he would have turned his attention to the horizon or the sky above, relishing the sheer size of it all. Now he seeks out miniatures with the hope of finding comfort in them: the buildings three thousand feet below, the moors so black and flat that they defy perspective, the prison and grounds, men running in ellipses around a track, the stain of suburbia.

The pilot shouts something and points to the right. In the distance a wood is being felled and they can see a tree lean and crash, then another, like matches.

'Surreal from here!' the pilot shouts.

'Yes,' he replies. 'Quail Woods. Falling.'

He leans forward and touches the shoulder of the pilot without knowing what he means by the gesture. A sense of grounding perhaps – he wishes to be back on the ground, and feels nauseous, and a little afraid. In any case the pilot must mistake his hand for a flapping neck scarf or even a bird gone off course, because he doesn't turn.

'My son!' he shouts. 'Down there, in the prison!'

The pilot nods and puts his thumb up; maybe he has not understood.

'I built that prison, the new part, back in the Sixties,' he calls into the wind.

'Yes,' the pilot returns. 'It's awful, I agree. Blight on the landscape.'

He leans as far out as he dare. Can he see his son? Can they see one another? He eyes with dim envy the mechanical, antlike grace of the men running round and round. That one is Henry. No, he is mistaken. That one, perhaps. That one? Impossible to tell, he decides. They are all thin from here, and besides, the wind blurs his vision. The prison is sliding behind them now as the pilot turns east and a limb of shoreline comes into view.

'My son went mad,' he shouts to the pilot. He wants to clear up this point straight away, given that the world has more sympathy with the madman than it does the criminal. 'For a while, after his mother died,' he qualifies. After all, the world has a short attention span even for madmen.

The pilot's word of reply is whipped away by the wind. It sounded a little like 'no', as if the wind itself, the very atmosphere, has simply disagreed with him.

To steady his lilting mind, he focuses on the

The Wilderness

Samantha Harvey

W F HOWES LTD

This large print edition published in 2009 by
W F Howes Ltd
Unit 4, Rearsby Business Park, Gaddesby Lane,
Rearsby, Leicester LE7 4YH

1 3 5 7 9 10 8 6 4 2

First published in the United Kingdom in 2009
by Jonathan Cape

A CIP catalogue record for this book is available
from the British Library

ISBN 978 1 40743 737 8

Typeset by Palimpsest Book Production Limited,
Grangemouth, Stirlingshire
Printed and bound in Great Britain
by MPG Books Ltd, Bodmin, Cornwall

FSC
Mixed Sources
Product group from well-managed
forests and other controlled sources
Cert no. SGS-COC-2953
www.fsc.org
© 1996 Forest Stewardship Council

pilot's thick neck and the roll of collar, wondering what that material is called. It isn't leather, but something like leather, and quite a common thing, the sort of thing he should know. The sort of thing he used to know. Gingerly he touches it and then pulls away, clasps his hands together and brings them to his chin. He closes his eyes and feels a slight churning in his stomach; if only they could go slower, or down.

Now he casts his thoughts out for Henry and all he gets is the usual clamour of data. Henry, after Helen's death, running across the field behind the Coach House with a carving knife, following the wing lights of a plane, shouting, 'There is God, you holy bastard, come back!' Some might say this is not a happy memory, but he would object that it is not the happiness of a memory that he is looking for, it is the memory itself; the taste and touch of it, and the proof it brings of himself. He reaches forward again in an attempt to attract the pilot's attention.

'Down soon?' he manages.

Another thumbs-up from the pilot, and a turn deeper into that mass of sky that seams with the sea, where everything is unmanageably large and wonderful, everything is *excessive*, he thinks. He consoles himself with confining thoughts of the prison, its four T-shaped wings and cramped cells.

They sail on; if he had more choice he would panic. As it is, where the engine's roar deafens him and the wind whips his limbs neatly into his body, he finds himself compressed into an involuntary composure, pinned back and down into his thoughts. At this moment there is just the image of Henry running manically across the field after that plane – the memory as vivid and isolated as a night landscape brought up sharply by a bolt of lightning – and then a converse image of Henry, sometime later after a period in hospital and drugs that made his hair fall out, tying on the apron Helen had once bought him and beginning a long, sleepy bout of baking: his specialities were *hamantaschen* and almond cakes from his grandmother's handwritten Jewish cookery book. The house smelt of hot sugar for weeks.

There is something about this utter deflation of his son that irks him more deeply than any other run of events, so that he can see him in ever-decreasing magnitudes, like an object receding.

The prison comes briefly into view again over the edge of the plane, then disappears. He closes his eyes. Some time ago, after the madness, Henry broke into three houses along his own street in the middle of the day trying to find either alcohol, or money to spend on alcohol, or something to sell to make money to spend on alcohol. It was such an inept attempt at crime – in one of the houses the occupiers were sitting having lunch – that Henry was caught and sentenced to community service, which he didn't do because he was always too drunk to turn up.

He told the courts that he was likely to repeat

4

his crime, not because he thought it was the right thing to do, but because he liked drinking and drink made him irresponsible. So then he was sentenced to prison and enforced sobriety; Henry accepted this with good grace and what looked almost like relief. Yes, he remembers the expression on his son's face – a short smile, a heavenward look as if to Helen, and then a comment: *my dad built that prison, it'll be just like going home.*

The crime was trivial, hapless and alcoholic, the downward spiral of it mapped loosely in his son's appearance. All his life Henry had been blessed with a plume of hair around his face, a plump – but not fat – figure, soft, mollusc features, a gentle height like that of a large leaf-munching animal, long eyelashes. He was pretty, his mother often said. But now he is hairless, thin. His eyes are still dark and bright, and he is still attractive if only one can get past the luckless look, but there it is – lucklessness is a kind of leprosy. You can't get past it.

Perhaps he does not want to see his son after all. The way the plane hangs and lolls on the air unanchored only seems to shake the giddied mind more, jumbling two names in his thoughts: Henry, Helen, Helen, Henry. Similar names – he sometimes confuses them. What if he one day forgets them completely? Then what?

Below them a bird flies, two or three birds. Far below that cars pass lazily along a road. The precariousness of his position is not lost on him, and the fear will not shake. He forces his mind down into the steep cleft of memory that always provides such comfort: him and Helen sailing along the beautiful flow of an American road on their honeymoon. A brown car, one shallow cloud in a deep sky.

But then very crudely and inexpertly the footage cuts to what he recognises as the beginning of a cruel montage of his wife's life, selected for tantamount pain and anguish. At first she appears in a languid sort of flash (persisting long enough to make the point without allowing the point to be explored); she is slumped at the kitchen table. It is that very particular slump strange with silence, the conspicuous lack of breathing. Oh yes, and the ring finger extended on the melamine tabletop as if severed from the hand, just, one must understand, for dramatic effect.

He forces his mind back to the brown car, and the cloud that seemed to follow them. Hours and hours like this, him and her, side by side and separated only by a handbrake, wondering why life had thrown them together. In the memory they see in unison with one pair of eyes, they eat, drink and feel the same things without knowing each other at all. The only time their attention divides is when they make love and his eyes are to the pillow and hers to the ceiling. Even then some curious and serendipitous force nudges a sperm towards an egg and the creation of a new pair of eyes begins, new shared eyes.

Who knows if this is love; it might as well be, it has the ingredients.

Then they are at the Allegheny County Courthouse. Helen stands on its Venetian Bridge of Sighs, eyes closed, freckled eyelids flickering as thoughts pass behind them. On one side of the bridge, he remarks, is the courthouse: here are the free and the godly, those who pass judgment. On the other side is the jail: the imprisoned, those who have been judged. The Bridge of Sighs is a moral structure, and he, as an architect, is becoming interested in just this: the morality, the honesty of a building. And his wife opens her eyes, shakes her head and tells him that a Bridge of Sighs is no more about morality than is a bridge between motorway service stations. She warns him gently: one should hesitate to cast aspersions. A person's morality is usually a two-way journey – it just depends which leg of it you catch them on.

He takes her hand; they are not on the same wavelength. Never; she is always a frequency above him, and as if to prove the fact he is about to begin humming out the Buddy Holly in his head when she starts quoting something from Song of Songs, chapter five. *My beloved's eyes are as the eyes of doves by the rivers of water, washed with milk* – then tells him that she believes she is pregnant.

He picks her up and spins her around, conscious that this is precisely what a man must do for his wife when confronted with such news. Does he feel joy? It might as well be joy, the buzz and panic

7

of it, and the sickly feeling that he is falling into something that has no clear bottom. Then her spinning feet smash an empty bottle left on the ground, at which she struggles free of him and bends to pick up the pieces. He crouches to help.

'Jake,' she says. 'We'll call the baby Jacob, after you.'

But he disagrees, having never seen the point of fathers and sons sharing names when there are so many names to choose from, and as an alternative he suggests something else, he doesn't remember now what.

'Henry, then,' Helen says. 'We'll call him Henry.'

'What if he's not a boy?'

'He is, I dreamt it.'

It is not that these surfacing memories just come. No, he casts around for them even when not exactly conscious of it, he forces himself into them and wears valleys through them. He plays games trying to connect them and establish a continuity of time. If it was their honeymoon they were newly married: this is what honeymoon means, a holiday for the newly married. He can nod in satisfaction about the clarity of this knowledge and can then move on. His wife was called Helen. If it was their honeymoon they were young, and he had completed his training, and Henry was conceived.

Here again is Helen, her bare shoulder beneath him and her hips sharp against his; she was only twenty then. They are in bed, then in the car. There is a handbrake between them; she lays her

8

left hand on it idly and he can see the ring finger, calm and static against the rush of road.

The news on the car's transistor radio reports that a monkey has just come back alive from a space mission, and images have been captured from the spacecraft. Inside Helen's womb Henry is a solitary blinking eye. Helen says that flight is the most excellent invention and that, through photographs, it will allow the earth to see itself from outer space.

'If nothing else,' she tucks her hair behind her ear, 'mankind's existence is utterly justified by this gift it will give to earth, the gift of sight, a sort of consciousness. Do you understand me?'

'No,' he contests after a pause. 'Not really. But it sounds thoughtful.'

Buddy Holly is still possessing his mind, and the tin-can voices from the radio (the word monkey sounding so strange and primal in that modern car on those wide roads). There is a sense of continued but happy absurdity at the way, with all the millions of people in the world, he is now Helen's and she his.

The pilot turns the biplane to the left and the airfield comes into view. 'We're going to begin our descent,' he shouts, pointing downward.

Very well, he thinks, staring again at the man's collar. The plane seems to pull back slightly and slow. Even up here, unhinged and feeling like a puppet swinging from a string, he finds the reserves to worry over the loss of that word. Leather? No, not leather. But something like leather. The word *skein* comes to mind but he knows that isn't right, skein is just a word dumped in his brain from nowhere; a skein of wild swans, a skein of yarn. It is not about forgetting, it is about losing and never getting back – first this leather word and then the rest, all of them.

The moors spread ahead of them, and behind them Quail Woods is being disassembled tree by tree. One must be careful, he thinks as he turns from the man's back and strains to see the land below, not to become too attached to what is gone, and to appreciate instead what is there. He eyes the small neat grids of houses below and finds, as he always has, that these spillages of humanity are not to be scorned for their invasion of nature but are to be accepted, loved even; he names some of the streets in his head and maps the area with compass points and landmarks, his hands now clasped to his knees.

At the point at which he expects the plane to descend, the pilot suddenly turns its nose upwards to the empty blue sky. 'One last dance!' he shouts. The wind rips through the cockpit as they change direction and the prison appears way down below at a tilt, as if sliding off the surface of the earth. Looking down briefly he sees, perhaps, a figure waving. Henry said he would look out for him and wave. He lifts his arm in response, less edgy now and more exhilarated by the air smashing against them and the disorientation as the plane lists and the scenery changes faster than the mind can map it.

They make a large, noisy loop. He feels sick and young, thinking abruptly of Joy in her yellow dress and blinking to find the vision gone. Joy, joy! *Nakhes*, as his mother would once have said when she still allowed herself some Yiddish. His mother would have loved Joy; would always have thought he made the wrong choice. He sits back and looks up, for the first time, to the sky.

As the plane slows it descends, too sharply. And with the slowing comes fear. He looks at his watch. For a moment he fails to understand what the watch hands are doing, where they are going or what for. He studies them like a child. Twenty to three, twenty to four, something like this. I have been unwell, he means to say to the pilot, as if to imply to himself: I am no longer unwell. It is impossible to accept that you will never be well again, and everything you have will be lost. A man is not programmed to think this way, he will always seek out the next corner and look around it in expectation that something, *something*, will be there.

He has been told not to think about it, and his son buys him a half-hour flight for his birthday so he can block it all from his mind. 'What?' he says. 'My birthday?' 'No,' his son corrects. 'Your – problems.' And he kisses him, all his plain, unscented good looks released from their mis-fortune for that one moment in that one simple

11

exchange. Henry no longer has to stand on tiptoes to reach his cheek. How old is Henry, he wonders, and for that matter how old is he? When is his birthday? What year? He can't remember at all.

He thinks of Helen tucking her hair behind her ear and reading from the Song of Songs. *My beloved's eyes are washed with milk* – and her feet smashing glass, and her picking at fish and chips in newspaper wrappings while she read the news. Monkey goes into space. Mother's milk gives baby brain damage. Israel attacks Egypt. Dog goes into space. Twenty thousand jobs cut at the steelworks. Monkey goes into space. Brain damage. Her picking at batter with her skinny fingers and then flattening out the newspaper saying, 'I'll keep this, this is important,' and him screwing it into a ball and throwing it in the bin. 'It smells,' he would say, 'and besides, tomorrow there will be more news.'

The plane drops towards the airstrip and he heaves a sigh of relief, recognising in the slow-down of the engine, the lengthening of its chugs, a familiar creeping desire to be getting home.

STORY OF THE HUMAN-SKIN BIBLE

It was the end of 1960 when his father was buried. He walked through Quail Woods with his mother who divulged no, or little, emotion. Sometimes she sighed or said 'asch', as if arguing against something in her head; sometimes she sneezed at the lily scent in her nose, sometimes she squeezed his arm and then, as he turned to console her, dropped it as if playing a game with him.

Some way along the wide track she stopped, knelt, and took a flask of coffee and two china cups from her bag. They were her best cups as usual, their gold rims slightly chipped. She poured two half measures, unwrapped sugar cubes from a napkin which she dropped in neatly, and handed him his drink.

'Thank you,' he said.

'To Henry,' she offered, raising her cup. 'For bringing the future when we most need it.'

'To Henry. And to Father.'

'And to us. Is it appropriate for me to be drinking a toast on the day my husband is buried?'

'In healthier cultures death is a celebration, Sara.'

13

'Ah yes, so it is. Perhaps we should offer the trees a dance.' She proffered her cup towards a tree and gave a bow. 'May I have this dance? No? You're feeling under the weather? Well, trees, we are all under the weather! Ha!' She spread her arms and looked up. 'All of us under the weather!'

He took his mother's arm and pulled her gently towards him. 'Tell me, what do you think of Helen?'

'She is too sincere for you,' she said after a short pause.

'Sincere?'

'You will become bored of her, just as I became bored of your father.'

'But Sara.' He was a little shocked. 'You gave him so much of yourself, you gave *up* so much of yourself.'

'As one has to, Jake, when one is bored. Give, give – you hope in all the giving that they will give back and then you wager, well, if they don't, at least you will both have nothing left to give. At last you will be equal. Your father and I were very equal by the time he died.'

He frowned. 'A terrible philosophy –'

'I loved him,' she said, as if sealing the debate. 'He was a friend. So there you have it.'

The edges of the woods were visible from this central path, and beyond them ploughed fields. In the car, on the roadside where the trees abruptly ceased, Helen would be waiting for them, leaning back against the new leather as she breastfed.

Today had been the first time Sara and Helen had met; it had been brief and cursory with all focus on the baby. They had each agreed that Henry was beautiful; they had reached a broad consensus about the way a baby's face is so general, made to a recipe of unbearable dearness, and Sara had added something about the way the dearness is at some point lost in a spurt of growth and features. She and Helen had looked at him and laughed as if to suggest that he was the living example of this loss. He had touched his own face self-consciously. In fact he was good-looking and they all knew it, and an appreciative silence followed as they all considered, he was sure, how very similar he and his son already were, how alike in mannerisms, especially the comic way Henry, only weeks old, held his hands thoughtfully to his chin.

All in all he thought the meeting between his wife and mother had gone well. It was a short encounter, yes, but Sara did not like first-time meetings to last long, even intimate ones like these. She liked to look, as if deciding whether she would buy, and she liked to go away and think before she said anything she might not mean. She had looked long at his new wife and baby, bowed, and said quietly, 'A privilege to meet you.' He had thought, perhaps, that she meant it.

'Is sincerity not a good thing, Sara?' he asked, throwing out the gritty dregs of the coffee.

'I said she was too sincere. Too much of anything

15

is tiresome, she will push you to acts of goodness that don't suit you very well. You are my child, I want you to be what you are and not what a pretty girl from the suburbs wants you to be.' She shrugged, and in her black mourning dress took measured steps, one two – three four, one two – three four. 'I have something for you,' she added.

As she crouched again, digging into her bag, he thought of how she was, or had become, a thousand acts of goodness herself, straitjacketing herself into Englishness, cooking the food his father liked, dispensing with the excess sugar and fat, shearing off her mother tongue, evicting her past, funnelling, tapering. Goodness could be a narrow state; perhaps she was right.

'How is Rook?' he asked as he waited.

'Rook? Oh, Rook is fine, of course.'

'And?'

She glanced up. 'And?'

He leaned back against a tree and turned his cup in his hand. 'Perhaps you could marry him.'

'We go driving together sometimes,' she said, looking away. 'We drive out to the coast to check if Europe is still there. We've checked across the sea so many times, we have never yet seen it, but we assume it must still be there. So we eat saveloys and wave at it. Hallo Europe, we say, nice to not see you. We are altogether *senile,* at least Rook is. I pretend, huh, to keep him company.'

'So is that a yes, or a no?'

'Jacob.'

'Mama.'

'You know I don't like to be called Mama.'

'Nor I Jacob.'

'Well then, aren't we both rebellious.'

By now she had abandoned her search in the bag. She slouched forward as elderly women generally do not, certainly as she generally did not, and gazed ahead blankly. Then, as if awakening, she took a shoe box from her bag that could not possibly have taken her all that time to find, and stood.

'Here,' she said, and smoothed her hair; it was still remarkably dark between the grey strands, and glossy.

He put the empty cup in his pocket. When he opened the box he found a bible. It was old, the leather weakened to the feel of silk under his fingers. They had stopped walking by now, and he knelt on one knee, his mother lingering above him. Then she crouched and put her head close to his; her hair smelt of lilies.

'It belonged to my parents,' she said. 'Why don't you have it, now that you're married to a religious woman? It's my gift to you both, maybe a wedding gift since you just ran away and married in secret.'

'Sara –'

'No, I'm not angry, I'm happy you did it that way. Too much song and dance the other way, too much money.'

He nodded, a little underwhelmed by the gift – touched and even excited that it was from his

17

grandparents, but without any wish to own a bible. The samovar perhaps, the praise ring his grandmother had used, the objects of charm and intrigue that belonged to an estranged world. But a bible? Was his mother mocking him?

'Helen will like it,' he said eventually, deciding to find in his mother's gesture some attempt at friendship with his wife.

'I doubt it, the cover is human skin,' she said. 'She may be too sincere for human-skin bibles. But you don't have to tell her.'

He coughed. Involuntarily his fingers danced across the leather, not wishing to rest anywhere. He eyed his mother then, assessing her, trying to show that he was not thrown by her games.

'My parents kept the bible out of rebellion,' she said, conceding to explanation. 'My father bought it for his bookshop – bibles sold very well in those days, people were afraid the world would end if they didn't pray hard enough. Then he discovered how it was bound and he kept it, as a rebellion against all this madness, this Catholic madness and hysteria. He thought it – how can I say it – belittled the Catholics, to have their precious holy bible bound with a precious holy human. Jews do not believe they are the only creatures that matter. Catholics not only believe it, they know it as a fact. He wanted to mock them. He had a dry humour.'

'I see,' he said, recollecting the photograph of his grandparents that lived on the dresser in Sara's living room. The picture showed a large, elegant and nervous-looking middle-aged man, standing next to a thin broad-grinning woman. He remembered how Sara polished the image with a flourish, saying, *Here, my father*, as if all history gathered up its skirts and kneeled at the foot of this man.

'I'll keep it for myself,' he said.

'It's very valuable.'

'I'll keep it. I won't give it away to Helen. You say I'll give myself away to her but here it is – here is me not giving anything.'

Here is me being your child, he thought to say. He put the box under his arm and began walking. The road was close; he could see the back end of the Mini parked up in the lay-by.

Sara laughed lightly. 'It is hardly that simple. The most important things are given without even knowing. We have a very strong tendency to give exactly what we can't afford, Jake, that's why I warn you. I sound morbid, but what sort of mother would I be if I didn't tell you the one thing I know.'

Just before they reached the car he put his hand on Sara's shoulder.

'Do you know,' he said to his mother, 'I think Helen and I will move back.'

He said it before he thought it, in fact he said it *hours* before he thought it, so that he was in the freefall of inebriated, unplanned speech. 'Helen would grow to like it here, she's already introduced herself at the church, perhaps I can do good things.'

He waited for her response, but none came.

19

She watched him with what he could only summarise as politeness.

'What is there here after all,' he went on, 'except moors and more moors? Peat and more peat. We need buildings, community buildings, facilities, places to swim, new schools. I see they're planning to extend the prison, that's a big project, to think how to contain people and at the same time how to re-educate them —'

'And punish them, I hope.'

'Punishment isn't the point of prisons.'

'If you say.'

He was always surprised by Sara's staunch view of things. He always fell into the misconception that a member of an ill-treated race will naturally be for freedom, naturally against bindings in human skin, naturally sickened by all that demeaned and failed to enlighten.

'Everything is falling into apathy here,' he said. 'And London has enough architects. It won't miss me. I feel like a child there, no, an orphan, a boy playing with building blocks.'

Sara stopped at the entrance to the woods and put her hand on the trunk of a tree. It was all pines here, pines and larches and that sharp clean smell of a place without history. He liked the flat sterility of it, and the idea that his home was something quite banal, quite blank, whose history was yet to be made, or never to be made. A place that was not sodden with sentiment. A place that was just coming alive with industry and gathering a population and looking ahead to a future it had no precedent for.

'Are you contemplating another dance?' he asked his mother, who stood at the tree in silence.

'My husband,' she rasped, sinking slightly. She was sobbing completely without sound. 'Shit,' she said. '*Shit.*'

He went to embrace her, comforted by her sudden sadness. She straightened and pushed him gently away. She wiped her red eyes dry. 'I am happy, Jake, that you're moving home,' she said then. 'It will make a nice place for a child.'

From here he could see Helen sitting in the back seat of the car, the door open, tucking her breast into the black sweater while the baby slept on her lap. A nipple vanishing into mourning clothes and her legs bent stiffly against the front seat. Hurriedly he shrugged himself out of his coat and wrapped the bible in it so his wife wouldn't see, and he wedged it in the back on the floor. They took their places in the car and he turned to his wife and the baby, leaned to them, made a noise like a pigeon, a low coo. The car smelt of milk and of dirty laundry shoved into bags. Together the four of them drove in near silence to Sara's home, with only the occasional comment from Helen – *the baby's watching you drive, Jake, look at that kestrel* (he contested, it's a buzzard, not a kestrel, they're very different), *what's growing in that field, is that the sea, over there?* She looked afraid, he thought.

Mama, he kept wanting to say, with nothing to

follow it. Mama. He called her Mama because it annoyed her – not because he *wanted* to annoy her, but because he had, he found, a marvellously perverse capacity for accidentally doing the very things she hated. And she had the marvellously perverse capacity to appear to love him more when he did something she hated.

He observed the mammoth clouds and steel sky, the open stretch of moors and the patches of mutilation where the peat was being extracted. The corners of his mouth kicked into a brief smile. Mama, he wanted to say as he turned to her in the passenger seat and saw a streak of yellow along the black of her hair. Mother, the lily has stained your hair. But he said nothing; leave it there, leave her to be ridiculous.

Eventually he had to fold his hands tight around the steering wheel so as to avoid reaching across and dusting it off. He could only conclude that not all relationships were simple.

Sara put the key in the lock and edged her way indoors. During coffee and then supper he weighed up whether he could broach the subject of the future. It was on his mind to ask her if she would go back to Austria; it would be an insensitive and hurried question but he felt he must ask; suddenly he felt he must know the layout of their futures. On the verge of his asking, as they were picking at a plate of biscuits, Sara eyed him and gave a low, short chuckle.

'I've forgotten the language,' she said. 'My own language. To think, I couldn't go back if I wanted to.'

'You haven't forgotten the language,' he said quickly. He had heard her that morning talking to herself in German while she put on her black dress and grey shoes, slotting the lily into her hair even despite his insistence that this was not custom, to wear flowers in the hair at funerals.

'I have. Every word of it.'

'But Sara –'

'Another biscuit?'

They all shook their heads.

He watched her closely for the rest of the evening. Of course she would not go back; her friends were dead, how could she bear the guilt of not being dead herself? She lived in a distinctly British house in, save for a few Austrian ornaments and pieces of crockery, a distinctly British way. Built between the wars, the house itself was the consciousness of Britain, the glass at its entrance stained with the bright painted colours of a galleon sailing into victory after the First World War, and every man, woman or child within those walls a sailor by extension, and a victor.

Of course she would not go back, and he did not want her to, but that evening he began to carry with him a frustration, that of a story unfinished. As a child there had always been myths and tales about *home*, and he had assumed that one day this word *home* would stop referring to something merely imaginable and begin to be real, and Sara would go back and reclaim herself, and he would reclaim the lost half of himself, and the story would be complete. Now of course, that place called home had been deftly swapped for somewhere else: this. There wasn't another half of himself. He deposited lilies into vases and let them crowd the dining table. He must accept it.

The evening wore on quietly. They listened to the radio and Helen disappeared upstairs for an hour or so with the baby. He thought of the bible and wondered what Sara had meant by the gift. Its beauty and relevance had grown in his mind; knowing that it was bound in human skin, knowing it was not, therefore, what it first seemed to be, and knowing that its cover contradicted its contents (for nowhere in the Bible could it say, *And their skins shall be stretched for leather*). He noted in himself, not for the first time, a liking for the perverse. He thought tenderly of how he might attach a building of clean prefabricated concrete to that excellent gothic manor that currently housed the prison and how out of keeping that would be, what a clash of ideals. How *iconoclastic* – a word he had learned well at university. He thought of his father's grave and which parts of his father's person would survive longest in this acidic Lincolnshire soil. Would he still fart for a few days in that coffin, still excrete fluids? How long would it take his polished leather shoes to decompose?

'What's that?' Helen asked as they readied themselves for bed that night. She struggled to pull her sweater over her head; he assisted.

'It's a present from Sara.' He threw the sweater over the shoe box.

'For you?'

He hesitated. 'Yes.'

'What is it?'

'I'll show you another time, it's personal.'

'Personal?' Helen queried, bending over a whimpering Henry in his pram. 'I'm your wife. What could be more personal than that?'

He stripped down to his underpants and climbed into the single bed. The spare room was not big enough for a double bed; there was a larger spare room but, against everything Sara stood for as a person, it was full from floor to ceiling with a lifetime of his father's junk. It would always be that way, he supposed. Sara would not suddenly defend her values against the man now, not after all this time.

'Come to bed,' he replied. 'I need you here, it's been a long day.'

She came. They made love quietly so that Sara wouldn't hear. Afterwards, while she slept, he thought intensely of hiding the bible from her as if it had become the very cornerstone of his independence. Perhaps it was the morose headiness of the day that left him so obsessed with the idea. In his grave, his father clung vehemently to his patent shoes and his pocket watch. Downstairs Sara clung similarly to her chipped coffee cups. Everybody needs a thing that is their own, he decided. Momentarily he was afraid of giving, feeling himself, as a man, to be a one-way river running into the sea of his wife, impregnating her so she could grow but not ever growing himself. To already be thinking these things, after less than a year of marriage! These were morbid night-time thoughts; in the morning he would be more cheerful.

At some point in the night he awoke to Henry's crying, then he slept. When he woke up again he discovered that the baby was sleeping belly down on Helen's chest. With all three of them in bed he couldn't sleep for fear that he would crush them both, and so he lay sweating in a pole-like stance all night thinking of the future. Against that thought he considered the monstrous tower block he was building in London. They had run out of money and stuffed its joints with newspaper; newspaper was a useless building material. There had been controversy about it and he had fought to prevent these ridiculous desperate measures, but had not succeeded. One day the whole block would fall down. He did not want to be there to see it.

In the morning he told Helen, 'We will move, leave London, we will get our things and come back.'

The day after that, before returning to London, he drove Helen and the baby out across the peat moors.

'I want to show you where I was brought up, maybe it will give you an insight,' he told his wife.

'I don't need an insight into you, Jake, you're an open book.'

He laughed and tapped the wheel. 'Only someone who needed an insight into me could think that.'

They drove along the straight, empty lanes that were laid out in a grid across the peat, Helen looking out of the window, astonished still at this landscape that was not London, nor like any countryside she had seen. She was full of questions which she asked with a sceptical note. What are those? Dykes? What's a dyke? This used to be an island? Will we sink, Jake, if we stay here long enough will it be an island again?

That morning, as they were packing the car, he had declared that they should come here to live. He told her. Had he asked she would have said no. No, passionately, definitely. And he knew he would not have been able to handle or manipulate those words, nor change her opinion. It was better, then, to cut off the possibility of objection and deal instead with the flurry of questions that would come. They had been coming all day, and all day he cured them with answers. Yes, there will be plenty of work, of course we can visit London, your parents, our friends. No, darling, we won't sink, we'll take root. Yes, we'll be happy, you'll be happy. I wouldn't do anything to make you unhappy.

She was afraid of moving to this odd, backward and (she hesitated over the word, then almost whispered it) *uncivilised* place. She said she could see too far. The great hourglass cooling towers were monstrous to her and the steelworks, though way in the distance, hummed like something at breaking point.

'What's the flame?' she asked rather fearfully, pointing to a chimney on the horizon from which a blue flame bellowed.

'Waste gas. Like an Olympic flame,' he replied, leaning across the handbrake to pat her leg, trying to cheer her up. She liked to watch athletics, she liked the speed, height and distance people could go for no reason but to go fast, high or far.

'Did you see it?' she asked, successfully distracted. 'The four-minute mile? I was with my daddy, we went to the cinema to see it, we had – oh, what do you call them? Those sweets with the mint inside and chocolate out.'

Yes, he saw it, the sinewy man stretching himself against the clock, and wondered, is this the best men can do?

'If a man could run as fast as an ant, for his size,' he responded, 'he would be as fast as a racehorse.'

'But that's irrelevant, he's not an ant. He doesn't need to be as fast as an ant.'

'All the same. You'll be happy here. I feel it.'

Their tour passed Rook's house, a bewilderingly out-of-place Italian Renaissance-style place painted in faded orange and dusk pinks, muraled walls showing cherubs, and an overgrown walled garden accessed through wrought-iron gates. The absurdity of its opulence, albeit aged and faded opulence, against these humdrum flatlands made it all the more astonishing. Helen held her hands to the car window. 'I love Rook,' she said. 'I love him for living there.'

'Rook loves himself for living there,' he commented.

He had never travelled the moors in a car before. Their blackness was unforgiving through a car window, without the fresh air to take the edge off it, with the flowers too small to see. He understood Helen's fear, and conversely her enchantment at the interruption Rook's house provided. She stared from the window as the scenery passed.

'Is *that* a kestrel?' she asked.

'No,' he replied. 'It's a buzzard. I mean it, they're very different.'

Then, further along, The Sun Rises appeared. He was genuinely taken aback. He had forgotten about it. If nothing else, life in London offered enough pubs and bars to never have to consider one solitary pub in the middle of some moors two hundred miles distant. And yet he had been here so many times; Sara had cooked her Jewish food here back when she still did such things. They had drunk – he was underage, nobody on earth cared. Sara had decorated the toilets with paintings of mermaids and slogans in German: *man ist was man isst.* You are what you eat. It was one of the few German phrases he knew. Rook had sat at the bar with a rope of sunlight falling around his neck, eating mussels, too drunk to speak, eyeing Sara with an unreadable expression. Love, possibly. Lust, or pity, or just drunkenness. Sara had lost all her relatives, her parents included, in the war. She was unsure of herself, wondering how to cook all the potatoes they had – as Jewish latkes or as English mash. Deciding who to be, where her allegiance lay. The Sun Rises had been a small pocket of belonging and energy in a sluggish time. How could he have cast it so easily from his mind? How strange, then, was memory – that a whole interval of one's life could be blotted out like the sun behind the moon, and then emerge again so intact!

In front of the pub he saw a woman. He knew immediately that it was Eleanor. She wore a turquoise dress patterned with blue flowers that fit her little better than a curtain; she wore a pair of Wellington boots. She seemed, as far as he could see, to be watering the bedding plants to the front of the pub although it had rained the previous night.

He sounded the horn and waved. For a time she looked up bemused, then waved back, then made gestures of annoyance that he had not stopped. There'll be plenty of time, he thought. He said it aloud to his wife. 'There'll be plenty of time to meet Eleanor.'

'The *e* is missing,' Helen said, pointing back at

the sign that swung above the door. It read, on the background of a faded hilly landscape, *The Sun Ris s.* 'It needs painting back on, somebody should do that.'

He smiled, watching Eleanor shrink in the rear-view mirror. They struck their way across the moors, past field upon field of beetroot and pota-toes, and at last reached the new tarmac corridor of the M1, his foot pressed onto the accelerator, and Helen fast asleep. They got home late, went to bed, got up, he went to work. When he left Helen was reading her bible at the kitchen table, her head dipped deeply, turning her wedding ring round and around her finger. That afternoon he handed his notice in. A month later they were packing their three cases and trying them out this way and that until they fit in the back of the Mini.

CHAPTER 2

Driving to work, he falls into the illusion for a moment that he is still in that Mini; the car shrinks to oblige the mistake. He misjudges the position of the gear stick in the thought that it is far closer to his leg, and his head and shoulders are stooped as they always used to be under the Mini's low roof. What frightens him is this – the way objects rush and trip over themselves to support his confusion. He looks around his car and tries to remember what make it is; he cannot. He opens the window to feel what month it is. It isn't a month. There aren't months. There are just happenings, a lack of signposts.

Why this *e*? Why this missing *e*? He laughs at himself. The brain stores billions of memories and some are obvious, of course – it is obvious that he will remember his honeymoon and his suitcases and his pilgrimage (this is how he thinks of it now), his pilgrimage back home. And Henry. Granted, some of the details are imagined or inflated or borrowed from other times, but the essence, as part of the story of himself, is undeniably right. But the missing *e*? It is with a struggle that he remembers what he did this morning, or how long ago it was that Helen died, and yet he recalls her saying those words: *the e is missing, it needs painting back on, somebody should do that.*

He pulls up at the side of the road, lifts his glasses and rubs his eyes. He has been doing this journey to and from work every day for thirty-five years. He pores over the map.

One day he arrived home from work, it was a Tuesday or a Wednesday, or a Monday. Helen was in the kitchen carving through salmon fillets while oblongs of sunlight fell in on her hands.

'They're old.' She put the knife down and spread her fingers. 'Are they really my hands?'

He stood by her side, picked up the knife, and folded her fingers around the handle. He kissed her neck, a neutral and warm contact but nothing more, and she tucked her hair behind her ear.

In response to these worries that she was getting old there was nothing more to say; he had said it all. You're beautiful, he had previously ventured (and meant it, she was more beautiful now, in the details, in the stories of the lines, than before). She had shaken her head and simply disagreed. We all get old, he had tried: to no avail. Me faster than most, she had replied. He had shaken his head, she had shaken hers back. Once or twice he had offered, Helen you're not getting old, and they had ended up smiling ruefully at the whiteness of the lie.

'It's like being injured,' she said, and rested the knife blade on the salmon. 'Suddenly I feel injured by the years, like I've been in a car crash.'

'What is this, Helen? You have to stop. You're fifty-three, it's not old.'

'I had a dream that you were leaning over a very beautiful bible, here at the table. What does this mean, Jake?' She cut through the flesh once and then again. 'That you're going to find God?' She laughed. 'At last, you're going to find God! And why would you do that?'

The expression she turned to him was unbearably sweet. Disarmed, he shrugged at it.

'I doubt I will, I'm not looking for him. The dream means something else, or nothing. It means you want me to find God. It means I need to, it means anything, nothing.'

She merely shook her head at him.

'I think it means, Jake, that I am not going to be here for very long. You'll be alone – you see, God finds those who are alone and in need.'

'And where are you going?' he asked, feeling querulous. He turned to take a plum from the fruit bowl on the kitchen table and Helen stole it from his hand as he was about to bite it. She sliced the plum in half and scooped out the stone, then passed half back to him.

'Look at this,' she said with a sudden child-like smile, and laid the salmon and the plum side by side. 'One is fruit, one is fish, but the flesh is so similar. This is where I see God, in these – in these consistencies between things.'

Discarding his half of fruit on the table he took the knife from her and held it close to her face. He had not wanted half a plum, he had wanted a whole one; he had not wanted it cut neatly, de-stoned. Certainly he had not wanted to hear her prophesy her own death, and moreover he had not, at the point where he saw her prophesy play before his mind in a stilted and sickening delivery of images, wanted to talk about the artistry of God in lieu, yet again, of a real topic of conversation.

'What is this, Helen? Didn't you once use to ask me about my day, and I yours?'

Her eyes, either side of the blade, blinked rather calmly. 'Yes, and you used to say, Do we have to talk about our days, Helen? It's so *superficial*, talking about days. Can we not just have a coffee and make love instead?'

The asymmetry of her face, divided as it was by the steel blade, captivated him. He had always thought of her as perfectly ordered, prettily symmetrical, delicate and unsurprising. She was, at this moment at least, not. Not delicate – her fearlessness made her formidable. Not pretty – too formidable to be pretty. No symmetry – one ear, he now observed, was higher than the other, one eye slightly wider, one cheekbone more threaded with fine blood vessels.

'Can we make love now?' he asked. He wanted to withdraw the knife, knowing the absurdity of it, but he did not want to restore her to the plainness of perfection quite so soon. He felt an urgent love for her; he thought, he had to admit, of Joy.

'No, not now.' She blinked again and backed away the few inches to the sideboard, and finally he placed the knife down. 'Besides,' she said, 'you didn't meet me to go shopping today.'

'Pardon?'

'I said you didn't meet me to go shopping today.'

He will never forget the way she brought her hands to her hips so as to challenge him not to lie. He did not lie.

'I'm sorry, I completely forgot. Are you punishing me?'

'No, of course not.' She sat at the table and leaned forward on her elbows, her hair crowding behind her ears and her eyebrows arched. 'You forgot last week, you put the coffee in the oven instead of the fridge, you sometimes forget my name.'

'What is this?' he demanded to know. He was angered now by the slipping of the conversation from plums to death to God to this, *this*, whatever this was. An accusation perhaps, though of what he was unsure.

'Can you say anything, Jake, except *what is this?*'

'If you could start making sense, yes, then I could stop asking you to clarify.'

She stood and took a bowl from the table. 'I'm going to pick some cherries.'

Then she walked bare-footed to the French doors, and slipped outside.

After her death he stared into the dark and demanded a ghost. He had read bereavement leaflets that warned gently of the appearance of the deceased, at the foot of the bed, out of the corner of the eye, a smoky presence you might put your fingers through. If such a thing came he was not to be alarmed – no, far from it, he was to be comforted. And so he waited.

Each night he sat in his study and looked through an album of photographs Henry had put together for her memorial. There is one of her on that same day of her death, after she went out into the garden bare-footed, and she is up the ladder in the branches of the cherry tree in her pinafore and shoes and socks that made her look like Alice in Wonderland. The more he sat in his study looking at those photographs, the more he became convinced that if she came back to life and he could ask her just one question, it would be this: when did you put your shoes and socks on?

The question plagued him out of all proportion. Maybe he was wrong about the bare feet. But he was not wrong about the bare feet. He *remembered* it. He would make himself a mint julep and swill it with the troubled concentration of a detective.

After closing the album he always sat back in his seat and replayed this scene: Helen bare-footed in the kitchen on her last day alive, slicing salmon and plums, making mention of his forgetfulness for the first time as if she had been saving this conversation – as if, before dying, she wanted him to know she knew that it was not just a bit of absent-minded ageing but dementia, an illness; that her knowledge of this would go some way to protecting him after she was gone.

This is where I see God, in these – in these consistencies between things, she had said. Did she really say this, or is it just the kind of thing she might have said? Were her feet really bare, or was going bare-footed just the kind of thing she would have done? And in perfecting that scene in the kitchen, has he simply perfected his version of it? And isn't it true to say that the more perfect the memory the less accurate it is likely to be? Like a nativity scene on a Christmas card, rendered so many times it now no longer represents anything of the real birth of Christ.

Dogged by these uncertainties, willing her ghost to come, he rid the house of milk, knowing Helen's near-phobia of it. For months he settled for black coffee and found himself remembering those days, so far back – before Alice's birth – when she did drink it, when she loved it, when her freckled skin itself was like cream dusted with cinnamon, when she would tell him his eyes were washed with milk, and when she loved the cherry blossom that curdled on the branches. But it was not to stay that way, and by the time she died her aversion to it was stronger than any aversion she had to anything; just the smell of it, she would say. Just the *smell* of it. So, in trying to lure back her ghost, he poured the remains of a bottle of milk down the sink and bought no more. She still didn't come. One day it suddenly dawned on him that he was being absurd and he bought a pint, put it in the fridge. Nothing whatsoever changed. The empty drudgery of the days went on regardless.

At night, occasionally, he would go through the photograph album once again and then try to feel the ghost or the delusion. He lay with his teeth gritted as his night-vision, still sharp, interrogated each pixel of darkness in the bedroom. Each pixel gathered with others in a crouch of wardrobe or flow of jacket or a heft of beam; the hand basin and the chrome arm of the record player caught a splinter of moonlight. In there, between there, from there, he calculated, Helen will appear.

There is a story his mother once told him about the murderer Luigi Lucheni. In 1898 Lucheni stabbed the Austrian empress in the heart with a shoemaker's file and killed her. When he went to prison he began raving and went mad, and he spent twelve years this way, in euphoric insanity, until he finally killed himself. In this time his only comfort was the regular visitations, *manifestations*, of the ghost of the beautiful empress. She came wrapped in fur, crouching at his side at dog level; she gave him dog vision. You can call me Elisabeth, she offered generously. She gave him access to the brilliance of sights, smells and sounds that humans perpetually overlook; she stroked him, he her. In whispers she explained how she had come back to the source of the sin that killed her in order to forgive it, to forgive him, and she told him that this close encounter with one's demise was the only way to heal the pain of being dead. The hole in her heart – a concise puncture that barely blemished the white skin of her breast – had begun to glow a little, and cool breezes passed through it. For the first time, she was happy. And he was happy, at last, he was happy.

(As an aside to this story, Sara also mentioned that Lucheni indirectly started the First World War by setting a precedent for the assassination of Austrian royals, which is what spawned the murder of the Archduke Franz Ferdinand fifteen years later, which is what flared the conflict between the Empire and the Serbian assassins, which is when Russia stepped up to defend their Serbian allies, which is when Austria mobilised its army, and Germany theirs in support, and France theirs in opposition, and Britain theirs in support of France's opposition, and so: a war. Sara dipped a wedge of cold potato in her milky coffee and said, *Hey presto* – a phrase she had just learned – *hey presto, Jacob, Elisabeth had a lot to forgive*. And she remained impassive, inexpressive, as if the war had no personal dimension for her.)

He believed, then, that if Lucheni – who had been ugly and craven by all accounts – got

Elisabeth, a ghost of Helen would not be unreasonable in the least. One bereavement leaflet seemed to feel so certain of apparitions that it listed them, as a compensatory effort, against the other possible symptoms of grief: physical pain (in the chest, as if one's heart is cleaved), a sense of injustice, a broiling anger, notions of hopelessness, an intermittent or abnormal appetite, sporadic loss of function in the limbs, extreme fear of, or else longing for, one's own death. And in return, one may see or get the distinct feeling that the loved one is there, at the foot of the bed, or in the bed, or at one's shoulder, a smoky presence. One may put one's fingers through it and feel the soul of the deceased, like moist remnants of dawn in the morning air.

Apart from that short-lived banishment of milk, he has never been a superstitious man; he awaited the presence as anyone would await the next step in a process. The chest pain came, the abnormal appetite, some anger promptly controlled. Confusion. In fact, it was more than this – it was clotting of thoughts, disorientation. A presence was the least a man in his position should now expect; it was not his privilege after all, it was his right.

He bartered with his solitude. The ghost did not have to be an apparition, nor strictly ephemeral, it did not have to bring lasting peace and hope, it could be real and logical, obvious almost, the outcome of a simple sum. It didn't have to creep in the dark, it could be felt in the day if Helen, who was not a night creature, so preferred.

He was open to possibility. After more than thirty years of marriage to a woman whose beliefs fired her every breath he had at least learned, for the sake of good-natured compromise, to be anything but agnostic, agreeing to believe anything in principle. And the more he lived by this compromise the more he found it served his natural attitudes. He would always favour something over nothing. He would always hedge his religious bets, preserving this something as just that, *some* thing, not this specific thing nor that particular thing. Helen would draw him into religious debate and he would, he always felt, evade it deftly by saying, 'Helen, take it up with somebody else – in principle, I don't disagree with you. Maybe there is a god, in principle you're absolutely right, anything is possible.' He meant it, and the integrity was part of what made the argument deft, that for once he was not trying to quell her constant musing by outwitting her but was doing so by being simple and honest.

Being so busy waiting for ghosts, he failed to notice then that the confusion, clotting of thoughts, disorientation, were burrowing deeper than the grief.

He lived by the leaflets. The leaflets said there was the chance of a presence, and on balance and in view of all he had been and was, he felt it was his due. But it did not come.

★　★　★

Entropy: this is the word his brain has been trying to hunt down for days, and suddenly it has arrived in a little whoosh of *eureka*.

Entropy is singularly the most interesting theory that exists, he mumbles to himself, propped in front of his drawing board at the angle, he thinks, of somebody who is always about to do something significant, but never quite does. The office is silent except for a rustling of papers in the other room, and is lit by a spill of light coming from there and outside, and a few desk lights people must have left on before they went home; the darkness stacked into the other areas is surprisingly deep and quiet.

Entropy – the theory that says everything loses, rather than gains, order. A cup of coffee will, with enough time, get cold, but no amount of time will cause it to get hot again. A house can become a mere pile of bricks of its own accord, but a mere pile of bricks will never become a house of its own accord. Everywhere nature's fingers unpick as if trying to leave things as they would be if humans never existed.

He stares at the drawing; it is not his, it was done by one of the junior architects and he has been asked to check it. Thornley Library, front elevation. A simple two-storey building whose only design hurdle is, as ever, the budget; but even so he has been gazing at it all afternoon, his pencil in hand, a stream of coffees getting cold as he tries to remember what it is one is supposed to do.

Should he change the lines somehow (but how?)? Should he put a tick in the corner? Now it is well into the evening and everybody – save for that mystery rustler in the next room – has gone, and he aches with inactivity.

Something makes him look up, and he sees a girl in the doorway to his left.

'Jake, would you like another drink?'

She is tall and familiar, brown cropped hair and a simple, kind face.

'A coffee, please.'

'Are you going to be here all night?'

'I have to deal with this.' He taps the drawing with his pencil.

'Well, I'm going in a few minutes, so you'll be left in peace.' She purses her lips into a smile and puts her hands in the pockets of her trousers.

'I won't be alone, there's somebody in the other room,' he says.

'What? This room?' She gestures behind her with a nod.

'Yes, I heard papers shuffling.'

With a tilt of the head she whispers, 'That was me.'

'Oh, really?'

Confusion passes across him, across his skin. He can feel it these days as a bodily sensation not unlike a rash. He wants to itch at it.

'So, coffee,' she says lightly, and turns.

He leans closer into the drawing board and hovers the pencil. Entropy. A house can become a pile of bricks of its own accord, but a pile of bricks will never become a house. Entropy. The arrow of time, time can only move one way. He taps, taps the pencil on the paper.

When the girl comes back with the coffee he shoves the pencil into his pocket with the accomplished efficiency of a man who is used to having something to hide.

'Here.' She pushes papers aside and puts the mug on his desk. 'What are you working on? Is there a deadline coming up?'

'Yes, yes. It's –' he sweeps the drawing with the palm of his hand and smiles. 'It's not interesting.'

'I'm interested.' She buries her hands in her pockets again as if she too is hiding something. 'I'm an interested secretary. Is that rare?'

'Is it very busy, being a secretary?'

'At times.' She shrugs gently and leaves the subject there.

'And what are you going to do, when you, when you're older?'

She laughs. 'I *am* older.'

'Of course, I'm sorry.'

'I always wanted to be a vet actually.' She sits on the edge of the desk. 'When I was a child I thought I'd be a vet in a monkey rescue centre, because I always had a fascination with monkeys, and I kept sticker books of them to help me learn the different types: chimps, orangutans, gorillas, baboons, macaques, spider monkeys.' She tucks her hair behind her ear in a way that reminds him of Helen. 'There are over a hundred different types. I used to know them all.'

The words peal against the silence of the office, exotic, forgotten; he thinks momentarily of the time in America when the old word monkey came strangely into the new brown car. And he grasps the last of her list: *macaques and spider monkeys*. He feels himself stash them away as if they belong to a world he does not want to lose, and to things which were once important and will be important again.

The girl passes his coffee from the desk. 'But I'm not sure what happened to that plan.'

'Maybe it wasn't ever a real plan, maybe it was just a fancy, an illusion.'

She nods. 'I think you're probably right.'

In the comfortable silence that falls between them he looks back at the drawing and, on an impulse, reaches for a pen on the desk and places a large, firm tick in the bottom right.

The girl glances at her watch and stands. 'Nearly nine o'clock. I'm going to get home. Don't stay too much longer, Jake.'

'In fact I'm going to stop now,' he says.

While he gathers things into his bag (takes them out again, puts them back in, wondering what stays and what goes), the girl turns the lights out around the office. A faint orange glow comes through the windows from the street.

'I'm sorry if I offended you just then,' he says. They leave the office and she locks the door, then they proceed down the corridor. In front of him her narrow shoulders, long back, green bag, stand slightly proud of the darkness, slightly vulnerable, and maybe it is this that makes him feel he has done her an injustice of some kind.

'Offended me in what way?'

'For –' He doesn't know what for. 'For the things I said.'

'About when I'm older?'

He nods hurriedly and makes a sound of assent; maybe this; he has no memory of it, but maybe.

She laughs again as they take the door out to the car park. Security lights come on and he sees a toothy smile, the bag now grass green, her hair behind her ears. 'I forgive you.'

'Thank you. I'm always – saying the wrong thing.'

Is he? He has never thought of himself that way before, but now he says it a sentiment rises to meet the statement and he feels clumsy, unlucky, very slightly sorry for himself.

She pauses and frowns a little in thought. 'I read an article recently about a man who set his girl-friend on fire. And then, in prison, the man decided he wouldn't eat anything except muesli, and it had to be a certain type. So his girlfriend visited every week and brought it to him in Tupperware boxes.' She looks keenly at him. 'He set her on fire and she brought him muesli.'

As she takes keys from her bag she smiles as if they are sharing a joke.

'So I think you shouldn't worry about anything. People can be very forgiving.'

Touching his elbow, she says goodnight and goes to her car. He goes to his – the only one left thankfully, or else he might have struggled to know which to choose. Can people be very forgiving, he wonders. Or did she say *women*? Women can be very forgiving. A man wouldn't have done that, with the muesli. A man would have walked away and not come back.

That night he wakes up hungry and goes downstairs in the dark, the word entropy loud in his head. There were times – there are still – when he would face the darkness of 3 a.m. and be terrified by the idea of entropy: nature dismantling every human object, and eventually every human being, until there was just an unfettered, cold chaos. Other people had God to protect them from such an outcome, but he had nothing – nothing except himself.

The kitchen is littered with aides-memoires: Keys on hook behind door. Turn oven on at wall first. Teabags in teapot, not kettle! In his tiredness he imagines his son weak and safe in his prison cell, wrapped in furs. He looks in the fridge for something to eat and takes out a box of eggs. He finds a saucepan.

If nature was so insistent on making a house a pile of bricks, he had once decided, he would become insistent on making a pile of bricks a house. One must always fight back, not in the hope of winning but just to delay the moment of losing.

If it was bricks-to-houses that he wanted to achieve, it would have been much more honest to become a builder. But there was something frightening in the vision of it – one solitary man battling against the tidal wave of a mammoth physical process, like that man and Goliath, like Sisyphus rolling the rock up the hill just to have it roll back down. (Always he has this image of Sisyphus, and the older he gets the easier it is to relate to that particular kind of penance: the acceptance of the pointless.) No, to become an architect and fight the process behind a drawing board in an office seemed less doomed than the builder's thankless task, more strategic and long-term.

So he went to London to university and then to work. He converted bombed ruins into high-rises, scrapyards into precincts, thistle-choked fields into schools; he met his wife in the ruins of a blitzed Victorian terrace and proceeded to carve an orderly life with her. She was young, sleek and suburban. All around them London was powerful with human endeavour. Entropy seemed to be a lame old process after all; it seemed never to encroach.

Now, when he looks back, he wonders – has he succeeded in holding back the tide? The prison is his creation; its codes and systems, its sequenced, numbered rooms, all of which act as a dam against the mess of the world. That in itself was a victory against chaos. He breaks eggs into the pan and throws the shells away. He then takes the shells from the bin again and stands with them in his hand with the idea that he needs them for the omelette – he can't remember if shells are like packets that you throw away or apple skins that you eat. Packet or skin, skin or packet? Or box. Or wrapper, or case? There are so many words, and so many actions that depend on the words, that it becomes impossible, when one begins to think it through, to ever know what to do.

He puts the eggshells in the bread bin instead. Think about it later, he resolves, mumbling to himself.

That evening – that Tuesday or Monday or Friday – he had watched Helen out on the ladder in the pinafore she always wore, and the socks and shoes; she looks like Alice in Wonderland, he had thought, and he took a picture. She was picking cherries from the tree with the familiar ineluctable energy that seemed never to leave her. So many times in the past she had come down from that tree, her fingers stained red, beaming – absolutely beaming at the bounty of it all.

He had told her, many years before when they first moved to the Coach House, about the Jewish laws of kashrut that dictated how the fruit of a tree could not be harvested until the third year –

that before its cycles can be interfered with the tree must know about ripeness and withering, until it becomes so adamant in its growth and so voluptuous with fruit that no amount of picking will disturb it. And for the harvester's part, the virtue of patience must be learned. The virtue of waiting for one's pleasure until the waiting itself doubles or triples the joy.

'Joy,' she had said smiling, 'is something I enjoy.' She had put the bowl of cherries on the grass and taken Henry from his arms. 'And waiting is my favourite pastime. Waiting for my little boy to grow up, him, waiting for him to climb the ladder with me and pick the cherries, what do you say, Hen, what do you say?'

She began to shower Henry's head with kisses, then sat on the bench beneath the tree and un-buttoned her shirt down the front. 'Are you hungry, Henry, are you a hungry boy?' It had begun to rain, large plump raindrops landing in discrete crystals on the leaves, but she had stayed there nevertheless and laid bare her right breast in the same way she laid bare packets of fish or cheese, with the same tender efficiency.

Whether she did, in fact, breastfeed there and then, whether this was, in fact, the exact occasion on which he had told her about kashrut, whether the rain had belonged to that occasion or to another, or many others, or none (for a thing that never happened can be remembered exquisitely, he knows) is beside the point. Kashrut and cherries were beside the point. As he watched her that evening in the pinafore, a much older woman, up the ladder, panic welled behind his eyes and he had what he now regards as his first true blankness. For a moment he forgot everything he had ever known, not just facts but the art of how to get facts. The utter blankness amounted to one solitary, stammering thought: what is it I'm supposed to do now?

It was a moment, that was all, of extreme disorientation, but though it passed it did not, he felt, pass fully. He reached under the bed for the human-skin bible and, kneeling over it on the bedroom floor, opened it at Psalms; perhaps he did not open it at Psalms at all, perhaps he scanned through page after page looking for something that might speak to him. He has remembered this evening so often that he has muddied it with his mind – but there it was in any case and however it came to be. There in Psalms it said, *Shall thy wonders be known in the dark? And thy righteousness in the land of forgetfulness?*

One cannot be expected to remember everything, and in fact remembering everything is a hindrance to living; if an event comes as a thousand details the brain needs to forget nine hundred of them in order to derive any meaning from that event. So a woman with dyed red hair, coarse skin and a pen in her hand has explained. But, she has also explained, too much forgetting is bad. He had wanted to take her to task over this: define *too much*, define *bad*, who do you think you are, do you think I am a child?

I'm going to say three words and I'd like you to repeat them after me: house, shoelace, picture. He does not remember what answer he gave, only that he wished for the woman to look away as he strove to meet her ludicrous demands; and he knows that he must, despite an effort, have failed to please her.

'Please draw a clock face on this piece of paper for me,' she had said.

'Analogue or digital?' he asked, looking her acutely in the eye.

'Analogue.'

He had drawn carefully; despite this the outcome had been unusual. He could see that what he had drawn was not a good clock face and that there was something wrong, but he could not see what, nor why. One day, he supposes, he will not even remember that he does not know or remember, and the ageless face of that woman taking his drawing and saying 'Right, Mr Jameson, thank you' will constitute for him neither hope nor fear, it will just be an unknown face.

Once he asked the woman with the fox hair what was meant by the missing *e*. It was just that he kept remembering it, and she seemed to have all the answers. She told him if he remembered something and he couldn't think why, he should let it go; it didn't matter. He was edgy and restless. He did not want to let it go. Then there is the cherry tree, he told her: they had once had a cherry tree in their garden, come to think of it they still might. And there was the human-skin bible. There was 1960. The year his father died, also the year Henry was born. She just nodded and offered a sympathetic smile, and rubbed her hand across her belly. He remembers that now, wonders if she had a stomach ache, or if she wanted to go home.

What if he did not remember that? He feels desperately unreliable. The bed creaks as he shifts his weight towards the centre, and instinctively he folds his arms around the body lying there. He decides not to be afraid. When he looks in the mirror he does not see an old man, nor does he see a brain that lacks logic. He sees himself, greatly changed, but undeniably himself, and he is grateful to this self for persisting this long. For years he saw in others what he thought was anger or hostility and he wondered why, then, mankind should be so incalculably reclusive, so intent on making life worse than it need be. Now he sees that this is not anger but rather a simple *refusal* to be worn down or away. The old man who looks in the mirror and sees an old man beholds also a man who has given up. This is not him. There are vast tracts of his life which he believes unassailable by disease, and strings of days in which he is no less coherent and lucid than he was as a twenty- or thirty-year-old. He is amazed, thus far, at the banality of this *land of forgetfulness*.

It is dark and late, although he is unsure how late. He moves his arm from under the other body's weight and puts his hand on her hip.

Eleanor, he mumbles, as if expecting her to wake up and make things right. Still uncomfortable he rolls to his other side so that he can see some night sky through the French windows. Out of sight are the branches of the cherry tree, perhaps heavy with cherries, or perhaps bare – he cannot think precisely, with his arm numbed like this and his brain half asleep, where in the year they are. The last clear recollection he has of today was looking at the map in the car, and even this, even this might have happened on a different day.

That evening Helen had stood so firmly at the blade of the knife, her hands on her hips, that he had been sure she would not be physically capable of dying. She had thought she was getting old, and yet her hands were oddly young and childish. He had asked this anxious question – what is it I'm supposed to do now? – as if she might step down from the ladder and guide him neatly back to himself. It was not meant to be the last time he would see her alive. On the contrary, it was the sight of her so solid and gallant on the ladder, her pinafore blowing in a new wind, cherries falling into her bowl, that propelled him into blankness, timidity and confusion. For the first time he did not find himself the better of the two, and for the first time he realised he might need her. He saw the wind pick up. He stood for a long time in a reverie, his hands to his chin, thinking he might go out and help her.

STORY OF THE CHERRY TREE

Their lives were in three suitcases, a suitcase per life. On their last full day in London he woke Helen up and suggested one final act before leaving.

'A last adventure,' he said. 'You choose, it's for you.'

'The zoo?' Helen said sleepily, hoisting herself up in bed and blinking at the window. A chilly, grey light struggled into the room.

'The zoo?'

'I had a dream I was at the zoo.'

'Is that where we should go, then?'

Gathering her senses, she tied her hair back and sipped water. 'Yes. We must go there, Jake. Could we?'

Generally they obeyed Helen's dreams. Her dreams tended to be practical and prescriptive, the kind that come clearly and vividly and settle arbitrary dilemmas without fuss. Her dreams had directed them to the cinema on several occasions – they saw *Breakfast at Tiffany's*, *The Hustler*, *West Side Story*. It had directed them to buy the Mini before anybody else they knew had one. To stock up on Gentleman's Relish.

So they took the Underground, stepping out of a city that was still tired from the night before, into the open gaze of macaques and spider monkeys. It was early on a cold Wednesday morning and humans were outnumbered by primates – outnumbered and also scrutinised with a gnomic scepticism, a pointed finger slightly bent or a deep frown that reached across the forehead, some scratching, some distracted eating.

'It's as I dreamed,' she said. 'Like a hallucination, to find all this here in the middle of London.'

Helen wanted to show Henry the aquarium, the hallucinogenic flashes of neon fish in water imported from the Bay of Biscay – everything borrowed and other as in a dream. She wanted to see all this one last time before they left the city and plunged themselves into a life of – what?

'What?' she had said one evening, quite suddenly. 'What will be there for us?'

'We can save money and buy land, we can build a house. It's cheap there.'

'Why do we need to build a house? We can buy a house, can't we? There's one just along the road for sale, that couple who are moving to Hackney. Our savings could help us buy that –'

'Our savings aren't for houses in Hackney,' he said. 'Houses in Hackney already exist. They're for new houses. They're for making new things exist.'

She dropped her shoulders. 'It's not that I'm saying we shouldn't go, Jake. It's just, what will we do there?'

'It's my home, that area. Now that my father is dead Sara needs me. I need her. Please, Helen, bear with me, trust me.'

She had bowed her head towards the book she was holding and had resumed reading. 'I'll try,' she said, and patted his hand when he leaned in to kiss her.

If nothing else, she knew when a game was lost. He had already had a job interview, and been offered the position, and accepted it, almost within the same breath. A day trip there and back, dropping in on Sara for long enough to visit the grave and then turn on his heel before dark descended. It had been hopelessly easy. Architects were rarely prepared to move to rural northern areas, not with the great London rebuild happening. In his interview he had been effortlessly impressive; he faced three men in their fifties, and talked at length about concrete. With a piece of paper he made a small, impromptu presentation of the possibilities.

'Concrete is a gift for the architect,' he'd said, curving the paper into a series of flowing shapes. 'By pouring it into moulds it becomes a very graceful material, you see, it has a freedom about it that other hard-wearing materials don't.' He formed it into waves, domes, folded it into triangles.

The men nodded – this was hardly breaking news but they agreed, wholeheartedly – and they asked him for a portfolio of work which he produced – suburban developments mainly, and six tower blocks in south London. He showed them series of shots of a Victorian street damaged by time and war. There it was in the first few photographs, a slum almost, with blackening brickwork and rows of drab doors and smashed windows. There, in the next photograph, in precisely etched detail, was the same scene flattened into red rubble. And there in the next set of pictures was the same location again but this time a silky-flat square of poured concrete with low, light, regular buildings around it bearing shopfronts and library signs, cafés, launderettes, bookmakers, Odeon signs.

The three men had nodded and run their hands over their chins; they said they would call him in for a second interview, and the next day a letter came that dispensed with the interview and suggested he start at his earliest convenience.

Walking through the zoo they saw animals churned from their enclosures while someone in overalls scrubbed their excrement from the ground. The tigers, having ripped up their meat with long, delicate teeth and claws, stood perfectly still and watched the few visitors passing; he scrunched his nose and stared flagrantly at them until their returned stare made him uncomfortable. An overbearing urge came to him to put his hand through the bars and beckon them, then to stroke their long spines and see if the orange hair felt different to the black. He resisted of course, but only because he thought, if he beckoned, they wouldn't come. Their stares were dignified and rejectful; he checked his clothes and posture and wandered on.

When they reached the aviary he passed the child to Helen and stood with his hands in his pockets. The aviary was newly built; he remembered having read about it, and about its architect Cedric Price. He had seen Price once, walking down the street near the Festival Hall – not that he would have known it was Cedric Price if his colleague hadn't pointed him out. He had always been rather ignorant about these things, a little parochial, clueless and wayward. Nor did he pretend to know what he didn't, in fact the older he got the more he valued ignorance as a kind of kudos in itself – that one didn't *need* to pad one's existence with trivia, or simply couldn't be bothered to direct one's attention into such small corners.

The aviary was a vast structure of glass held aloft by tension cables and aluminium castings. He had never before seen so much glass in a building; the sheer rise of it, the complexity of its frames, the very over-engineering of something made for creatures as blasé as birds. The very over-engineering of something that was supposed to emulate a simple sky.

'Look, Henry, look,' Helen was muttering. 'Look at that, look at those birds! What sound do birds make? Do you know? Do they go cheep? Cheep-cheep?'

Henry looked startled, but apparently not by the birds or the tower of glass, more, perhaps, by the general rigour of being newly alive.

He seemed to remember then that Price had

been an imposing man, black-haired, a sincere intelligence – not a tenth as imposing as his creation, admittedly, but then that creation now seemed to lend its grandeur back to its maker, as if its only function were to add to that which had given it life. In retrospect, through the convex lens of memory, Price became a sudden god of sorts.

Cedric Price, architect of the birds. Jake Jameson, architect of the high-rise tenant. Architect of Harold Macmillan and his winds of change. What did the birds know, what did the tenants know, of philosophy or politics or the aspirations of one man, and what did they care? The real function of the building, he thought in that moment, was to please and bolster the architect, nobody and nothing else. He stood for a long time simply taking in the angles of glass, enjoying the mathematics that held it there and the humdrum screwing of metal into metal by way of sums scrawled on paper. The way it decided what sort of life the birds should lead, and the way it half led that life for them.

'Do you think it's big enough for the birds?' Helen worried.

'Yes,' he said. 'It was built precisely for birds.'

'Do you think they know that's the sky out there?'

'Yes.'

'So they must miss it.'

'But they don't have a memory.'

'Why would they need a memory?' she frowned.

'You don't need a memory to know you're trapped.'

'They're not trapped, Helen – there's sky outside and sky inside, and a pane of glass between, which is just a collection of atoms like air itself, or like rain. Glass is liquid, just liquid. The birds live happily as the glass tells them to, like they live as the rain tells them to, like they fly at certain altitudes because the air tells them to.'

'But –'

'You must understand.'

He went to put an arm around her waist but she gave him the baby and walked towards the glass until her nose was against it. There were one or two people ambling some distance from them, but otherwise the zoo was struck with early-morning silence. Against the brightness of the glass his wife was part-silhouette, her smallness, slenderness tucked neatly inside a brown dress – a sparrow, he thought, or a thrush, something very English, and something lovely not in its entirety but in its detail. The way she tended to consume minor moments by tapping her toes or scratching a very particular area on her right cheek.

He turned from his wife then to see that approaching the aviary was a man with a large cage of birds, not parrots, too small, but audacious and colourful nonetheless, and the man put the cage down heavily while he opened a glass door, and went inside.

Helen marvelled: 'Where did the door come from? I didn't see a door –'

True, neither had he. It had appeared and then swiftly disappeared in a trick of glass and metal. Once in, the man began releasing the disorientated creatures, tipping them out of the cage so that they stuttered on the air and then flew any which way in an outpouring of colour. Both Helen and Henry were staring openly at the man as he ushered the birds out with his small white hands, Henry reaching his own hands out in exploratory swipes at the space around him.

At that another three men came, carrying containers. They, too, stepped in through the invisible door and began laying down trays of seed and fruit salad, flinging tubs of cockroaches and mealworms up onto platforms above their heads. The birds came from their perches and boxes, slapping their astonishing wings, singing, squawking, diving, rising in trails of prime, high-pitched plumage.

Helen was rapt and childlike. She gawped as children do when they've no idea of social mores, and he in turn stared at her pointedly while Henry blinked at a glint of sunlight that the glass had thrown him, and one of the men glanced up from feeding the birds and waved to them, holding Helen in his sight for a moment longer than necessary. The whole zoo had become a busy junction of scrutiny, a hall of mirrors, even the sun had rid itself of cloud to observe and be observed. It all had the unruddered perspective of a dream. Was this how his wife dreamt? Was it the sort of thing she dreamt about? Was he giving her what she wanted? Would he ever? What was it that she thought while she stood there gawping? What did she see?

He kissed her unexpectedly – kissed the back of her neck, kissed the baby's forehead. He pulled the collar of her dress down a few millimetres and kissed the top bone of her spine; he wanted to tell her, all of a sudden, that he loved her. As he lifted his head he saw birds rising to the top of the aviary and watching everything at once with rapid, cocked vision.

'We should get breakfast,' Helen said, turning to him with a resolute look. 'Is there a café here? Coffee and toast. I want a cigarette too, do you have yours?'

'Yes,' he said, surprised. He had only seen her smoke once or twice before.

Two cups of Nescafé, six pieces of toast, orange marmalade in plastic pots, two cigarettes, and a piece of Battenberg cake which they split into two squares each. Helen liked the yellow sponge, he did not. They disputed it – do you save the best till last or plunge straight in for what you like. He said the best should always come last; she laughed, shook her head and breastfed while she ate and smoked, dropping cake crumbs on Henry's forehead.

'When we go,' she said, tapping her cigarette into the ashtray, 'I want to live in an old house in the country. I want us to find our favourite place there, somewhere in the house, and whenever I stand in that place I want you to notice me.' She stirred her coffee without looking away from him. 'When you stand there I'll notice you. I'll say, "There's Jake, my husband, my Jake." When we stand there together we'll make sure we look one another in the eye. The first time we find that place we'll make love there. We'll leave a stain. No one will know it's there, just us.'

He smiled and held her gaze. 'I thought you didn't want to go.'

'I don't. I'm watching that cherry tree there.' With her cigarette she gestured out of the window behind him. 'It's very early in bloom. It made me think – I don't know.' She shrugged and looked beyond him, but not at the tree. 'It just made me think, what's the point? What's the point in holding on.'

'We can come back.'

'No, we can't think of it that way. When we go, we go. We find our place in the house and we act as if it was ours all along.'

Having just inhaled a ball of smoke he let it out quickly in anticipation, almost excitement. 'That's how I feel, Helen. We go. We stay. We make it home. To Henry it will always be home.'

She rested her cigarette in the ashtray, finished her cake and took Henry from her breast, smoothing down her blouse.

'*And they took their journey from Succoth, and*

encamped in Etham, on the edge of the wilderness,'
he said, leaning back, waiting for her response.
'It's from Exodus, Helen. From the Bible.'

She raised her brows. 'You think I don't know
that?' she teased. 'I don't like the sound of *the edge
of the wilderness* very much. Couldn't you have
remembered a different quote?'

'We'll leave this great sprawling city of Succoth
behind, and on the edge of the wilderness we'll
find a cherry tree –'

'And it won't be a wilderness any more.'

'It will be ours.'

'Yes,' she said. 'Yes.' She picked up the cigarette,
and looking at it distrustfully, took one last drag
and put it out.

Instead of taking the Underground they took
the bus back through the city so that they could
see it one last time. He wanted to look hard at
the new world of tower blocks, eructations of
concrete, structures escaping the sky.

'Did you see how those monkeys looked at us?'
Helen said as they moved along. 'Did you see how
perceptive they are? They see everything, they see
us truly.'

He nodded. 'Yes, they're uncanny.' He formed
rings around his eyes with his fingers. 'Their eyes
are like this, can you imagine human eyes being
like this? Terrifying.'

'The first monkey has just come back from
space alive, did you know that?' Helen said. 'And
there are some images of the earth taken on that

space mission. If nothing else,' she tucked her hair behind her ear, 'mankind's existence is utterly justified by this gift it will give to earth, the gift of sight, a sort of consciousness.'

Eventually he rested his head back and let the motion of the bus carry a Buddy Holly tune through his mind, eroding the words and thoughts: thoughts of Helen and how she had excited him just then in the café by the mere fact that they had *agreed* on something vital. It was such a powerful state, to be in agreement, like two streams meeting to form a river. Thoughts also of how strange it was, getting to know her. They had married so fast and unthinkingly, not so much through passion but through mutual and unspoken logic. What was the point in two people being alone? He desperately did not want to be alone. And now he would have to justify their marriage, both to himself and her. Today was the beginning of that.

Thoughts of the baby, the baby that meant more to him than he could justify or quantify, and for whom he felt an almost painfully dense love; so dense, so graceless, that he sometimes wondered if it could count as love at all. Thoughts of his mother and dead father. Thoughts about the aviary, which culminated in an effortless knowledge about the permanence, the coercive and perfecting permanence of a building, the permanence of a home, of going home, and of being home.

★   ★   ★

Sara was in the kitchen when they arrived, negotiating the complexities of her coffee machine. They deposited their three cases in the living room, brushed the long journey from their clothes, and took coffee with her. It was, indeed, a matter of *taking* coffee, as some take the papers each morning: with the adoring rigour of a ritual. He kissed his mother and, with barely a word, took the gold-rimmed cups from the cupboard – proud to intuit immediately where they lived – then laid them out on the sideboard.

They exchanged pleasantries about the journey. Helen trod the orange living room carpet with the baby in her arms, stepping between their sparse belongings and humming or repeating *sshhh*, even though the baby was silent. Then they sat, he and Helen on the sofa, Sara across the room in her bentwood chair. The china cups, though slightly chipped and tarnished, clinked with a hushed clarity that shored up mislaid moments of his childhood with such concision that he was disorientated briefly.

'So you will be looking for somewhere to buy, once you have started work?' Sara asked.

He glanced at Helen. 'Yes.'

'And what about building?'

'We still intend to, in a few years. We'll save, then buy land, a piece of moorland, sit on it for a while and then build.'

That wonderful interlude of agreement between him and Helen had revealed its drawbacks quickly enough. He had realised soon after how he had in fact just agreed to live in some state of rustic dreaminess rather than the self-conferred modern splendour he had planned: the glasshouse to end all glasshouses, the white sunlight on the panes, skeletal against thick black peat. He had, with one cigarette and the mention of inappropriate sex, consigned his reality to a dream. But he told himself it did not matter. There was time. Time reaching forward, time going backwards – more time than he had ever had in his life.

'So you'll need to stay here for – what? I don't know, a few months maybe?' Sara asked.

'Just for a month or so – until we find somewhere to rent. Then we can look around properly. It will all be quick, Sara.'

'As you wish.'

When Helen brushed her hair behind her ear the gesture seemed to carry an undercurrent of irritation. 'You don't mind us staying, Sara? It's an awful pain, all three of us.'

'If I minded I would not have invited you. It isn't my way. And if I want you to go I'll tell you that in a second.'

Helen reached for her hair again to find it already behind her ear. She smiled with visible effort and sat. She put Henry stomach down on the sofa, between them.

'Look at these.' Sara took something from a drawer in the dresser. They were photographs, square Polaroids which she handed to them. 'It's a house about six miles from here, a coach house. The woman who owns it is a friend of mine. She lost her husband a few months ago and she wants to sell. It's a bit – ratty tatty, but a good house. She wants to find good people to buy it, it's not the kind of a house that appreciates complete strangers.'

The photographs showed a long narrow building with a white façade, dating, he estimated, to the early 1800s. Perhaps the monochrome images bequeathed to the house a mystique it did not really deserve, a cloudy wistfulness to its old age. He saw through it; he did not especially like it. The two photographs of its interior showed large rooms and splendid supporting beams, frowzy and disordered decor, bad plaster work. *Ratty tatty*, as Sara had said. Woodworm, he thought; joist problems; the lintels are probably shot through with holes; likely it will need re-roofing.

'It's absolutely the most perfect and wonderful house I've ever seen,' Helen said, caressing the pictures.

He knew the deal was already done, even before Sara mentioned they could have it for less than two thousand pounds, and even before she went to the kitchen and returned with two glasses filled with what she informed them was cherry wine, and even before she declared that the wine was made with fruit from the cherry tree in the garden of the house, and even before she produced a final picture – in case they were interested – of the tree itself, its blossom the colour of mallow (the monochrome image could not subdue that creamy pinkness), its branches as slender, Sara observed, as a tamarisk tree.

Helen put her hand to her mouth in measured delight. 'As I envisaged it,' she said.

'And also,' Sara added, 'Rook is coming for dinner.' She rested her cup on her palm and seemed to test him for a response.

He raised his brows. 'Rook?'

'He visits me from time to time.' Her eye twitched and she held her fingers to the offending nerve. Long fingers, elegant face – the sort of face he would expect to see in tall women, when in fact Sara was far from tall. 'Anyhow he's coming at seven, and already it's four. Will you excuse me in that case? I have a lot of cooking to do – make yourselves welcome.'

'Just as I envisaged it,' Helen repeated, rubbing her hand up and down Henry's back.

Then, if Rook is coming, he must have a bath, he thought urgently, and he must have a piss. It was the coffee machine, the compressed shot of hot water and then the trickle of liquid as it passed into the jug. It always made him need to piss. And the business with this cherry tree and the house they seemed suddenly destined to buy. He excused himself. He hadn't seen Rook for over a decade.

CHAPTER 3

He knows the route to The Sun Rises like the back of his own hand. He knows without any conscious thought when to change gear, when to slow down or speed up, which potholes are deep enough to avoid and which areas flood, specifically which areas, down to a few metres or so. Sometimes the puddles have frogspawn in. He knows to avoid them at certain times of the year and he knows, by light, colours and instinct, that it is probably that time of year now.

Eleanor has a newspaper on her lap; when he glances across he sees that the headline is something about a plane disaster, there is a photograph of something mangled. He thinks of Helen. Her love of flight always made her morose over crashed planes, because planes belonged to a perfect world of height and freedom that was not supposed to fail. She would have been upset now by those pictures in Eleanor's paper and he would have tried to cheer her up with some platitude or another. Maybe she would have been upset by Eleanor herself, wondering how X could be put in Y's place as if Y had never been. He hopes she would have been upset; he is. He glances back at the newspaper.

'What's the story?' he asks.

Eleanor puts down the pocket mirror she has been frowning into, looks at the paper, sighs and tells him to hang on a minute. 'Something about the Rwandan president being killed,' she says. 'In a plane explosion.'

'Will there be a war?'

She folds the paper and picks her mirror up again, rubbing her skin with her fingertips. 'I don't know. It doesn't say.'

It worries him, war. It seems like one of those things that, now he is unable to follow the news properly, might just creep up on him. He was always so aware; now not so. There was always some control over the workings of the world when he could see what was coming.

Silence settles between them as Eleanor combs her fingers through her hair. *Memory*, Helen used to say as they drove. He would give her a memory. This was his homeland and she wanted to get to know it through the eyes of his childhood. He drives on and his stomach tightens. It strikes him as strange and sad that whenever he maps out his own history it converges on pain. He has known so much more than pain – and yet recently everything pivots on the tragedies and wrong turnings.

He doesn't know if Eleanor has truly sunk into oblivion over the past or whether she is just pretending. Either way, it obviously isn't important enough to her. But to him it is. While she inspects her hairline he entertains horror. This is the precise route he took that night, from the Coach House to The Sun Rises, 1967, the week after the Six Day War had ended, it was hot. War, you see, and bombed airfields and Egypt's planes blown to nothing by Israel, and Helen angry for an entire week as if they would divorce over this: this war. As if it were his fault.

How full of rage and horror he was when he drove out here and decided to make a play for Eleanor, knowing Eleanor would never refuse. All he could think about was Alice. To salve the blame he had loaded on himself he decided to run to Eleanor's bed, and there she was, of course. Of course she let him in. And then he left.

He cannot decide now how long it was before he and Eleanor spoke again. He was embarrassed. He spent months disgusted with himself, and when he checks now to confirm when that disgust eased he is not sure that it ever did. He is embarrassed, that decades later Eleanor is what remains. Their past seems so dull and grubby, and their present so – inexplicable. He wonders if he should have brought her along tonight.

They pull up at a junction and wait. In the mirror her eyes become ringed with dark brown and expand in size. She emerges and changes under the nib of the eye pencil as Helen had used to do. In the late Sixties Helen had worn her eyes large

74

and black; her once brown legs had turned ravishing white from the bad northern weather and her knees had seemed to be exposed bone. They are so uncannily different, Helen and Eleanor. Eleanor is plump and her make-up is a mask; he prefers her without it. He wants to tell somebody there has been a mistake. He searches his pockets for a cigarette, finds the accelerator and pulls off.

Eleanor dabs her cheeks in the failing light. 'Are you excited?'

Dear Eleanor, to think that somebody could be *excited* about their own retirement dinner.

'Nervous,' he replies. 'It's a bit like going to your own wake.'

She sniffs and puts the mirror on the dashboard. 'I don't think I'll ever retire. Don't think I'll ever be able to afford to. I'll be digging my own grave to save money.'

She grins; the smell of her perfume edges into his senses as if through a wall of sponge, just some of the smell permeating and the rest lost. What does she even *do* for a living?

'Everyone retires. I tried not to – but there comes a point when it's necessary for you to be eased out. It's a system.'

He worries suddenly that he has forgotten the car keys, quizzing himself to think where he might have left them, before realising they are in the ignition. Eleanor clears a blemish from the windscreen with the cuff of her blouse. She turns to him.

'I'll look after you,' she says.

'Sara used to call retirement the Sabbath days,' he says, ignoring her. He does not want to talk about being looked after or to look across and catch her eye as if they are sealing a joint fate. '*The Sabbath Days*, the days of rest. No gathering manna, no ploughing or reaping or pressing –' He frowns out of the window at the moors and the cooling towers in the distance, ejecting broad plumes of cloud into an otherwise clear evening. With his thumb and forefinger he makes a small circle. 'No pressing those things, not plums. The other things.'

'Grapes?' Eleanor ventures.

'Yes. Grapes.' Embarrassed still, he forges on with his point. 'No ploughing or reaping. No cooking. She called them the days of rest.'

'No cooking? Then I'll have to cook for you. Oh Jakey, poor you, it'll be beef sandwiches every day and frozen hotpots.'

She puts her hand on his thigh and squeezes.

'There was something about a man not eating muesli,' he begins, on the periphery of a memory he cannot quite place. 'Did you tell me about that, the man who wouldn't eat muesli, or was it meat?'

'I don't think so.'

He pauses, interrogating his brain aggressively for the clarity that sometimes comes out of temporary confusion, but this time it doesn't come. After a lifetime of well-founded reliance on things just fixing themselves, he finds it disturbing to accept that they are more likely, now, to stay broken.

But where was he? What had he been thinking just now, before that other thought?

Eleanor squeezes his leg again and stares lightly at him; he has often asked her not to stare down his foolishness like this as if in great alarm, or, worse still, great sympathy. Her voice, saying something calming he suspects, is somewhere in his head but he is now noticing the plants that push through along the dykes, and tries to conjure their names. Brooklime, he recalls. Labrador tea. Funny that he should remember such trivia.

She scrutinises him as if trying to establish from the way he sits or the expression on his face whether he might let himself down terribly this evening.

'You alright driving?'

He nods.

He must have seen Henry recently because he remembers it, and everything remembered happened either very recently or very distantly; something he must get used to now that there is no middle distance as such.

The moors spin past, the peat dark grey and puddled along the dykes from heavy rainfall. When he saw Henry he showed him the letters. They've been coming ever since Helen died, he explained to his son. They just come and come. All addressed to her: look. Helen Jameson. Look.

There were six or so inmates in the visits room; *Are any of these thieves?* he had asked. A shrug from Henry. *Nobody asks what you're here for,* Henry had said. He found this information unbelievable, but let it pass. He could not abide thieves. Murderers, adulterers, heretics, junkies, kidnappers – not ideal, but the world needs its irregularities – it is too perfectly spherical, too perfectly perfect without. God is too easy without the challenge. But thieves disrupted the oiled mechanisms of give and take that he, personally, took as the most human of human traits: the ability to recognise value, fairly trade, to save for what seemed important, to spend on what seemed immediate. To give, also, and to provide.

Each of these six inmates, except Henry, was being visited by a woman. One of the women had a child who played sullenly with his father's fingers, lifting and dropping them. He recalls a black couple whose quiet conversation was casual and sporadic as if they were waiting together for a bus. How loyal women are, he had thought – loyal and patient. His mind was drawn to his daughter, he wanted to talk to Henry about her but had no idea what he would say – could not bear, more likely, Henry's casual regard of her. *About Alice,* he wanted to say. *Let's talk about Alice.* Instead he put his hands to his chin and tilted his face upwards.

As he slid the letters across to Henry he looked at the grey walls, the refectory along the wall to his right – no, left, no. Right. He remembers that the woman at the counter looked drowsy as she piled bars of something on a rack. He sipped his tea, usually refusing tea on grounds of its tasting like wet clay, or old wood, but there at the prison it is always strangely delicious – strong, sweet, still hot in the stomach and homely.

Helen was my mother, my mumma, his son had said, cradling his cup in his hands just as Helen used to. *Do you remember I used to call her Mumma? And she used to call me Bubba. And now you sit here and accuse her of having an affair!*

He and Henry had disagreed about the letters; he was sure, is still sure, that if they read the letters they would find infidelity in them. Only a secret lover would keep writing to his beloved after her death, not knowing that she was dead. The thought is painful to him, so much so that he sometimes feels pity for this poor man, who must by now be worried, mustn't he? The lack of replies must be eating at him.

Henry was not interested in the theory and put the letters aside, yawned and rambled about prison life. They saved their fruit rations, he said, and fermented them with Marmite and sugar to make wine; he asked if he could be sent some Marmite, they had stopped selling it at the prison shop.

There was an argument about who knew Helen better. He remembers he had tried to pull the chair towards the table to impose his view, but the chair was rooted to the floor. In the effort he had done something, spilt his tea or knocked the

79

letters to the floor, it is unclear now, but one of the women had looked around at him as if apologetic, and he had felt, again, something like unworthiness or failure in the slow tired blink she gave before she turned back to her husband.

The argument – the argument had been so familiar. He can't with any honesty say they definitely had it this time, more that it is just an argument that is always there for the having, regurgitated so many times it could be scripted. He sometimes wonders if it is the only conversation he and Henry have really had since Helen died. It is an argument over who knows her best, who is more like her, who loved her most. The debate tires and upsets him; how can he even approach these questions? Helen was his *wife*. Compacted in that word is a whole planet of intimacy, not to mention the fact of choice: that he and Helen chose one another in a way that Helen and Henry never did. Slept together, too. Made Henry. Henry is secondary to Jake-and-Helen, a by-product.

Henry gathered the letters then, from the floor or the table, and patted them tenderly into order. He began to talk about a German poet in his block who had a wife at home with long blonde hair and eyes like planets. The poet wrote his wife a hundred poems a day. People write when they're lonely, Henry said, and it would be no good just writing to yourself, what you say has to be said *to* someone. Days when the poet couldn't get his post sorted in time to go out he went mad. Henry smiled as if at a fond memory. He said that maybe those mysterious letters were just from somebody lonely exploiting Helen's charity.

He must have been looking away from Henry during that speech, because he remembers now seeing him suddenly as a stranger: restless, warring, and vulnerable in his – what is the word – jail costume? It occurred to him that, given a choice of who he should be, his son had been launched into a dilemma he had not yet solved. The baby was in him, and the boy, and the man, the old man, the wise, the embittered, the arrogant. His hair had not grown back from whatever it was that had made it come out, either the drugs or the prison razor. There they both sat, more hairless than ever. He had no idea how to relate to his son. They could not pull their chairs closer, and there was no way of bridging the gap. The table and chairs were all of a piece, arranged so as to never be rearranged.

He put the letters in his pocket before he left. Henry whispered something: *There,* he said, *see that man, he's the one who set his girlfriend on fire.*

As he listened to Henry whisper he looked at the clock and saw its fast hand trip forward; and it started near the four and, by the time Henry stopped speaking, it was near the eleven. In that time Henry had told him about how the man would eat nothing that had been in contact with meat; he would eat only muesli which his girlfriend brought in plastic boxes. Yes, that was where he had encountered that man, in prison. He is relieved; he remembers sharp words with Eleanor when he came out into the car park where she was waiting, because she wanted him to tell Henry about his illness and he could not. They quarrelled, but gently. Everything is always gentle now, even violence and quarrelling. He looked at the prison and felt the stab of pride that he had built it and that it was still standing. Eleanor coughed when she started up the engine and punched at buttons to get the radio working. It was raining heavily. The moors were puddling around the dykes.

All of this he remembers and can see as plain as day – he just can't say when it happened. Like a photograph that cannot be placed anywhere specific in the album.

His colleagues are sitting around the long oak table and when he walks in they turn and some of them hold their hands together as if they are going to clap. He eyes the bar, the stone floors, the mirrors behind the glass shelves, the window through which the rope of dusty light always used to sling itself, cutting in angles over Rook's figure on a barstool, and he decides he will not succumb to that last refuge of the old – nostalgia. It sounds like a disease, a weakening of the body. Neuralgia, nostalgia. And besides, he is here to look forward, not back.

Whenever he sees these people together, out of

context, he is instantly compelled to think of them as he has always done, as the *council corps*; they have always thought of themselves as a muted collective, low in flair and kudos, striving onwards in mediocrity. He realises, as he places himself and Eleanor amongst them, that he has come to feel this too. He has become a member of a group that doesn't know whether to stick together for safety or fly apart for escape.

He sits amongst them: all architects except for one, a girl. She waves across the table at him and he waves back, though he is certain they've never met before. There are so few women in architecture that he would remember if they had. He always wondered why more women didn't become architects, and he never came up with an answer, except maybe that women forget to think big, and for this reason they are not engineers or aeroplane builders. An inbuilt humility means they never imagine they can create something bigger than their own bodies, whereas with men – well, all he has ever wanted to do is just that. And despite his own standards, he would still maintain for this very reason that one of his ugly and defunct high-rises is better than no high-rise at all.

'Drink, Jake?' This is Fergus, his peer he supposes. Fergus with his lank and rangy physique and pale Irish complexion. Before he can anticipate it Fergus is leaning across the table and clutching his forearm in a gesture of solidarity. 'What can I get you?'

'A bourbon,' he says. 'With ice, and a little sugar

if they have it.' He offers a twenty-pound note which Fergus declines. He insists, but Fergus is adamant.

It becomes clear that this evening is to be his, and this means that it is all organised for him, and he just has to sit here and behave. In his wallet is a packet of mint which he now lays on the table in a vaguely petulant frame of mind. He considers that he could drink until blind – yes, what an idea! Drink mint juleps until eloquent, like he has so many times at this very table.

Over dinner he is fretful at first, worrying about Eleanor, worrying that she is out of her depth and that these men, who have all known and liked Helen, should be offended by his replacement of her. But this feeling wanes as the bourbon relaxes him and as he learns that if he is indeed being inappropriate there is a perennial pleasure in that. He would like more of it. Prompted by Lewis, one of the younger architects, he indulges in talk of ideals. There is an unspoken creed to being a member of the *council corps* that says one cannot afford to have architectural ideals. Even theories – even theories without the slightest ambition – are aggravating.

'The modernist project,' he says, 'is not just about lack of ornament – it's about the lack of a *need* for ornament. Think about decoration in general: every time it occurs it occurs in order to cover up for a crime. The ugly woman. Mankind putting its clothes on after it ate the apple.' He pauses for a moment. This was once his wife's argument also, the one ideal they both believed in. 'Think how many criminals have tattoos.'

'Adolf Loos,' Fergus says to his surprise. 'You're quoting his theory, Jake, am I right?'

He nods; of course the architect's name had abandoned him but yes, this is his theory.

'But it's just meaningless rebellion,' Fergus continues. 'Look where Loos lived – Vienna, which is a beautiful city. He just got sick of beauty, like being full up on a huge chocolate cake. Doesn't make chocolate cake bad. It certainly doesn't mean we should destroy every chocolate cake we find, am I right or am I wrong?'

What Fergus is alluding to, he assumes, is the period of architecture for which they are both part responsible, the decade of obliteration in which wrecking balls defied hundreds of years of history and replaced them with concrete. In which tower blocks were built to be lived in by the most unfortunate until the best inventions in demolition techniques ten or twenty years later allowed them to be brought down in front of applauding crowds. In which bright new towns spliced the landscape with right angles in order that people could move from the expanding twilight of cities. In which the manor house now known as Moorthorpe Prison had suffered an extension so ugly that even at the time, and even over something as profane as a prison, people had been outraged and petitioned against the violence done to beauty.

Lined up on the table are three bourbons; he drops mint into them, stirs them with his finger and knocks one of them back. Fly apart, he thinks. Fly apart.

'You are wrong,' he tells Fergus. 'Architecture rests itself too much on the principle of beauty. A building must be beautiful because it is first worthy, and not worthy because it is first beautiful.'

Lewis, sitting opposite, leans forward with his elbows either side of his plate. 'So you'd honestly screw someone worthy before you screwed someone beautiful?'

Eleanor laughs. It is the first sound she has made for ten minutes or more, and he supposes that she has laughed out of a need to contribute more than out of appreciation of the joke. He dislikes it when Lewis – not the most masculine of men – assumes the stance of the predator; despite himself, he dislikes the infidel trait that he sees in other men, as if they think they can live by their own rules alone.

'You miss my point,' he says, 'if you think it is about screwing people. Architecture is at the heart of life, it's life wrought into something permanent.' He turns his hands as if manoeuvring a great lever. 'It's not just how to build but how to be *moral* and to use your brick, your concrete, your steel honestly, without tricking people, without treating them as if they are children.'

He is not sure how well he even understands what he says, and how much mass has been lost from the argument over the years. Nevertheless it gains stature as he speaks it, warming him to his profession as he has not been for years, unearthing that good faith that drew him to it in the first place. He drinks down another mint julep and considers Joy in her yellow dress gazing out over the ocean from the glass wall of her home, sipping a julep – never gulping, always sipping.

'I was going to build a glass house once.' He cuts steak away from the bone and chews it ponderously, wondering if he has an attentive audience.

He begins telling of the glass house he had always wanted on the moors. A little like that famous one in America, he says, and a flurry of nods and *Philip Johnsons* echo around the table. But better, he says. Better than that. He tells them how he had intended to dredge the water from the peat; at first the structure would sit out of sorts in its sponge bed. But gradually over decades the peat would begin to dry, it would be smothered and heated by sediment that would crush out its water and slowly, another century later, it would become brittle coal, then the coal would harden until it was a tough, glassy graphite. A polished glass house embedded in polished ground. And at last the land would have adapted itself to the structure. This man-made coercion of the landscape is what is rightly called architecture and the rest is called only art at best – at worst, modelling.

When he has finished speaking he assesses the three or four faces looking at him, sees interest, and so he goes on; he tells them that the building that inspired him the most is the bird place at London Zoo, a great iceberg of glass. While he gestures its size and angles with his arms, some quizzical and troubled stares meet his, the words Cedric Price are muttered; Lewis asks, *Is it made of glass? Surely not? Surely the birds would die, isn't it made of some kind of mesh – some kind of –* and Fergus interrupts with the assertion that it is a mighty piece of architecture, yes, who could fail to be inspired?

From their enthusiastic nodding he can only assume everything has gone well; he stands. 'May I make a parting speech?' he says.

A choral yes passes up and down the table. He meets Eleanor's eye and sees her apprehension. She is sitting up straight, twitchy and almost – very uncharacteristically – birdlike.

'I would like to say only this,' he states. 'You do not create a building in keeping with its environment. You create a building that gives the environment something to aspire to. Beauty is not the point. It just happens to slowly become the point. Is this not like life? I am going to spend my retirement seeking beauty. That's all, thank you.'

He does not exactly mean this, or rather, does not know if he means it or not. Seeking beauty? As if it can be found in the cupboard under the sink, or in one's sock drawer. But there is something very marvellous in being blindly profound, and everybody agrees it seems, raising their glasses and toasting him. Now when he looks at Eleanor she is relaxed and heavy once again in that cloak of needy devotion.

He has little idea what he just said; but that, he thinks, is because he is drunk. Nothing more.

Before they leave he decides to go out into the garden, and is confused to find it changed: where once had been a neatly, cleanly filled rectangle of poured concrete, surrounded by a low wall and open view of the moors, there is now a – what is its name? – the glass shed, the glass part, and it is cluttered with tables and large sweating plants. People are eating at the tables and look up at him as he wanders in. Unsure of how to get out again he panics and stares at their hot, flushed faces.

Then he sees on the floor, by his own feet, some footprints embedded in the surface, dried fossils of prints that are making their way out and over the wall that is no longer there. One set is large, the other smaller. He smiles before he has had time to guard himself from the tender swipe of the past, and then Eleanor comes up behind him, not seeming to notice the footprints at all, and guides him back to the others.

In his memories he is often travelling, riding uninhibited down motorways at night, down the brand-new M1 hushing and empty, along an American highway in a brown car with his wife. Flying.

When he is driving in those memories the roads are always like this: black and quiet. The car swishes; everything feels soft, overly soft. His eyes are always closed even when he is at the wheel. There is certainly no danger, only a secured sense of going home, though home is not necessarily the bricks and mortar of the Coach House or the fluorescence of a motel or even the flat open landscape of his childhood. It is an eternally imminent concept of home whose proximity brings fantastic comfort until he begins to realise that it will only ever be proximate and will never arrive. Then there comes a longing and nothing to satisfy it, a neural restlessness.

It is the drink perhaps, more than the softness and darkness, that brings the longing now. Here is the urge to touch Eleanor, an urge inflamed by bourbon. An urge to reach across to the driver's seat and find her arm and to feel the movement of her leg pushing down the clutch, just to feel that she is alive. To touch the girl in the pub whose name he has forgotten; to touch Joy. He has not thought of Joy for days, nor her letters about her dear husband. What is the man's name? His brain is too soaked for this. Silas, that's his overblown name. *Silas*. Now he thinks of Joy, and that picture of her in her yellow dress. Thinks of fucking her, and enjoys the deliberately crude shape of the thought before it passes into reverence – reverence of her distant, almost ghostly being.

It is like a whip slicing through him – the brakes, the bump, the sharp whistling sound from Eleanor's throat, and then they are still, at a forty-degree angle to the pavement. Eleanor's hands clutch the steering wheel ineffectually. He assesses himself – he is fine. She is fine too, eyes blank, very still, but fine. He looks back. A shape is lying in the road but he cannot identify it – not human, he thinks with relief, but what?

'Hit a dog,' Eleanor is saying, tearful.

He leaves the car and sees the dog there – it is black, its knees delicately bent and its head tilted up as if trying to escape the body's predicament. It is, he finds himself thinking, just a dog. There is no collar. When he strokes behind its ears his fingers come away with blood. The dog stares without movement but makes a small noise, no more than a song of the breath. It sounds like a tired woman humming a baby to sleep.

Eleanor is kneeling next to him in the road weeping, randomly generating different types of lament. 'Oh no, Jake – oh goodness – oh Lord – what have I done? What have I done?'

He can think of nothing else to do; he picks the dog up and it screams. Has he ever heard a dog scream before? Surely dogs do not scream? The sound is similar, he thinks, to the noise his children used to make on their cheap plastic recorder.

He lays the creature on his coat in the back of the Land Rover. Eleanor, pulling herself together, asks where they should go, and he suggests the police station, the only place he can think of that will still be open.

At almost 1 a.m., forms filled, the dog alive but sedated on a vet's table, they pull up outside the dark shape of his house and get out of the car.

In contrast to his own lucidity Eleanor looks exhausted and distressed. She makes her way up to bed. He is as lucid as a bright day, and un-affected by the dried burgundy blood that is still on his fingers or the scream that lingers in his ear. Restless, he stays downstairs and helps himself to Helen's Barley Cup. The jar must have been there for months – years; the best-before date is July 1993, but what, he wonders absently, is the date now? It is difficult to believe they are so far down the century already; how time leaves you winded and stupid! He drinks from a dirty mug because the sizeable mug collection that the family has acquired over the years has formed a sullied congregation at the kitchen sink, or in the kitchen sink, or on the table.

When he gets into bed he cannot sleep, and instead churns words through his head: Silas, Helen, Eleanor, Alice, Fergus. It dawns on him that these words are all names. What then, is the differ-ence between a word and a name? How similar they seem: Silas, for example. How similar to *silence*, and how without physical grounding. He repeats it, not as a name any more but as a tool with which he sharpens the claws of his memory. He simply must not fly apart, he thinks. It was wrong of him to drink so much, and to indulge his thoughts the way he has.

He turns on the light and begins a letter to Joy in his usual pseudo-aristocratic style. Dear Joy, One thinks one is going mad at last, one lies in bed and repeats the word Silas. One thinks, perhaps, that one takes after one's son after all, though one resists the idea.

Eleanor rolls over and groans. 'Turn the light out,' she says.

'I'm writing.'

'What?'

'Epistles.'

'Oh Christ.' She nestles her arms down under the blankets. 'What's an epistle?'

'A letter, Ellie. A letter.'

He knows that she likes it when he shortens her name; she gives a contented sigh and slips into an easy childlike sleep.

It is good to write to Joy, he can tell her anything. Letter after letter, year after year, she invents herself as someone perpetually unpredictable. She never thinks, says or does the obvious. When he told her about his diagnosis – writing the word Alzheimer's carefully, copying the unfamiliar spelling from a book – she wrote back and said only that she has prepared a spare room in her house for when he slips into oblivion, and has told Silas that her formative lover might be coming to stay. She has festooned the room with coloured cushions and may paint the walls orange – her favourite colour – as if expecting the arrival of a new baby. She did not say, how terrible. She did not say, you must tell Henry.

Perhaps he is mistaken, but he has felt Henry coming back to him slowly since Helen died, leaning on him, confiding a little more, looking at him with a depth of empathy he had never shown before. Even Henry's requests for money have been reassuring in his ability to provide it. He has never been richer, never had, he supposes, more to give and so few to give it to. He can now see his son, not as an enemy or a stranger, but as an edgy child, *his* edgy, frightened child. Their fractious little chats are the most honest encounters they have ever had. Fatherhood must come in cycles, so that you create something helpless that needs you, and you watch it grow until it is so big it needs you again, like a sunflower that grows to six feet and needs staking. Henry needs him, he decides; depends on him.

When Alice was born one of his first thoughts was that one day perhaps he would be able to give her away in marriage. This was a cause for celebration, because it thereby implied, did it not, that until then she would be *his* to give away? He was standing at the foot of two or so decades of ownership of this exceptional being. She was his, *his*!

94

He loved her for that (though not that alone); he loved her exultantly.

Eleanor is the voice of unreason if she thinks a father will allow himself to disintegrate into a dribbling, idiotic babyhood in front of his children. And there comes that feeling again that this will not happen to him, it will not go that far. He will not let it go that far.

Though he is cheered by the thought, the letter to Joy does not proceed terribly well; he feels suddenly exhausted and puts his head heavily on the pillow. He thinks of the dog, the needle entering its vein, thinks of oblivion, and hopes the creature is resting soundly.

STORY OF THE MISSING *E*

Gracious with age, improbably tall, dressed in a pin-striped suit that must have been three or four decades old, Rook manifested himself in the living room with a filthy and charming smile. He kissed Sara on either cheek; 'My queen,' he called her. 'Sara, my queen.'

Then he took Helen's hand and gave it the sharp, faithful treatment of his lips – a kiss, a wide crooked smile. At last he turned.

'Jake, my son, my favourite son.'

'Rook.'

They hugged, a lofty and lopsided affair. Rook had brought the sugar in with him, his clothes smelt as the air often did – that heavy burnt smell of sugar beet from the factory seven or eight miles away. After time it would work its way into the clothes, skin and hair of everybody that lived here, just as the peat would work into the nails, and the flatness into the attitude. It happened to everybody, everybody, that was, but Sara, who seemed impermeable. It therefore struck him when Rook carried the moors into Sara's house that a cocoon had been penetrated. He sat on the sofa, on top of the photographs of the coach house, with his legs spread. Sara brought him cherry wine, leaving the bottle on the coffee table in front of him.

'You've got a boy.' Rook looked around the room. 'Where is he?'

'Asleep,' he answered.

'Of course. Babies sleep – I forgot.' Rook wheezed a laugh; same wheeze, he thought. Same laugh. Same amusement at his own behaviour.

'Henry doesn't sleep a lot,' Helen offered, pulling her chair towards the coffee table. She tucked her skirt underneath her as she adjusted her position.

'Henry?' Rook grinned. 'What a fine and regal name, like my own. Charles, that is, not Rook. Say it: Charles. It always sounds regal even if you swear first. Fucking Charles.'

Wheezing, tittering, he reached for the bottle of wine and poured into each of the glasses. When Helen leaned forward and covered her own he leaned in further, lifted her hand towards him and turned it palm up. He ran a long finger across her palm, a finger livid with the life and anger of old age.

'I'm a soothsayer. Sooth says you drink tonight.' Then he placed her hand carefully on the table and filled her glass. 'Henry,' he repeated, nodding appreciatively. 'Good name. I'm a royalist. Did Jacob tell you that? To the bitter end. Don't believe in politics, it's all buggery, that's the truth. It gives the illusion of freedom, *freedom for the people.* Truth is the people don't want to be free, they want to be owned by someone better off than them. They want to be pets, you ask anyone, you ask anyone what their fantasy is – it's being tied up and *looked after*. Yes, I'm a royalist. I'd let the queen tie me up any day. In fact I have. She's a busy woman, used silk and a slip knot. I let myself out after.'

Rook glanced up towards the kitchen where Sara was cooking, gulped his wine and made a contented sound in the back of his throat.

'Don't you think the queen's a beautiful woman?' Helen ventured, smoothing away her smile with the hand Rook had touched.

'And so are you,' Rook replied. 'What a relief that Jake didn't choose a mangled peasant for his lady wife – he always had that in him, a taste for the perverse.'

'I know,' Helen added with a quiet air of collusion. 'I'm discovering, aren't I, Jake?'

'Discovering?' he asked his wife lightly, returning her gaze. 'Discovering what? What perverse thing have I ever done?'

Helen inclined her head demurely, he thought, to one side. 'It's not what you do, it's just your way.' Then she squared her head and shoulders in resolution. 'I'm a royalist too, Rook, from this minute.'

'Of course you are, beautiful girl. Of course you are.'

He saw Sara light the candles of the menorah in the back window. The point of the menorah was to allow those outside to see in, so that the light became a flagship of faith and pride in one's faith. But of course there was nobody in the back garden to see in, and nobody beyond the back garden, and nobody for miles. What a suffocated little gesture it was, he thought; how the flames gulped at the air and then seemed to shrink in on themselves in denial of their own light. Years with his father had reined Sara in. Years of objection to that menorah, years of compromise. She shook out the match and hushed back to the kitchen. Against the orange carpet she looked like a waft of smoke in her grey suit.

The breathtaking sweetness of custard that she used to stuff the *sufganiya*, and the breath-stopping syrup of boiling jam inside the *hamantaschen*, and then the smell of pastry that forgave everything – the baked scents of his childhood that created a memory understood by nobody else, just him and Sara. Next to him Helen was telling Rook about how she had dreamed she owned the most beautiful bible in the world, and how when she opened it the pages were made of water and the parables floated through them as fish. Water from the Bay of Biscay, she was saying, and as she spoke Rook was fashioning a fish from a piece of old blue paper he had taken from his pocket, which he handed to her with a ceremonial bow.

'Here, princess.'

She held the fish in her palm and examined it. 'This is so wonderful,' she said, and kissed the back of Rook's hand.

He could still smell Rook, the ambivalent, industrial sweetness welded in his suit jacket. He began to get a feel for the old man again, his grainy temperament, sour breath, yellow fingertips, green eyes that didn't need (or wouldn't tolerate) glasses, and his endless giving – how he was always making and giving, his long fiddly fingers folding, bending, snapping, wrapping, tying as if driven by some hyperactive need to expel his heart through his hands.

The food was fatty, creamy and sweet. It had been so long since Sara had cooked like this. He was reminded of how she had used to conjure up these feasts, always with some apology, trying to disguise the Jewish theme of the food as mere coincidence. After all, there were potatoes everywhere, so it made sense to have latkes, hasselback, hash, dumplings, potatoes mashed and roasted with garlic, crisped, layered, baked, re-baked, twice baked, stuffed. After all, the fishing ports were not so very far away, so it made sense to have gefilte fish, lox, tuna with fruit *tzimmes*, trout with cream sauce made with the fat of the fish, haddock stewed in milk. After all, there was a lot of milk, a lot of cheese, until the war closed in even on their piece of apolitical black turf. She did not use these excuses now but simply put the food down in hot dishes, presented them with gleaming cutlery and fine china, and asked them to eat.

'Sara, my queen,' Rook bowed, straightening his shambly old tie. 'You have done us proud.'

Sara smiled and muttered, 'Asch.' She had always prospered in Rook's company. She bent forward and poured him more wine, her ringed finger clinking on the bottle and her mouth open by just a margin when usually it was closed implacably.

'Are you from here?' Helen asked Rook, sipping at her wine, dissecting her fish with the impeccable cutlery that she manoeuvred with her impeccable manners. He had not really known how impeccable his wife was until that moment, a revelation that made him want to throw her a cigarette, tie her in silk, see her slump at the table in drunkenness.

Rook grinned once more. 'If you must know,' he said with a swish of his knife, 'I'm from Italian stock. Real name's Asanti. Fredo Asanti.'

'But you're called Charles –' Helen began.

Rook swigged. 'All I like about Italy is the olive groves and the criminals.'

'Oh.' Helen scratched her cheek.

'Italy is a country that's got itself obsessed with politics and corruption. They're blind with it, all of them.'

'Except,' Sara said, 'those men who tried to kill Mussolini. You don't mean they were blind. You like them so much.'

Rook held up his glass suddenly. 'You're right, Sara – to the men who tried to kill Mussolini!'

For the sake of it, they raised their glasses. Fervour beamed in Rook's eyes. Suddenly he laughed as if deeply amused by something, then stopped and turned.

'And what, Jake, do you think of fatherhood?'

He considered considering. He considered applying himself properly to the subject matter and explaining how very strange it was, how vivid was the idea of a child and yet how remote was the reality now it had actually come, how *impertinent* it was of Henry to have his own character when once he had been the random collision of an accommodating egg and an ambitious sperm (his sperm, *his!*), how he loved him, how he was in some way afraid of and for him. But he knew that Rook was on his own course and that whatever answer he gave would be immaterial.

'I like it,' he said at length.

'Yes, and so you should. Parenthood is unpolitical – oh, of course it becomes political, that's when it goes wrong and the trouble begins. But at first parenthood is monarchy. King, queen, and their wee little prince, and none of this manure about freedom and votes and agendas. No, it's just there. Ma and pa. You can't choose them. Ma and pa are your nation, your history and your language and all the rest –'

'Not for you, Rook, Charles, Fredo, whatever you are called,' Sara chided, waving her hand. 'There is nothing unified about you. You don't even know what language you speak, huh?'

'But you have a point,' he told Rook, propelled into thought. 'It becomes *political*. One day Henry will start to think he has rights himself. We won't be enough for him, or right for him. Too right wing or something. Our policies will bore him. Maybe he'll divorce us.'

'Of course he won't,' Helen was quick to add.

They were approaching a point of saturation with the food, merely toying with it. Helen had stopped some time ago and Sara had never truly started; Rook was picking at the *kishka*, modelling his napkin into a boat, he himself was de-fleshing the bones of the fish with greasy fingers.

'We need to clean up The Sun Rises,' he said suddenly. 'The place looks a mess.'

'The sign is missing an e,' Helen added, pushing her glass away. She looked a little drunk.

Rook chuckled and let his head rock back. 'The sign is missing an *e*! You're a funny girl.' He reached over and took Helen's hand.

'It is!' she said, flushing.

Rook tried for a compassionate look. 'Tell me which *e*.'

'At the end of *rises*.'

'Then we must find it!'

Helen assessed Rook for two or three seconds, trying, maybe, to gauge what sort of person this old man was requiring her to be. Her eyes flickered bright hazel and she crossed her arms. 'Where can it be?' she giggled.

He had never seen this accommodating trait in his wife before. She was mild and gentle to a fault, but never ingratiating. But now she smiled as

Rook opened another bottle of cherry wine and poured some into her glass, and she drank as if wanting little more than to please the old man.

'Rook, I'm serious,' he stated, straightening. 'We need to help Eleanor clean the place up, there are all these workers at the steelworks now, and the beet factory, and they all need somewhere to drink. And poor Eleanor –'

He trailed off. It was customary to refer to Eleanor as *poor*. Poor Eleanor with her roguish uncle, poor Eleanor with her lank hair, poor Eleanor with her matronly figure, poor Eleanor with her overgrown garden, her crooked teeth, her propensity to laugh in the wrong places, to become desperate like a dog, to suffer for her love, and to cook badly – to do most things, on the whole, badly.

'Poor Eleanor indeed,' Sara said. 'Did you know that her uncle has gone? About two years ago now, he just left overnight and she thought he left her nothing. She didn't hear from him.' Sara began collecting plates from the table. 'Then she found some piles of money under her bed that he had put there for her. It was about a thousand pounds. And she came here and she cried and she said she hated him because all the love in her world had been taken and replaced with a thousand pounds and she would have liked it better if it had not been replaced at all.'

Helen hiccoughed and shook her head in grief. 'Poor Eleanor.'

'You do not even know her,' Sara said in her disorientating, even tone. 'Save your sympathy for those you know need it.'

He was spared of having to jump to his wife's defence, or conduct some dreadful *telling off* of his mother for her lack of tact, when Rook took Sara's head in his hands and stroked her cheeks with his thumbs.

'That's it, Sara,' he said quietly. 'That's it.'

It was as if he were taming a pet, and it was uncomfortable at first to see his mother controlled like this. But as the gesture went on (beyond, he decided, its appropriate limit) it was clear the control was both ways, that there was a meticulous but overbearing love between them. The gesture was so gentle it was hypnotic, even for the watcher. Sara did not recoil from it.

'That *e*,' Rook said to Helen, besieging the mood with a new humour. 'Let's see if your boy Henry has it.'

Helen nodded and stood, flattening creases from her dress. The two of them went upstairs.

They had been gone twenty minutes or more. The wine was almost finished, and he was full of *hamantaschen* and had jam in his teeth. His mother had made coffee and was not talkative, and after an attempt to draw her into conversation she had fallen into a doze on the bentwood chair.

'They say, Sara, that Israel should never have been created in the first place and that they are

105

set on nothing but threatening the Arabs. Is this true, do you suppose?'

Sara had only sighed. 'Perhaps.'

'Maybe there's tension – of course – but Israel is so involved in its own growth, its socialism – confidence can easily look like tyranny.'

'I don't think we can say,' she whispered. 'I'm so tired. Asch, it's useless, I'm getting old. What a useless pastime, getting old!' And she closed her eyes.

He went to the dresser and picked up the photograph of his grandparents. They were on the cusp of middle and old age when the picture was taken, and an odd-looking pair. Arnold was tall; without his straggling beard and nervous look he might have seemed much younger. He was shabbily dressed also, but maybe that was just a symptom of the time (1920 it said on the back of the photograph) when Austria's krone had crashed and thousands of them would not even buy a meal. He had symmetrical scars on his left and right cheeks, inch-long diagonal slivers of silver skin that invisibly influenced his face into a more aquiline shape than it perhaps really had. Sara looked like him. Henry even looked a little like him, in that rough grace. Arnold's wife, Minna, was thin and dark-haired, crookedly good-looking with a mole on her right cheek. In the photograph she stood next to Arnold with a broad closed-lip smile and a straight back, holding a praise ring – an old embroidery hoop with ribbons attached.

Upstairs he could hear Helen and Rook moving about; there was laughter. Once Sara had told him stories about her younger life, about how she was behind the lens in this photograph, and how she was the first of all her friends to have a camera. She was nineteen. She liked to take photographs of different scenes and then find numbers in them (a door number, a tram number, a date on a calendar or a painting), then she would add these together and the sum would be the number she would have to find somewhere in the apartment or the city: her own treasure hunt. She could not take another photograph before she found it. Patterns were important to her. Limits on chaos.

He knelt and opened the doors to the dresser. In there was the praise ring his grandmother had been holding, and the hammered silver samovar and tea set that Sara claimed was the first thing she saw when she was born, an intricate silver seder plate, a Star of David keychain, fine cups and saucers. He looked to see if his mother was asleep; she was. When he picked up the keychain he found he was examining it as he would an alien object. Even as an adult he did not feel he had permission.

When he was a child an ancient boat was found buried in the peat near his house; its hull was a perfect black skeleton of long, strong spine and curved ribs, they thought it would probably be seaworthy with a little patching. Looking on he could sense his connection to it, but the sort of connection that comes without privileges, where all you can do is examine, observe, detach. So with these keychains and plates and all this silver; the only way he could be worthy of them was to remove himself from them. Like the boat, familiar and strange in one breath. He looked again at his mother. Her eyelids were heavy and dark and the shadows hard on her face. For a moment he thought she looked like his father.

He closed the dresser doors and stood. In London he had left disputes about land. Being an architect seemed to be one long dispute about land. As he shut away his grandparents' belongings he thought again of the narrow columns of news he was reading about Israel, and of Sara's seemed indifference. The starved desire of a man for his home. He felt along with those men who wanted to find their patch of turf called home. He stood in the centre of the room, hearing Rook and Helen above hurrying from room to room, more laughter. He drank down another glass of wine.

War is around the corner, he thought. The insight comforted him. Peace was becoming very popular, but the idea of peace made him uneasy. The fool believes in it. The wise man is edgier. In the photograph of his grandparents the gold frame seemed to say it all. The peace and beauty they thought would save them in fact locked them in a moment of time from which they never escaped. The photograph saddened him. He observed and examined it. Where did they belong? And him? Where did he belong? He felt that he had come home, and he was drunk but that was not the only reason for the sensation. If he could get land he could provide for his family in the proper way; if there were a nuclear war, say (he was not being negative, just pragmatic), they would be safe here with land. If there was not, they would still be safe here with land. If the house was glass they would be safe and happy; they could see what was coming. The image of birds lifting through the air of their handmade home coloured his thoughts and strengthened him – the idea that he could *put colour* here. The past was always black and white, but the future colour. He was happy to be home, if only he could tie these strings together; he kissed his mother lightly on the forehead and went outside.

In the garden he pulled himself up onto the wall and stood; from his vantage point he could see the outline of Sara's aggressively clipped hedges and shrubs, and into the next garden, neatly turfed, and out across the fields to the steelworks churlish on the near horizon. Steel and sugar, he thought. Such mixed exports, as if the people here really had no idea who they were.

He heard somebody in the bathroom, and then the lights went out upstairs. He didn't know whether Rook had gone home or had settled on the sofa or had gone to Sara's room. It was too far, he decided, for him to have walked home, and if he had arrived here by car certainly there had been no sound of the car leaving. Rook's manifestations never had a history or a process, he simply issued from nowhere one minute and dispensed himself to nowhere the next.

The clouds of smoke that rose from the factory chimneys were tin-coloured, and to their right the orange gas flame seared the night sky. He had always found these sheer, hard colours rebellious and brilliant, strangely clean. It was so unlike the sugar factory clouds that, dispersed in the toxic lights, came up neon orange and yellow and faded eventually into something sickly. He remembered standing on this wall as a child, watching the flame, brewing the courage to jump, and then one day finally jumping and landing two-footed, with a plump thud. But surely no; he had never lived in this house as a child. That was not a memory at all but a fabrication, perhaps a dream. He was drunk, he realised, on holy cherries. Still, he held his balance on the wall and tasted the residue of wine on his tongue.

It was plain jealousy, with Rook; he could see that now. All the teenage years of warring with the man had suggested a complex power struggle between them, when in fact its cause was simple. He was jealous of Rook for winning Sara's love. At the same time he genuinely liked and respected the man for that success, and of course like and respect were integral features of the jealousy. Sara should be with Rook; it wasn't just that she loved him, it was that she loved him in a difficult way, with risk and insecurity, the sort of love she had always lacked with her own husband, and the sort that was equally returned. Despite Rook always meaning to him the loss of his mother, he also denoted some kind of deeper discovery of her, and he found himself hoping that Rook had gone off into the darkness of Sara's room, that they were together there now.

But when he heard the scuff of shoes he knew it was Rook and was hardly surprised. The tall figure appeared as a shadow and remained so. Neither of them spoke. Rook rolled a cigarette with a series of deft flicks, lit it and handed it up.

He smoked, crouched on the wall and handed it back to Rook without a word. The menorah was still burning inside the window. Its message was striking: here we are, here we live.

Seeing Rook's eyes gleaming judgment in the darkness, he was taken by a thought.

'You think I've failed,' he said.

'I do?'

'In coming back from London.'

The old man's eyes looked up at him. 'On the contrary, *you* think you've failed.'

'On the contrary.'

He looked away from Rook.

'London was too easy. It's full of pioneers. You can see where pioneers are by the colour they leave everywhere, do you understand me? The lights and the way they fill in all the black spaces.

There isn't a black space left in London. Here though –'

'So you're here to colonise.'

'The potential here –'

He extended his arms to the darkness.

Rook coughed. 'What's this big idea that we're in control of our own characters and destinies anyway, Jacob? Much easier to give in to the pull.'

'Maybe.' He took the cigarette again. The jealousy surfaced on a new, convenient level. 'What were you doing with my wife?'

Rook straightened suddenly as if he'd had a brilliant idea. 'Isn't she *great*.'

'I think so.'

'And that she gave up so much for you. Brave girl, to take the plunge. It's a responsibility my boy. Now of course she's yours to look after. All yours.'

He rolled the smoke around his mouth and frowned. 'Gave up?'

'Her engagement.'

'Engagement?'

He thrust the cigarette back to Rook and shifted his weight, rubbed the smell of sugar from his nose.

'You do of course know about her engagement, Jake?'

'To who?'

'A good man of the cloth, a *believer*. Her parents were very keen. Very disappointed when she chose you instead. Still, you are an architect I suppose. That's something.'

They muttered humourless laughter together; Helen's father had nothing but disdain for architects, England was going to the dogs and it was the buildings that were sending it there; buildings were not what they used to be, progress was peril, the road to hell was clad in cement, and so the rant continued along this same weak vein. He looked along the top of the wall and felt incensed.

'I've got no idea what you're talking about, Rook, and to be honest I don't even believe you. Why would Helen tell *you* that when she hasn't told me? It doesn't make sense. You never make sense.'

Rook shrugged and wandered away from the wall. 'Believe me or not.'

'Why wouldn't she tell me?'

'Everybody has a secret life,' Rook whispered. He took a red leaf from the hedge he was standing next to and burnt regular holes into it with his cigarette. Then he pushed it up against the shadows on his jacket. 'A ladybird, Jake,' he said, coughing, peering down. 'See it?'

'What do you know about him then, this man?'

Rook flicked the cigarette into the hedge and put his hands into surrender. 'Ask your wife, my boy. Ask your wife.'

'Oh for God's sake, you started this.'

'*You started this*,' Rook mocked.

On an impulse he jumped from the wall and lurched towards Rook, thumping the man's chest. Rook laughed thinly and lashed out, swiping his leg from under him. He pulled Rook down with him and they scrambled ludicrously on the ground, both knowing that they could have stayed standing if they had wanted; that it was part game. He knew also that, unlike their fights when he was a child, he could now probably kill Rook without much trouble. They dug punches in one another; he felt Rook's knuckles pushing into his face, not punching but grinding almost, as if he wanted to wear him down to sugar.

It would be easy to stand up now, throwing the old man off him, shrugging, swinging a ferocious punch to his head. He could break every subservient cycle of his life, bring the glass house into being with one sterile and excellent act of violence. Pinning Rook to the grass he thought of Helen's giggle earlier, and the way she crossed her arms like a child; he entertained jealousy, suspicion, he doubted his wife and jabbed Rook in the ribs for it. He tried to feel jealous about his wife's *man of the cloth*, but the emotion kept redirecting itself instead to Rook, to the fact that Rook had got her to confide where he couldn't.

Then he stood and let Rook give him a savage kick on the shin, accompanied by a wheeze of apparent joy. Rook stood, and they flailed their arms again in the dark. Some punches found their target, most didn't. There was a little blood at the corner of his mouth that tasted pleasant; this was where he always knew that the fine and confusing line between fight and play was crossed, and that play had won. When one of them bled Rook always laughed and he always followed, and Rook would take the blood on his fingers and say watch, watch it turn from scarlet to burgundy. And they would do so, utterly detached from the violent fact of the fluid and how it had come to be there.

Rook did not reach his fingers for the blood this time. He sat on the grass and gave out steam on his laboured breath. He was laughing as usual.

'Get me up, Jake,' Rook said, and then when he was up the old man sauntered off as steady as a racehorse, went round the side of the house and was gone.

In the bathroom he washed the blood away and found a small nick in his gum, nothing to worry about. He got into the single bed next to his wife and tried embracing her, then tried to lie in such a way that he was not even touching her, then tried a casual hand on her stomach. He opted for this last position, feeling a restlessness in her gut and sensing that she was not properly asleep. Henry began rumouring tears, moaning in sleepy bubbles, but soon settled again.

He felt arrestingly alive. He was awake and twitching with ambivalence. There was the sense, first, that he could fly apart from all he knew, and those splinters of his being would fall into the resolute shape of the glass house and embody a future. Then there was the opposite sense of falling into the peat, becoming it. He must have been drifting into sleep because he did indeed feel the descent of himself and saw Sara's face before him, saw himself bowing to her amongst the trinkets he had found in the cupboard, and telling her, I want to be your son. Won't you have me? Then he came out of the strange sleep and smelt his wife's soapy hair, stretched his legs; his feet hung over the end of the mattress.

A little while later Helen got out of bed, groaned, went to the bathroom and was sick. In between retching she sobbed and sniffed. He got up and tapped at the bathroom door, putting his fingers to the small throb in his gum.

'Are you alright?'

She made a sound, neither negative nor affirmative, and eventually he left her alone, thinking how he had never succeeded in making her drunk, even at their wedding, even on their honeymoon. While he waited for Helen to come back he leaned over the side of Henry's cot and watched the child sleep. That man, the one she was engaged to? Was it true? He felt bewildered by it. Flattered and awed that she would have severed all ties with another man without a word, just to be with him. He stroked Henry's forehead, passing his thumb back and forth, back and forth.

When Helen came back they got into bed and he turned away from her, pulling her arms around his waist. She gripped his hands.

'The missing *e* is the death of me,' she groaned.

She smelt of mint where she had tried to scrub away the taste of her sins.

'Did you find it?'

She squeezed his wrists. 'Forgive me, Jake.'

'Of course,' he returned. 'I forgive you.'

CHAPTER 4

Over his mint julep he consults this bible, the skin soft under his fingers. It says very clearly that adultery is a sin. *They have committed adultery, and blood is in their hands, and have also caused their sons, whom they bare unto me, to pass for them through the fire, to devour them.*

Without fully comprehending the meaning of the words on the page before him he knows that they speak of unrightable wrongs. He bends forward at the kitchen table, turning slowly.

The letters are in a stack, a veritable brick, in plush cream and pastel envelopes. He cannot be sure exactly when they started coming or how long he has been biting his nails over them in this state of overwrought indecision, but there has been an increased urgency to their arrival so that now they arrive two or three times weekly and the handwriting becomes more hasty and desperate. Whatever Henry might say, it is a man's handwriting, constricted and reticent, and it leans the wrong way which suggests the man is left-handed like himself. This only adds ammunition to the theory of the affair, since Helen liked his own left-handedness. She liked it that his

118

ring finger belonged to his more active and capable hand, as if that might mean that he would be an active and capable husband. She decided that left-handedness denoted sensitivity and that her active and capable husband would still, beneath all that physical brawn, have the soft innards of a clam.

Who is this man? What does he want with Helen? Were they intimate? If so, how? Why? *When*? When faced with the unknown, or with particular troubling outcomes, it is, to use one of Helen's favourite words, *healthy* to be moderately afraid. Well, as he sits here now he is petrified by the letters; he bites his nails, becomes irritated with himself, and drinks the mint julep in anxious instalments as if it is a thought he is chewing on. The fear is not concerned with what the outcome of the letters might be, but rather the notion that, whatever the outcome, he will deal with it wrongly.

If Helen were having an affair will he be obliged to forgive her? After all she is passed away, gone to the other side, *departed*. Here are yet more choices of expression, and he could go on. Pushing up the daisies, kicked the bucket, met her maker. Such a spread of options before him only heightens the fact that, looking up at the utensils that hang along the kitchen wall, he cannot name them all. Masher, knife with teeth – sawing knife? Perhaps no, but then what? – peeler, whisker. He looks out to the garden and the thing that the washing hangs on. Windmill. Wind thing. Wind washing thing.

Helen has *had her innings*. She has *given up the ghost*.

If she was not having an affair and was only up to something of the utmost purity (if this shaky left-handed man is the grown-up and grateful orphan she had secretly been supporting all her life, or if he is her priest), then is he, he wonders, supposed to be angry with Helen nevertheless for concealing something from him? Is he supposed to write to the man and tell him the news? Are they supposed to become friends?

The trouble with right and wrong, he thinks, is that one is usually disguised as the other. He finishes his mint julep and thinks of a myth he knows about two travellers who knock on the door of an elderly couple and ask for shelter. The elderly couple welcome them in, scour a dining board with mint and prepare the travellers a simple meal. The travellers turn out to be gods in disguise and, so impressed by the hospitality of their hosts, give them a temple in exchange for their *ratty tatty* house.

He can only assume this is a lesson in being good and doing the right thing, but the right thing in one situation is the wrong thing in the next. If the travellers had turned out to be murderers, letting them in would have been the wrong thing. Besides, it seems terribly unfair that one should be judged in secret, that gods should sleuth around searching out their unsuspecting victims. He, perhaps, is being judged second by second by his formless wife – an exacting, unrevealed ghost, and a kind of god herself.

He had always told Helen this myth when she said he was drinking too many mint juleps; he would point out how mint is a symbol of home and humble goodness. And then he would wonder, if humble domesticity is so prized a virtue, did that elderly couple even want a temple? What is right, what is good? What use is truth? What constitutes a happy ending?

Eleanor picks up a plastic container of red fruit and rattles it.

'Do you like raspberries?'

'I love them.'

'So we'll get some, then. Did Helen used to do anything special with raspberries? Jam? Could try to make a tart.'

He digs his hands into his pockets. 'I don't think we had them. They weren't her thing.'

'Shame,' Eleanor says. She drops them into the basket.

It is true, Helen did dislike them. He recalls her once tasting one and taking it out of her mouth. *Hairs*, she frowned, *texture, not right*. She had given him the chewed remains of the fruit and smiled; he had eaten it from his palm. But he doesn't in fact remember if *he* likes raspberries.

As they round the small shop he examines the food and realises that this is true for most things, and that his likes and dislikes have become

121

peripheral trivia. A shoulder of beef behind glass. Some – what are they? He reads the label: clementines. He looks back at the beef, remembers a precise time he had it in a sandwich with the hot white sauce, what he was wearing (blue nylon trousers, hair thick around his ears), where he stood (by the piano), who with (Helen, playing Irving Berlin, Alice on her lap); the memory of the food is more real than the present, and in this memory he loves it – the taste and warmth of the meat, the fondness of the moment. But that slab of pink meat behind the glass, a lining of blood around its edge, makes him feel sick now. Vertigo overcomes him. He glances across to Eleanor to tell her but decides against it.

She loads the basket with dirty vegetables and he can't help but think how like her it is to have dirty vegetables. Always digging, her hands always a little sullied, her clothes too. She unloads the basket at the counter and pays while he stands and watches. When the supermarkets came Helen was glad to be out of these awkward little shops. Into the clean and bright! You could get everything you wanted in one go. Eleanor struggles with bags, holds one out to him.

'Any chance you might help?'

He takes one, and then insists on taking them both. They get into the car, he into the driver's seat. The air feels thick and congested. Caught in it is the thought of himself as a young man, he is tall with dark hair and a leather coat, dark blue nylon trousers, he is composed, beautiful some say, his skin tans the moment it sees the sun. He attracts stories, he wears them, and they are what make him alive. As he drives away, Eleanor chatting to herself, he wishes he could be more sure about the point of the missing *e*. So strong and sharp is the memory of it, and of the minutiae: the leaf that looked like a ladybird, the keychain, the deep orange of his mother's carpet, leaves elsewhere, a stain in the shape of a leaf, leaf banisters, woods. But what of it? What was its point? So sharp, and he has made a story around it, but now he thinks about the story it resolves nothing. Nor is the tale necessarily true. He has begun to worry about the truth, and to become protective over it. That young man is nothing if he has no true stories. Just an empty and ongoing present.

Driving, though, he feels at ease. Today there is something he has to do. In these new restless, workless days there is something he has to do. He must remember a list of words beginning with D. The drive home passes in anticipation of it – finding the list, constructing patterns to order the words in the mind, applying some discipline and logic. Then sitting down to the test, a thing he has always enjoyed doing. There is a hope, more than a hope, that he will pass it. Impossible that he will fail.

At home he helps Eleanor unpack the shopping and then takes a circular route around the house, beginning in the kitchen, coming through to the hall, ascending the staircase (letting his fingers bounce lightly against the leaf shapes wrought into the banisters, relaxing), following the landing to Henry's bedroom (leaving his footprints on the chocolate carpet), ducking through the secret door, crossing his own bedroom (past Joy's letters, which he eyes suspiciously, not sure why they are lying there on the floor), picking step by step down the pine treads of the second staircase into the study (cold, draughts caught behind the books), shoving his weight into the jammed door that opens to the living room, coming back to the hall, and standing.

All the while he repeats: discard, devolution, demolish, dish, decrepit, drone, dynasty, diamond, drastic, day, develop, drip. As a method for remembrance, the circular route works. It sets his brain into a loop, and, if he concentrates on the nothingness of the loop, the turgid pointlessness of it, he finds that forgetfulness, having wilder gardens to explore, does not bother with him.

The more he is able to remember, the more the exercise brings him peace. There is a satisfactory quality about gathering the words into his mind, filling him like stones filling his pockets. He has seen a programme, at some point, in which a man gathers dark grey stones from the shore and his children count the stones into the deep pockets of his coat. They are learning about the relation-ship between size and weight. If one pocket has small stones and the other large, he leans. At one point the balance is so uneven that he lies on his left side and his children have to grapple underneath him to remove the excess stones from his left pocket until he is standing. They comb the beach for stones that can form pairs. They become obsessed with the task of making him as straight as a plumb line, as if he is suspended from the sky. One shoulder is tilted; they remove a stone and replace it with a pebble. They add a shell and he is almost there; they add a few grains of sand and he squares himself, miraculously balanced, perpendicular to the horizon.

Demolish, drastic, drip. Each word a stone, one in this pocket, one in that. Day and demolish here, drip and develop there. Each word, he imagines, straightens him. He begins to feel their weight sincerely. There are moments when the sheer challenge of his illness feels blessed; he rises to it and the elevation brings new air to breathe, and memories come sharp as shards from nowhere, like this man and the beach. He thinks now, as he often thinks, that perhaps he is not ill at all, or if he is it is very mild, or his case is quirky and reversible; it is, after all, not like him to get old and unwell. He was always going to be assassinated in public like the Empress Elisabeth. He was going to haunt his murderer as Elisabeth haunted Lucheni. There was simply no option concerned with fading away in cautious, anxious increments; it is not *like him* to forget who he is.

He can see Eleanor through the kitchen window,

in the garden heaving up weeds; he thought she had gone out, or that she was not here today at all. He can't remember waking up with her this morning and her putting on that pearl-coloured suit jacket and trousers she is wearing now, tight over her broad figure. Her hair is illogical and her shoulders rounded against the effort of gardening.

The letters are still there on the kitchen table, forgotten about. Each time he comes back to them he has to begin the whole logical process again, fumbling with them, feeling unease fold itself up into fear, calculating the outcomes, then, in response to it all, wandering away in a state of pure distraction, his moral vigilance gone.

He makes coffee, pouring the grinds in, releasing the handle, hearing the water shoot through. Then he crushes ice, thinking that by now it must be late enough in the day for his first mint julep, and he assembles the drink with a careful adoring rigour. He sits. It is his greatest pleasure to have a mint julep in the afternoon followed by coffee and to see the evening in slightly intoxicated, his brain responding to the chemicals in his blood and the sense of life being to hand, and something waiting around the corner.

The water trickles through the coffee machine. He fidgets against the need to urinate. Eleanor comes in from the garden and washes her hands, commenting on the smell of the coffee. It occurs to him that there is little or no smell, not of coffee, nor of the delightful sugar, mint and bourbon of the julep, nor the generic smell of the house, nor, he discovers, his own skin. There are smells perhaps, but they are ghosts. He puts his mug down on the table and breathes in deeply, closing his eyes.

'The cherries are coming,' Eleanor says with a forced brightness.

He is relieved by her brightness and forces his own, smiling and pushing his breath out through his nose. She runs her hand over his head and down his arm, holding his hand, then she comes behind him and presses her chest against his head, stroking him.

'Have you learned your words?' she asks. 'We'll have to go soon.'

He brings his hands to a prayer position. 'Dynasty, develop, drip –', he pauses, 'demolish, diamond, depend, desecrate, dilapidate.'

Eleanor walks to the tap and pours herself some water, spilling it down her as she drinks.

Poor Eleanor, he thinks; it makes him feel better to think it. He repeats it to himself as he watches her sponge up the water with tissues. Poor Eleanor, *poor Eleanor,* and feels the coffee wake him to a sense of himself as a tall man, a good tall man, a free man who can get up any time he wants and walk away.

Eleanor waits outside as she always does. He has been here before, he knows the room, and he knows the chair he has to sit in. As he takes a seat

127

opposite the young woman the anticipation of before is replaced with a sudden fear and boredom. She is a woman, also a doctor or some such person. He wants to please her, he will not please her. The letters spring to his mind then sink back into a grey confusion. The woman's hair is as red as fox fur and she looks like, out of that uniform, she would not want to be here at all asking this deranged old man what day it is. Her green eyes offer no solace. He coughs.

In the fifteen minutes that follow she takes the role of a ringmaster. He jumps, as obligingly as possible, through her hoops. She holds up objects: what is this? And this? What is this called? She makes notes and instructs him to fold a piece of paper in half, in four, into a triangle.

A triangle?

With the paper in quarters he looks to her for encouragement. He knows what a triangle is, it has three sides. How to make it from this? She tells him not to worry and asks him to count back from one hundred in multiples of seven; he does so until he reaches seventy two and then is overcome with a weary anger, like that of the tiger who burns his paw going through a ring of fire and reflects long enough to wonder why on God's earth it must do this useless thing.

'Why am I here?' he asks suddenly. She looks at him long, a little pitifully, as if she is unsure what level the question is functioning on.

'We have to keep track of where you are,' she

puts her fingers lightly to her temple, 'so we can make sure you have the right medication and the right care.'

He nods.

'And where am I?'

'Where we would expect,' she says, leafing through papers in his file. 'It's rather routine.' She lets her pen swing loosely between her fingers like a pendulum as she thinks. 'You had a list of words Jake, beginning with D. Can you tell me some of them? Any of them.'

She sits back in her chair, combing her fox hair with her fingers. How old is she? Young. Youngish. He contents himself that she is middle-aged, feeling that many people are middle-aged, the middle age being that which one sinks into on this great mattress of life. She looks beached, he thinks grimly. Cast like a horse. He no longer likes her. She would once have been pretty but now she is just irritating, and he is not going to pass this test. He can't even recall what it is she wants him to do.

'I'm sorry, could you just repeat that?' he says.

She nods in a businesslike fashion, but she looks unravelled. 'You had a list of words beginning with D. Can you tell me some of them?'

He feels like an old tiger winding its jaded flanks around the ring, spying the scarlet-lipped woman from the corner of its eye, and seeing its weariness in her own.

'D,' he says, tapping his fingers. He closes his

eyes to recall his loop of the house, the leaf banister, the draughty books. He wreathes like smoke up and down the two staircases. 'Day,' he ventures. 'Dip.' He is standing at the shore filling his pockets with stones; there are no children, only an ocean hushing out his logic with its expansive to–fro. He feels becalmed. 'Dog,' he says.

After a long pause the woman leans forward. 'Any more?'

'Yes, yes, there are a lot.' Sitting up straight, he joins his palms and strokes the bristle on his chin, giving his whole body to his mind. 'Do,' he offers tentatively.

She puts down her pencil. 'That's fine,' she says.

He still has each of Joy's letters, a vast number by now. Letters from America, American stamps, their prices going up with the years. Here under the bed they are shored up in an almost violent darkness, sheathed in a leather satchel displaying the letters J.J. Instinctively, like an animal checking its territory, he smells the envelopes, particularly the small patches of semi-transparence where Joy (also like an animal, leaving her mark) had used to drop scented oil. The paper, once so ripely perfumed, gives little or no smell now.

What a gruesome mess. Secret letters from Joy to him. Secret letters from a man to Helen. Joy is a secret from Eleanor, Eleanor from Joy. Helen had a secret engagement; he kept it a secret that he ever knew about the engagement. The fox-haired woman – he is keeping the badness of it all a secret from her. Is this a normal life? All these deceptions; he will not be able to maintain them when the brain goes. Maybe it is the deceit that has rotted the brain. Already he is unsure whether Eleanor knows about the letters to Helen, or whether he has spoken to her about them. He feels the insufficiency of himself, the completely unsatisfactory way he has lived his life.

Yet when he opens Joy's letters at random and immerses himself in the words – not the meaning of them as such, just the words alone and their shapes – they do not feel deceitful, but rather the most honest thing in his life. Maybe they are pathetic, maybe they are, but they make him happy. The early letters, being the ones he has read the most, are thoroughly compressed in his mind, their contents rich and resinous. In those letters he and Joy were still able to draw on their physical memory of each other, and he could reference the fading of a bruise she had seen, and she could reference the fading of the hair dye that had been so new and red on their night together.

For a time it was always about fading. There was nothing they could say about their relationship – which had not even lasted twenty-four hours – except to express the loss of it. These are not the letters he wishes to find; he has lingered enough over the stench of loss – for it is a stench, no matter how sweetly packaged – and he has grown too old, surely, to spend time being unintelligent with love. He wants to read the letters as they evolved into something more reasoned – those letters in which he was most himself.

After some weeks of writing back and forth across the Atlantic, he and Joy began to play letter chess, the games continuing for weeks or months and Joy habitually destroying him; he had never been good at having too much thinking time, the more he thought the less bold he became and the more he would venture off into fool's errands with his pawns. While he went about defending his king she rampaged across the board with her knight and wiped him out.

Around these games the letters became more confident, more neutral, more pragmatic. Joy told him what clothes to buy to make himself modern. (He had so wanted to be modern, and she, with her startling red hair and rimmed eyes, and her androgyny that dismissed all notions of bellies and hips he had once held dear, was modernity in human form.) When he could, he took her advice. Helen liked the clothes Joy recommended; he came to believe that the three-way arrangement brought about a harmony that two people alone could never accomplish.

What pleased him in Joy was that she showed herself to be a factual, practical person; she was fed up with women who skewed all they saw with the wide curves of sentiment and empathy, as if their thoughts could not come straight but had to be filtered through their bodies first. She said she was homesick, so had bought herself an American dictionary and book on Californian history to indoctrinate herself against England. These tactics having not worked well, he informed her that America was a huge grid. Each township was originally six miles square, that is, how many? How many square miles, he now wonders? He can remember the letter perfectly, and the stolid exhilaration he felt when he wrote it, and yet the sum disintegrates in his brain. Fifty? A hundred? A thousand? It is so painfully frustrating to not know; but he is tired, increasingly tired and agitated, and he has never been able to think clearly when tired and agitated. All the same, six miles square. A huge grid, a huge pattern like an immense chess board. To counter her longing for home she had to stop seeing America as something that was never quite England, and start seeing it as a game she needed to learn to play.

Then came the confessionals – the lighthearted list of everybody he had slept with prior to Helen. It wasn't a great number, but enough, he was thirty-two after all. (He could not make that list now – names all gone, a few faces remain as a sort of puppetry but they could belong to anybody.) Joy had no such list. At twenty, he was her first.

Amongst the letters here is a little package wrapped around with elastic bands which, when opened, contains leaflets and pages of text entitled *AIPAC: American Israel Public Affairs Committee*.

133

Joy's husband was Jewish. He doesn't even know if the man is still alive; in any case he belonged to *AIPAC* in order to lobby for Israel's rights – he knows this because he reads the leaflets in front of him. At the time these leaflets, and Joy, and her husband, had unwittingly granted him permission to honour his past, not by running backwards to find it, but by standing up for its future.

He remembers that Joy would send him the latest news from the Committee, and indulged him where others would not in this path towards himself he so wanted to follow, and through it they became allies in a joint cause. There seemed to be so little difference between allies and lovers – or at least one seemed a condition for the other – and they are still allies now, he thinks. Joy is always on his side, always fighting his war; heaven knows, Joy has been the only person in his life who has even recognised there is a war to fight.

It was two years or more before Joy sent any photographs of herself; he had kept asking, trying to stave off her demise into ghostliness. The photographs, of course, he still has. Joy in the bright bleached Californian garden, Joy on a sun lounger in the garden, Joy eating lobster on a sun lounger in the garden, her hair no longer red but (interpreting loosely from the black and white) a far more civilised earth brown, flooding to her elbows. Joy's over-long over-tanned body clung to by a pair of shorts and a cotton shawl and a man – her husband. He struggles for the name briefly and then decides to let it go. Joy's body adorned by a ball gown and hunks of ruby and a man, her husband. Joy's body wrapped in a faux fur throw that does not become her and is bought, and owned, as she is herself, by a man, her husband. Joy's body, wrapped in nothing, clung to by nothing except some shadows and light. Joy's naked body in front of a photographer's tripod in a series of modest poses that use cushions and armchairs and silk screens and Indian fabrics, all of which are chosen specifically to strike against her skin in the most flattering and tastefully sexual way. Joy's naked body in a series of immodest poses that use the same cushions, armchairs, screens and fabrics as nothing other than gratuitous props for one inevitable sexual overture that he found amazing, and amazingly unbearable.

She sent pictures of her husband too, as if she expected him to show them to his children or pin them on the cork board in the kitchen. He inspected the man – his slick and charming demeanour and leaking intimacy. He was a man with undeniable charm; he had not thought this was Joy's taste, and then realised that he had no idea what Joy's tastes were, or even who she was. He might have fallen out of love with her there and then had it not been for one photograph of her standing in a car park, just standing, looking blankly away from the camera clearly unaware she was under the lens. She looks thin, a little haughty, a little *fuck you*. To him, this was Joy – the woman who in her most unguarded moments was guarded, and in her most inelegant moments was elegant. And into that aloof, black, white and grey metallic tarmac scene he could, with confidence, inject some colour. That dress she was wearing was yellow, he knew it, he knew that dress. He, in the spirit of the pioneer, in the spirit of the man who illuminates through his knowledge, could put colour where it was not. Joy in her yellow dress.

In a letter written a few months after the photographs came, she said that it was no good, she did not belong. America had her but did not want her, it just tolerated her presence. Had he seen the photographs? Did he see the costumes she wore just to entertain this gruelling, demanding America? She was playing the game at full tilt with all her faculties attuned, dressing up, playing up, learning the accent, learning to spend dollars without converting. But it was a game. Perhaps she would come home, she didn't after all think much of – the man, her husband – anyway; perhaps she would come home and live in Rook's eccentric house or find some of her family in Italy.

He drafted a reply. He told her that because America was divided into square grids, every so often there had to be an extra bit of land that wasn't a mile square, to account for the earth's curvature, just as there is an extra day in the year every so often to account for time's curvature (and this day, he added incidentally, is Henry's birthday).

He suggested the bit of land she lived on must be one of those extra bits that did not quite fit, which was why she could never make America feel like home.

She wrote back jubilantly. Of course, she would move. The problem would be solved. They had already started looking.

He was equally jubilant at her happiness. He told her that since money was no object she should move to somewhere with a great deal of glass and a view of the ocean. She could stand there on a shag-pile rug and sip martinis.

No, no, she wrote. Not martinis – the rage these days, the thing you drink if you want to be modern, is mint juleps. At the bottom of the page she wrote out the ingredients and a few quick instructions. Mint, ice, sugar, bourbon. The smell, she wrote. The smell – heavenly! Once you've smelt the sugar and mint, you will never, dear Jake, go back to martini.

These branches and leaves look like chaos, but they are not. There is a pattern. Each leaf has a pattern, and each bit of bark, and each pattern in the leaf has a smaller pattern. And the patterns are repeated, and the patterns of the patterns are repeated.

He walks the wide path looking above him at the tree canopy. The branches lattice in mad arrangements across the sky. The sky is pristine with light, it is true sky-blue, and he is warm under it, hot even. Sara insisted that there were patterns here, and that the madness had methods finer than the eyes could comprehend. Mathematics held it together. Clasps of numbers cohered what the eyes saw as separate. Of course he agreed; he went so far as to say that the logic going through the leaves must proceed infinitely through all things, at which she called him reckless for his choice of expression. She did not believe in words like *infinite*; it was that very optimistic carelessness in Helen that she balked at. One does not see infinity, one cannot put a value to it, nor measure it in stones.

He enjoys looking up. Upwards, being on the vertical plane, is not connected to time. He is troubled by the recollection of Eleanor talking to the fox-haired woman, nodding, her arms crossed, and that look of sympathy softening the wrinkles around her mouth. Apparently he is struggling with numbers and shapes, but his words are good – his ability to label things is still very good. He cannot accept this; he realises that he has no real wish to label things. If he can no longer call a tree a tree, it is sad, pathetic, but the tree will go on. But if he can no longer calculate or piece together through numbers then the invisible sense, the sense behind the apparently chaotic stray of branches and leaves, is gone. Order will be a dream he once had that has melted like glass, slowly and quite imperceptibly.

He sees himself sitting in the chair trying, failing,

to make a paper triangle. Rook would ridicule him now for this dysfunction – Rook who was so canny with those fingers that could fold infinite objects into being. And now Sara would chide: *Infinite, there you go again, Jake!*

He wishes, more than anything, to not be drawn down by his situation. They say that on balance he is where they would expect him to be, that is, his demise is reassuringly predictable. The simple enormity of it grips him and rids him momentarily of feeling, and when he surfaces again it is to a vista spread before him of arable land and beyond that the black strip of the moors. The path ahead is strewn with felled trees. The wood is gone.

How dizzying it is, to come here to Quail Woods only to find that it has no wood. How dizzying for something to turn to nothing. What day is it, how long since he saw the fox-haired woman, or Henry? He recalls, from his childhood perhaps, a view of woods from the air and the trees being felled, their trunks stacking up on the ground like matches. But it cannot have been Quail Woods; Quail Woods has been here quite recently; he remembers walking here with Sara on the day his father died, and drinking coffee between these now recumbent trees. It is not a memory, at least not his memory. Maybe, like the man on the shore, it was a programme, or maybe, he thinks, disappointed with himself, he made it up.

Wondering what he has done with Eleanor, and

why he wore a jumper on this increasingly hot evening, he turns around and makes his way back to the lay-by where the Land Rover is parked.

That night he chaperones Eleanor to the bed and allows her to help him remove their clothes. As they make love he watches her face, the V of creases at her eyes, the pores of skin on her flaccid cheeks, the stubborn mouth. Is this really her? He struggles to relate this woman to the memory of an old friend.

Under the bed Joy's letters ghost into the darkness, and downstairs the unopened letters to Helen listen to the creak of the bed. My life is a slow-motion mistake, he thinks. Then he buries his face in Eleanor's; her skin has the neutered centuries-old scent of the human-skin bible, some musty religion packed inside. He goes after that, the musty religion. Astonishing how a pensioner's body can still seek and find a god in this curious old act, and still believe in that god's promises, even when they have been made and broken a thousand times before.

In the morning he has an idea, or at least recognises an idea that has been distilling. He goes to the telephone book, wracks his memory for a name, and makes a call. Wrong number. And again, not this one. Eventually he has some success. The vet tells him that to the best of his knowledge the dog brought in two months ago is well, recovering from an operation to its leg. No owner could be traced and nobody came forward, so she was taken to a dogs' home. He calls the home. She is still there, is he interested in taking her? Maybe, he will come and have a look.

When he arrives they show him her enclosure and, to his surprise, he recognises her at once; she is standing, a white bandage round her black leg, as if she has been waiting for him. A swell of possession arises in him. She is flesh and blood, as black as wet tar; when he puts his hand out to her nose she nudges his palm with bold curiosity. They tell him she is called Lucky. He grimaces. All rescue dogs are called Lucky. When they call the name, a hundred lopsided, empty creatures must come running all at once.

STORY OF THE WOMAN
CLOTHED WITH THE SUN

Helen scrubbed the sign down and painted it. She painted a naked woman whose skin glowed with sunlight, her arms held aloft and the sun a furious ball of yellow in her hands. She had stars above her head, and stood in front of a black landscape, the steelworks in the far distance, with the graphite smoke emitting from the chimneys. The words in black across the woman's legs, with the missing *e* painted in: *The Sun Rises*.

'And there appeared a great wonder in heaven. A woman clothed with the sun, and the moon under her feet, and upon her head a crown of twelve stars.'

With this declaration she scratched her cheek and stood back to assess her work.

He observed the painting, it was sweet, a little childish. Not skilful at all but the brushstrokes were so plain they were utterly irreproachable. He could not fault her anything, ever. Could not ever question her goodness. He sat on the grass by her side in the afternoon heat and smoked.

The Sun Rises was in an odd place, thrown

into the middle of the moors without bound-
aries, except for the arbitrary knee-high wall
somebody had put around the back garden. In
fact the land that The Sun Rises, and therefore
Eleanor, owned had always been in dispute, and
perhaps it had no right to any land at all, but
gradually it took it anyway, edging the forty or
so yards to the road at the front, and spilling out
of its low walls at the back. From where he and
Helen sat on the small strip of grass at the front,
and with the pub's back and front doors open,
he could see right through the building to the
rear garden.

Already that morning he had washed down the
pub walls inside and out, nailed chairs back
together that had been left broken in the cellar
for years, glossed the doors and skirting boards,
scrubbed the stone floors, secured window latches,
fixed the cisterns, put locks on the toilet doors,
oiled the bar hatch; Eleanor cleaned the windows
and sills, the glasses, the spirit bottles, the pumps,
polished the last pieces of brass that remained,
and she watered the beds at the front. They fit a
till to replace the shoe box stuffed with crumpled
cash.

The day before, they had spent the entire day
hoisting the waist-high weeds from the small back
garden and flattening the ground. Then at seven
that morning, lucky enough to have a hot dry day,
two men had come and poured concrete onto the
layer of hardcore and sand that covered the soil.

By now the concrete was beginning to dry and its whiteness shone against the peat.

He looked for Eleanor but she must have been indoors. He turned to his wife and pointed out to the steelworks with his cigarette.

'The Sun Rises is so called because the sun rises over there. And we used to be able to see it, before the smoke from the chimneys botched the sky. So we decided, together, to call this The Sun Rises, as an affirmation. That the sun does still rise.'

Helen returned his smile. 'That's nice,' she said. 'Who's we?'

'Me, Eleanor, Sara, Rook, Eleanor's parents, when they were still alive.'

'And what happened to them? How did they die?'

'Her mother died before the war of – pneumonia, or something like that, and her father wasn't around much, he didn't cope with the loss and wouldn't come home for days at a time – then he got conscripted when the war came and was killed in, I don't know, '42, '43. Her uncle – her father's brother – came to look after her but he never wanted to be here. Then he left too.' He shrugged and inhaled. 'Eleanor says that every man in her life is useless and always will be.'

Helen shielded her eyes from the sun and squinted at her painting. She added some colour to the stars above the woman's head.

'So she believes she'll never find the man she wants?'

He shrugged again, not knowing how Eleanor viewed her love life, and not interested either.

'She will find him.' Helen put her tongue out in concentration. 'She will.'

He leaned over and kissed her shoulder.

'The concrete looks good don't you think?'

'I think it looks strange. I preferred the grass.'

The weeds, he wanted to correct. Helen had a habit of lumping different things together under the same word, as though the act of being specific pained her: in this case all things green and growing were grass. But to him they were weeds and it mattered, suddenly greatly, that the garden had choked and shrunk underneath them.

'When I was a teenager, a few years before I went to London, I used to dream about doing this place up. I remember seeing all the factory workers come here on their bikes and sit at the bar, or out in the weeds at the back, trying to get a bit of fresh air, talking about blast furnaces, torpedoes, rolling mills, crucibles –'

Helen pouted a little. 'Those words mean nothing to me,' she said. But she had stopped painting and started listening avidly as she always did when he talked about the past.

'And I always thought how bad it was that after twelve hours sweating in a factory there was nowhere outside for them to sit, I mean properly sit with space and air around them. Just weeds.'

He stubbed his cigarette out. Helen took the butt and tidied it away in her pocket.

145

'I thought they looked quite pretty.'

'Before the war it used to be grass and we sat out there in the summer – Sara used to play the violin and Rook the harmonica and we would sing –'

'I didn't know Sara played the violin,' Helen said.

'She did. She used to do a lot of things. We would sing – I still remember it – *Komm doch mein Mädel, komm her geschwind.*' His singing voice was dry and dusty, and he couldn't remember when he had last thought of this song. '*Dreh dich im Tanze mit mir, mein Kind –*

'*Hör, wie die Geigen locken zum Reigen,*

'*Komm doch, mein Mädel, zum Tanz geschwind!*'

He grinned at Helen and she returned it, reaching over to touch his knee.

'It was a Hungarian dance – you had to sort of twirl round and round until you were dizzy and fell over. And I remember – I was always allowed to stay up late. There were money spiders – that's what I remember most about it now. Money spiders, everywhere. In our hair, on our arms and legs. Sara always said they were lucky.'

From the corner of his eye he saw Eleanor coming out of the pub towards them. She was carrying a bottle of something and some large glasses.

Helen glanced at her and then away. 'My mother said that too.'

'But maybe not so lucky after all. The war came.

146

No more of it. The grass turned to weeds and the spiders went.'

Helen watched and waited for him to say more, but now Eleanor was here he didn't want to. He felt, as he always felt, that a past was too intimate a thing to share with Eleanor, that her drab misfortune was infectious, and a meanness in his character detested the thought that their two lives might seem bound. She had of course been there, too, in those days. Money spiders had climbed up her arms. She had stayed up late with him. They had sometimes slept top to toe in the same bed. He would sleep facing away from her feet.

Eleanor stood behind them and spread her arms, bottle sloshing and flashing in the sunlight.

'It's the wilderness! It's the bloody wilderness!'

She flapped her arms about, her feet rooted in their Wellingtons to the peat. '*Christ*,' she said. 'I'd do anything to get away from here, and you come here by choice. Left London for *this*.'

Helen laughed. 'This,' she said, stretching her own arms. 'Look at it, it's heaven today.'

And it was. He took in the scene: enormous blue sky, wild flowers, sun silvering the water in the dykes, the distant gas flame of the steelworks almost invisible against the light, and the three of them equally dwarfed by mile upon mile of sun-blurred horizon.

He recalled his conversation with Helen in the zoo cafeteria: *We'll come to the edge of the wilderness*

147

and we'll make it ours. He dug his heel into the earth.

Helen went back to painting, still smiling. Her arms were dusted with colour. It was mid-afternoon and hot. As he watched her, she struck him as a different and more purposeful woman without a baby in her arms. Her body, always mummified by blue blankets and clinging limbs wrapped in terry towelling, reappeared solo in a definite, young shape, and her legs were revealed thin by the jeans which she had rolled up her shins.

Eleanor sat close to Helen, removed a jar of mussels she had stashed inside one of the glasses, and poured three drinks. Gin. Without taking her eyes from the painting Helen took the glass offered her, knocked the drink back and put the glass down.

'This is the woman clothed with the sun,' she told Eleanor, who had leaned in over her shoulder. 'In the Bible the woman clothed with the sun is the people of God. And with her in heaven is a red dragon with seven heads who is waiting to devour her unborn child. The dragon represents the non-believers, the people who think they're not of God.'

He realised then that he had closed his eyes, and that he always closed his eyes when she began talking about the Bible. Now he opened them again to see her smooth her hair apologetically at the bad news.

'The unborn child is Jesus,' she said, 'and the

seventh head of the dragon is the Rome of the future, the Rome that is going to kill him. The Roman – Pilate, of course.'

Eleanor squinted her face into scepticism.

'Is that supposed to be true?' she asked.

'Yes, Eleanor, all of the Bible is supposed to be true in its own way.'

He rested himself back onto his elbows and witnessed himself in Eleanor, the churlishness and refusal to be bought with words. *In its own way.* This was such a lazy answer, he thought, and yet Helen obviously thought not. To her it explained everything, and so fully and satisfactorily.

'But after the woman gave birth to Jesus,' Helen smiled, 'she entrusted him to the kingdom of heaven, and she escaped to the wilderness.'

As she looked around her at the moors her smile persisted, but it was a not a delicate smile, not incidental as he had always thought, but serious and persuaded. Her peace was a tangible weight.

'During the war we built a bomb shelter in the garden.' She scooped a mussel from the jar and was pensive suddenly. 'I used to play in it. When the bombing got bad we – me, my mum, my daddy, my brother – lived in the shelter for a week. I remember it as one of the very best weeks of my life because we were all together, absolutely *for* each other. We never argued you see, because we didn't know when a bomb might drop and whether our shelter was any good. Mother prayed.'

She drew her legs up to her body and fixed her

slightly excited look on the yellow woman she had painted.

'Bombs missed us. We began to assume that the prayers were making us immune. Then one night a bomb blew the door off our shelter and took off one of Daddy's feet. Mum lost her religion for five years, until her congregation convinced her again, or bullied her, I don't know which. I watched my daddy for weeks, struggling without his foot, going to work and getting on with it. He was a doctor, he had to keep working.'

She turned her head up towards the sun, warm and rich as it eased past midday.

'Unlike my mum, I wasn't in any doubt. I suddenly knew God existed because he'd saved my father. And that man with only one foot was still my daddy. If he'd had no feet, no hands, no legs, he'd still be my daddy. So we can't be our bodies alone. And if we are not our bodies we must be something else.'

'Our brains,' he said.

'More than that, Jake.'

'Why more than that?'

'His soul shone out through his eyes. I *saw* his soul.'

'In your own way.'

She held her gaze on him for several seconds too long, not with anger or irritation, just as though he were a formation of light she was suddenly interested in, or as if she were waiting for him to finish his sentence. He hadn't known

150

about her father's foot; he wondered what else she didn't tell him. Footless father, secret fiancé. They had married so fast. Perhaps he didn't know her at all.

Eleanor crossed her legs uncomfortably and tapped her bare knees.

'Honestly, I don't have your strength to believe.'

Helen leaned over and put her hand on Eleanor's knee. 'You have all the strength in the world. You especially, of all people. It's plain to see.'

She stood and picked up the sign. Then she climbed the ladder and hooked it back in place, wavering, humming. He was afraid she would fall and he thought he should go and help her.

'With this sign, I call the woman clothed with the sun to The Sun Rises,' she grinned as she descended. 'I call the People of God to the wilderness.'

'I hope the People of God drink a lot,' Eleanor answered.

'The People of God do everything, they are everyone.'

He stared up at the sign; it looked good in situ, and the woman seemed to be staring straight back at him, precisely at him and nowhere else. He winked at her.

Then later, Eleanor straightened her legs into the quiet strip of sunlight and smoked. Rook was there and Helen was not. They sat on the low wall around the bright rectangle of concrete as the sun set.

'Cannabis,' Eleanor said, passing it on. 'I have it for the aches in my back. It's not just for black people any more.'

He straightened his legs along the wall too, sun-filled, dusty and tired after the day of work. He held the cigarette between his fingers; of course, it was not a *cigarette*, but he was so ignorant about drugs that he had no proper word for it. This had all just been beginning in London when he left, he had started to see it, people smoking in parks here and there, a sort of immature excitement gathering that had not been present before.

'Thanks,' he murmured.

He smoked, loosening instantly, and passed it to Rook who was folding minute paper birds from cigarette papers – elegant long-necked cranes with wings bent and poised for flight.

Rook refused. 'Too old. You shouldn't smoke that, you bad children.'

Fuck off, Rook, he thought happily. With a hazy concentration he inspected the long tight roll of tobacco. So much more interest in an object you have no word for. He inhaled more before passing it to Eleanor.

His mind was milky and he wasn't sure how he came to be here, where Helen had gone, where Rook had come from. Having worked his way through much of Eleanor's bottle of gin, and having eaten only mussels all day, he was drunk and hungry; he was optimistic too. He had the sudden feeling that all his decisions had been

152

right, coming here, marrying Helen – that a potential chaos was being fought back, and that Helen was instrumental in this – no, necessary to it. That peace he had seen in her earlier, it was a peace missing in himself. Somehow it seemed she had a wisdom that could presage and protect them, a wisdom he should not mock.

'We did good work today,' he said. 'We made a difference.'

He looked up at the rear wall of The Sun Rises and then across the silken concrete and out over the moors. He loved the way this low, random wall marked man from nature, how there was so little separation. So little, but enough. Under the concrete the few remaining weeds were dying. The peat glowed in the sunset as if on fire.

'There's so much we can do,' Eleanor said. She sat upright for a moment to clear a path for inspiration. 'We can start doing food. Why don't we get some tables and those chequered tablecloths?'

Rook flew one of his paper cranes across the garden where it landed and nestled the tip of its wing in the wet concrete. 'We can bring back the debating groups.'

'You know, the red and white ones, and candles in bottles. Sara can do the cooking.'

'We can have snail races.'

'We can have book clubs, Nescafé, we can have dances –'

'We can start an assassination club.' Rook swilled whisky around his glass. 'We can jointly and

153

democratically decide who to kill, and then we can fashion weapons from unlikely objects and go forth and murder. Being humble folk it may be messy at first but practice will improve us.'

'We can begin,' he cut in on Rook, tired of this nonsense, 'an action group. A pro-Israel lobby group.'

Rook laughed. 'This is Lincolnshire. You might not find many supporters.'

'On the contrary, areas without any strong leanings this way or that are good fertile ground for this sort of thing.'

'Why would you want to?' Eleanor asked, slumping her body weight onto her knees and gazing, as though longingly, at the creamy concrete beneath her. She looked tired.

'Listen, it isn't enough just to give a people a block of land and then deny them their history. They're surrounded by countries who deny there was ever a Holocaust. What the hell are they doing there, then, if there wasn't a Holocaust? Why didn't they just stay in their nice European apartments? Has it ever occurred to you that they might not *want* to live in Israel any more than you and I do? Maybe they'd like to go back to Vienna or Berlin – the places they were born. And now everybody says the Jews are a – what was the word I heard? – an unscrupulous race. A naturally *unscrupulous* race. Why? Because they won't settle for being trampled? Because now they've been given a piece of land and have to live with the hatred of their neighbours they would like something more?'

It was the first time he had ever really voiced these views. Anger – albeit an anger that was blunted with smoke and drink – surfaced, ebbed and surfaced. He was angry, not because he cared about a distant race, but because he wanted to defend his mother, and his mother, if she were here now, wouldn't want him to do so. She would shake her head and say, *Asch, Jacob, you would be better not worrying about it, you would be better starting up a wine-tasting club.*

'We don't want to become too – political,' Eleanor frowned.

'Take this place,' he argued, 'your uncle left it to you, a building, some land, a business. It's all very well, but do you want it? Is it enough, without any love, or –'

He gave up on the thought. The word *love* had slipped out with the smoke and he wished it might disperse with the smoke.

'No.' Eleanor pursed her lips tightly around the sound. 'But I'd be stupid to think it's not enough when it's all I've got.'

He felt slightly ashamed by the question, but then kicked the shame away. By Eleanor's argument nothing would ever improve or progress, it was a terrible, overly humble, defeatist thing to believe.

Rook slung his legs over onto the moors side of the low wall and stood, cracking his knuckles.

'For pity's sake don't start up some ridiculous Jewish group, Jake. You'll upset your mother.'

'She might want to come along.'

'She will not want to come along.'

They eyed one another for a few moments and then he stood too and picked the butts off the wall. It was time to go home to Helen, he thought, and get some sleep. It had been a long day.

'We could have a vegetable-growing club. A poetry club!' Eleanor, laid out along the wall, clapped her hands in fantasy. 'We could be the hub of the community. We could have coffee mornings with custard, apple cake, apple strudel, ice cream, chocolate sponge –'

In that moment he suddenly missed his father. He looked at Rook and was angry with him for his flippancy. For all that was disappointing, violent and rigid in him, his father would not have joked childishly about assassination clubs, and he would have spoken up against the triviality of poetry and ice cream; his father was a man of strong political ideals. Circumstance meant that he could only live them through the impotence of nostalgia, but he defended them viciously in that domain, locked in his mind, locked in his colonial anecdotes. Ice cream would never have been on his agenda.

These thoughts closed down. It was the only real stab of grief he'd had for his father and even then it didn't quite reach its object. The poor rotting man underground, the man who once took him to see the Blue Diamonds flying overhead in

156

formation. He struggled and failed to find love in the grief. He just wanted an ally.

It was almost dark now, and the pub looked a little forlorn without any customers. Tomorrow, when the paint was dry and Eleanor opened up as normal for lunch it would be a new dawn. He felt for her, *without love* as he had put it. If they could make a success of The Sun Rises it might change things for her. As he offered her a hand she sat upright, frowned deeply and looked up at him as a child might.

'Is that a storm coming?'

On the horizon a barrel of black cloud was rolling in, a wind beginning to blow up.

He nodded. She held on to his hand but did not move.

'Can you hear the sign swinging?'

'Just,' he said.

She shivered. 'Sounds like someone's hanging.'

'Rich and nasty imagination you have, Ellie.' Rook put his leg over the wall and tested the concrete with his toe.

'I often think I can hear people hanging,' she went on. 'Then I wonder what it was they did, who they murdered, and why. Then I can't sleep.'

'Nasty, nasty. You should think about pleasanter things my dear.'

'But it isn't actually unpleasant. It's quite comforting, to think about a crime being punished, do you know? Every person hanging is one less that can kill you – I like it, it makes me feel safe.'

He and Rook looked at her in dismayed sympathy. He helped her to her feet; she was dozy and loose with smoking, and she wrapped her arms around him. Like a small child, he thought. Like he had grown up and she had not. The wind picked its way across the moors and seemed to shove itself suddenly through the tunnel between the open front and back doors of the pub, and gusted into the garden.

Then, as though dealt up by the wind, a figure appeared. Rook turned and was taken aback. There was silence. All three foggy faces turned to behold it: a tall woman in a yellow dress. She was separated from them by the pool of concrete. The yellow of her dress was outrageous against the angered light. His first thought was her resemblance to the woman Helen had painted, and his second thought was, at closer scrutiny, her lack of resemblance to anybody he had ever seen. He took time to absorb the amber eyes and long face, the ears that protruded from her hair, the wide mouth that reminded him of Rook's, and the orange scarf around her head.

'Darling,' Rook said with tender surprise.

'Granddad.'

She winked. That state of her face, on the brink of ugliness and beauty, was the most interesting of all states. He saw it sometimes – rarely – in a woman's face, and had even seen it in a man's. It was sometimes there in thin cats. One day soon, he vowed, he would build himself a house that was in that suspended state. Glass – gleaming and unforgiving.

'This is Joy,' Rook said.

They nodded in her direction. After a hungry pause Rook cocked his head. 'What do you think of hanging, darling?'

She tilted her head slightly to one side. She managed to look deeply interested and at the same time deeply aloof, and intelligent at the same time as vacant. Her chin rested on her hand in consideration.

'I don't like it,' she reflected at length.

'Is there a reason?'

She fixed them all with a firm gaze. 'It breaks your neck.'

A gunshot sounded out on the moors. Poor Eleanor breathed the word *Jake* – an involuntary betraying sound that fled from her mouth before she could stop it – and jumped into good posture at his side. He could have sworn she whispered a do-or-die *I love you* in his ear beneath the crack of the released bullet. In this spot where there were no trees, a leaf blew in across the white concrete, drifted to the pair of feet closest to the back door – a pair of yellow silk slippers at the end of eternal legs – and stuck.

CHAPTER 5

O r no. Maybe the gunshot did not come like this. The leaf. Maybe not. Maybe the run of events is not precisely like this; but it is the curse of age to be confused, let him curse it back with improvised clarity. *Nakhes*, it sounds like. The gunshot is delivered in two snapped syllables: *nakhes*, joy.

He loves this memory to range into his mind, the yellow dress gathered in tight to Joy's small waist and then falling impractically to her feet, so unfashionable that it seemed it must be before its time. The straps that revealed the entirety of her long arms. The image is sticky on his memory like pollen on a bee, and happy, and invisible, and secret. The happiness of it is deep in his gut.

And when he tries to place himself in the picture, in the concrete garden, the man he sees is one he likes. Usually his memory of himself as a younger man renders him sleek like a sea-cleaned stone. It paints him as Helen saw him – a man who is attractive in the way that men are usually not. Long-lashed, doleful. To his mind (though Helen never meant it this way) this began to mean unchallenged, dull and overly accepting. Unruffled by resistance of any sort. Inert. But in this memory of first meeting Joy he is alive, with some of that electric energy that Rook always seemed to possess, with a fractious expression, with extra height and agility: he is a match for her.

Now he doesn't know if that rendition of himself is romanticised, or if the other is demonised. Even looking at the few pictures of himself doesn't settle the dispute in his mind – and in fact he barely recognises himself in them. They don't correspond with either mental image. He is giddy with the sensation that nothing, *nothing*, not even himself, is certain. And then he begins to wonder if perhaps this is a godsend, and that he can protect himself by filling in the gaps with what he would prefer as opposed to what was.

The story of the soldier comes to him. He is a child and Sara invites their blond-haired neighbour for dinner. It is wartime and the neighbour's husband is a soldier on leave from his duty in France. Over a meal of chicken soup and dumplings, and heaped plates of dry-roasted potatoes, the soldier tells the tale of how he was in a bombed hospital and the building collapsed, leaving all but him and a foul-smelling Frenchman dead. They were trapped for a day and night, these two soldiers.

A year later the neighbour and husband come to dinner again. The husband is on leave, but hopes that this will be the last fleeting visit – there

161

are signs that the war could end. He retells the story of the Frenchman. This time the one day of entrapment becomes four, the hospital a school; the Frenchman weak and maudlin to the point of near-death.

Another year later and the war is over and the neighbour and ex-soldier invite them for dinner. The beleaguered soldier tells the story again. The four days has become a week; the Frenchman weeps at night about his beloved estranged dog. The two soldiers are sustained by a leaking water pipe that has conveniently surfaced in the tale.

The next time the story comes out it is years later and the soldier drops by to say he and his wife are moving to London. Jake is moving to London too, Sara tells him. To study to be an architect. The soldier stays for one of Sara's now famous coffees which she makes strong and luxuriously milky. She hands out hot *hamantaschen* and the soldier asks if he ever told them about his encounter with the Frenchman. They say, perhaps.

He tells it with expert flourishes. The week has become a fortnight. The Frenchman's estranged dog has become children, the Frenchman's wife beautiful, the water infected, the den smaller and hotter, death closer.

The poor exaggerating soldier. It was clear that the man was at no point lying, just deluded, just craving after a drama in what had, for him, been a war of fairly undramatic, inevitable, unnarrated loss.

They always joked about it, he, his father and Sara. He picks up a black-and-white photograph of Helen when she was pregnant with Alice. There is such pressure to remain true to the facts, and it seems so important somehow, so vital to preserve events and people as they really were. But he knows how memory can make a shattered dream come true. Sometimes he loses the strength and vigilance to stand up to its forces, and thinks he would do just as well to let it transform the past as it wishes.

Under guidance from the fox-haired woman he sketches up a timeline of his life with places, major events and people along it. She instructs him to make simple logs such as who he was married to, who his children are, and what his profession was. She escapes his derision with a reasoning hand that slices the air – the gesture says, *you'll thank me for this one day*. So he bows his head and says he will do as she asks.

The timeline raises questions. When was he born? What was his father called? Who is older – Alice or Henry? Certainly Henry came first, yes, because there were many times of three people. And if Henry came first that possibly makes him younger – one is a young number. But Alice, too, was young, in fact she was the youngest of all things. Here she is as immediate to him as a prime colour, and he marks the event on the timeline: 1967. She is wearing a blue dress with a large felt strawberry on the front – Helen had even stitched in the yellow specks, the – spots that one finds on a strawberry. His daughter is breathy and excited after tripping around the garden after Henry and a toy plane, and she comes to him, chirping *Jape* in an attempt at his name, and her fingers fiddle at his knees to get his attention.

Something moves: the dog. She yawns from her place on the floor, snaps her jaws shut and then contemplates him. He blinks to find he is just standing here in the kitchen with a pen in hand, and he can feel the vacancy on his own face, the typical elderly glaze. No idea how he came to be standing when he was sitting. Hasn't he even forgotten to breathe? His nails are bitten.

He sits down again to the timeline and hovers his pen. 1967: that was the year of the Six Day War. Agitation overcomes him. He can still just about grasp this war, its mechanisms, its reasons – something about it still makes sense to him. The Israeli planes attacked Egypt at sunrise, so that, with the sun behind them, they were difficult to see and distances difficult to judge; he has always had that image in his mind, of the planes silhouetted against a large sleepy orange ball, just as the steelworks are silhouetted. And Helen furious that the sun should be misused in this way for such ungodly crimes.

Then it transpired that hundreds (thousands? Lots. Is thousands lots?) of Egyptian soldiers had died, while most Israeli soldiers were unharmed. Support for the underdog is never to be underestimated, he knows. He knows from years of marriage to Helen that whatever is losing is suddenly loved. And there was Israel, the tyrant, and Helen hated it until the hatred began to feel like it was directed at him personally, and as if the tide turning against that land was the tide turning against his own stupid beliefs.

1967. The day after the short distant war ended he had taken his family to Quail Woods, it was June and hot even under the patchy shade of the trees, and Helen was a little irritable and perturbed. Extremes of temperature always made her so, where they had the opposite effect on him. He liked the feeling of being pushed to a limit, and that day the heat had caused him to wake up from a night on top of the sheets resolute and hopeful. He scooped Alice from her bed, kissed her and carried her downstairs. She liked cornflakes with a little side bowl of mashed banana and jam, so he made it for her as was the ritual and they sat down to eat.

Then, over coffee, he heard on the radio that the Six Day War had ended and Israel had won territory. The body count began: so many Egyptian soldiers dead. Numbers were reeled off. The BBC doubted its own news: impossible that Israel could have won; their correspondents must have got it wrong. For a while the news wrangled back and forth between fact and disbelief until the victory became undeniable.

Helen came down from dressing Henry and sighed over poached eggs, swilling the coffee viciously around her cup, and after a tense silent breakfast he suggested a walk in the woods – anything, anything to get them out of the house.

'Everybody needs to know what or where their home is,' he said as they walked the wide dappled path.

'Agreed,' Helen nodded, 'but their home is ultimately within themselves.'

'No, Helen, stop that. It's about land. Israel was given to those people as a home and they have to fight for it.'

'Not like this.'

Helen walked bare-footed along the path in her miniskirt, blotched in the green and yellow camouflage of the sunlight as it fought through from above. *Military light,* his wife called it. He carried Alice on his shoulders so that she could become a tree. And while they walked she needled her fingers through his hair, chirping, Jape, Jape, as though he were in fact the tree and she a bird in its branches.

'They said at school the other week that Israel was going to be destroyed and we had to pray for it,' Henry offered suddenly. The content of the sentence made his voice all the more high and childlike.

'They said that?' Helen instinctively reached for

Henry's hand but he didn't go to her. 'They shouldn't be saying things like that to children, for heaven's sake.'

'Did you pray, Henry?' he asked suddenly. Helen blinked at him in anger and shovelled her hair behind her ear.

'Everybody did. We always do when we're asked. We pray for everything, last week we prayed for a girl who's got chickenpox.'

'Chickenpox is fine,' Helen said. 'Politics is something else. Feeding politics to six-year-olds is wrong.'

'Six-year-olds have brains,' he told his wife. 'I don't see the problem.'

Henry ran ahead and threw pine cones at targets on the tree trunk – a knot in the bark or a red cross painted to mark the tree as fit for felling. Most of the trees were marked, and dotted about like bright mushrooms – though there were no men to be seen – were the yellow hard hats and jackets of the fellers.

'The woods are going to be cut down,' he said.

'Yes – it's so sad.'

'Sad, because this land is our home.' He looked hard at Helen to make his point. 'We don't want to lose it. Do we?'

'So would you kill for it?'

'Of course not.'

'Well, the Egyptians have been killed for the same.'

'It's over. By all accounts that little war is over.'

'Little war!'

'It was six days long.'

'Well, it's not little, and it's not ever over for the people who grieve!'

'It's been three years,' he said, trying to splice the mood. 'Three years since Alice was born, and it's a lovely day, and as of today the war is over – and our own kashrut is done – we'll go home and get up the ladder and pick cherries. We'll make, I don't know, a pie. We have everything now, it's complete. A house. Two children. Cherries. Each other.'

He pointed out onto the horizon through the trees, the infinity of its straight line now broken up with clumps of his own handiwork – houses, the prison with its fence barbs suspended like a swarm of flies, and a general suburbia gaining ground.

Alice whispered in his ear: *Jape, I want to pick them.*

He kissed her cheek, of course, of course, whatever she wanted she could have.

'The only ripe cherries will be on the highest branches,' Helen said tersely.

'Then we'll get an extra tall ladder. We're not afraid, are we, Alice?'

He stood in the middle of the path, between the yellow hats and coats, and closed his eyes to the gunshot. Helen turned her face up to the sound and shivered as though she wanted to shrug off the aggression the shot had left in the air.

'You look just like a soldier,' she said. 'The way you reacted to that gunshot. You look so – serious. So intent. Dressed in that military light.'

'I'm trying to work out what's on the other side of that sound.'

'Peace,' she said. 'There's nothing quieter than the quiet after noise.'

Jape, Alice whispered to his ear. *I want to pick them.*

He decides to make coffee. The dog stands, stretches and comes across to him; she rests her head on his knee. Knocked you down with my car, he thinks. Don't remember, but know I did. Am told, am told you came out of the blue. She observes his thoughts move across his face. Every one of his movements seems to interest her. She appears beguiled. Scratching the back of his head he strokes her until she lies out flat and closes her eyes, and he crouches until his legs are stiff – a minute or ten or twenty. He becomes absorbed – to the obliteration of all else – in the blue-black shine of her coat and the slowing rise and fall of her ribs.

He reads the name tag on her collar: Lucky. Yes, of course. They have become hasty friends as if neither can see any point in delaying or assessing. Back at the table he works again on the timeline, thinks he might have a coffee, stands, crouches to stroke the back of the dog's ear with his thumb, tells her, silently, that he is terribly sorry for running her over, returns to the table, thinks he wouldn't mind a coffee, stands, concludes that he needs to urinate. Urinates, and returns to find the dog barking at the coffee machine, which is banging with dry heat and a crack working its way up the glass. Fool that he is. He switches it off.

'I'm sorry about that,' he tells the dog. She winds back down to a curl on the floor and soon sleeps her mouth into a long, accepting smile.

STORY OF THE FAILED ESCAPE

'**I**'ve decided to start up a group. I'm going to run it from The Sun Rises. A lobby group for Israel.'

Sara sighed and looked up at the branches.

'You have foolish ideas.'

'We might touch on CND too. Or something stronger even, the Committee of 100. The issues are all bound up together.'

'You are not a pacifist, Jacob. You have a hawk's eye for war, since you were a boy.'

'CND isn't about pacifism, neither is Israel. I'm not talking about growing our hair and loving our neighbours, I'm talking about the real world.'

Sara touched one cheek then the other with her large white hand. 'My father, Arnold, had a scar across each cheek. Here, and here.'

She met his eye and then turned to face the path again.

'Fencing scars, Jacob. From his days at the University of Vienna. Look, let me show you.'

Under the shelter of a tree she dipped her hands into her bag, allowing them to swim for a long time in the blackness before she pulled out the photograph that he had seen so many times before.

'Here, my father.'

She presented the image to the dull light of the woods with a flourish: here is where it all begins, the gesture implied. Here in this picture is alpha and omega, and you would be wise to know it.

Then she touched the monochrome cheeks of her father tenderly, just as she had touched her own. 'Do you see them, the scars?'

Yes, he saw them, the silver glints along his cheekbones, tribal almost.

'In his first term at university Arnold was beaten up a few times by fools. *Dummköpfe.*'

She spat the word. Giving it in German seemed to do a greater injury, something to do with the hardness of it. *Dummköpfe.* Fools.

'And of course the fools usually got away with it. It was to be expected.'

'*Die dümmsten Bauern ernten die dicksten Kartoffeln,*' he responded parrot-like, with some of the very little German she had taught him.

Sara looked at him as if to say, *you remembered*, and she put her arm around his waist – but the look and the gesture were wary. She wanted him to remember? She didn't want him to? Had he done wrong?

'Fools are often lucky,' she translated. 'Yes. You are right. It is a queer law of the universe. If the clever man jumps into the canyon he falls to his death. If the fool jumps into the canyon he falls into a boat and sails off down the water.'

She pocketed her hands and went on.

'The beatings were not very serious things, just punches in the stomach, a bit of hair pulls and calling names: Jewish shit, Jew scum. It was standard. But the Jews had to learn to defend themselves, and so they started fencing.'

She tilted her head back.

'Look up, Jake, look up at the branches.'

And so he did, and they walked in this way, the summer drizzle finding its way thinly to them; he could hear its delicate fall across the leaves. Their own faces were wet with it. He wiped his cheeks every few moments, and Sara scrunched a lace handkerchief into a ball and pushed it into his hand.

'Here, have this. The rain's on your face.'

He thanked her and she hummed something briefly.

'The fools didn't even mind Jews,' she then said. 'Their lecturers were Jews, their doctors were Jews, their friends were Jews. It was just that they wanted to fight something. You know this feeling, Jake? You just want to fight something.'

'Yes, Mother,' he muttered, wiping his face roughly, surprised suddenly at how well he knew it.

'What I'm trying to tell you, Jacob, is that my father and the other Jewish students practised until they were so good at fencing they couldn't help but win. They won everything.'

He turned to check her expression, expecting a smile, but she was in fact frowning.

'This is the Jewish problem,' she added. 'Can't help but excel. When you really excel at something you make one friend and ten enemies. My father didn't know what it was to lose, and when defeat came he couldn't recognise it.'

He nodded, feeling the silk of the handkerchief in his palm, the luxury of it.

'We were beaten, Jacob, as a race. We had to start becoming individuals, and our lives have been better for it – my life is better for it. It is safe and free. You have to leave it alone. These groups, what good are they? You must leave it alone and save the energy for your family.'

Family! *She* was his family. That man in the photograph was his family. Why must she always forget it? And anyway, he was entitled to his own projects. As an adult he was allowed to do the things other adults were doing.

'Eleanor is happy for me to use that large table in The Sun Rises,' he continued unhindered. 'And I think I could probably recruit a few people from work.'

They ambled onwards with no company for their thoughts but the patter of rain. After a minute of walking she took the flask and gold-rimmed cups from her bag and went through the ritual of coffee, a ritual he now saw as defunct if it harked back to a part of her she had deleted. It was an echo, that was all. The thing that made the sound was gone.

'Sara, there's room in this world for idealism. Your father and mother stayed where they were because it was their home and because they believed they had a right to be there. Why *should* we recognise defeat? Why?'

Sara was perfectly upright as she walked, and quiet for so long that he thought she either hadn't been listening or simply couldn't be bothered to answer. Eventually she turned her coffee out to the ground with an anxious flick of the wrist.

'What is better? To give up what you are and be alive, or keep what you are and end up dead? What you are is mere circumstance anyway. It isn't that important. What address you live at, what clan you belong to, what name you go by, what day you set aside for worship, what you worship. It isn't more important than being alive.'

She stopped in the middle of the path. Her face was anguished.

'They could have left Austria. Everybody else was leaving through the ports and escaping – my mother and father had the chance to leave and they didn't. They could have *left*, Jacob.'

He stepped forward to offer her his hand but she gestured him away.

'For my father the truth was a burning building and he was always searching inside it, even though it was safer to get out. I assure you that to persist with an idea that has run its course is stupid and will cause nothing but harm. All this talk of Israel! What clue do you have about Israel?

175

What about your own home, your wife, your dear child whom you spend little enough time with as it is?'

An image of Joy's naked back played over him, her chalk skin tight across the spine. Sara collected herself, tucked the cup back in her bag and held his gaze.

'I am telling you and you must listen: where you are from, what is yours, what is home – sometimes these are not the point. The truth is not everything. You have to know when it is time to walk away.'

CHAPTER 6

The mysterious letters to Helen rant at him from their pastel envelopes, but the more he is faced with them the less he knows what to do, except to cover them with an object – a plate, a salt cellar, or whatever comes to hand – so that the other woman, Eleanor, can never find them.

The letters bring to mind a vision of him and Helen in bed one night talking about jealousy – or no, there is more to the story than that. It begins in the garden of the Coach House and it is a Saturday, perhaps five years ago. He hazards a cross on the timeline. Helen is reading in the sun while he is putting the finishing touches on a model plane, sticking the solarfilm to its bright red wings and fuselage. Henry arrives unexpectedly. Though he lives nearby, Henry doesn't visit often – instead he and Helen meet for cups of coffee, or Helen goes to see him in his damp little flat that designates the triumph of his independence, and they appreciate his baking. But he rarely comes here. Seeing him, Helen jumps from her seat to hug him, repeating, Henry, Henry! How nice! While Henry returns, Helen, you look so well, what are you reading?

They bow their heads together over her book like two children, their small hands pawing through the pages, their dark hair touching. The sun coppers the outer strands of their hair like fused wires.

'These are some of the paintings I'll see when I go to Paris,' Helen says.

Henry puts a hand on her shoulder. 'Show me.'

The book is about art, a subject they are both interested in. Helen likes the turn-of-the-century paintings and the pictures of downtrodden women in shabby rooms, or a poor man smoking in a bar with nothing but his shadow for company, or paintings of dancing girls and prostitutes, young women with drooping eyes. *Marvellous!* Helen always remarks, tracing her fingers across the colours. *Amazing!*

'Paris?' he says, interrupting them. 'You're going to Paris?'

'Yes Jake.' Helen turns the sweet oval of her face to him. 'With my Bible group. Surely I told you?'

'No, you didn't.'

'Oh. I was sure I had. In any case, you don't mind.'

He goes back to making the plane. 'Of course not,' he says.

That night he writes to Joy at length, and his words are fuelled by the image of his wife and son conspiratorial over works of art, and how anything, even the racy and demoralised paintings, appear innocent in her grace. He is excluded from her, and this distance makes him love her more, and love Joy more. A win-win situation, perhaps. In bed that night Helen has difficulty sleeping because of the feary *imps* in her chest, a queasiness, a worry about old age that comes only in the dark. He asks her about Paris and she kisses his forehead and says she is sorry for being remiss about telling him. Fine, it's fine. But he finds himself picking a fight as if he wants her to be doing something wrong to salve his own bad conscience. He quite wishes she would confess to a secret affair; years and years of writing to Joy are eroding even his own astonishing ambivalence. But she will not fight. Are you jealous? She asks, smiling with curiosity, and some of the worry of age falling from her face.

Jealous! He tells her he does not suffer from jealousy.

Her response is the comment that base feelings are perfectly acceptable sometimes – she likens love, honesty, loyalty to flowers, and jealousy, greed, hatred to weeds. To pretend the weeds are not there is more destructive than to admit they are there and tend to them.

He nods and agrees, but insists he does not suffer from jealousy. She says something about Moses and the Mountain of Solitude, but he is not listening. Instead he is considering whether to tell her about Joy, maybe just to see what her response will be. She is saying something about the Ten Commandments. Before he has the chance to confess anything she is asleep, so suddenly, as if she has a disease that abruptly shuts her down.

Now, leaning over his timeline, he thinks he might look up that section about Moses in the bible, his human-skin bible, and find out what it was she was trying to tell him. When Helen died he marked in his bible all the passages that she had marked in hers. Maybe those passages held a code, a message she had left for him, a greater reason for these days than eating, sleeping, shitting, breathing. He was mad back then, he spent months poring over the quotes, ordering and juxtaposing them, and he learnt them all until their sense was completely washed out by overuse.

He jerks his head up, thinking he has heard some movement in the house, and finds his heart beating hard. Helen? The other one – the other woman? When he looks for the dog he sees she is still sleeping and is comforted again by her long peaceful breaths. Perhaps in a moment he will make himself a coffee or a mint julep, something to relax him.

Somewhere, here on the timeline, is the felling of Quail Woods when he was a child. He will have to mark it. He had been with Sara who had brought with her a flask of coffee as usual, and the two of them had been looking up, always up, until, unexpectedly, the branches above them thinned, and when they looked ahead the woods were horizontal rather than vertical. Sara had breathed in sharply and murmured, *Dreck! Fallen like matchsticks!* He remembers the loud drone of a plane overhead. And scattered around were the yellow hard hats of the foresters, but no men. Yellow hats everywhere, this is what he remembers. The event is difficult to plot exactly on the timeline but he guesses he had been about nine or ten, and so he makes a mark near the beginning and stands to make coffee.

The dog will have to fit somewhere on this timeline too – she is certainly an *event* – but where she goes is mysterious, whether it be a day, a month or a year ago. He offloads a cross where there is a space, though in fact there are many spaces – his life is not very well inscribed with events. There are entire decades he doesn't remember at all, and which have slid off the great mountain of his life into the valleys below. And then there are curious, bloated memories like this one of Helen and Henry poring thicker than thieves over an art book in the garden, with the sun catching their hair.

Then the recollection of his mother in that wood with those words: *You will cause nothing but harm. I am telling you and you must listen.*

Then the recollection of a gunshot which explodes his muggy ennui and levers open the air to provide a place from which he will never be excluded. His place. His moors. Every happening, every person, every defining instant, every sense, has succumbed to this black gravity of the moors and to a flag of yellow like a flame in his brain setting him on fire. His whole life would appear to be an object hurtling towards a miniature window of time: Joy feeding a mint into his mouth, putting on her yellow silk shoes and wrinkling her nose up to the weather swarming down the rattling old windows. *Going to go to America as soon as I can, leave this rain behind,* she said. Him, sucking the last bit of flavour from the mint, in no doubt that she had the courage to leave and wishing he had it himself. And then his life passes through that window and comes out the other side altered, as if a piece of glass embeds itself in him during the transition and digs in deep.

Now it is coming out. He is who knows how old; it is who knows what year; it has been who knows how long. There are letters to Helen from another man; *are you jealous?* she asks from some dead place. He sees her hair touching Henry's in the garden and he thinks, yes, jealous of everything that ever touched you – sunlight, God, and death itself. But I am not jealous of the letters. The letters are my last chance at forgiveness.

The glass is coming out of his soul (if he has one, if he does), and with it the pain and sin, and with it the dream. Out goes the baby and the bathwater and the whole lot. Instinct tells him to hold on even if it is pointless. He makes another mark on the timeline: gunshot. Bang. That first gunshot was 1961. He makes four attempts at writing the number next to the line and the last attempt is good, neat for him, and clear.

STORY OF THE FIRST
GLIMPSE OF HEAVEN

Helen stood in the centre of the room and looked about her.

'So this is where you were born,' she said. She seemed pleased, he thought. Her voice was keen.

He nodded, yes.

'It's so – humble.'

'I suppose, yes.'

Humble it was, more so now in its dereliction than ever before. The Junk, they used to optimistically call this house, because it always looked as solitary there on the moors as a boat battling the oceans from China. Looking at it now he was taken aback by how small it was, and how derelict, and it was sinking into the peat so that one half of it was shrugged low like a hunched shoulder. Now more than ever, as it sank, and as it came closer to resembling a pile of useless rubble, it lived up to its name.

They stood in what had been the kitchen, a low room about ten feet by ten feet, separated by an unstable wall from a similar room to its left.

That was a supporting wall. It would come down before long, what with the gradual collapse of the foundations into the peat. The peat acted like a sponge, pulling solidity into it. It was certain that the whole thing would collapse.

Before them, against the supporting wall, was a staircase that had not existed when he had lived there as a child. The staircase was open to the kitchen, without any banister. It was being pulled akimbo by the shifting wall – this not helped by the fact that it had been badly built in the first place without proper support underneath. It, too, would come down. He took it all in impassively, and then broke the silence.

'These stairs are new.' He banged the falling plasterboard that flanked them. 'We used to get up and downstairs by a ladder on the outside wall.'

Helen raised her brows. She had not lived like this as a child; she was from middle-class suburbia and besides, was ten years younger than him, born the very year the war had started. Things were different when she was born, a decade made a difference.

'We hardly belong to the same generation,' he said.

The statement was a crude summary of a flurry of thoughts about time and childhood. It came out rather nonsensically.

'We belong to different generations? So Henry is both your child and your grandchild,' she joked, spreading a picnic blanket on the kitchen floor, stubbornly seeking pleasure in the face of this squalor.

Sitting cross legged, they took food from the knapsack – some sandwiches, some Battenberg cake, apples, a flask of tea, and for him an inch of whisky at the bottom of a bottle. It was chilly; she pulled the edge of the picnic blanket over her knees, took the Battenberg cake from the bag and smiled.

'So what do you think, Helen?'

'Of what? Of this? Of knocking this down?'

'Yes.'

She took the clingfilm from the cake and handed him some.

'We can't ever afford it.'

He glugged back a mouthful of whisky and felt it warm his throat.

'We can't afford it now, but we will.'

'You're obsessed. You get obsessed with ideas, Jake, and I never feel there's anything I can do to stop them. I don't even know why you ask me.'

'There'll be a steel frame, not timber, not the timber A-frame of the Coach House, a discreet steel frame with a flat roof, glass walls, all glass with masonry walls either end.'

'We'll feel like fish.'

'We'll feel like pioneers.'

Helen watched him dissect his cake.

'You're eating the yellow sections first,' she remarked.

'Yes. I don't like them.'

'So in that case you leave them till last.'

'No, you save the best till last.'

She, too, was eating the yellow sections, because, he deduced, they were her favourite: the same action, opposite motivations. Like all things they did? Like getting married? Having a child? They both ate with strategy, a cube at a time, peeling the marzipan away.

'You don't like marzipan?' he asked.

'It's horrible.'

'Then you'll be left with it and you'll wish you'd eaten it first.'

'I won't wish I'd eaten it first, because if I'd eaten it first I'd feel sick and wouldn't be able to eat the rest.'

He shook his head and smiled. 'No, no. It's like a sacrifice. Making an initial sacrifice before the feast – to appease the gods of hunger.'

'Gods,' she laughed, leaning forward and whispering. 'You and your little pagan gods.'

He watched her eat, nibbling cake from the white napkin. Then he stood and wandered into the next room, a cramped and dusty space, ramshackle, cables hanging loose.

'Jake,' he heard her call. 'Come and eat.'

'In a minute.'

'Come now.'

He stood still, gazing at the floor where an Indian tiger skin had used to be. His father had been such a fool, a colonial throwback to days gone and better forgotten. They hadn't been allowed to set foot on the tiger skin, even though it had taken up a large part of the room. When Sara had gone into labour, and there was not time to get her from the middle of the moors to the nearest hospital thirty miles away, she gave birth here on this floor. Not on the precious tiger skin, in case of blood. No, not on the tiger skin, on an old blanket.

Babies turn their heads when they emerge. He and Sara agreed that the tiger's mouth, mid-roar, must have been the first thing he saw when he was born. Then she would tell him that the first thing she saw when she was born was the silver of the samovar glinting in a winter morning, and the first thing she heard was the singsong alphabet palindromes of their maid: *en, oh, peh, kuh. Kuh peh, oh, en,* chanted for comfort as the birth pains climaxed and Sara's eyes and ears appeared. It was important to know the very first things perceived, she said. They held the secret. They would be the very last things perceived.

Helen's voice came from the kitchen. 'Jake! We were in the middle of eating.'

He sniffed at the memories. He dug at the crumbling stone floor with his toe; rain had started drumming on the patches of corrugated tin roof.

The whole lot could go, the whole house. It reminded him of denial and negation. Sara's religion hidden, Sara's trinkets shut away, Sara's past leaking potent in splintered stories when his father was out. Small, charming and murderous stories, that was all he ever got of his mother's legacy. Then they dried up. The war shut them up. Something on his father's side of the battle was won for good, and not only did Sara curb herself, but his father too. He stopped defending his values, he stopped hitting out, stopped ranting. With nothing to fight for (Britain doing noble battle, his side victorious beyond doubt) he lost any recourse he had once had to human interaction, let Rook – with his gift for human interaction – edge further in, became quiet for almost twenty years, and then he died.

Helen appeared in the doorway with her hands on her hips and the picnic blanket draped over her arm. A bird flew up behind her and out of the room, she looked back at it rapt, childlike, then turned to him.

'I agree to all this' – she wafted a hand – 'all these glass dreams, if you agree to have another child.'

He laughed. 'Wow.'

'Don't wow me. Come on, yes or no.'

'Well, I suppose –'

'Great. Come on then.'

She brushed stone dust from her pleated skirt, scratched her cheek. 'Come on.'

As she climbed the stairs she pulled off her knitted top. Shadowing her, he focused on the ladder of bones that formed her spine so that it was as if he were climbing, not the stairs, but her – her physiology, her very structure and make-up, ascending the pathway to her brain, a brain so very different to his. She thought in different ways to him. But for this moment at least they were thinking the same: Henry is not here, the rain is thrumming, the atmosphere is right, another child would be sensible, yes, and fun, and good for Henry. Yes.

She reached the top of the stairs and peeked into the bedroom.

'You met Rook's granddaughter didn't you?'

He stopped. 'Yes.'

'Eleanor said everybody in the pub talks about her. Was she really that beautiful?'

'Beautiful?' He felt hot and guilty. 'Unusual more than beautiful.'

A gunshot. The silken white concrete at his feet. And then Joy's long thighs along the musty old sheets, the way, afterwards, she had risen from Eleanor's boat-like bed and knelt at her shoes. And how, as she peeled the leaf from their saturated yellow silk, she had said in a bruised voice, *Going to go to America as soon as I can, leave this rain behind.* And licked the leaf for good measure, and stuck it on his arm.

'And now she's gone off to America,' Helen added. 'So brave – she's so young – younger than me isn't she? I'd like to have met her.'

'How do you know she's gone?'

'Rook told me.'

'When did you see him?'

'He popped by yesterday while you were at work.

He taught me to play poker. Not for money.' She ventured to the door on the left. 'I think he wishes she hadn't gone, sometimes I think he's lonely. Jake, can I tell you a secret?'

He nodded blindly.

'Our trip to America, our honeymoon – it was lovely and everything but I was homesick most of the time. I could never live outside England.' She spread the blanket down on the floor of the bedroom. 'Does that disappoint you?'

Shaking his head, he thought, so Joy has gone. He should have been relieved. That night he had arrived home and taken deep breaths in the garden. He had splashed his face with cold water. The gunshot still rang loud in his ears and Joy's dress in his mind; Joy's tendency, that he had discovered like a delightful truth, to tilt her head and fold her ear in half when speaking. He had been given his first glimpse of heaven and it had been yellow and completely impelling. Without meaning to he had woken Helen up, leaving rain-soaked clothes on the bedroom floor, and, seeing the leaf stuck to his arm (a birch leaf, silver birch) he swallowed his guilt and peeled it off, half expecting to see a wound under it or some evidence of wrongdoing, but saw only his almost young skin. Even the mere edge of spring had brought a tan to it.

He blinked and brought his attention back to the room, to Helen looking around, her arms folded to guard off the cold. She looked strange here in her bra, misplaced. This had been his parents' bedroom, once. Not so different in some ways, still bare and drab, only then it had been mitigated by the multiple blankets and cushions Sara depended on for the illusion of luxury. A section of the room had been annexed as a bathroom, incredibly small and now shabby and fungal in corners, the porcelain of the washbasin cracked.

Helen squeezed into the bathroom and closed the door. He heard her use the toilet, which no longer flushed; she was desperate, she said. By the time she had come back he'd smoothed the picnic blanket as large as it would go and without undressing, they made love. As he ran his hands over her back he found himself thinking of where she had come from. He had been to her house once – a mock Tudor house in a neat and hushed cul-de-sac, nicely groomed parents and a back garden with a loop of lawn around a silver birch. Her parents said that as a girl she had used to peel off the bark and glue it to the wallpaper in her bedroom, and she bolstered this story with her own memories – the white chalk of the bark on her fingertips, and the fishy smell of glue.

For his part, here in this room, he could smell foxes, milk, a mix of stench and scent. He gripped the hem of Helen's skirt. He was making love, he thought, in his parents' bedroom. Five nights before he had been with another woman and did not regret it. So now he was one of those men he disapproved of. He clutched the back of his wife's thighs and littered her neck with messy, roaming kisses.

Afterwards they tipped the components of the picnic into the knapsack and left. The rain had stopped and the moors were steaming slightly where the sun had begun warming the soil. The sight of it filled him with renewed ambition. The day after his adventure with Joy he had gone to work and been told that he would be the lead architect on the design for the new prison. Lying in bed while Helen slept that night, he thought of it intensely. He knew how it would be – not the terrible Victorian design of herding prisoners into cramped wings, like animals, and leaving them solitary. His would have four wings, T-shaped as he had read about in a recent journal, each wing reaching out from the central hub of the prison like a free limb. And each wing would be its own community, more like a public school than a prison. In the day the men could move amongst each other, at night they would be separated.

Helen said it sounded horrible. T-shaped wings? Sounded dark and dingy. Why did he want to work on such a horrible project? He told her: a prison dictated its own design like almost no other building: the size of the rooms and windows was set to a maximum, the width of the walls, the breadth of the staircases, the number of doors and windows, the regimented oval of land around which those men would run – these were all given. There was nothing less satisfying than a building

193

which permitted its architect total freedom – much better was a building that exerted limits and challenges. To Helen it sounded far from pleasing. But it was not supposed to be pleasing; it was supposed to reform and moralise. Not punish, but moralise. This was the modern way.

Helen had sighed when he told her this, pulled her nightdress back into order under the covers, and assured him that he should not cast aspersions. A person's morality is a two-way journey, whether they appear good or bad depends only on which leg of the journey you catch them on, she said.

He had contested: he did not care whether the prisoners really *were* good or bad – this wasn't a question for the likes of him. He only took the agreed assumption and acted on it.

Perilous, she sniffed, and lifted her arm above her head to sleep.

'We should call them Conception Events,' Helen said now as she got into the car. 'Trying for a new child – *Conception Events*. What do you think?'

'It sounds hopeful,' he agreed.

'I wonder if Henry is okay, he's been with Sara all day. We shouldn't have left him.'

He wished to ask her, Why the sudden change – you weren't worried about Henry before – is it the house? Is it because we lived like peasants? Do you think Sara wasn't a good mother?

'Henry will love her,' he said. 'She will love Henry. We won't be able to tear them apart.'

'How will Henry love her?' Helen muttered, turning her face away. 'Not the most easy woman to –'

'Love,' he finished.

Helen faced him. 'I'm sorry,' she said. 'I really am sorry. She's your mother. I don't even know her.'

She settled her gaze on him for a moment and then, probably realising he was not going to speak, resorted again to the window and the view: the landscape she thought would sink beneath sea level if left unguarded.

He started the engine and drove off, the Mini gathering a bit of speed on the perfectly straight roads. If only he could press his foot down hard on the accelerator and churn along at eighty, ninety! It seemed a way of laying claim to the place. In London he had always felt the city was a living entity that he could, perhaps, rub along with or even, with his buildings, nourish – but he was always superfluous to it, no matter what he did. Now, for example, now it would be oiling along, grinding along without him. Whereas here, these moors, that house, had been waiting for him all this time.

His wife was right in what she said about Sara. It was difficult to love a woman so bound by her own limitations and losses. But he was beginning to understand that Sara did not wish to be loved, she wished only to survive. Love to Sara was what he was to London: perfectly redundant.

When they got back to the suntrap house they found Henry propped lavishly against the arm of the sofa, and Sara throwing and turning the praise ring, moving round in her long brown dress in inexpressive circles; all her animation was contained in her wrists, which moved the praise ring, and her mouth, which formed sounds.

'*En, oh, peh, kuh. Kuh, peh, oh, en,*' she was singing with a sweet and clear voice.

I have caught you out, he wanted to blurt. Caught you being yourself! He thought of all those leaflets he had made advertising the new lobby group, stacked up in his study against his mother's wishes, all the petition forms he had drawn up, the reading and research he had done, the sense of purpose it gave him, and how he was right not to stop.

Sara turned to them. 'I am teaching your child the alphabet,' she said. 'Say it Henry, say what you've learnt.'

The baby looked about him perplexed and managed one fat sound, 'Ma,' then a slimmer one, 'Mi.'

Sara, standing in the square of light that came through the window, shook her head at the smiling baby. 'No, no, dear child. Phonemes are next week. This week is the alphabet. But you are a clever child, a clever and wondrous child, are you not?'

'He's five months old.' Helen paced towards Henry and picked him up. He had rarely seen his wife so brittle and agitated. Conversely, he rarely saw his mother so relaxed in another human's company as she had been for that brief moment with Henry, before they interrupted the scene. Sara linked her fingers and half smiled.

'Every month is a gift. Every month is a month he won't have back. Your child is a genius. Don't overlook him.'

Helen stroked the downy silk of the baby's hair. He stood in the centre of the room trying to command a presence, mark himself as the axis of this little set-up. Sara was watching him keenly as if she knew all too well what he thought. Could she tell where they had been, that they had made love where she had also made love, slept, read, embroidered mythologies? Could she smell their sex, like a rude smell that intrudes in the middle of a perfectly good reverie?

'I mean it,' Sara said when Helen had gone upstairs to change Henry. 'He's a special child. Don't overlook him.'

The Conception Events did not pass Henry by; he knew what his parents were doing, as if he understood something of the gravity of it. He did not want to be replaced or added to, but nevertheless he was silenced, as if awestruck, as if something wonderful would come whether they each welcomed it or not.

The nights passed with solemn committed attempts at a child. The prison was his first serious project, and with this, and the new child that must surely be on its way, his life seemed to be moving forward. They listened to Buddy Holly. *Buddy will be the first thing this child ever hears*, Helen observed. *She'll come out screaming, Buddy Holly! It'll mean Joy! I'm alive!* And when the record was finished, revolving on the turntable, he noticed he was recalling the gunshot. The leaf. The leaf, the gunshot. The sight and sound of them had begun rushing into almost every silence. Stuck whispering in its grooves the record would send him off to sleep. It is nothing, he told himself. Joy is gone, it all amounts to nothing. Don't think of it.

After a fortnight of the Events Helen said she had been having some peculiar dreams, that maybe they would come into some money.

'We will?'

She set her head on the pillow and closed her eyes. 'Mmn,' she said, drifting, her speech loosening. 'I think.' Her knack for plucking sleep from nowhere was astonishing, one moment talkative and the next torpid and heavy-eyed.

'Buddy Holly,' he whispered into her ear. 'Eureka.'

'Yes,' she whispered in return.

'And when we do, we'll build a house, do you want that, Helen?'

He stroked her back and arms and let an urge for her abate. She didn't answer. He lay for half an hour and thought of the wet peat that had been caked to his shoes, Joy's white hand carving angles in the darkness. *Here would be a good spot.*

With the factory behind like a frame, d'you see it? With the sun rising behind.

Again he asked, 'We'll build a house, Helen. Glass. Something for Henry to be proud of. Do you want that?'

'Ssshh,' she said in her childish sleep-voice. 'I'm having a dream, I'm dreaming about Alice. Alice under the cherry tree.'

'Who's Alice?'

'Indeed,' she whispered, smiled, then let sleep take over.

CHAPTER 7

He is late. He scurries from the bed and dresses fitfully. Sometimes there is this urgency to *get out*. Get out, deconstruct this big sleepy being that dwells in bed and *get up*. Eat, get out. What if he could get up at this point before the dream of Joy began so that he did not have to dream it for thirty-five years? What if the moment packed itself into a gunshot and died with the sound? Before he leaves the bedroom he glances at Eleanor who sleeps on, the cumbersome shadow of himself that he has left behind, as if he must sever himself from her to form a new day.

Today at least there is a reason for this urgency, and as he descends to the kitchen he wonders if his hair is acceptable this morning, if Alice will approve of the way he has gone thin and grey on top and of this funny round-shouldered thing that has happened to him. Well, she will not approve, but she may accept. She may smile, put her fingers through the grey strands and say, 'There is still a little black underneath, Jake.'

It has been so long since he saw Alice; when he

pictures her he always tries to put her in the context of a place and to imagine the objects that surround her, but in fact all he usually gets is the image of her stepping off a bus or train that has come from a place he has never visited, and then stepping back on it, to the place he will never visit, and her separation from him becomes so apparent that he would rather not picture her at all.

He forces his book into his coat pocket, a book by a man named Seth Hansen about restoring old architecture; he notes the name because Hansen sounds like *handsome* and the words intertwine until he can no longer tell them apart, and until the author is imagined as a striking, knowledgeable, middle-aged man despite his photograph that suggests otherwise. Hansen, handsome. Different words, same words.

In the garden Lucky dozes comfortably on the grass in a triangle of brand-new morning light, her injured leg heavy on the grass. The corrugation of her ribs catches the sun in bars. He must feed her, he thinks, before she gets any thinner. Feed her, and then walk her, that's what you do for dogs. He mustn't forget.

'Lucky,' he calls through the open door.

She is still. Dead? He panics.

'Lucky!'

The sleeper wakes, possessed of an instant wit, and trots inside. She sinks to the floor at his feet and rolls over, a flash of white streaking up her belly by way of invitation for him to stroke her, which he does. She closes her eyes. He stops. She half opens her eyes and shoots him a look of betrayal. He strokes her again. Whole days have passed like this, he is sure. Whole lifetimes.

In the glass of the cupboard door he runs his fingers through his hair. It is always a test of nerves to see Alice after a long absence. Daily she grows more beautiful; monthly the acceleration of beauty is so marked it makes him laugh with pleasure; yearly the phenomenon becomes indigestible. It makes his heart ache. It sends a dull pain down his left arm that he long mistook for heart disease, thinking he had inherited what his father had. His heart is fat in his chest and his fingers tingle with the wasted energy of a love that has never found proper expression.

He retrieves a piece of meat from the fridge and takes it from its wrappings. It is a breast of lamb, clean and unbloodied. He hurls it into the garden and Lucky saunters out, circles it, sniffs, begins licking suspiciously, looks to him for approval and only settles to it when he nods, yes, yes it's yours, it's safe, eat it.

The dog's eyes close, her tail twitches on the grass, and, utterly consumed, she rips at the shreds of meat so precisely that it looks like she is sewing them together.

The bus station is empty but for a couple of men in uniforms eating bacon sandwiches, the fat yellow in the bread. He realises he is hungry.

Both excited and nervous at the prospect of seeing Alice, he buys a coffee and paces, trying without success to get an overview of himself in the glass of the waiting room. For passing moments his reflection is there, but is promptly broken up by blocks of daylight or a loss of focus. Slightly underfed, is all he manages to glean at first; or, if it can be counted, if it is not too obvious, old. Old, and yet well, as if there is nothing wrong with him at all.

The uniformed men stand and one comes to him. 'Waiting for a bus?' the man asks.

'I suppose it could be construed that way,' he replies good-naturedly.

'Which one?'

'It gets in at eleven.'

The man scrubs at his chin briefly with the back of his hand. 'Well, it's – not even, let's see, not even eight.' The poor man makes a pretence of looking at his watch.

'I didn't want to be late,' he explains.

The man laughs. 'Yeah, well. You aren't.'

So he waits, and the light shifts. It appears from around the back of the bus depot and begins filling the bays, and now people arrive and do what he can only think of as *people-ish* things. It is as if their repertoire is limited to a fistful of verbs: arriving, eating, drinking, talking, smoking, standing, sitting, waiting, going.

For a short while he reads; or at least looks at photographs of buildings with a sense of fondness and urgency as if these old *ratty tatty* structures were dying people that need his charity. Victorian, Baroque, Edwardian, Georgian: they sound so worthy of life. But before long his concentration gives and the dog enters his thoughts. He wonders what she is doing, and feels guilty about leaving her, after all, he ran her down and got her into this predicament with her leg. What if she can't get to her feet, if she's hungry? Did he leave her food? Water? He finds that the hand in his jacket pocket is clutching two inches of envelopes, inside of which are the letters. Read them? Don't read them? Read them? No need to read them – any fool knows what they say. Helen was a good-looking and intelligent woman, and a marriage is small in a world obsessed with love. Don't read them, but keep them within reach always, in case. Just in case.

A warm day is gathering. He looks at his watch and studies the hands but cannot fathom how a hand here and a hand there – and another edging continually behind them – is supposed to reveal the time of day. While he stares his breath flutters and anxiety rises in his chest until finally he gets up, buys another coffee from the vending machine, and stands and waits.

Alice wants to introduce him to her new partner, who is a poet. Well, good, in a way; he was always worried that he and Alice's partners would tread on each other's toes or compete in man-talk. With a poet, though, it will be obvious from the outset that they will have nothing in common and that they may as well not even try. And sometimes friendships grow in this way. Yes, he is hoping for friendship, and he is pleased with himself for becoming gentler with age. Where before he might have objected and worried about the logistics of a poet supporting a wife and child, he now only hopes there will be a child, and is prepared to let the logistics go.

With the bus station filling with people he feels he is in the way and makes again for the bench. The coffee is now cold. Hot, then cold. Full, then empty. Dark, then light. These are becoming markers of time – often, without them, his brain would not know how much time had passed, or even *if* it had passed. They are proofs of time. He cradles the cup and taps at its beige plastic. His nails are bitten. The pads of flesh at his fingertips are as pink and new as the day he was born.

Alice has warned him: don't expect too much, she is on her way somewhere, she can't stay, she would love to, she can't. Well, he is used to this *en route-ish* style of fatherhood; his children have never been *his* children, not in the way this watch on his wrist is, or the hair that has begun absenting his head, not even in the way the food or the bourbon in the cupboard is his. One's children are too huge, too much, one loves them too much, kills them with too much love. *Impossible* to possess a thing that possesses you. He opens out his hands. It is such a small thing now, this constant, wholesale relinquishing of his children, so routine that it feels prosaic. They have simply been on a lifelong passing-through. Now they are – what? He does some quick, slovenly calculations. Thirty, or thereabouts. They have truly passed; there should have been some sort of ceremony for it. Anyhow, a bus comes in. He waits with interest, but it is not Alice's bus. Another comes, and then another.

Here she is suddenly, squinting from the bus's interior gloom. He has woken up without knowing he had slept. He must have heard her voice somewhere at the rear of his consciousness, that quiet singsong of it behind the one-way glass.

Observing her step off the bus with a tall blond man who limps (limps? Limps! He must admit to a small surge of triumph), he notes that her hair is longer and darker than he had remembered it. His memory had logged it as blonde and fine like the hair of a child. She is more adult than he had remembered and her face more serious. More angular and exceptional, but otherwise, in all the core detail, she is just as he has always known her. Just the same.

She hugs him and stands back. 'Meet Seth.'

'Seth. How are you? I'm Jake.' He extends a hand which the poet clasps.

'I see you're Jake. Didn't take a lot of deducing, right?'

'Seth and I only have a few hours,' Alice tells him with a slight southern accent that makes her sound aloof. 'So we could have lunch – and Seth wants to see some of the projects you've worked on.'

'Very well. Whatever you want. A restaurant for lunch, or home?'

Alice brushes an imaginary thing from her eye. 'I don't feel like going home somehow. Maybe when I'm not in such a rush, when I can do it more justice. Dwell a bit.'

A little relieved – the place is scattered with a thousand slipshod thoughts, a hundred forgotten tasks – he nods. 'Yes, dwelling would be – better.'

It is a bright and decent day, warm enough away from the breeze that has picked up. On Alice's impulse they buy sandwiches and two flasks of coffee – there is a bakery which lends out flasks and cups for a pound a day, a service there is no real call for in this area. They use the service out of pure nostalgia. It used to seem the epitome of adventure when Alice and Henry were children, to walk into the town, buy sandwiches and cake, rent a flask of coffee, and camp down on a piece of green, lie back, talk about the shapes of the clouds.

'Constructing a building is similar to constructing verse,' the poet says, rolling a cigarette.

This irritates him immediately; similar how? One you do with a crunch of numbers and a pile of materials, the other with a pen and an edgy relationship with reality. He says nothing, and eats.

They have a spot on the bank behind the Edwardian building he had been campaigning to save: St Hilda's, formerly a school, shut down in the 1960s, used for the last two decades as a place to run classes for the deaf, which have now been moved to the new community centre – a building he also had a hand in and is not especially proud of.

'I've been trying to secure its future,' he tells Alice and the poet – Saul, Seth. The name will not rest in his mind. He gestures with his sandwich towards the building.

'Its future as what?' the poet asks.

'A school, preferably. But most likely it will just become flats, in which case we'll – they'll – sell it to a developer. At least it would still survive that way. But a school would be better.'

'And are they succeeding?' Alice asks, pouring coffee. 'In saving it?'

'Yes, maybe they are. Maybe they are.' He eats the sandwich, enjoying his hunger. 'I want to see it secured, the demolition plans binned, all that rubbish cleared out.'

'Why?' the poet asks. 'Why not let it go?'

'Because I don't want to.' He hopes a debate isn't on the horizon; he just wants to eat his sandwich and drink his coffee, to sit here with his knees drawn up to his body, unchallenged.

'But if it doesn't make sense, right, to spend all that money when you could make something new and *better* for a little less, then why don't you want that?'

'Because my career was to make buildings, not keep knocking them down.'

'And part of creating is destroying –'

Yes, yes. He knows this. The man could be dictating from his own soul. Create, destroy, destroy, create. A see-saw, a tide, life, death, poetically tilting from one pole to the other. And yet this so-called poetry has created nothing, or little, he can now put his name to. The creation of some high-rises in London, now mostly, yes, poetically, destroyed. Some concrete leisure centres still standing. Some uninspiring schools packed to twice their capacity and annexed by Portakabins. A prison, his son inside. But in general, above what stands, there is all that no longer stands. The poet wants to see some of his buildings? There *are* no buildings to see. They are gone. A faint programmed guilt at the shamefulness of what he built, and a mounting amnesia over them (did they ever actually exist?) are what he has left of his career. If he wants to be stubborn at this thirteenth hour, and stop washing along with the current, if he chooses to fight even if his cause is pointless or misguided, then he will.

Alice offers him half of her sandwich and he accepts gladly.

'How do you feel about retirement, Jake?'

'It's fine,' he tells her. He has no idea if it's fine. The poet has put him in a bad mood. After a pause he flattens his hair to his head, hoping it does not look too ridiculous. He finds his fingers are digging, digging away at the grass, soil in his nails. 'Every day I feel – things become thinner,' he says. 'The world becomes thinner.'

Alice frowns. He watches the butterfly-wing dip of her brows. 'Thinner? More' – she gestures an I-don't-know with her slender hands – 'more – temporary?'

Silently he blesses her. Like her mother, she is always keen to understand. She does not, ever, belittle with triteness and scorn. The poet throws the cucumber from his sandwich and, without drama, grasps the air with a fist.

'There *is* a thinness to things,' he says. 'I think jobs distract us from it. As soon as that distraction is gone the days look – flimsy. We look at ourselves and feel flimsy. Who are we, what are we meant to be, all this shit. This is the shit we spend our lives running from.'

With this declaration the poet stands and wanders off towards the building, casual even with his limp.

He wants to shout after the poet now and tell him about the CND and the Israel group he ran from the table in The Sun Rises, the group whose name he can't bring to mind. They did things. They were *effective*. When he thinks of those meetings he can remember nothing except for a couple of faces that may or may not have belonged to that table at that time. He remembers how, years later, he organised blood donations for the Israeli soldiers going into the Six Day War, and he and those people around the oak table all gave theirs. Henry's school announced that Israel would be destroyed, so Henry emptied his money box and gave its contents to the cause. He knows that what they all did was idealistically extreme, for a greater good, and he knows he was respected for it. He knows the poet would respect him for it, and he would call after him now, but the poet seems otherwise absorbed.

'How did he get that?' he asks, watching after the man. He clutches a stone in his palm.

Alice inclines her head. 'The limp?'

'Yes.'

'We had a bet. I bet that you would ask about the limp when Seth wasn't listening, and he bet you'd come out and say it in front of him. I think he had this idea of you as a brash, formidable man who would have no qualms about pointing out his faults. Anyhow,' she shrugs lightly, 'it looks like I won.'

The dug-up earth in his hand comforts a slow, drunk feeling that is beginning to occupy him. 'I see,' he says. 'And did you have a lot of money on it?'

Again she smiles. 'It was a sportsman's thing. We try to keep money out of everything.'

'Next time you bet on me maybe it would pay you to bring money into it. You know me, after all. He has no idea.'

He pats her leg and she passes him his coffee. The wind becomes restless and blows their hair. Full of DNA, hair, a single strand can tell a child who their father is. Alice's flickers out long and fine. Just one strand of that hair knows about him, can testify to him. He is in every part of her.

'I have this dream,' he tells her, or at least tells some invisible vanishing point beyond her. 'That there's a woman in a – what do you call it? The place with the food.'

'Kitchen?'

'Tins and jars, things that don't go off. Sara has one. We don't.'

'Pantry? Larder?'

'Yes, quite. She is naked, Alice, and she has labels which she sticks to the jars. She goes up and down the rows of jars. But when she reaches the end of one – line – row – the labels have already fallen off the first jars. It's endless, Alice. Her job is endless.'

'Like Sisyphus rolling the boulder up the hill,' Alice says. She pulls a shawl over her thin shoulders. 'Just to watch it roll back down again.'

'I dream it again and again.'

She leans to him and strokes his temple. 'Dreams are good for us, Jake. Even bad ones. Ride them. Do you know how? Focus on the jars, say, or the woman, and say *this isn't real, this isn't real.* Let one part of you step out of the dream. Remember you're its master, and not the other way round.'

He sees his daughter blink her lilac eyes. When they reopen they are blue. With her head caught just there they are bluegreen.

'And the woman gets older,' he says. 'She starts young and –' He gestures curves with his hands. 'In the end she's old. She looks like a fucking plank of wood.'

Alice smiles, seeming surprised.

'Your mother was afraid of growing old. Your mother was not afraid of anything but growing old. She was –' He frowns and seeks his train of thought. 'Was she old?'

Alice is pensive. 'Fifty-three. That's not old.'

She engages his eyes for a moment with a look that is worried, that is sympathetic, that borders on suspicious. He smiles to distract her and, returning the smile, she retrieves her hair from the wind and sets it in place behind her ear.

'Alice, I'm afraid I have a disease. I have Alzheimer's.'

She brings her hand to her mouth; on anybody else the gesture might show gossipy surprise, but on her it seems only to press back any words that haven't had time to be considered.

Eventually she takes her hand away. 'I saw something in your eyes, before. You aren't yourself. I knew something wasn't right. I thought you just seemed lost, because of Helen.'

'I am lost.'

The relief, to have told her, is so immense that he is heavy and warm with it.

'How long have you had it?'

'Two years,' he says, though he is not at all sure of this. It isn't a lie; it is his best shot at the truth.

'So what does it mean? Can you manage?'

'Yes, for now. I have – that other lady. She helps out.'

'Eleanor?'

'Is that definitely her name? It doesn't seem right somehow –'

Alice takes a careful sip from her drink and puts the cup down.

'I haven't told Henry,' he says. 'Just you.'

'Why not Henry?'

'Because I have to look after him.'

She crawls the two or three feet to him and puts her hand on his cheek.

'Then I'll look after *you*. Don't worry, I'm here. You see? I'll make sure you're alright.'

Her look is all Helen's; capable sympathy. Somebody who knows how it all works. He clasps her hand and swallows a grief that has welled in his throat.

'It's my brain, Alice, I feel like all my wires are being unplugged one by one. No, not even in an order, just unplucked. I need to keep it all together. I have to stash all the documents in one place quick before they blow away, do you understand? You could help.'

'I'll take time off work, come for a fortnight or so and we'll go through everything you need, I'll read up on it and we'll go through everything.'

'When will you come?'

'Let me organise it –' She takes her hand from his cheek and sits back on her heels. The poet is wandering towards them in his own world, concentrating, his hands translating some train of thought; he seems to be calculating something.

Alice looks across at him and then back, then presses her palms on her thighs.

'Jake, is it bad timing to say this now? Me and Seth are going to have a baby.'

For the moment he is shocked. A flock of birds lift from nowhere and crowd the sky as if they, too, are shocked. They stain the air with prime colour and beat their wings. He sees, behind the birds, the poet receding again, scanning the brick-work of the derelict building. Alice? His child? Having a child? How extraordinary and miraculous that this could happen. He finds a stone in his palm, wonders where it came from, and pushes its reassuring shape into his coat pocket.

'Everything will be alright,' she nods. 'I'm going to look after you.'

'You are really having a child?'

'Yes, Jake, really.'

'Buddy Holly,' he grins, gripping her knee. He is – yes, he recognises this feeling – he is exulted.

'Eureka,' Alice breathes. She tips her head back in gentle laughter and draws her hands into a prayer.

Waking confused, he turns to the woman, to Eleanor. Quite dislodged, she seems lying there – plucked from old time and put into new. She doesn't belong; he doesn't belong. Vertigo, he feels like he has vertigo. Is he still at the bus station? Has Alice's bus not come yet?

No, he is somewhere familiar. The room is half

lit through the single curtain drawn across the French windows and he hears birdsong. He sits up and frowns into the pixellated light, gripped now by elation, and now by a morbid disappointment that quickly becomes anger. By the bed is his book he has so struggled to read these last weeks. He fails to remember what it is about, but picking it up it falls open at pages on the restoration of an Edwardian school, and a photograph of a small – what is the word? People with signs refusing to allow the bulldozers in.

Was all of it a dream? Is the dog real? Did he feed her the lamb, and has he *ever* fed her lamb, and has he ever even fed her at all? I bet I have killed her, he thinks. In the dream he was fighting for a building and it felt so good to have a cause, a corner. Where is his corner? He searches out the shapes and objects of the bedroom and finds them momentarily unfamiliar. Where is Alice? Where is his *corner*? Which is his war, which side is he on?

As he lifts himself from the bed he realises that the illusions of his sleep have spread to every edge. There was no such time on the grass with Alice, with the poet. He may have been to the bus station or he may not have, it may have been today or five years ago, because time is not considerate enough any more to make itself clear.

There is no poet. There is no grandchild coming. No Alice. There is only now. Now! Like a punch in the face. And now again. Now is so endlessly small and inadequate. Now there is the urgency

216

to get up, get out, get away from Eleanor, shoo away the heartbreak of the dream with a coffee, some water – he is so thirsty – maybe a mint julep. Drown it. He is breathless with trapped tears. He has never dreamt so vividly. He wishes never to do so again.

STORY OF THE CUT-OUT SOLDIERS

In the next room Helen was saying goodbye to the members of her Bible group, who slipped out through the French doors of the study and appeared in the garden with their King James's tucked under their arms. Then he heard his wife call out, 'D, you've forgotten your notebook,' and some chuckles and the clean, succinct contact of young lips on young cheek.

D, she called the man, and yet to call somebody by their initial seemed too familiar for a Bible group. Then he considered that the only other person Helen might have called by their initial was God himself. D was honoured indeed. What was he? Devil, Dream? Was he drastic and disastrous? He tried idly, over his shoulder, to get a view of him through the window but the man had gone.

When Helen came into the living room this is how he was, his neck craned as he fluttered his hands over the piano keys, Henry sitting stoically in the crook of his arm.

'What's that you're playing? Is it *Three Blind Mice* or something?'

'It was meant to be Debussy.'

Helen laughed and then put her hand to her mouth.

'It's difficult one-handed,' he said.

'I know. All my life is one-handed.'

On the left side of his body was the baby; on the right side, in his pocket, a letter from Eleanor. With Helen close by the letter felt the heavier of the two, so much so that it made Henry weightless; he tightened his grip on the child and stretched his little finger to the octave below; he was not anywhere close to being good enough to handle Debussy – such strange chords and fingerings – but he wasn't interested in starting anywhere lower. Better, he concluded, to be very bad at a difficult thing than very mediocre at an easy thing.

'Well, Jake,' Helen said. 'What do you think?'

'Of what?'

'Of –' Her expression changed, less curious, more excited. She reached for Henry. 'Haven't you been upstairs? Don't you know?'

'If I say, *know what?* will that give it away, that I don't know?'

'Follow me.'

She beckoned him out of the living room, into the middle room from which the stairs led. They climbed together, he following her. The letter shifted silently in his pocket. Henry babbled at him over Helen's shoulder and pointed in great excitement at the wrought-iron birds and leaves of the banister. He glanced out of the landing window at the road and the church. The church bells were ringing, six o'clock, he thought, though there were never six chimes, always waves of them one after the other breaking on his eardrums. He looked at the back of his wife's shin-length rayon dress as it moved along the landing. He looked at the small stain on the carpet where the roof sloped at the eaves and piles of blankets were stored. Henry pointed wildly at the walls, the blankets, the stain, the doors, the webs, and laughed in bubbles.

They went into Henry's room, across its chocolate-brown carpet, past translucent mobiles, a light blue cot, wardrobes along one wall stuffed with unpacked boxes of photographs, Christmas decorations, clothes. To the right was a low inner door – a secret door, Helen had remarked when they first looked round the house. They bent double through it and were then in their bedroom. If they had taken the other stairs that led to the bedroom directly from the study, where they had almost begun, they would have been here a minute ago, but Helen liked the game of the double staircase. She would enjoy it, she had said, when there were two children in the house and they could run around, up and down the two staircases, in loops like birds flying.

'Look, Jake,' Helen said, pointing unnecessarily at the bed. 'Look what Sara gave us.'

In the middle of the bed, on their faded pink

blanket, were piles of cash – neat structures of ten-pound notes.

'What is this?'

'Some money from your daddy's death. She was going to give it to you another time, when she – passed away, I suppose,' Helen hesitated to give the notion some respectful space. 'But she wants you to have it now, she said what use would it be to you in twenty years? It'll be too late then.'

He approached the money and handled it. 'She came here today, and gave you this?'

'One thousand pounds. Your daddy was richer than you thought.'

He said nothing. Henry made an aimless grab for the paper and then put his fist in his mouth.

'We should go and thank her. Perhaps we can have her round for dinner?'

'Yes, if she'll come,' he said.

He was not as shocked as he thought he should be. In his mind he was always going to be comfortable; to see his bed awash with money was not as incongruous as it was for Helen, who had chosen him, perhaps, for his lack of comfort. Despite his profession there had always been a whisper of poverty about him. He attracted all that was insalubrious; it was his gift that his wife most cherished – the gift of a house with cobwebs the length of legs, of rising damp, of an edge to her billowing and unchallenged world view, a mild demon that proved her god.

'It will help us when we have another baby,'

she said. She rested Henry amidst the piles of money. Perhaps she was trying to envisage how they would look in luxury. Seeing her small, worried smile he took her in his arms and nodded. He would have been shocked by all this had he believed for a moment this was, as Sara was claiming, his father's money. As it was he had other ideas.

'I'll see my mother tonight,' he told her.

Sara didn't speak, but went to the kitchen to make coffee. He waited, out-staring the orange carpet before feeling the inevitable urge press his bladder. The letter was hot in his pocket; he skim-read it again as he stood at the toilet, unpicking Eleanor's handwriting. By the time he came back downstairs from the bathroom Sara was placing a tray on the coffee table. She plumped up the cushions on the sofa. She was wearing the dress he most liked to see her wear, a long brown wool dress with a dark yellow belt, and a run of four fake buttons at the neck.

'Sit, sit,' she told him.

Coffee came, and sugared ginger.

He took the plate in the flat of his hand. 'Thank you, Sara.'

'Don't mention it. I was about to have coffee and ginger anyway. I always do before bed. It's a strange little habit I've picked up.'

'Yes – I mean for the money.'

'Oh, that.' She sat across the room from him in her chair and pushed her skirt along her thighs as if trying to shoo it away. 'Thank your father, not me.'

'Well, I can hardly do that.'

'Asch.'

'It's a lot of money, Sara.'

'I suppose you are going to offer it back, and then I will refuse to take it, and we will bicker like this for five minutes, and I will win, and then we will be in the same situation we are now, yes? So let's agree not to do this. Time is short.'

She popped a cube of ginger in her mouth. It was typical of her to diagnose time like this: time is short, time is running out, there's no time, the time has passed. He ignored the comment.

'I wasn't going to argue, Mama, in fact I've already decided what to do with the money, if you approve.'

'Good.'

She smiled and put her plate on the carpet, the ginger neatly consumed, and took her gold-rimmed coffee cup from the tray, ran her finger round the rim until it settled on the chip.

'I want you, Helen and Henry to be comfortable,' she said.

'Of course.'

He waited for her to ask what it was he had planned, but she only chewed in apparent thought, surveying the fireplace from a distance as if she were deciding whether she liked it. He tried to remain composed – easy at any other time with any other person, but with his mother – never easy. Never easy. Hysteria flickered in his gut and he swallowed. If he were hysterical, would he get a reaction then? An emotion? Or just this: this woman facing her own silence?

'Aren't you going to ask what I plan to do with the money, Sara?'

'Must I ask? Can't you simply say?'

Yes, he realised. He had been stupid, childish. Why did he have to wait for her prompt?

'I'm going to buy the Junk.'

'Oh.' Her expression gave nothing away; it was neither approving nor disapproving, kind nor unkind. 'And what will you do with the Junk?'

'Knock it down and build another house.'

'You have a house. Perhaps you could do some little improvements to it. It's, what is the word, ratty tatty.'

He smiled, then stood. 'But if I buy this land I can build the least ratty tatty house you've ever seen, something completely new and fresh.'

She gave out one unamused laugh, again, not unkind, not kind. 'As you wish,' she said.

With his coffee cup cradled in his hand he knelt at her feet.

'If you hate the idea I can do something else with the money. Invest it for Henry's future, say, or take Helen around the world. She's always wanted to fly.'

'She would be afraid to fly when it came to it, and the rest of the world is not so interesting, Jacob, only different people doing the same things in a foreign language. Build your house. Do well, make it comfortable, make sure you succeed.'

He stared up at her face with his hand on her knee. He had a faint sense of humiliation, that she should now be telling him to do the very thing he had already decided to do. It was a constant choice, a battle. Hysteria or composure.

He straightened and sat back on his heels.

'Where did the money come from?'

Sara shrugged and pursed her lips. 'The bank paid out far more money than I expected. Lucky, yes?'

'The bank that father worked in?'

'That's right.'

'That was very generous of them.'

'You say generous, I say fortunate. I always think if you have had bad fortune in your life then you will have an equal amount of good fortune. So here is mine, and I'm giving it to you because I'm too old for fortune. At my age everything is already decided.'

'It isn't father's money, is it?'

She put the coffee cup on the floor near his knees and rested her large hands on her lap. 'Jacob,' was all she said.

'It belongs to your aunt in Austria – what was her name? Schorske? Aunt Schorske. I remember you telling me about her once, she was the only one surviving, wasn't she? So now has she died, Sara?'

'As a matter of fact, yes.'

'This is decades of family inheritance in one lump sum that's now sitting on my bed.'

Her eyes dipped, her shoulders fell a fraction, her hands sagged in her lap. The change was by parts of degrees but he saw it nevertheless and it startled him.

'When did she die?'

Sara shook her head.

'And you didn't go to the funeral?'

He ought to stop, of course, what with his mother diminishing visibly before him, and Eleanor's letter in his pocket leaving him no moral footing at all, but he could not stop.

'It's a transaction, isn't it? You exchange your past, with all the difficult feelings you can't bring yourself to feel, for some money, and then you give the money away and wipe your hands of it. Simple.'

Rich coming from him, he knew. He relied himself on the very idea that emotions were disposable, just as Sara had taught; emotions were asphalt roads, the more extreme the emotion the straighter the road. The straighter the road the faster one could travel, shuttle, shuttle one's way into a sort of charmed oblivion. He had no rights, no *grounds*, to be pushing her into a sentimentality he dare not feel. But his voice looped back to him thick and calm and it convinced even himself. Sara stood lightly and went to the window, closed the curtains.

'Everybody wants to know about money, where it came from, where it's going. Money money.'

'Yes,' he said, feeling more together now in his small triumph. 'We make too much of it. I'm sorry.'

She could not look at him. 'You shouldn't keep it on your bed,' she murmured.

'You're right. I'll put it in the bank.' He paused. 'The one father worked for.'

'Sums like that get stolen, if you tell people you have it, you lose it. In a small place like this.'

Still with her back to him, a brown-and-yellow figure against brown-and-yellow curtains, a gracefully whittled figure blending increasingly with its surroundings, she began humming. He remained on his knees, twisted so that he could see her better. Then from the humming a chant broke almost inaudibly – a signal of her distress, as a chicken will pull at its own claws.

'I'll go, Sara.' He rose to his feet.

The chanting stopped. She turned, smiled and nodded.

'I'll let you know how I get on with buying the house. Maybe you can help me plan the building –'

She flung her hand up, but flung it slowly in a way nobody but she could. 'I know nothing about architecture,' she said. 'It's all the same to me. You go ahead.'

He dug his hands in his pockets. 'Fine. I'll – go ahead.'

He thought to carry the cups and plates back to the kitchen but decided against this one subservient gesture, not at this stage when he had established some command. He must leave while he could, before he felt so desperately diminished or guilty that he would have to stay and lie awake in the spare room and worry for her well-being.

He hugged and dwarfed her.

'Goodnight, Jake,' she said, fighting gently free.

'Goodnight, Sara. And thank you. Helen thanks you too.'

Sara nodded. 'She thanked me herself. Will you be alright to let yourself out?'

'Yes, quite alright.'

Despite this, Sara followed him to the hallway.

'Are you okay?' he asked.

She nodded. 'Of course.'

'Is there something you want to say?'

'Not at all.'

But for a moment she had the look of a stray dog, lost between these walls, not shielded by them. He recalled her suddenly as a young woman sitting with him on the dyke bank, their bare feet numb in the water and in her hand a marshfrog. *Little invader*, she called it, and let its green head ooze from her hands; its whole body, like a great drop of oil, slid into the dyke. It laughed into brown water. He had been able to smell his father's Makassar oil that she had rubbed into the ends of her long dark hair, each strand thick and strong as a violin string. Her stern brows had butterflied at some moment of pleasure in the frog's freedom.

She seemed, standing before him now, to carry

an outline around her like that of the cut-out soldiers he had played with as a child. Everywhere she went an invader. Little invader, getting littler. He stooped one last time to kiss her. They were never happy, either of them, unless they left the other a little bit less alive.

CHAPTER 8

The fox-haired woman runs her finger over a diagram of the brain.

'Many things are happening here,' she says. 'Do you see these tangles? These are fibres that twist together and choke the neurons.'

'And what is a neuron?' he asks, adjusting his glasses lower on the nose.

'A cell. It transmits messages to the next neuron, and the next. There are billions of them. Without neurons we can't think, Jake.'

'Very well. Go on.'

'These shadows here are called plaques, they're another common sign of Alzheimer's. They are a kind of rash that develops between the neurons. Between them, the tangles and the plaques, it becomes very hard for the neurons to transmit any messages at all. It's like trying to kick a ball through a bramble hedge.'

'I see.' He folds his hands together, thankful that somebody is taking the trouble to explain. 'And is this my brain?'

'No, this is a diagram. From a textbook.' She shows the cover of the book to demonstrate. 'We don't know what your brain looks like, we can't know, but we can predict that it will be beginning to look like this.'

'I see. Well then.'

She stands and pours him a glass of water from a jug on the shelf behind her. He watches carefully.

'My mother used only ever to rely on the things she could count,' he tells her. 'She always said we were made up of cells, just so many of them, we are just a lot of them. But we look like so much more. But we in fact aren't.'

He smiles and the fox-haired woman nods.

'But you could count the cells, if you really needed to, and you would see then that they were – that they were –'

He loses the thought, pinches his fingers in frustration.

'Your mother had a point.' The woman hands him the glass of water. 'On the other hand, cells don't explain everything.'

She pulls the chair out and sits. 'So, Jake, how are you feeling?'

'Neuron,' he says. 'What did you say a neuron was?'

She rubs her eye then folds her arms across her chest. 'Jake, much as I think your curiosity is wonderful, I do find it's better not to talk about these things. It's confusing, and a little frightening. It's better to address the practical issues.'

'I'm not frightened.'

'Well, that's good. That's good.'

'Is this a different room?' he asks.

She pushes the water closer to him (as if this, this water, will solve everything) and he nods his gratitude.

'You mean, to the one we're usually in?'

'Yes.'

'It's the same room. Exactly the same. We'll always be in this room, Jake. If we move – and I don't expect we will – but if we do, I promise to tell you, okay?'

He smiles. 'That's good of you.' He goes back to the picture. On the adjacent page is a different brain, larger and whiter. 'This is a normal one I take it.'

Sitting again, she makes brief eye contact with him and pauses before she speaks. 'That's right. You can see how it has no plaques or tangles, and it's bigger. The Alzheimer's brain is atrophied.' She looks at him and raises her brows a little as if to see if he has understood. He wants to understand, so he nods. 'Shrunk,' she says. 'See how it's shrunk?'

He leans on his elbows, running his hands through his hair and feeling himself become agitated, desperately wishing to stay afloat, to say something intelligent. 'Why has it shrunk?' he asks.

'Because the tissue begins to wear away.'

'And what was it you said before? About brambles?'

She touches his arm. 'I think we should stop there, don't you?'

She has a look about her that he has seen a million times recently: pity, and then relief that this problem is not hers.

'Do we have to do that test today, with the words and the dates?'

'We did it when you first came in.'

She puts the flat of her hand on a pile of papers and he sees some awkward writing, some childish drawings. Sweat dusts his forehead, a bead of anger, a ball of frustration at the forgetting. He leans over the picture of the brain, and something dawns on him.

'These shadows,' he points at the dark, shrunken diagram, 'remind me of the markings put on trees before they're cut down.'

Quail Woods, he thinks, was cut down. Leaving an emptiness. Branches gone, patterns gone.

She looks up to observe, then goes back to her writing. 'Yes I suppose they do.'

'It makes me think the brain is marked up when it is old and no longer any use. I'm no more than a tree. I've been marked up. I've been selected.' Resting back against the chair he draws his palms together, firmly now, as if, for once, he means it. 'The brain is finite, this is what you mean to say. I understand exactly what you mean to say.'

For the first time in his life he feels the hand of God on him, a surge of religion which abates again like a chill wind. She gathers her fox hair into a band and casts him a concerned look.

'That's the bottom line I suppose, yes.'

Any moment now, he supposes, she will write something about his wayward digression into logic. The patient is not supposed to be logical; it is much easier for everybody if the patient behaves and tries not to understand. He feels like letting himself loose in the room, having an adolescent outburst, turning the shelves of books on end. Then going to the next room, and doing it again. *Fucking books!* And again. He tries to make out what she is writing, but he cannot. Odd, the way words sometimes make no sense any more. Odd the way he wants to gather them up like sheep and stop them escaping him. He goes to drink his water, but the glass is already empty.

They come into the kitchen and the woman, Ellie, Eleanor, lifts the lid of the kettle, takes teabags out and throws them in the bin.

'Teabags in the pot, not the kettle,' she says kindly.

She goes to the door, bends to take the post from the floor and hands him a letter. 'Another one from America.'

'From Joy.'

Her hand goes to her lower back. 'From Joy.'

She puts a coffee in front of him and leaves the room. Inside the envelope is a picture of Joy as requested, though he can't recall requesting it. He reads the date on the letter, July 1994. Strange date, implausible, looks too heavy at the back end. The picture shows her sitting somewhere, in front of a large window, looking through the things, the magnifying glasses that make distant birds close, or that one uses to spy. In fact not much of her is visible at all, what with the magnifiers and the shadows and the glare of the window behind.

He understands why she hides from the camera; she doesn't want to age in front of him. They must always be young for each other. Where the handwriting loses curves and gains angles, where the dates creep up, where the black ink becomes blue biro and the photographs go from black and white to colour, they are both silently embarrassed and apologetic at having let time invade.

Her letter is long. It has a plot, something about a trip to Phoenix and the lack of grass there, and the question she poses: how can people live without grass? He doesn't know the answer. Maybe he doesn't know about people any more. But he could live without grass, he thinks in a minute of panic, he could live without anything if he could have his thoughts back.

A swarm of cells, a mass of dying strangled cells. Bramble hedges, unwholesome growth that chokes. His mind sees a garden being strangled by weeds which climb up and over the walls, suffocate the flowers, split the paving, cover the house, reach their wayward tendrils through windows and find the people sleeping and pick at the locks of their hearts, unpick them until they are just dismantled machines. He could live without grass. Without growth and green. Having never been to

Phoenix he knows what it is like, a huge orange desert stabilised by the sun, it never ages or changes, its dryness is trustworthy, its earth is as hard as stone, nothing unexpected comes. He suddenly yearns for this place he has never seen. His thumb traces to the end of the letter and rests on the signature; *All my love, Joy.*

When he takes the letter to the study, rummaging to find the secret place he has always stored Joy's letters, he finds a box file that contains all the literature he made for his group: *LIPAC: Lincolnshire Israel Public Affairs Committee.* Yes, he remembers the name now he reads it – it seems grand and over-important, and he smiles.

There are leaflets with a logo of a rising sun on the front and a schedule of meetings inside, and notebooks of minutes from meetings, and a list of names and signatures with his own at the top, and letters to the government lobbying for pressure to be put on Palestine to fulfil Israel's demands, which he reads now with a faltering understanding and a disbelief that these words could have been typed by his own hands.

What was the point of it all again? If he had a map he would not even know where to begin to look for these countries. The inspiration these leaflets and letters had once provoked in him is felt so dimly now, and with immense shame he cannot quantify but which suggests to him inspiration cannot be worth its consequences – it is better overall to keep one's head down and say and think nothing.

He misses Joy, suddenly. Then he simply misses everything. He puts the literature and the letter back into the box file, puts his coat on, calls the dog and leaves the house.

After an hour of walking he realises he has no idea where he is going, except that with all the talk of Phoenix he wants to travel. Yes, travel! But where to? The dog trots silently at his side, and every now and again he bends to look at her collar and rediscover her name. Lucky. Of course. Stupid of him to forget. So then, if he wants to travel he will go to one of those travel offices and tell them, and they will find somewhere for him to go, so long as dogs are allowed.

He finds himself now on a main road with the rushing cars tipping his balance. It doesn't feel safe; he wraps his hand around the letters to Helen in his pocket and finds his mind tripping from one thing to another. Henry, the felt strawberry stitched into Alice's blue dress when she was a child, Helen's feet smashing a bottle, the royal blue nylon trousers he used to wear, the smell of Makassar oil. As a child, sitting in the back garden of The Sun Rises with Sara, his father, Eleanor, Rook, some others now faceless, singing while Sara played a little old violin and Rook a harmonica. There were always money spiders, he suddenly remembers, in the long grass, up and down their arms, in their hair. What a strange warm memory to come from nowhere!

The main road comes to a roundabout and he recognises where he is. From here he may as well go on to Lincoln since there will be travel offices there, he is sure he has seen them in the past. But where to travel to, he wonders. Maybe he doesn't want somebody to decide for him, maybe he will choose a place now and tell them that's what he wants, and take the cash from his wallet and seal the deal in a moment. And then go, tonight. If dogs are allowed.

What about Rome? It sounds closer than Phoenix; by all accounts he doesn't recall any grass there, but then maybe he hasn't been. He imagines Luigi Lucheni setting out with his sharpened shoe file on his search for somebody to murder. Hot streets and high walls. Amphora pots and crucibles built into the walls; water running through tufa stone. Architecture he has studied and used to know in depth, because one had to, because they were told everything derived from it. Architrave, pediment, pole thing, porch.

The light seems to be failing and he ought to press on, so he walks faster. The dog begins to lag behind. On the horizon the sunset is long and red; he loves this, these elongated sunsets, he loves how flat they make the land. He sees the cathedral perched on its hill in the distance, a sight he hasn't seen for months or years. He used to come here sometimes with Helen to the pictures to see *Quatermass and the Pit*, and *The Hustler*, and that film, that film whose name he doesn't remember but which had no beginning or end. You could walk in at any time and begin the story and it would make sense – and they did this, they watched it several times from different starting points.

The idea of the eternal story delighted Helen and perturbed him. If a thing went on for ever, how could one ever know its centrepoint, where its weight settled? It seemed to him to not be a story at all. It seems to him now far too resonant of the way he is beginning to think, the motifs that repeat in his mind like subliminal messages, someone hypnotising or doping him. Birds flying, the missing *e*. That little keychain; Star of David. Suddenly, now, the word plutonium from nowhere: plutonium; what a funny word to spring to mind, and an image (that surely doesn't go with it?) of a blue peg with an elastic band wrapped around it. And now Joy's yellow dress. Cherry blossom adrift and homeless across the air, almost invisible against grey sky.

He turns to see a bus approaching from behind and waves it down. He lays some coins in front of the driver, takes the ticket and finds a seat. The driver calls him back to say he has forgotten his change. (Forgotten more than my change, he wants to say, but takes the money and sits again.) As the bus makes its way through the town he struggles to recognise the streets he is in. Somewhere around here was some office space he built in the mid 1960s, since knocked down. Somewhere a community centre, since replaced.

He belongs to a period of architectural amnesia, he thinks, holding the dog's head to his knee to steady her. Most of what he built has disappeared as if it never existed. The prison building is the exception, he still counts that as a success and spares a thought for Henry cooped inside there, until the thought becomes envious: to be inside there too, to be safe, to be with his son. To be there playing chess with his son, to know which side you are on. His breath forms on the window.

Out of the bus, he and the dog begin searching the quiet streets. No travel offices to be seen, and his legs are beginning to ache now that they have had a chance to rest. Finally, as he is beginning to fret that he is lost, he finds one of the travel places. The front is all window with pictures of beaches and mountains. He tries the door but it won't open. With his head to the glass he sees that there is nobody inside, and when he looks around him, up and down the street, the story is the same, everything closed. It is quite dark.

I want to go to Rome, he thinks sulkily. He and the dog scour each street hoping to find something open. He starts to feel hungry and the hunger addles his thoughts. What was it his mother wanted him to do with that money? It always felt like a test: did she want him to spend it and rid the family once and for all of its European past, or did she want him to spend it on something that would prolong that past?

And then there is the letter from Eleanor which he realises now he had quite forgotten about – just

240

as he forgets about Eleanor he supposes. And he shouldn't do this; Eleanor is all he has. Did he drop it at his mother's house? It got somewhat lost in all the drama of the money. It had seemed so heavy with portent there in his pocket while he tried to play Debussy, and then it slipped from the picture. And then there are the letters he clutches now from Helen's lover, which he knows (and is happy for the absolute certainty of the knowledge) must not be opened. And Joy's letters, strange, intoxicating Joy, a surge of yellow in his mind. He is hungry and thirsty and can't think any more.

The streets become a jail; he is lost. One street just looks like another, and he finds himself climbing a hill steeper than his legs can manage, so that he sits halfway up catching his breath, stroking the poor dog's head and wondering at what point he became an old man.

Hours must be passing. At the top he buys an ice cream just before the man packs up for the day and drives off. The cathedral is at his feet, the square empty but for a couple treading their way across with a packet of crisps, and darkness is falling fast. There is nothing he can do to get home, or get to Rome, there is nothing he can *do* for himself or for his dog to make this better. Once he would have been able to solve any problem or navigate through any city, and now he doesn't know which way is home, or how far it might be – only that he is exhausted.

Another hour of walking around and he finds a

bus; he came on a bus, so he must be able to go on a bus. Another half an hour and he is somewhere unfamiliar. A few questions to passers-by to find out where he is, a blast of panic in the middle of a narrow street in a narrow town on what feels like the edge of nowhere, or worse still the edge of everywhere, as though another step will scatter him far and wide beyond himself. A slow, aching trail through the small town, past the fish-and-chip shop, blinded by a memory of Helen by the fire: *monkey goes into space, Egypt, Israel.* Freckles on her eyelids that she could never see. The static crackle of her petticoat as she took it off, little green flashes in the dark that made her gasp – *my petticoat's flashing!* Maybe he could get some chips, but he has lost the confidence even to do this, wondering what he would say to the person behind the counter. Maybe he will cry. Here. Sit here and cry?

Another few minutes of moving forward, because moving forward is the instinct, and now there is a police place. He goes inside.

'I'm lost,' he says. 'I need to get home.'

Some activity and showing driving licences and identity, establishing addresses, raised brows – he must have walked some fifteen miles before he got on the first bus, is he okay? Yes, but hungry, and the dog is thirsty. Both are given water, and then put into a car and driven across a now deeply dark flat landscape. Shame descends. He has done a bad thing. The police are involved.

Gradually the motion of the car relaxes him, his legs relax, his head is heavy on the back of the seat, his hand a hot weight on the dog's head. So grateful for the police car that is taking him home, so very thankful. Though the dog sleeps soundly next to him on the seat, he is awake for the journey. The police drop him off outside the house, coming to the door to make sure this is where he lives, and to explain to the woman what has happened. She nods at the door in her dressing gown while he shuffles past to sit at the kitchen table; from here he has a view of her back. Wide back, short hair coerced into a band. He fidgets. Already the last few hours are hazy. If she asks, what will he say?

When the police go she sits heavily opposite him with her head propped on her hand, just looking at him – in anger? In dismay?

'You wrote me a love letter once,' he says.

'I did.'

'I don't know what I did with it.'

'You burnt it. I found a corner of it in your grate.'

She stands and wraps her dressing gown around her. 'If you want to escape from me save yourself the effort. Any time you ask, I'll go.'

As she leaves the kitchen he sees bottles floating on the sea. Hundreds of bottles with messages inside. Today, or sometime this week, he went to see the fox-haired woman and talked about cells. In his brain are countless cells – countless, but not infinite. To say infinite would be reckless. Inside each cell a little piece of him is packed, and every time a cell dies a piece of him dies. His past is just an electric impulse. Static flashes on a petticoat. Gradually he is being scattered and lost – hundreds of unread messages floating out across the sea.

STORY OF THE LOVE LETTERS

He crouched on the bedroom floor, spread out the paper and drew plans. A large cube of glass here and another smaller one here, joined by a corridor. The low elevation, the seamless joints of glass, the lights embedded in the ceiling. An Irving Berlin record played through and began rotating silently as he worked. He glanced towards the money under the bed and set his thoughts back to the evening after they had decorated The Sun Rises.

He replayed it: Rook and Eleanor had gone to stay at Sara's house; Eleanor often did this because she hated to be alone on the moors, and that night she was paranoid and spooked because of all they had smoked, and because of Joy's odd appearance at the door, and the likeness of her to the sign. She couldn't get it from her head that Joy was a ghost. The two women had not taken to each other at all. Joy had expressed – with her lazy feline lack of expression – huge enthusiasm for staying at The Sun Rises alone in all that darkness that was so lacking in London, where she lived, from which she was escaping for a few days. And so it was

245

settled, and it was just him and Joy left there with a storm coming in and the rain beginning to fall.

After Eleanor and Rook had gone, then, Joy had set foot on the white garden, realised that the concrete was still setting, and drew her foot back. She hopped onto the wall instead and walked around it to meet him. It was windy and getting dark, and in the distance Rook and Eleanor were making their way on bikes along the road. She sat on the low wall and, with long young fingers, folded her ear in half.

'I've run away from home,' Joy yawned. 'I can't decide whether to go back or go to America.'

He looked up to the heavy sky. 'America.'

'Oh?' She arched a brow. 'Have you been?'

'On my honeymoon. I recommend getting a car and just driving and driving until you reach the sea.'

'And then?'

'Driving back again.'

She inspected the fine layer of concrete on the bottom of her silk shoe but seemed unbothered by it. 'You don't have to stay and look after me, by the way.'

He laughed at that, at the idea of looking after this woman. Then the rain had begun to fall, fluttering at first on the wind and then coming sudden and heavy; his thoughts were still muffled from the *cigarettes* they had smoked, and by contrast the rain was cold and soothing. He had no urge to go indoors.

'Let's go for a walk,' Joy said, jumping from the wall. 'You know the way animals huddle from the rain – well I can't bear that, huddling. The rain has to be faced.'

She grinned and stalked out of the garden, across the concrete, and he followed, leaving their two sets of prints across it. As they walked he told her about the glass house he wanted to build and they linked hands – some solidarity against the rain perhaps, or some instinct to play their parts without unnecessary loss of time. They trudged half a soaked hour to a place from which they could see the Junk, a sunken house like a forgetful old man making his way somewhere, and behind it, in the dusk, the line of birch scrub like thin white limbs. And behind that, the great chimneys of the steelworks and the gas flame aglow in the rain, purple and unextinguishable.

'Yes, here,' she had said. 'Build your house here, so that the house is framed by the factory, d'you see?'

She cut a rectangle in the air with her long arms. There was a coarseness about her, an enthusiasm that overlooked the mud on her hem and shoes; her dyed red hair was the rebel in a massive flat conformist landscape. He both liked and disliked the crude words she used to describe the house that she envisaged there, he liked and disliked it that she so easily shared his vision – excavate some land, the water table is so high here (look at the rain pooling already underfoot) – build a floating glass house like a lantern, hang silk in its windows so it glows against the black, green silk, purple silk, yellow silk. He liked and disliked her, and where the like and dislike met and cancelled out there was him, himself, some lost person found.

'Green silk, purple silk, yellow silk,' she said, and turned amber eyes to him. Two molten cast-offs from the sun, he thought. Two coins. Planets.

'You're immortalised,' he said without thinking.

She wiped rain from the end of her nose and flicked the drops into the torrent around them. 'At last!'

He smiled. 'The woman on the new sign of The Sun Rises is you.'

What was he saying? What nonsense. What a dishonour it was to his wife, from whose imagination the painting had come.

'Apt, then, Jameson.' (It was not the first time she had called him by his surname, as if they were partners in crime.) 'Because I fully intend to be an alcoholic when I grow up.'

'A good ambition.'

'May as well have ambitions you can achieve. My family is full of not-quite-but-almosts.'

He stared out across to the Junk, felt rain run down the back of his neck. Joy wrapped an arm around him. 'I don't think you're like that, Jameson. You'll make it.'

'We're huddling,' he said, and moved away.

With Helen he would never be so abrupt, too protective over her, too concerned with keeping her happy. Joy just smiled, shook the affection from her hands and laughed one single *ha!* as if she had caught him out.

They made their way back to The Sun Rises. Reminded of it by the mud that was caking their legs he began talking about the myth of the golem, how the golem, in Jewish mythology, was a creation of the holiest of holies. The holy man would make himself a golem out of mud to prove that he, like God, was capable of creation. Then he would bring the creature to life with spells; the golem, brainless, without its own agenda or heart, would serve the holy man as a slave serves a master.

'*We* are virtually made of mud,' Joy had said, flapping the sodden yellow material of her dress. 'Never mind the golem.'

They ran the rest of the way. Back at the pub they filled Eleanor's bath deep with hot water and got in fully clothed, shoes and all, until the water was brown. What he did not mention to Joy, what he would not want her to know, was that Rook had always joked – in a perfectly serious way – that he was Rook's golem, his dumb unfinished creature. And it had always seemed to be a harmless childhood game, all those play fights, always losing to Rook even when he could have won, always being controlled one way or the other. The thought of it through adult eyes sickened him. Then there he was in a bath with Rook's granddaughter, and it could go any way. Any way he wanted it. Rook had no part in this even though Joy was one of his own, his clan – he had no part in what happened next.

They had peeled their clothes off and climbed into Eleanor's huge bed dripping, ignoring the untidy lovelessness of the room around them. Outside the bedroom window the new sign banged and swung in the wind. No words were spoken at all, none were needed, and anyhow the creak of the ancient bed did enough to fill the silence. Never, never, had he felt so utterly aligned to another human being. Afterwards, as she rose from the bed and bent to her sodden dress, he bent with her.

'I love you,' he said.

'And me you, all of a sudden.'

She had taken the leaf from the silk of her shoe and stuck it on his arm. He thought of how they were positioned, hunched double on the edge of the soaked bed, their heads pressed together.

'We're huddling.'

She smiled like a cat, like a cat that has just seen an open door.

'That won't do, Jameson. That won't do.' She sat upright, stretching out her long spine, her skin taut and chalk white. She stood, pulled on her yellow dress which clung to her skeleton. A gunshot rang out over the moors – deer culling, he thought. Deer killing. And he briefly weighed the words for their difference while Joy cocked her head towards the rain pelting down the windows, then narrowed her eyes.

'Guess what,' she said, 'You've persuaded me. I'm going to go to America.'

He leaned forward a fraction and touched her hair. 'Don't.'

'I'm going to go to America. Going to leave this rain behind.'

So that was then, and some short time after that Joy went without a word, and some time after that came the money, and the paint on the sign outside The Sun Rises faded a little in the heat of the summer. Some time in amongst these times Eleanor's love letter came, declaring what she would never declare (or so she said) to anybody else, and saying also that she knew about Joy without him having to say a word – she knew, she just absolutely knew – instinct and jealousy told her so.

Eleanor's take on his encounter with Joy was painfully tender. As she saw it, Joy entered the garden as tall and unapologetic as a sunflower, wearing a yellow dress and yellow shoes, and he, some dashing quixotic figure exhaling smoke, decided to deflower her. And when the moment came it was unequivocally wonderful, because the sunflower succumbed to his charm, and he to hers, and they were suspended from themselves and from time like dandelion clocks floating on the breeze. When they landed reality hit. He went back to his wife, she went to America. There was no remorse, only happy memories that would begin eventually to feel like dreams. He wondered how accurate this would prove to be, whether remorse would come. And he wondered how many times Eleanor had gone over and over the scenario in her head, poor Eleanor, relaying it with spelling mistakes, promising she would tell nobody what she knew.

Though she intended for her words of love to hit hard, they instead landed on him so lightly. Toy words. So insubstantial compared to his compressed, shrinking, infinitely dense memory of Joy.

Joy didn't write. Nothing came. He decided to cast her memory aside. The more he reflected on it the more he thought of how impassive she had been, and he wondered if he had perhaps taken advantage of her. She was very young. Rook's *granddaughter*. And he Rook's son in all but blood, in all the ways that were supposed to count. There was a sickly feeling of perversion, if not incest then something else which he could no longer put down to mere infidelity. As he read the lovely scenario in Eleanor's letter he was forced to confront its opposite scenario, that he had perhaps forced Joy into sleeping with him. Of course he hadn't forced her – but had he? How could he know for certain?

Even more distressing was that he did not feel guilty, neither for Helen nor for Joy. He felt new. Visions of his glass house buoyed him until the Coach House began to bleach out around him, and when he and Helen took to their Conception

Events he focused on his sudden hunger for another child and on the being that would become Alice. Helen had described her (you think hard enough, she said, and your thoughts will be the case). Pretty, average height, she will have long fingers and small ears and lilac eyes, a little elfin, honey skin, freckles, her father's strong nose. All this was very well, he thought, but not enough. She would have Joy's height and arrogance, she would not be all good and all God, and lilac eyes were fine but Alice's eyes would be indecisive and refuse to settle for lilac alone.

Upstairs the money sat under the bed in surprisingly few neat piles – a thousand pounds did not look much when it was stacked. It had been there for some weeks, and in those weeks he had made investigations into the ownership of the Junk, except that the task was far harder than he had imagined. The house belonged to a woman called Mrs Crest, but nobody could find her. She had bought it several years before, in 1956, but never lived there, and left it to fall to its current state.

He chased up all the possible leads until they ran dry; he made enquiries, rural communities had strong grapevines – but nobody knew of Mrs Crest. Some had vague memories which turned out to be mistaken and some knew Mrs Crest senior before she died, and there was an illegitimate son, or daughter, or no, that was a different Crest or maybe even a Croft, no, to be honest nobody paid much attention to those decrepit little houses. They were much more interested in the people on the new estate with the car, or the people who were going on holiday to Australia by plane (it was taking them three days, they had to stop all over the world). Nobody went on holiday to Australia by plane, if they went there they stayed for good. Mrs Crest, probably, had done this. Probably never coming back.

He took his wife and child across the moors and drove them right out to the prison, wanting to show her where the new building would be, wanting to show her for once what he did.

'I suppose you could just – well, *have* the house and land,' Helen suggested in the car, in response to his long exposition of the problem.

He smiled. 'Steal them?'

'No, use them. And if Mrs Crest ever came back you could sort it out with her then.'

'And if she didn't?'

'Well, then no harm done.'

'Helen, God would not approve.'

'Don't simplify everything. Right and wrong come in shades of grey. You always try to simplify things to on or off. You're, what is it? Binary. You're Binary Man.'

He laughed and wound the car window down to throw his cigarette out.

'If you've tried everything you can to find her Jake, and she's just disappeared, then – well,' she looked out at the manor house ahead, the stone lions at the gates, and played with her wedding ring.

'Those lions are very striking. Are they to protect the prisoners from the outside or protect the outside from the prisoners? Anyway, about Mrs Crest, it's just a suggestion.'

'It's a really charming suggestion. I mean, what's property anyway? Why not just take what you want and then just *settle* it afterwards if needs be. No harm has ever come from people taking land from each other.' He shrugged in jest. 'It's just land. The Palestinians, they don't mind. And that footpath we got rid of when we built those houses in Bromley, the local community didn't mind that at all, that's why they campaigned for two days in the rain to get it back. *Pedestrians shouldn't be walked all over!*'

Helen glanced at him and tucked her hair behind her ear. 'It's just a forgotten little piece of land, Jake.'

'And with those words a thousand wars have begun.'

They drove past the no-entry signs and parked by the manor house in bays marked *no parking*, where the first foundations were being dug up against the manor. Land for the grounds was being levelled, the topiary uprooted, a small fountain removed, the security fencing marked out by stakes and tape in a wide circle as far as the eye could see. As they walked around Helen became sullen and hugged Henry who, always deferential to her, was sullen too. She was upset by the idea of imprisonment, she was upset by her inability

255

to conceive straight away, she was tearful with pride at her husband's work, even if she could not condone it, she said the flatness no longer scared her but made her melancholy. She said she was sorry for being such a terrible wimp, and she smacked a kiss on Henry's cheek.

And then a month later a letter arrived from America. In it Joy said that she had got his address from Eleanor and that she hoped he didn't mind her writing, but in the two months since she had left England she could not stop thinking of him. She even recalled a bruise he had had on his leg. She had met a man in California, a rich man who owned vines, and she was wondering whether to marry him – what did he think? If she did she would have to become a Jew, have a proper Jewish wedding (what if, she joked, she became his golem?). Did he think that was too big a step? Should she?

The letter caught him off guard. He had not expected Joy to think of him and his bruises, or at least to think of them only in hate. He put the letter in a satchel and stuck it under the bed with the piles of money, as if under-the-bed had become a mythical place for all expectant things, as if Mrs Crest herself would turn up there. As he drove out to get fish and chips that evening he mulled the letter over in his mind, his heart reeled despite his head knowing better; Joy, he repeated to himself.

He came home and Helen poured him a beer,

made herself a cup of tea, got forks, salt and vinegar for the chips. They ate in front of the fire, and when they had finished eating Helen fed the fire with the newspaper, making the flames spit with fat. *Last woman in Britain hanged. Dog goes into space. Fifty thousand jobs lost. Russia tests nuclear device. Monkey goes into space.* He watched the news burn with pieces of fish batter. Helen leaned forward and took a triangle of paper that had dropped down through the grate, not that day but some day previous, and she asked what it was, the writing on that corner of paper. He told her it was a letter from Eleanor simply because he couldn't manufacture a lie any faster. Saying what? She asked. Saying that she is in love with me, he replied. Poor Eleanor, he had not meant to make her emotions public, it just came out in the rush of things.

Helen frowned – why are you burning it? she asked. You should never burn love letters. Love letters are okay? he asked. Yes, they are okay – so long as they are one way. She patted his leg, put the corner of Eleanor's letter back into the grate as if that place of salvation was where it rightfully belonged, and turned the lounge lights off. Except for the firelight they were in darkness.

Look, she said, pulling up her skirt, taking off her petticoat. As the satin rubbed against her stockings the material flashed, green sparks of static. It was such amusement to her. Look at me flashing!

He smiled and watched the flames, drenched in chip fat, glow a similar green. Then she redressed, turned on the lights, sat looking into the fire. She confided that she'd had a love letter – a love note – from a man in her Bible group and she would keep it for ever. D? he asked. She was surprised – yes, D, how did he know? Short for devil, short for disaster? Short for David, she said. He raised his glass of beer. Well then here's to David. Helen raised her cup of tea. And here's to Eleanor, poor Eleanor, and to being loved.

The fatty flames snapped, wafting bad news and smells of vinegar into the room.

Yes, they toasted in unison.

Here's to being loved.

CHAPTER 9

Time speeds up, rushing headlong into conclusions, then it stops. There is something teenagery about it. Something uncomfortable and maladroit as if it has not learnt how to pace itself with space.

'No,' she says, and her words are the first indication that he has been saying something out loud. 'No, Jake. It's you, not time. Time is just as it was. It's you, we have to help you relearn, like I've been telling you.'

She sits at the kitchen table beating eggs. Embarrassing, but he cannot remember her name. So desperately embarrassing because he sleeps with her, he knows her, she is not a stranger.

Since he dragged the police into his disease things have changed; suddenly he is a liability, suddenly nothing he says or does can be trusted, as if it used to be quite an informal kind of illness and now it becomes official. The timeline is a mass of crossings out and corrections. He feels to be the supremely unconfident author of his own life. Question marks appear against words, then he deletes the question marks, thinking that if he doesn't question the truth there is no question about it. It is only *him*, as the woman says, only him who is confusing things.

He bruises mint into the sugar solution with the back of a spoon and leans his senses into the sphere of the crisp sweet smell. Of course, there is no smell. Every day he wakes and thinks, today I will smell again. Some primitive optimism stirs: today I will smell again! And visions come, as if to correct that optimism – Henry as a warring adolescent in tight jeans and black boots, and that constricting shirt he always wore as if he were trying to commit suicide by his clothes alone; in the vision Henry's childhood is breaking from him like rocks from a cliff-face, and the boy's adulthood is the result of some avalanche of which he, the father, is the unhappy cause. And of course this has nothing to do with being able to smell and not being able to smell, except for the sense of guilt, that the lack of smell is the punishment for bad parenting, for somehow allowing his son to lose his childhood. Or taking it away.

'It's early for mint juleps,' she says, watching him make the mint syrup.

'We used to drink mint juleps at four in the morning,' he counters.

She smiles and pinches salt into the egg mixture. 'Have you taken your tablets today?'

'Yes,' he nods, and sits, allowing Lucky to rest her head on his knee.

'Let me check.' She goes to the cupboard, to

the small box in the cupboard, and opens it. 'The pills are still here,' she remarks. 'Which means you haven't taken them after all.'

'Oh?'

'I'll get some water.' She tips the pills from their bed of – white stuff, white wool – onto her hand and goes to the sink. This is her system, to section off two pills and then go back to check he has had them, as if she is tracking the behaviour of a badger in the garden, the strange snuffling behaviour of some night-time creature.

'I don't want them,' he says. 'They give me a headache.'

She sits and pushes the glass towards him. 'Is that why you didn't take them?'

'I thought I had taken them.'

'Yesterday, Jake, I found pills in the bin.'

He shakes his head. 'I didn't put them there.'

'You mustn't lie. Honesty is everything.'

'I'm not lying. I didn't put them there.'

'Well, anyway. Have these.' She taps the table. 'It's important, they're keeping you well.'

'I didn't put them there. I just thought – I wasn't sure. I didn't *put* them there.'

Already he cannot think what *they* are, where *there* is, nor what exactly they are talking about. He repeats the line, it comforts, it seems to have meaning even without his understanding it.

She smiles faintly, her scrutiny deep with good intentions. She is wearing wide-awake and all-seeing make-up around her eyes.

'You just wanted to get rid of them. I understand. They give you a headache, darling, I
understand, but you must take them, they're doing
you good.'

He rises and pushes his chair away roughly. 'I
didn't put them there!'

Fuming, lost, he wishes for a beach of stones
and solitude, and him in a long coat facing the
ocean, him coddled in a coat and miles of windless
isolation.

'This is insane behaviour from you, testing me,'
he says. 'I am not obliged to put up with it, I have
a busy day.' He begins clearing plates and cups
from the table and piling them in the sink.
Stoically, she takes them out.

'These are clean,' she says. 'We haven't had
breakfast yet.'

He eyes this woman – this stranger, friend, those
pearl-pink nails resting assured on wide hips, that
firm regard, the silver thing hanging around her
neck, the small cough that raises her chest. How
dare she presume to be half known to him and
half unknown. Darling, she calls him, and the
word breaks his heart. Struggling from her gaze
he takes a cup and smashes it against the wall,
then stares with clenched fists at the mess.

'I didn't put them there,' he says.

'Your grandfather had a scar here and here,' he
tells Henry. 'Across both cheeks. At university the
Jews would be challenged to fencing matches, and

if they lost they ended up with a scar where the other man had made his mark – to show he owned the Jew. To –'

'Stake out his territory.'

'If you like. Territory. Yes, territory.' He straightens himself tall in the chair. 'Of course the Jews learned to fence. They turned out to be better at it than the others. Success is the Jewish disease.'

'All success is a disease, Jake.'

Within moments the pause in the conversation becomes insufferable; the noise of chatter around them and a child babbling encroaches on them. He used to love silences. Now they are just flood-plains for questions and doubts, in which the seep of continual panic makes itself known.

Henry has a bruise on his cheek, blue and rude. Neither has mentioned it yet except obliquely but it looks, he thinks, painful and has started to spread beneath his eye. He wonders what happened to the photograph of his grandparents. The fencing scars on his grandfather's cheeks had appeared silver and symmetrical, like tribal scars. Next to him his wife, holding her praise ring with a crooked smile that suggested she might, at any moment, throw the praise ring in the air, twirl around and catch it. Henry has that look too, that mischief.

'What is your surname?' he asks Henry suddenly.

'Jameson,' Henry says, and interlocks his hands at the end of outstretched arms, peering and serious.

'Yes, Jameson, that's right. The same as me, of course.'

He smiles and stirs the tea with his finger. It's hot; he withdraws his finger in surprise. It is gratifying and logical for him and Henry to share names – he can see himself in his son's face, in the dark eyes, black almost, and the long lashes, the straight line of the lips.

'How did you get it?' he asks, waving a finger in the rough direction of his son's cheek.

'Just a fight, nothing important.'

'You shouldn't fight,' he hears himself saying. 'You really shouldn't fight.'

Henry scratches at his stubbled hair and frowns. 'Sometimes you have to. Like you just said my grandfather had to – he'd have been cut to pieces otherwise. It clears the air, it establishes order.'

'Yes, but you shouldn't fight.'

The conversation echoes in his ears as one he and Helen would have had, with the roles played by different actors – now he is Helen, and Henry him. But Helen would have said it with such force, giving anecdotal evidence and quoting from the Bible. The *Reasonable Book* she called it. The Reasonable Book favours peace amongst men, tolerance, gentility, turning the other cheek. He, on the other hand, says it merely as a lazy platitude because he is unable to think. *You shouldn't fight, you shouldn't fight.* It sounds right, after all – broadly acceptable, harmless enough, a wisdom given by a parade of faceless ghosts moving through his brain. He rests on his elbows, places his chin on entwined fingers. 'How did you get the bruise?'

Henry laughs. 'I told you, it's not important.'

Rage again, rage from nowhere – just looking at Henry's shorn head heats his blood, and seeing the shallow hills and wells of the skull that used to be covered by dark silk curls, and the lost beauty of the face, and the new beauty of age and fear, and the bruise. My child, he thinks. Straightening his shoulders again, winging them back, he pushes the bag he has brought across to Henry. Provisions, as they used to say. The things one provides.

'You don't like my hair,' Henry smiles. After a pause he adds, 'You were staring at it as if you wanted to put it in a bag and drown it.'

He shrugs as he so often does now – a large vacant shrug. 'I think it's quite difficult.'

'I'd grow it,' Henry says, 'but they like you to keep your hair the way it was when you came in, so they can identify you easily. I'd like to grow it.'

'They don't want you to reinvent yourself,' he says, remembering this word, how Helen had said it to him on their second or third date while sitting on bomb ruins in Stepney, running her hands through his newly cut, oiled hair. *You've reinvented yourself. For me?* She is hopeful and happy. *Can you reinvent yourself,* he asks her, *if you didn't invent yourself in the first place?*

'Exactly,' Henry responds. 'We're supposed to stay as we are, to prove we're useless, to prove

265

to society we're useless so society can feel useful in comparison.'

And what did Helen say in return? He trawls his knowledge of her for an answer, feeling that he must end her sentences now that she can no longer end them herself, and that he will lose her if these memories fail him, lose her completely.

'Henry, I tell you about your grandparents because it's important for you to know who you are and where you come from.'

'Is it?'

'Yes. There was a lot of money – there was very much money given to us when you were a baby, and it was from your grandparents, and their parents, and theirs. And it should have been yours and Alice's but I have failed you. In failing you, you won't ever know about them.' He reaches forward. 'None of that will *belong* to you.'

Henry gathers in the top of the canvas bag and holds it to himself.

'It would have made no difference.'

'It would have helped you –'

'Be Jewish you mean? I'm not Jewish. I know about it all, my grandparents, Sara – all those weeks and months I spent with Sara cooking, we talked a lot. She always told me I was going to be amazing, some brilliant achiever.' His hand alights on his head briefly and then sails down, slaps a thigh lazily. 'I know about it, and you're right, none of it belongs to me. I haven't worked out yet what belongs to me. This place I suppose.'

He looks around almost affectionately. 'This place.'

They sit quietly for a moment.

'So what happened about the letters?' Henry asks. 'Have any more come?'

'No, no more. I have them, here, do you want to see them?' His hand cradles them in his pocket and he goes to put them on the table.

Henry bars the offer with his palm. 'I don't want to see them. They're Helen's. It's like putting her underwear on the table or something.'

Yes, he thinks. Rather like that. Rather an exposure.

'I opened them,' he tells his son, 'and I know who they're from. A man called D, David.'

Henry narrows his eyes. 'Last time you were here you gave a long speech about how you wouldn't open them – it wasn't morally right, an unopened letter is the property of the sender, etc etc.'

He has no recollection of those words or that visit; it is bleached out like the pattern from a tablecloth. No recollection of when he last saw Henry, no traceability for his own words.

'Well,' he replies eventually. 'I did read them, and the sender is a man called D. It's short for devil.' He smiles, feeling genuinely amused for a moment. 'And he was your mother's lover, another Bible lover, he used to come to her Bible groups. I've met him in fact.' He adds, dishonestly, 'He's extremely ugly.'

'Her lover?'

'Yes, and the letters are very animated.'

Animated, he thinks, but not at all erotic. He leans forward, puts the letters on the table and spreads his palms on the – what is this, what can it be called? – this table plastic. 'They are about Moses and the Mountain of Solitude. And the Ten Commandments. You go up the mountain to pray, and down the mountain to have sex. You see, you have to go down the mountain sometimes. D says there is nothing wrong with what he and Helen did. It's about weeding. It's in the Bible.' He bangs the table softly as he says this. 'It's in the Bible.'

His son looks quizzical and forlorn, and so he reaches forward and takes the small hands, overwhelmed by a need to protect and restore, and be a father, a good open-minded father.

'Henry, she will have had her reasons for what she did,' he assures.

They sit like this for some moments and he is surprised that Henry does not recoil, or that he himself does not. Henry appears to know nothing about his disease – surely he would recoil if he did. The timid little child was always afraid of infection by others. He would whip his hands away now if he knew his father's mind was rotting, but because he does not there is a sense of victory, over the disease itself and its captious, jeering nature: something is only a fact, he tells himself, when a lot of people know it. Until then it is an unfledged rumour.

There is clatter from the – the tea place, the

268

teashop; the woman has dropped something and its smashed pieces mosaic the floor. He sees the liquid spread, hears some ragged applause and a quiet opera of sounds he cannot place, sees everything as if in slow motion and for the first time. Seeing it miraculously, roundly, sharply, red, blue, white, quiet. He blinks at leisure. The experience is new, he thinks, as if he has just fallen to earth. Everything mint and unreasoned.

In time he relinquishes hold of his son, and Henry turns the letters in his hands.

'They're not even opened, Jake.'

'Let me see.' He takes them from his son and observes the sealed *V* of paper. 'No, no they aren't, you're right.'

'So how did you read them?'

'I don't know, but I did read them. I remember it.'

Henry leans back and looks around.

'When I get out of here we'll go flying. You know that flight I bought you – we'll do it together next time.'

'I must have fastened them again,' he says quickly. 'Yes, I definitely did that. I used the sticking things.'

'I'll be out in about five months. Maybe less. We'll go flying.'

'I used the sticking things – that's right, let me see –'

Henry draws his finger to his lips to signal silence, then reaches into the pocket of his trousers.

'Here, Jake, I got you a present.'

On his son's palm is a glass dome, and inside the dome is winter. Loose white, like snow. Inside, navigating the snow, is a mother and child. They hold yellow hats on their heads against a wind nobody else can feel, and their yellow scarves snake up on the same wind, to confirm its direction. It blows across them, left to right. Their long coats are as white as the snow and the yellow is everything, all the colour in the world, the yellow is what makes the white white. Henry shakes the dome and holds it between thumb and forefinger. Without the scarves and hats the mother and child would be phantoms in the flurry.

Henry hands it over. 'Here,' he says. 'My cellmate was given it by his grandma and he threw it away. I took it out of the bin, I thought you might like it. The poet wanted it – because I had it, such a fucking *child* – he tried to take it.' He gestures, *yours, have it*. 'That's what the fight was for, if you must know.'

'For this?

'Yes,' Henry says. 'For that.'

STORY OF THE MUFFLING SNOW

'**B**ut even if you could find Mrs Crest and buy that land, how could you build on it anyway?' Helen asked. 'It's foolish.'

She held Henry above her head, both of them grinning and gurgling, then she turned and became serious.

'I'm sorry Jake – but it is a little foolish. Isn't it? You can't build on the peat. It's useless, when I just walk on it I sink –'

He sat on the sofa, his knees wide. 'Have you seen the plans for the new M62? It goes right across the Pennines, across miles and miles of peat moor. Do you know the lengths they'll have to go to just to be able to stand on the peat and cut it out? If they can do that, Helen, I can do this.'

'You said yourself that there's land for sale everywhere all around the moors. Just not *on* the moors.'

'Right, not on the moors.'

He took a mouthful of cherry wine; it was raw in his throat.

'Why must you always prove yourself?' she asked.

'I want something good for us.'

'This is good. Everything we have is good.'

Some emptiness made itself known to him; a hole, a distinct yearning for something more than this. 'I just want it,' he said, spreading his arms. 'Glass, coloured silks, a sea of black. Some sense of achievement and –'

'Control,' she said, hugging the baby. 'Power.'

'No. Satisfaction.'

'You're spilling your wine.'

He looked down to find there, on the carpet, a wine stain. 'Satisfaction,' he said, correcting his hold on the wine glass. 'When did you start walking on the moors anyway?'

'While you're at work we go, don't we, Henry? We love it. It's magical.'

She began waltzing the baby slowly around the room. Beyond her the late evening sun glared through the window, holding her in silhouette. Birds flew up behind her in the garden, startling colours flashing and beating on the air.

'Sometimes we go and see Eleanor,' she said. 'Sometimes we talk to the peat cutters, and they show us what they've found. Little wooden Bronze Age tools and Roman whistles. From time to time, Jake, they find whole trees preserved in the peat, did you know that? Birches and oaks.'

He nodded. 'Yes, I did, yes. When I was a child –' He dismissed the sentence and passed his eye over the stain. That sensation in his gut again, yearning, fear of nothingness. 'So – you're happy here?'

She stopped her waltz and smiled. 'Yes. We're happy. And you?'

We, you, as if Helen and Henry were one, and he a quite separate other.

'I'm happy enough, yes, but I want this house. I'll show you the drawings. Let me get them.'

'All you ever want is what you don't have,' she said mildly. 'All you ever think about is what is far away.'

I remember how orange your hair was, he wrote. *How long will it take for the dye to fade, or has it already? Will it fade or will it grow out?*

And in answer to Joy's question, in her previous letter, about his bruise, he wrote that he got it falling from the stepladder whilst cleaning the windows. Anyhow it was gone now, that bruise. He wrote that he loved her, he did it, he braved the words again without even knowing if they were true, and in the process of writing they became true. A gunshot, a yellow dress, hair tangled over her shoulders, a woman with a man behind her eyes. Joy; he repeated her name to himself as he sealed the envelope and penned out her Californian address in his tall, stiff letters.

D, he heard as he crossed the drive to the car. *D, see how Henry loves you? He's so happy with you!*

Helen and her Bible group were gathered in a circle of chairs under the almost-bare cherry tree; it was late in the season to be outside. They were wrapped in Helen's blankets and the cold, failing light seemed to dignify their struggle with the large questions. Always the large questions, he thought. Every week they took the Reasonable Book and bartered with it: how do we reconcile anger with God? How do we best protect our children in a dangerous world? Is it right to hang a man or a woman for a sin? An eye for an eye – but doesn't that eventually leave us all blind? What will happen to me when I die? My hands? My soul? Does it say in Revelations? Where? What page, what verse?

Henry was cocooned in blankets in the man's arms, D's arms – and D was smiling and nodding as the conversation moved around the circle. Today they were discussing Jerusalem. What little he had caught of the conversation revealed their abstract view of it, a city of peace, a city that symbolised man's redemption. What absurdity, he thought. A city is a city, nothing more or less than the people and buildings that make it up. There is no timeless miasma that hangs around it perpetually restoring its spirit; its spirit is only flesh and bricks.

He said so. 'There are probably nuclear weapons in Jerusalem as we speak,' he offered as he opened the car door. A shudder passed through the group. *Nuclear weapons* was a phrase to shrink from, this was the Sixties, nuclear weapons were for earlier, cruder times than these.

'Jake,' Helen warned.

They eyed him with disdain, D especially. Good, he thought. D was a good-looking man in a closed, harmless way, and Helen looked astonishing beside him – something of D's tameness freed her of her own. They looked like they understood one another. She was beautiful with her legs curled and her body lost to the blanket; he only knew her lap was there because the bible was resting on it, otherwise she was a swirl, a question mark, an open question. Her almond freckled face appeared as a beacon of hope and health in the ill light. Beautiful, he thought, terrifically so. 'Helen,' he said, content to leave her this way, with D. Beautiful with D. 'I'm going to post a letter, I'll be back soon.'

'Yes,' she said. 'Of course. Be as long as you need.'

'You'll be alright?'

'I'll be more than alright.'

After posting the letter he kept driving. The ridge pulled him in its direction and he assumed he would stop there, that the pull would end and he would linger long enough to recollect his time there with Helen, earlier that week, when they had flown the plane. As an early birthday present she had given him a model glider attached to a bungee cord; once propelled only God knew where the plane would land. They had taken it to the ridge, Helen running and shouting, *There it goes! Chase it!* How she loved the dream of flight. Every escapist urge in her converged on the wings and engine of an aeroplane. He thought he would stop there at the ridge and fondly recall Helen of a few days before running along its spine with her heels flicking behind her, but he did not seem to want to stop. He continued beyond the ridge further than he had been for years, right out to the sea.

Theirs was a long and frozen coast. Seals littered it. He hated to see them, thinking they must be cold and bored simply lying there with their great gelatinous eyes. There was often snow in the air even when the day was warm elsewhere. As a family the three of them had come here when he was a child, he, Sara and his father. His father had seemed proud of his English coast (as he thought of it, *His English Coast*), and afraid of it also, because at the point at which the tide met the sand England was truly jeopardised. It became no-man's-land, then at some point Europe. It became everything of Sara that he neither knew nor understood.

Regardless of the weather they would lay a table-cloth out on the sand and sit a little way back from the seal rocks. His father ate fish and chips with – when he came to think of it now – jealous, nationalistic enthusiasm, and he and Sara followed – Sara always bringing a plate from her bag to put the food on, discarding the newspaper by folding it small enough to go in the pocket of her coat. Once done, she would eat hungrily and squint out across the sea. He never knew which to follow, Sara's strenuous long-range gaze, or his father's absorbed, squirreling attention to everything near. He tended to settle for the middle distance, finding there two dozen pairs of seal eyes blinking into their own horizons. He would eat and read the paper over his father's shoulder. *Dog goes into space. Israel. Dog, monkey*; the three of them would eat in peaceable silence.

Now, pulling the Mini into the car park, he followed the path through dune grass and came out onto the wide stretch of sand. The tide was out and the sand was tinged grey by the threat of snow. There were already fragments of it sharp on the wind. Ahead, standing with their arms linked, was a couple. They were distant and beyond the seal rocks, but he knew without doubt or hesitation who they were. The shorter one, in a long coat, barely moving, was Sara. The taller one whose legs seemed impossibly long against the endless horizontal landscape of beach, horizon and low sky, was Rook. Rook's arms were pointing over here, over there. Sara turned her body to follow their direction, and then the two of them walked a few paces forward towards the sea.

He thought they would, at some point, stop and re-enact the family picnics of old, Rook sliding in seamlessly to take the place of the father, a few memories walking in to take the place of the child. Only this time both arms (the long and the short) would point out over the sea and both minds and mouths would dream of what was beyond. Hallo Europe, they would say. Nice to not see you! But their collective mind would see it. There would be a lot of keen talk and laughter, and swapped tales of Austria and Italy which would pass between them like small electric shocks.

But in any case they didn't stop for any such re-enactment. They walked on with linked arms towards the sea. Snow blew in from the north. No use looking out over this sea for warmth and comfort. America was the other way, and California the other side of it. It was not wrong to be in love with Joy; it may seem selfish from an outside perspective, but it was not wrong for him to strike out for something he wanted where it caused no harm, where it could come to nothing. He did not even want it to come to anything, he just wanted something for himself. Sara and Rook had always had one another. Look at them linked like particles. Nothing could break them.

The sky was thickening with snow and the flakes hurried inland with the waves. Sara and Rook kept walking. And they kept walking. They were ankle-deep in water. He dug his feet into the sand and watched, perplexed, while the seals snoozed on. Then they were knee-deep. Sara pulled her coat tighter; Rook took his off and put it over her shoulders. Then Rook was waist-deep and Sara in up to her chest, then armpits, Rook's coat fanned out across the water. He took a step forward in alarm and waited for them to spread their arms and start swimming.

All that remained of Sara was her dark head,

and of Rook his head and shoulders like a bust the waves had sculpted. With one wave Sara's head was gone. He ran forward and called out but the snow rushed into his mouth and muffled the word. He stopped. Rook was gone too. Surely their heads would come back up and their bodies would be swimming. Nothing. He ran forward again. The snow muffled the sea. The white sky left the water black and quiet.

CHAPTER 10

Eleanor turns briefly.

'Your mother and Rook didn't drown,' she says. 'Where did you get that idea from?'

She goes back to digging the compost. The cherry tree is thick with leaves and the tight red fists of new fruit; birds hover above its branches. His eyes blink at the aggravated bash of the birds' wings.

'I can think what I like.'

'But it isn't true.'

He sits on a fold-up chair Eleanor has put out. He knows it isn't true, but he feels belligerent. Can he not *say* things that aren't true? If there is no freedom in words and thoughts then where is there freedom?

And anyway in a sense it is true, in that Sara did finally drown when they scattered her ashes over that very same sea, a vision that comes to him now at a slow swoop: Sara is dead (when did she die?), Mother is dead (how did she die?), Mama is dead. Some part of him knows this should matter more than any other thing, and yet he meets the forgotten news with bareness. Alive, dead; there is a profound difference, but he does not know what it is. It affects him, but only as a news bulletin from a distant land.

Eleanor crouches and, holding a piece of bread for the birds, waits for them to fly near. They flap to the ground, hop, but they will not come to her hand.

'Don't you remember that winter,' he says, 'and the muffling snow, and we had to clear it away. You must remember that.'

'The muffling snow.' She chuckles. 'I do remember. I remember everything.'

He folds his arms. 'Well then.'

It is not that he thinks Rook and Sara did really drown that day, nor that he is confused, just that it is a scenario he has run through countless times and whose tragic slant has become addictive to him. Had this terrible thing happened everything he is might be viewed differently perhaps, with more conse-quence and sympathy, as one might view the mess in a room differently when one discovers it was made by a burglar. Somehow it is not enough to just go wrong in life, to just get things wrong. There has to have been a terrible drama that sets the stream of errors in motion. Had Sara and Rook walked into the sea that day, he would be exonerated. Everything, every other thing would be excused.

'It would have been tragic if they'd died that way,' Eleanor says, watching the birds. 'You need to get the idea from your head.'

'Tragedy is a good thing,' he counters. 'Interesting thing.'

She sits upright for a moment. 'How can you say that? Haven't you had enough of it to know better?'

'I haven't had it at all.'

'Your wife died! Your wife died of a stroke at the age of fifty three. She was perfectly healthy and happy, then suddenly she had a stroke and was gone. Believe me, that is tragic.'

'Death is only tragic when it happens to people under fifty. Death over fifty is just life. It's not sad. Nobody allows the sadness, you just have to get on and cope.'

She extends her arm further to the birds, hunches her back.

'You lost a child.'

'That was my fault, so it isn't tragic. Tragic is when nobody can help it. Comes from the sky. Comes like a downpour.'

When she tries to speak he turns his head away slowly until she is discouraged enough to stop.

'Jake, you seem to think so badly of yourself,' she says eventually. 'How can you think it was *your* fault? You seem to think everything you've ever done is wrong. You're a nice man, you've always been such a nice man.'

He needs the toilet; he can't remember where in the house it is and if he will need to go upstairs, and then if so, which stairs. Two sets. One has to choose carefully. A nice man. Poor Eleanor, she is always so mistaken about everything, so deluded.

'I know you, Jake, I know everything you've done, and you aren't bad. What horrors are you building in your head? What fantasies? What for?'

He keeps his head turned from her and stares into the blankness until his eyes are dry.

'Tell me what you think, Jake.'

Suddenly he feels too confused to answer. Everything seems disbanded and rolling away too fast to fetch.

'Won't come,' she says finally of the birds, and, frustrated, throws the bread on the grass.

He comes to his feet, scattering the birds with his sudden movement, and picks up the bread piece by piece. Then he holds out his hand and stays perfectly still. If he is a nice man he will just die, as Helen was a nice woman and died. The fates clear away the nice first, and then get into the real business with the wicked. I don't want to die, he thinks. I want to go home. I do not want to die before I have got home.

The breeze needles his hair, his brain empties thought by thought, and he feels himself become slowly inanimate. Mindless, motionless, a stopped clock. Even the need to urinate has gone. The birds approach. Hours and days pass without breath or thought. He begins whispering Irving Berlin: *I've got a great big amount saved up in my love account; Honey, and I've decided, love divided in two won't do.* A smile takes his face and he can feel it lift him. One by one the birds take the bread from his fingers.

In the actual memory it is November and the sky is so full of snow it seems unable to support itself. The sea is black. The threat of snow muffles the mind. The couple stops walking, Rook takes Sara's hands and kisses each one, and Sara kneels and opens her bag.

He decides he will observe them quietly, and so he eases the distance between them with a few steps. Even if they turn they will fail to recognise him with the sun setting behind him and leaving him in silhouette. They, in contrast, are washed with a coat of matt evening light that leaves them plain but for the blue tint of distance. Sara takes a flask and cups from her bag – white porcelain cups with gold chipped rims, he knows – and laying the cups on the sand she pours coffee. She stands; they drink.

Crouching, he looks to his right along the beach. A few seals sleep in the high, drier sand, but the colony must be mostly out at sea. The smell of them remains, like a litter of dog pups. When his father died Sara was at this beach, swimming in the frozen water, eating chips and saveloys with Rook, drinking coffee; she reasoned that the brine eased their creaking joints and the cold was good for the soul. His father had been dead for five hours before Sara came home and found him slumped at the kitchen table. Watching her and

Rook now he gets the impression that they are rarely apart. That they seem washed up on the shore, that a mistake has brought them here to England, that some rectifying will take them back to their homelands, and that he will be left. He suppresses jealousy; there is no use for it.

Rook then takes Sara stiffly in his arms, and she eases herself into them, and he watches the two of them waltz formally around the centrepiece of their coffee cups on the sand. They respond to one another like a muscle responds to the brain. In contrast to everything he sees around him, every relationship and happening, they do not look arbitrary. Each leaf has a pattern, he remembers Sara once saying. And the patterns are repeated, and the pattern of the patterns are repeated. The leaf is a billion numbers that defy chance.

Of course, Sara and Rook had once been all chance, meeting in The Sun Rises, Rook sitting in that dusty rope of sunlight popping mussels into his mouth, Sara the uneasy alien holding a child in her lap and twisting her thick Jewish hair. But they used the years as a filter through which all chance was forced out. Now they are bound like the wooden couple that waltzes in and out of the cuckoo clock every hour. Is it love? Yes. It is not that it might as well be, but that it can't be otherwise.

His mother and Rook waltz wide across the sand, in and out of the snowflakes. They are both skilled dancers. Sara used to go to waltzes as a child when she lived in Vienna; he feels, as he squints against the incoming snow, that he is looking through the muffled haze of time and beyond himself into the past. He is taken by a heat-giving happiness. If Sara and Rook walked straight into the sea now, if they did! This lone man standing on the beach, small in the bigness of it all, watching with a jealous heart as his mother goes to her death in love, and takes her (and his) past with her, this poor rootless man, no wonder he loses his way, he is an effect without a cause; poor man.

But his mother just dances. She seems happy. He isn't a poor man, he is quite a rich man, an architect, a father, his mother is happy. He'll have to make and answer for his own fate after all. He stands and, giving them one last glance, turns back to the dunes and the car park.

Why are you so anxious? Helen read.

If his memory serves him, she pressed her thumb into the cushion of skin between his eyes. *Jesus asked his disciples: why are you so anxious?*

She smoothed the creases from his brow with her thumb. *Do not be anxious about anything. It will not add a day to your life.*

He told her he had just seen his mother at the beach. That was nice, she replied. Did seeing his mother make him anxious?

If only he could have told her then! Helen, a man is anxious because he has too much time and

286

not enough to think about. A man is anxious because he has lost too much time and has ended up thinking about all he should have thought about when he had the time.

With the dog following him he moves through the house, up one staircase and down another, kicking at objects that get in his way, shouting at a fluttering curtain, at the chimes of the church clock, throwing his weight about only to make certain that he does still have weight. He does, and when he feels it he bears it joyously: this, then, this body is not lost. He is disorientated by the memory of the beach and the seeming nearness of it, so close to his thinking that its waters could be at the top of the stairs and its snows filling Henry's chocolate bedroom.

Eleanor is there and then not. He sees her hunched over and he is moved, wants to put her up straight, hold her, talk to her about the past. Then he sees pink nails, make-up, and gets the giddying sense of the stranger emerging and eclipsing her. And then he thinks he must have made a mistake because she is hardly Eleanor at all except in outline; if he could grab her and hold her still she might remain as he knows her, but she moves, and the movement confuses him.

Things are getting worse, have got worse, suddenly. Everything is quite wrong and the pills make his head ache to the point of sickness. He is possessed by a sudden boredom that greys the colours. If only he were a child, he thinks, but the thought ends there.

He is furious at useless implements that he can no longer name, at Eleanor who is not steady, who is solid and then disintegrates to his mind, at the coffee machine that perpetually boils dry for lack of water, at the shifting world – the days into nights and restlessly back again, the plates in the sink in the cupboard in the sink in the pill box, the headache in his head and out of his head, the nausea, the rage. To say that all the change is in him is unreasonable and infuriating – that he must be questioned, manoeuvred and ultimately culpable, that all this is his fault but that despite this there is nothing he can do. Everything must now always be his fault. If only D's letters were opened; if only something were Helen's fault too and she could share this burden.

The rage comes so hard, so often – starchy, white rage with no give. Always lately there is a feeling that he must escape and get home, and when he can't he feels hopeless. This morning's rage comes because Eleanor tells him he does not need to wash the windows, he did it yesterday, the day before, the windows are clean. Besides, it is raining, washing windows in the rain is pointless. Pointless as the naked woman and her jars, point- less as the man rolling the rock up the hill (though what man, and what hill, and where did he hear of it?). And yet the icy shine of the glass has pleased him, as has the sight of the windows harnessing the light, as, too, has his reflection appearing through his own labour as if, at last, Helen has answered his question. *You did invent yourself, you are always inventing yourself.*

In rage at Eleanor's charge of pointlessness he has hurled a bucket of soapy water across the garden; now, guilty and apologetic, he watches her through the gleaming window picking it up and tidying it away, just as she tidies away the fragments of cups and the burnt food and the tins of fish he puts absently in the freezer: the multitude of little arrangements she makes out of his derangements. Eleanor, his external memory, his conscience, his nurse, his cleaner, his cook. She thinks he fails to notice, but he notices. He sees her clearing traces of him from the face of things, and the way her life seems to have become little but an apology and recompense for his actions. Around her all his doings lose substance as if she simply absorbs them. Such broad hips and shoulders on which to rest the weight of his errors.

Sorry, is what he seems to say to her most. Sorry about that. Most of the time he can't even be sure what he is apologising for. Always she ruffles his hair. Never mind, she tells him.

She does not seem to age. Never beautiful, she is still not. Never young, never old, nothing to lose, she has the vigilant indifference of an automatic sprinkler system that floods a room whether or not there is a fire. He does not even remember fully how she came to be living here – what sleight of hand was this that removed Helen and left Eleanor? There is a fog around her. His fog, she will say. Why my fog? He will respond. Why must all the blame be mine? Because (she will attach her hands to her hips) that is the nature of your forgetting. Fog. That is the weather in your head.

He is ashamed of his adolescent moods. The shame is never greater than this, now, as he returns to the garden after his looping, looping like a caged bird up and down the double stairs, to find Eleanor, poor, watchful, vigilant Eleanor sweating hunch-shouldered against the humidity waiting for him. He can do nothing for her; in truth he is growing afraid of her and of what she is beginning to see in him. He sits on the wall around the raised flower bed with the dog laid across his feet; he checks her name tag: Lucky. Unusual name, he can't imagine why he would have named her this, it doesn't seem like a thing he would do. But then his life doesn't seem like a thing he would do either, not at the moment. He lets his fingers dig the soil.

The air is soupy. A van pulls up at the gates and Eleanor goes to it, he cannot hear what she says to the driver but she walls her body off by hugging her arms across her chest. She is always this way with strangers; they talk – about him? Are they discussing his behaviour? He has done nothing; whatever they think, he has done nothing. He digs in the soil and collects, digs and collects. After a time Eleanor comes away from the gates and relaxes her arms.

'He wanted directions,' she says, and returns to her gardening.

He takes a new pocketful of stones upstairs to the bedroom and rests them with the others at the foot of the French windows. The dog pursues, his canine shadow, the shadow of the part of himself that is still noble, he thinks. Her sheer blackness is brave and her thinness willing. In whatever tight and unlikely spot she lays she makes it home. She settles here by the heap of stones and he sits on the floor next to her, pushing the heap taller until it holds its shape. Perhaps that man did not just want directions. Perhaps they are planning to take him away. He must get more stones. Needs more. Build it up here, build it back here, make it higher, yes, and get some of those stones that have fallen out of Eleanor's armfuls of weeds around the compost. Get some of those off the grass; get things in order.

That night he makes some advances on Eleanor in the bed, biologies born of habit: she is warm and unfathomable under cover so that he is reminded of a time he cannot place, in which he once discovered her body and was surprised by how he liked it. When was this? Which episode of the past? How long has Eleanor been here? He remembers being relieved by how she opened her arms to him in complete trust and how he entered, dumbfounded by her huge, undutiful breasts (Helen's were egg-like in comparison, and obedient and firm, biology-textbook perfect; Joy had no breasts, only ribs and nipples): here suddenly was a world of breast! A universe of breast! Unshielded and staring at him adoringly. And behind that adoration all he could hear, and all he can hear now, is the deep long moan of failure. *I should not be here, I do not belong here.*

Finally the two of them settle for just holding one another. He is without energy, she is always afraid of doing something to make him unhappy or agitated. They just hold each other with locked limbs.

'Will we be getting something for my headaches?' he asks.

She wraps her arms tighter around his neck. 'Tomorrow we're going to the clinic again, we'll ask about the headaches.'

He separates himself from her and settles on his back. If they are going to the clinic tomorrow he ought to see to his timeline, in case the woman there asks. He tries to remember what that woman looks like and gets a picture of a teacher he had at school, Mrs Webster, her image flashing in front of his eyes after half a century of absence. What musty corner of the brain keeps these images? What nudges them out?

As they lay there he can feel Eleanor's lack of sleep, like Helen's in the last few months. Helen had always been able to sleep so easily, and then suddenly, as if she knew that her time was short, she would lie there and breathe in loud circles to alleviate what she had begun to call the imps in her chest. Pain, no, not pain. Worry? Was she beginning to get old? Look at her hands – were they an old woman's hands?

There used to be a painting on the wall opposite, he suddenly recollects. Now that he goes to define it, he cannot, except that it was dark, and perhaps of a woman slumped along a dirty mattress. Very often Helen and this woman would look at each other as if they were one and the same person, but born into different rooms at different times in different light conditions. And very often she would sigh, and say, There is not very much that separates one human from another.

And towards the end of her life she said this more and more frequently. Instead of sleeping soundly when the light was switched off she began to turn from one side to the other, and then, as she was falling asleep, gnash her teeth a handful of times, and make disorientated comments about a 'poor woman', a 'fine line' and a 'ruined bed'. Perhaps she even muttered the word D. Yes, and he would not have known to listen for it. Yes, the more thought he gives it now, the more certain he is that she must have mentioned that name.

He gets up and dresses.

'Where are you going?' Eleanor asks.

'To make coffee.'

'Come back soon.'

He sees her white fleshy arms and disc of face in the darkness, nods and goes downstairs. He turns on the coffee machine. On the timeline he makes a mark, November 1961, Rook and Sara at the sea. At 1967 he blackens the mark he has put next to the Six Day War, and he wants to write there: Alice dies. Yet – yet he cannot. It doesn't seem that it can possibly be true. Now more than ever it seems to be the most absurd outcome, something he has made the case through his very fear of it. He doesn't want to approach the memory. Maybe it is not true. And if it is true, maybe the disease will make him forget it before he can be sure of it. Like cycling off a cliff on fire. If he bides his time – if he winds slowly towards the edge, he will lose consciousness before the ground disappears.

He makes another mark: 1980, painting goes missing from bedroom wall. Nothing in him can vouch for this claim; in all honesty he can remember nothing at all of the last twenty or so years of his life. The gap on the timeline is ominous and looks better with this careful little detail, inevitably Mrs Webster will be pleased. Then he puts on his coat and pushes D's letters into a pocket, summons the dog and leaves the house, thinking he will go and visit Henry. The prison seems suddenly safe and homely, everybody tucked in their T-shaped wings and forced into communities. There are not these loose times, and Henry is probably waiting for him.

He cuts across the main road and past the church, and, gripping D's letters, delves into the heavy darkness of the lane opposite. Beneath the letters is something else, smooth and hard; he cannot identify it. At first, when he takes it out and holds it on his palm, he is puzzled. A snow thing? Crystal snowball thing. He shakes it. Slowly he remembers where it came from, that Henry gave it to him for his birthday some years ago, and as he remembers that day (snowy, and they were walking in the woods) warm nausea breaches his stomach.

The crystal snowball tells the story they all know, he, Henry and Alice, the story of their beginnings: it is the end of the 1800s, a shoemaker and his daughter venture out into the Austrian woods in the snow to find mushrooms, and discover in their path a child wearing a lace hat and yellow shoes with a bullet hole in her head, the mother with a yellow hat, yellow shoes, yellow foam in her mouth and a revolver by her side. She has shot her daughter and then herself, for what reason nobody knows. Gory photographs and speculation make the papers every day for a week.

A man called Arnold is sitting in his chair, feet on a stack of books, a Siamese cat in his lap, a coffee in a chipped gold-rimmed cup in one hand and the corner of the newspaper in the other: he is trembling as he reads. It is Vienna, Strauss is dead and the century is closing. He touches his silver fencing scars. How could a mother kill her own child? Closing the shop he rushes home through the snow to his wife, finding her twirling a praise ring with a twinkle in her eye. He takes her to bed. Must replace a life for a life, he thinks.

Life is fragile, even when times are good, life is fragile enough to leave a child in yellow shoes dead in a wood. They call their lovemaking Conception Events. She, Minna, thinks of love and life, her belly full of fried fish. He, Arnold, thinks of the dead child. Somewhere in the clash of these opposite thoughts Sara is conceived.

Twenty-eight years later Sara fights back the death in her, thinks not of the bullet hole but of the yellow, and her son Jacob is conceived. Thirty years after that Jacob takes the hand of a slight freckled woman in the bombed relics of Stepney and invites her home. The woman looks at the church of St George opposite and nods her consent. She is thinking of Jesus, he of bombs, London bombed and bombed, London rebuilt. In the midst of their uncertain hopes Henry is conceived. Two years later she is thinking of the cherry tree, of fate. He knows little but yellow, a yellow dress, the sun glinting off the glass of his extraordinary would-be house. In the midst of a yellow autumn Alice is conceived. Out of the story a family grows: here they are, one, two, three, four.

The story has not ended then. By virtue of their existence Alice and Henry are fighting for its happy ending. He and the dog wind on at random, he now realises, along the dark street; he has no idea where the prison is. The lip of the moors opens out just ahead in an expanse of no-building, nothing. There is a choice, to go out into this nothingness or to go back home. Ambition and fear rub up in his bones; he looks back and sees a figure running towards him, a woman; large, cumbersome, running, and a breathless voice that calls, *Jake?*

He shakes the snow thing again. Thinks of his son, his history, the birth of his children. In the snow the woman and child dig in their heels, hold their yellow hats and stride on.

ANOTHER THING ABOUT THE MUFFLING SNOW

'*A*nd Jesus said to his disciples: why are you so anxious? Do not be anxious about anything.' Helen was wrapped in a blanket by the fire. He took her a cup of coffee, sat by her side and watched the page as she read aloud.

She reiterated, as though to herself. '*Do not be anxious about anything.*'

He pushed her back gently onto the rag rug she had made from old towelling sheets. Now they had new cream sheets from her mother, sent in parcels with sachets of detergents she recommended and soft toys for Henry, and little paperback guides on housekeeping. He lifted Helen's nightdress and took the bible from her hand.

'The house is so cold,' she said.

'I know, I'm sorry,' he replied, putting her hair behind her ears before she had a chance to. 'I'll get more wood so we have plenty – some ash, it smells good when it burns.'

The snow from the sea was just beginning, three days later, to come inland, and the moors were locked rigid inside white-grey skies. He took his clothes off and pulled the blanket around them both. Alice had to be made; an urgency began to invade the situation, one that neither could rightly explain, except that they were waiting for her as one waits for a dinner guest who is running six months late.

Two days later and the snow came in earnest, bleaching all description from the moors so that he squinted out at them and struggled to find perspective. After digging out the snow around the Coach House he managed to get the car to The Sun Rises and help Eleanor. The journey of two miles took him over an hour, the wheels grinding and slipping. He had to stop occasionally to dig the road free of drifts. When he pulled up Eleanor was there shovelling snow from the pathway, heaving, her hair was soaked and her bare legs screaming white in the gap between skirt and boots.

'Wear trousers, Eleanor,' he said, getting out of the car.

'Why?'

'Because it's three degrees below, that's why.'

'I never wear trousers.' She handed him her shovel. 'Here, have this, I'll get us a drink.'

As he dug he looked out across the moors at the white desolation.

After he and Helen had separated from each other and the blanket that night and she had gone to bed, he had looked at a passage from the Bible that she had gone on to read aloud. It was alien and senseless to him, and it annoyed him. Upstairs he silently retrieved the human-skin bible and opened it at this passage, surprised almost to find the same words there. It did not feel like a bible to him, nor like anything God had been near. He relished the wrongness of it and that it dared to be wrong. Reading through the verse he saw the words anew, *his* words, *his* bible, his own religion.

And the city lieth foursquare, and the length is as large as the breadth: and he measured the city with the reed, twelve thousand furlongs. The length and the breadth and the height of it are equal.

Digging now, and starting to sweat inside his jumpers and suede coat, he saw the moors through the steam of his breath milkier and vaguer than ever. Eleanor brought out two cups of strong tea and a bottle of whisky. *The city was pure gold, like unto clear glass*, the human-skin bible had said, and he had caught on that phrase, coupling *gold* and *glass* into an irrevocable mental image of Joy inside his house, simply standing as if not to disturb what he had made. He dropped some whisky into Eleanor's mug and then his own.

'You'll die of the cold,' he said, rubbing her back briskly.

'Won't,' she smiled. Her hair was stuck to her face, her nose and cheeks red.

'Seems arrogant, doesn't it,' he said, picking up his shovel again. 'To think that we, with these bits of metal, can fight back all that snow.'

Eleanor leaned forward heavily on the shovel

and scrunched her nose. 'Not really.' She gazed at him as if preparing to go on, but then looked away and scratched inside her nostril.

'Sometimes,' he said, 'when it snowed like this, me and Rook used to fight in it. We were always play fighting. Or at least I think it was playing.'

'I remember.'

'We sometimes came away with nose bleeds.' He shrugged. 'Difficult to know the line isn't it, between play and violence.'

Eleanor gulped her tea and banged the snow from the shovel on the cleared ground around her feet. The sound was stolen by the muffling snow.

'It's about power,' he said. 'Us with our shovels against the snow, and those fights with Rook – it's about who's more powerful, Ellie.'

She sniffed and smiled at him. 'Ellie,' she whispered, shaking her head as if grateful to discover it was her name.

'I could beat Rook to a pulp now.' He arched an eyebrow. 'Not that I want to. Just knowing I could, though, just knowing that means something.'

'I hate power. Dangerous thing,' she shrugged. He nodded.

'The things you can do to a person when you have power over them – it's shocking.'

'And the things you can do *for* them, Ellie.'

She shook her head vehemently. 'No. That's not power, to do something for someone. Power's always against.'

She scraped the shovel across the ground. He put his tea on a patch cleared of snow, took the shovel from Eleanor and went to the sign that hung outside the pub. He bashed it with the back of the shovel until the snow began falling in clumps, and continued to do so until the image appeared – the woman with Joy's cat-like eyes beckoning the yellow from the sun with her long arms, her long hair, her naked defiance.

'There,' he said, and hit the shovel against the iron arm of the sign to make a sharp, metallic sound that the snow couldn't take.

Three days later, and even despite the weather, the concrete walls of the prison were up, the T-shaped annexes slotted onto the sides. It had been twelve weeks from drawing board to realisation – twelve weeks. A triumph.

The public's resistance to the building was short-lived and limp. The people who resisted were the ones who would never go to prison nor have sons who went to prison, and it was easy to persuade them that the prisoners themselves deserved nothing more than these terrible buildings, and that it was a subtle part of the punishment. Architecture affected the mind, he told a journalist. It was an external consciousness; if you put a man in a godless building he would feel godless, when he woke, when he shat, when he slept. The journalist omitted the part about shitting but kept the godlessness.

'And what is your dream building, Mr Jameson?' he asked.

'We got this building up within twelve weeks and a small budget,' he replied. 'I'm more interested in reality than dreams.'

'Of course you're not in the dream business, we all understand your constraints – but if you *were*, hypothetically?'

'My dream building is one that exists, as opposed to one that doesn't.'

The journalist nodded. That conversation, too, was printed. He felt himself become an accidental working-class hero, a five-minute burst of undeserved fame. The day after completion he took Helen there to see the prison, and they walked thickly through snow around what had once been the landscaped grounds of the manor house. Helen became quiet when she saw it. The concrete looked ashen against the shrill white flakes – ashen and dead.

'Jake, it's awful,' she whispered.

'It's utilitarian. You can see the way we've created these annexes with the idea of allowing people to congregate –'

'But it's awful, and what you said in the paper about godlessness was awful.'

'I didn't mean it, I just said it. You know that.'

'Why say what you don't mean?'

'Why not respect me, my job?'

She sighed. 'I do, I do respect you.' She handed him the baby and fastened the button of her coat collar. 'Those towers you built in London, they were terrific. I mean, so impressive and new. But this –' Her gloved hands struggled to push her hair behind her ears, and she sighed again. 'Maybe I just don't understand it. That's all it is, it's me. Yes, it's me.'

They walked around to the other side of the grounds where the view of the manor house was still unspoilt. They stood for a long time gazing up at the windows of the house. Despite how he had come across in his interview, he did believe in beauty, and he did believe that his building would do these men a service, otherwise he would not have built it. When he saw the grey-white flow of concrete he saw protection for them as much as he saw imprisonment. It was his own take on godliness, and he wanted to explain this to Helen but thought it would not be enough for her somehow. He took his coat off and wrapped Henry inside it against the cold, kissed his cheek.

'One day we should go back to America again,' he said. 'California, where it isn't cold.'

'California, where all the dreamers go, where there is fruit and gold and grapes and sunshine!'

He looked hard at her. 'Well, don't you have any dreams?'

'Jake, we live by my dreams!' she said with an incredulous smile.

'No, I mean aspirations. Your dreams are more like instruction manuals – I mean *aspirations*.'

'Something I want to do or create?'

'Yes.'

'I create all the time, I created Henry –'

'We.'

'We created Henry. And let me tell you something.' She pulled her woollen hat down over her ears. 'I think creatively. If you even *think* loving thoughts about God, that love becomes instantly real in the world. Each thought is an act of creation, a – little birth.'

He shook his head and let Buddy Holly rotate around his thoughts. An act of creation? Creation of what? He didn't understand what she meant when she said these things, and he was tired of feeling stupid for it. He was tired of feeling that their inability to have another child lay in his misunderstanding of some religious equation that was just too abstract for his simple mind.

Later that night they went to their Conception Event with a weary anger. Helen was angry because the baby would not cry any more and she never knew what he needed or when. The crying, she said, made the milk rush up her body ready for feeding, but now without that cue she often had to make the child wait; she felt angry with herself and the uselessness of her body which refused to conceive. His anger was at her, or at her ridiculous arcane God that he did not understand, or at the piece of land that he could not get his hands on, or at her dreams that had predicted Alice but never delivered her.

They tried night after night, week after week.

The winter became intolerable except for the glorious smell of burning ash wood in the grate. Damp began creeping up the walls of the prison annexes and the builders were called back to assess; they blamed it on the architects who pushed the project through too quickly and with too tight a budget. The architects pointed out that they had been given both time limit and budget and were just doing their job; they blamed it on the council, the council blamed it on the government and Harold Macmillan, who was shrouded from the accusation by greater political distractions and rafts of snow.

'Meanwhile,' Helen said, 'the prisoners shiver.'

'Yes,' he replied, removing her nightdress, wondering why she couldn't for once come to bed naked and let him warm her, 'but don't think about it. Think about what is far away. The stars, the monkeys in space. Concentrate on what is far away.'

Outside the snow continued to fall. As they made tired love Helen tightened and asked, *What if one of the prisoners dies from the cold, I feel like something awful will happen.* He ignored the untimely question, they were supposed to be thinking about *life*; he had the sensation that the snowflakes were blossom, and that the blossom was eating away at substance. And Mrs Crest was buried under a mound of muffling snow, calling out with a silent snow-filled mouth. And then that the money under the bed was torn into flakes; he imagined handing it over to get his house and being laughed at, and that the man laughing at him looked like Rook, with the same crooked attitude.

Eventually he thought of the unparalleled form of Alice, and he forced his attention back to his wife.

CHAPTER 11

'Do you know why you're here today, Jake?'

'Why?'

'Yes. Why do you have to come here?'

'Because I get headaches.'

She purses her lips and nods. 'Yes – but do you know why you're getting headaches?'

'Because I have brain damage.'

'In a sense, yes. You have Alzheimer's. And the tablets we give you for that are giving you headaches.'

He squeezes his hands together. 'I know that.'

Nodding, she pushes an orange file away from her as if it has displeased her somehow.

'So I'm going to go through the usual with you, and then we'll discuss what to do about your tablets, okay?'

'That will be fine.'

'So, tell me Jake, what day is it?'

He has practised this, but hesitates now under the pressure. 'Thursday, or thereabouts.'

'And what year are we in?'

'That's,' he nods repeatedly. He has practised this too. 'That's – quite difficult.'

'Roughly?'

'I think – I would guess – I don't know.'

'And could you say what the time is?'

He brings his palms together and exhales, closes his eyes. 'Well, it's certainly recent times.' He opens his eyes again and looks appreciatively at her fox hair, the way it bronzes today in the light. 'Ask somebody else, they'll know.'

She puts her hands in her lap.

'I'm going to name three objects and I want you to repeat them after me. I want you to listen carefully Jake, because in a few minutes I'm going to ask you again. Okay?'

'Right.'

'House, shoelace, picture.'

'So, then –' He squeezes the skin between his nose, rubs beneath his eye. Thinks. Thinks with all the pointlessness of a tiger thrashing about a cage. 'Piston. No, not piston. House. No, no I'm afraid it's gone.'

She writes something. The way she writes with unconcerned purpose makes him think he is doing not so badly, perhaps.

'Now Jake, tell me what this saying means: *people in glass houses shouldn't throw stones.*'

'It means,' he stands and begins pacing the room as he analyses the words. 'It means that –'

'Jake, sit down again.'

She holds the arm of his empty chair – empty as if it had never been occupied, nor could be occupied again. How will he sit there, if it is empty? It is a blind, mole-ish trust that brings him scuffling back to the seat. The fox woman smiles and gives him a moment to get comfortable.

'*People in glass houses shouldn't throw stones.* Tell me what that saying meant Jake.'

'It means, I would imagine, that people in glass houses shouldn't throw stones because the stone will hit the glass and not the person they were aiming for. It might even break it. It depends on the size of the stone.' He finds himself tapping fast on his leg. 'Glass can be rich.'

'Expensive.'

'Expensive.'

She pulls back the orange file, opens it and takes some paper from it which she passes to him.

'Read the words on this page and then do as it says.'

He sees the words CLOSE YOUR EYES. He reads them over and over, untangling and understanding them, looks up at her with a smile to indicate to her that he has understood, then hands her the paper. 'Thank you,' he says. 'I've done as you asked.'

She makes a mark on her sheet and thanks him in return.

'So now can you tell me the three objects I asked you to remember?'

He considers this carefully. 'Piston, stones – the other thing.'

'Can you remember the other thing?'

'No, not at the moment.'

'That's fine.' She writes; he knows what she is doing – writing scores. Rating him. 'Now,' she says, 'please repeat after me, *No ifs ands or buts.*'

He sniffs. 'No ifs or buts.'

'Okay, can you tell me Jake, are you left or right-handed?'

'I'm left-handed,' he says promptly, confidently.

She goes back to her writing. 'Good. Good,' she murmurs. When she finishes she crosses her legs and rests her arms on the desk.

'I'm thinking of taking you off the medication. How do you feel about that?'

He is surprised. 'Am I improved?'

'No – not exactly. You are fine, but the tablets can only help with so much and after that there's no real need for them.'

'But I only started on them a week or so ago.'

'Not quite. You've been on them for two years.'

He sits in a long silence, conscious of his posture appearing too dejected for her, or too dry, or too shambled.

'What do the tablets do?' he asks suddenly.

She runs her hand across her upper lip and frowns. 'It's complex.'

He tips his head to one side and watches her touch her fingertips to her head.

'The tablets make your brain cells work better – but eventually Jake, there are not enough cells left, no matter how well you make them work.'

'Why aren't there enough cells?'

'Because Alzheimer's kills them. This means

311

there aren't as many, which means there aren't enough messages going back and forth.'

He nods. She talks slowly, as if picking each word from a tall tree.

'The tablets can't stop the cells dying. There is nothing we can do to stop that – but – but they make the cells that remain work harder. The problem is, the disease overtakes the tablets after a while, and then, no matter how hard the cells work, there just aren't enough of them any more for the tablets to make a difference.'

He circles his hand impatiently. 'Tell me in the real terms.'

'Those are the real terms.'

'No, in real things. Didn't we used to talk in proper language, in mother tongues?'

His stare is that of the bully, and he knows it. The stare he used to give Helen when he wanted his way.

But his stare is returned coldly. She closes the folder and puts the lid on the pen to declare an end. 'I have explained,' she says.

'Again.'

He slams his hand down on the desk and, without flinching, she finds his eyes perfectly and speaks into them.

'Very well. In your brain there is a chemical called acetylcholine, which acts as a lubricant, if you like, that allows messages to be communicated between neurons.'

He nods. He likes the way her eyes fix on him.

'Increasing the amount of acetylcholine in the brain increases the ability for neurons to communicate. Acetylcholine is broken down by an enzyme called acetylcholinesterase. The medication you've been taking restricts that enzyme. But it only does so temporarily; after a certain point – a point I suspect you have reached – the drug loses its ability to stabilise the enzyme production.'

'How interesting and extraordinary,' he says. 'It's – it's like entropy. Houses can't build themselves, that's the thing. That's the thing we're facing. Can't build themselves.' He finds he is firing the words rapidly, and that they are met with a frown. He stops. 'And?'

'That's it.'

He brings his hand once more on the table. She blocks him with another of her tough looks, clears her throat and continues. 'As the levels of acetyl-choline decline –'

His eyes are locked with the fox-haired woman's as her big words come out stubborn and steady; he has the sensation of going down a slide, and at the same time watching himself go down that slide. Some part of him is just the cool observer, and when the sad little thrill has finished he will collect himself and wander off for coffee. The woman, meanwhile, is still talking and he has missed something she said. He brings his hands up to his chin.

'Meanwhile the neurofibrillary tangles and the

plaques worsen, and the medication can do nothing whatsoever for these. What you have is neuron loss, neurotransmitter loss, the destruction of synapses – no drug can recover what the brain erases.'

'I understand,' he says, containing her wide, hard look.

Gracious, important words between two adults. Not a single one of them remains to his memory, nor ever even found its target, but he and his fox-haired friend have engaged in the game, both knowing it is a game. They played. There is something about that, the playing, the meaningless movement of a knight here and a rook there.

'Before you go today, I'll speak to Eleanor about what we've discussed – the tablets and so on. We can ease you off them gradually.'

He nods. Though standing, and tugging at his jumper for buttons in the mistaken idea that he is wearing a coat, he does not let her escape his stare.

'Why do I have brain damage?'

'It's a disease, we don't exactly know why some people get it and others don't.'

'Did I get it in an accident – did I hit my head? Some people have brain damage from accidents with the car.'

'You don't have brain damage as such, Jake, you have Alzheimer's, and it's a disease.'

'I know that.'

Holding the door handle, she bends to pick some

discarded paper from the floor. She screws it up, puts it in a – container. Takes it from one place, puts it in another without any apparent reason. Again, an emptiness as if the paper had never been there. And the next moment, seeing the emptiness, forgetting *what* was there – a pen? A shoelace? And interrogating the blank space, and feeling the eyes water as if trying for a lifetime of pointless tears, and then out of the door.

'Did you know, my dear,' he says, addressing his fox-haired companion, 'humans are the only things that ask why. Do you think that is our curse?'

'Do you think we are cursed?' she asks.

'Yes,' he replies.

Without the headaches he feels better generally, more alive and astute, lighter. He and the dog take longer and livelier walks through thick, reddening countryside and a season he can name: autumn. The dog has a dear love of chasing, and anything he throws she will run for. Each time she sprints off up the road he stops doubting that she will come back and knows, absolutely, that they are not about to leave each other. He has remembered the art of wolf-whistling from his childhood at the Junk, when the moors would take even the most piercing of sounds and one could whistle all day without the smallest effect. Now, like a reply coming decades after the call, the dog flies back to him up the lanes.

And for the first time in years, before going to bed, he undresses and looks himself up and down in the mirror as if facing the enemy at last, and takes in what he sees with a tender, bewildered humour. Some prodding and pushing reveals that everything that was once functional is now redundant – the muscles that used to form the hard slab of stomach are now slack somewhere deep inside a round of pale fat. The legs are still long and sturdy, but the energy that used to flow down them has got trapped in the ex-stomach, and now, when he considers it, they hardly want to move at all. The eyes still shine, but they don't see very well. The genitals, once so instrumental, are now just part of the confusion. He holds them and experiences, for a moment, the great electric lurch of dream and desire; it flashes up through his body and forces his eyes closed, and then is gone as suddenly as it came.

At the top of each of Joy's letters to him there are numbers, like so: 16.8.89. 18.12.62. 12.2.76. He takes a selection to the telephone and tries to dial them. 16.8.89. The telephone has no full stop, but in all likelihood that is just a way of writing and won't affect the number reaching the exchange. Multiple attempts fail, even when he tries to put some of the numbers together: 16.8.89.18.12.62. It fails too when, thinking that Joy may have encoded them as a particular and peculiar secret between them, he mixes them up: 16.18.89.62. All that comes back is a dull hum on the line.

How he would like to talk to her! There are things he must tell her. Once they got talking they would find their theme and there would be no end to the flirtatious, anecdotal flow of it. Well, if he cannot telephone her he will write. Paper. Where does Helen keep paper? Things for writing. He finds one on the sideboard in the kitchen.

In the first few years of letters to Joy he described to her Luigi Lucheni, a man looking up to the ceiling of his cell and knowing he is in the centre of a vortex. It is this thing called The Big Death – everybody in Austria is dying in preparation for the new century. By 1900 there will be nobody left; it is a cleansing, time purging itself. The musicians are all going (Brahms, Sara used to chant: Brahms 1897, Strauss 1899, Millöcker 1899), the two archdukes, the yellow woman and her child (lying dead in the woods, a gun in the mother's hand and her egg-yolk shoes running from her feet), and of course the Empress Elisabeth with her black hair gleaming, Elisabeth who Lucheni has killed with his own hands.

Elisabeth's ghost huddles next to the murderer, and she tells him that in The Big Death there are two sides: those who will survive and those who will die. It's a war of man against circumstance. He need not be scared, because she will save him from circumstance. She covers his body with her mink coat and her perfume settles round his neck.

All this was once written to Joy in dark nights in the study, the paper lit by a torch on his desk, and as he had written he had dug out the newspaper clipping that he had found when he was around eight. It was a cutting from the *Neue Freie Presse* showing a picture of a short man in a black down-at-heel suit and hat, flanked by police. The man's face was set in a scowl and his clothes were too big. Amongst the columns of foreign words he found one he recognised: Lucheni. Lucheni, some kind of heroic figure and perverse super-hero whose story had become one of his first memories. When Sara had told him the story of Lucheni it had never occurred to him that the man was real, and then suddenly there he was walking out of myth and into life.

As an eight-year-old he had stood on a chair and looked into his reflection in his bedroom window; he moved a leg to the left, back to the centre, practised distributing his weight into the most casual, thoughtless pose possible. Like Lucheni? He took a butter knife from the drawer and pushed it into his chest, then imagined his chest belonged to somebody else, that he was in the middle of the act of killing. Now like Lucheni? He pressed it into the old pillows on his bed, or into his kidneys and soft pockets of his body. He pushed it into the peat, and into a hard-boiled egg. Sara said that Elisabeth had come to the cell purely to forgive Lucheni. Every time he stabbed an object he then looked at it and wondered if it forgave him, and what forgiveness felt like, and why it made Lucheni so happy.

In a reply to this letter Joy confirms that she has never yet had to forgive anybody, or been forgiven by anybody, so she can't answer that query. With this statement he remembers how young she is, and he is both dismayed and nourished by the fact. One day I'll haunt you, he says, so I can forgive you every one of the sins you haven't yet committed. One day I'll haunt you, she says in a letter that crosses his, so I can forgive you the sin you committed with me. They laugh about the duplicated sentiment and the word *sin*; they are both uncomfortable with it unless they can mock it.

Still, Joy is quietly impressed with Lucheni, and is uncharacteristically girlish about his plight. Mad? Hanged himself? Isn't there a happier ending to this tale? But he tells her that he never meant to say so much about Lucheni, and has drifted from the central point of The Big Death. The content of their letters begins behaving like their convoluted letter chess, in which mail crosses mid-Atlantic and his pawn, that she has already swiped from the board with her rook, takes her queen, which has already moved out of the pawn's reach.

(And then she tells him incidentally that Rook is so named because when he was a child he went through a period of only ever moving in straight lines; maybe this was why Rook eventually migrated to the peat moors where all lines were straight? In his next letter he agrees, but it is too late, the point has moved on.)

It goes on, the flurry of letters. But I must tell you, he writes again, about the relevance of The Big Death. He drafts it all out: his religion. His grandfather Arnold sitting at his desk in a deep, richly stocked bookshop, a Persian (or was it Siamese?) cat on his lap and a white (or was it black?) coffee in his trembling hand. In Sara's accounts Arnold always arrived via this same evocation: this big, nervous death-hunter trawling the news in the *Neue Freie Presse* for yet more reasons why he and his young wife needed urgently to have a child.

He writes about the Conception Events, in which Arnold and Minna would spend days and nights in bed trying for a child, snacking on fried fish and *hamantaschen*, and eating *sholent*. He writes to say that at the end of The Big Death came a life: his mother's life, as though she were the resurrection of all those dead.

This is his religion, he states in one of those eureka moments in which a man suddenly understands what kind of thing he is. The religion is ultimately Christian but without the problem of Christ. It allows him to understand his wife and to place himself in time. Granting him his Jewishness, it also explains a darkness in him and Sara, a seed of death in their stomachs which they treat with strong coffee. A seed of Lucheni in his brain, Lucheni who started the First World War which led to the Second World War which led to the extermination of their family: a seed in one's brain that grows into one's own extinction. *An explanation, Joy*, he wrote, *as to why I can never love Helen completely, because there is no darkness in her.*

As he writes all this, at his desk in the sharp torchlight, he sees himself as that squatted Lucheni in the vortex of time, waiting for Joy, his sin, to come and rescue him from his sins. He craves her perfume, the weight on his neck of the fur coat her wealthy Jewish husband has bought her; he waits for her.

In the next letter, under torchlight, he offers to come to California to be with her, and build a glass house overlooking the ocean, a house with a seamless steel frame and liquid walls. All she needs to do is say yes and he will leave everything and be there.

Joy never gets this letter, or at least he assumes so, because her reply does not acknowledge it. She tells him about an argument she has had with her husband and how a barbecued lobster ended up in the swimming pool. She ends by instructing, Knight E5 to F3. Perhaps, he concludes, his letter was dropped into the mid-Atlantic by mistake.

He wakes with the idea that Helen is downstairs, and then realises that he is not in bed but at the kitchen table clutching a pen. The residue of a dream plays and replays an image of Alice appearing in sunlight from a bus. Always dreaming of Alice, always seeing her beauty through the haze of recent sleep. He stands from the table.

'Helen?'

There is nobody in the kitchen except the dog, who comes to him and presses herself against his leg. He pats her back heavily and goes to the living room, also empty. He finds, without knowing how, that D's letters are in his hand as if an extension to his own fingers. The envelopes are filthy, crumpled, but give out a certain heat and reassurance.

'Helen?'

He checks in the study. He is not at all sure if he really expects to find her; something tells him she is definitely not here and that she is dead. Dead of a stroke they say, whatever that is. But dead? Does this mean she can't be here? What does it mean? Surely she is here, she has always been here. You were not faithful, he thinks with some relief – our score is not settled, and so you cannot be gone. We need to both be here so we can start again.

He holds the letters to his stomach and goes from room to room. He gets lost, he picks his way back. Perhaps she is with Henry, stroking the child's hand and hair as she whispers, *sshh bubba, sshh*. He thinks now of Henry, coddled by Helen, always loved in her arms or on her lap, having stories, cooking, their hair catching sunlight.

322

Henry is the daughter and the son in one. Unreachable by the law or by the general filth of systems. Helen will save her child from systems. They look at art books, cookbooks and bibles. He calls her Mumma, she calls him Bubba, and with those downy words they draw the world around them.

He makes a breakfast of toast and butter, curious as to why there seems to be no light outside yet. Maybe it's – the late season. The late season is so often dark.

Then, by the living room's unlit fire, he sits and eats, and lets the television flicker in the background. He recalls a letter burning in the grate and a hundred fat-soaked newspapers, salt and vinegar on his fingers. *Monkey goes to space. Israel does a thing. Egypt.* If he waits here, the dog's head balanced on his leg and her black body curled out across the carpet like a contorted shadow of himself, Helen will possibly come.

He draws his knees to his chest and crosses his ankles, a difficult position for a man of his size, but he finds balance on his sitting bones and roots himself to the ground. He has no headache. Life seems closer: somehow his mother seems closer. His shoes are on, and a pair of trousers and his coat. This surprises him. He closes his eyes and an image of himself comes, kneeling over the human-skin bible. Outside Helen wavers on the ladder in her pinafore as he turns to Psalms and reads. *Shall thy wonders be known in the dark? And thy righteousness in the land of forget-fulness?* The emotion of it is so pressing, yielding the feeling of something terribly lost and lost over again, that he squeezes his eyes tighter. The memory is clear and godly, so clear that it barely has the quality of a memory at all, but more that of – what is it? The feeling that one has been here before, and that time spirals rather than flows. He has been here before, he thinks. He will be here again.

His mother is close. Is she dead? Alive? Dead. He is certain he remembers her dying, and the recollection is peaceful and fightless, almost as if she did not die at all but just moved restfully from one sitting position to another. She told him a story, then or some other time, about milk. About how there were once children who were born and were perfectly healthy until they drank their mother's milk, but in that milk was a disease that damaged their brains, and they kept drinking and kept drinking the very stuff that gave them life, and all the time it was taking their lives. Until they were blank and empty. Until their pale skin was a shore of washed-up milk.

Why would she tell him this story? He wonders if it relates to the woman and child in the woods. Or if it relates to nothing, just another unexplained story that she told as she always did, as if she were for ever showing him grains of sand but never showing him the beach.

Then other images play: a flock of coloured birds

flying up into a pyramid of glass (surely not a memory, more likely a dream). A brown car passing like silk along an American highway. Quail Woods being cut down, the trees massive to his small child's mind. Alice in a blue dress with a large felt raspberry that Helen had sewn onto the front and Henry running in the garden after a plastic plane. Sara pouring endless streams of coffee as if to substitute for affection, her large white hands handing him a cup, handing it over, handing it over like birds in flight. Now those brain-damaged children again; how he feels for them, and how sick he feels to think of them at the breast dying piece by piece.

Then his wife comes to him in a form she has so often come to him. It is a fantasy. She is wearing a miniskirt, that miniskirt that he so well remembers with the red stitching on denim and the small pockets that were good for nothing. He had always imagined that it was theirs, not hers. It was something they might take from the cupboard some rainy afternoons, use for the duration of lovemaking, and put away again. An erotic agreement between them.

He is still surprised by how unsophisticated this fantasy is, and how the more elementary it is the more arousing. His fantasy requires that she is naked from the waist up, dressed only in the skirt, her hair plain and her eyelids tinged yellow, and her head directed to the centre of the living room, resting on the human-skin bible. The room is empty and featureless, the fire out, a cup of water near to them that they never touch. There is no before or after, no baby, no milk, just that lone unmitigated act.

STORY OF THE LITTLE DEATH

The wrecking ball buckled the face of a house. Along the Edwardian terrace other houses were being pulled down with hydraulic excavators and cranes; they could not demolish them fast enough. It was a bleak scene – the buildings' masonry twisted and their brickwork crumbled, and the house interiors were black, rotten and forgotten. The snow around them was dirty and the air dusty. He covered his face.

Hardly old at all, these buildings, but not worth living in as they stood, and too expensive to restore. They were not war-damaged themselves, but they reminded one of war damage, reminiscent of that starless, hungry time of his teens and towns that looked beaten up and sick. No, the sooner the rows were gone the better – their poor condition did nothing for the area except cast an austere shadow, and the ground they occupied was relatively high and drained, close to the steelworks. It would provide a good housing site for the influx of workers. He was wondering at a clean modern development based on the big ideas of the Thirties;

when he talked about humanity, comfort and provision Helen approved. Yes, she said, that's better, that's good.

She had encouraged an excited discussion about the possibilities – a sort of village, as Mr Rowntree had made for his workers, with everything they needed at hand. But more modern, he had interjected. Yes of course, she conceded, more modern, good roads and places for cars, they could even have a coffee house and a Chinese restaurant. He had been thinking more along the lines of uncluttered horizontal and vertical planes of white poured concrete and roof gardens faced at the sun, and buildings centred around sets of perfect squares so that every house was aware of every other house, to create a –

Close community, Helen had offered.

Quite. Everybody in their own space, but conscious, on a bigger scale, of their shared life.

Helen had been enthusiastic. She still was. He observed the demolition and made site notes, kicked the snow away and dug his heel into the ground to get a feel for the soil. Had the sun been out, this whole small plateau would be drenched with it now. It received thirteen or fourteen hours of sunshine a day in the summer which meant that with careful planning and decent construction the houses could be warmed through without the need for much heating, and would not suffer damp problems.

He walked back to the Mini and put his notebook

of ideas on the passenger seat. Somehow he did not see it happening the way he planned. Somewhere between the ideals and the reality an ingredient would be lost. Money, probably. He did not have the heart to tell this to Helen, or even the heart to tell himself. He turned the radio on – Buddy Holly. He thought of the money under his bed and, charged with the need to trade it for something extraordinary, tapped his fingers as he drove away.

That weekend he and Helen argued, properly, for the first time.

'The house is so cold,' she said, pulling a blanket around herself.

'It's old, what can I do? You wanted to live here.'

'So is it my fault, that we're cold?' It seemed to be a genuine question, so he answered accordingly.

'In part, yes.'

She gave a crazed smile he had never seen before.

'Is it my fault it's been snowing for two months?'

'Of course not.'

'Is it my fault we haven't got any of those gas heaters – everybody has them, except us. Is that my fault?'

'I wouldn't say so, I'll get some. If you want the house to smell of gas that's fine.'

'Jake, they won't make the house smell of gas. Cheryl has one and it's fine.'

'Who's Cheryl?'

'A friend from church.'

'What is it with you, that everywhere you go you just *make friends*? You didn't want to leave London because you were happy, and now here you are with all these friends, seemingly *happy* –'

'Is that a criticism?'

He sat at the piano and played a few high ironic notes.

'Anyway,' Helen said, 'I'm not happy. I'm cold.'

'Is that my fault?'

'Yes.'

'Good. And good that everything isn't absolutely one-hundred-percent brilliant with you.' He turned to her and ceased playing. 'Because your perfection gets a bit wearing sometimes.'

He saw her body stiffen. 'How terrible for you,' she said slowly and quietly. 'How you have suffered in my hands, poor man.' He had never seen her appear so pale and blank. She tugged at the blanket until it was tight around her.

'Everything is supposed to be easy,' he said. 'What with me making decisions to carve our future, and your dreams to guide us. What a perfect combination we are! But your dreams are failing us. Where's Alice?' He stood from the piano stool. 'Where is she? Why can't you just accept that you're not perfect, you don't *know*? You're going blind into every day just like the rest of us.'

'I don't know where Alice is,' she said. 'I don't know.'

'That's right. And here we are running after

something that doesn't exist, so why don't we give up?'

'Because it does exist.'

'It doesn't.'

'Jake, it does. Why don't you trust me? When you said we were coming here I trusted you.'

'Yes, but you have reason to trust me because I do everything I can to *make* the future and make it certain, I control it. You just predict it, where's the control in that? At best – if your predictions are right – all we are is victims of them.'

'No –'

'And at worst, like now, gullible victims.'

He went to the fire and fed it with another wedge of ash wood. It was not even that cold, if she only dared to shrug the blanket off, face and challenge it.

'You have to stop playing God,' he said.

She marched to him. 'You're the one playing God. *I control the future. I make it certain.*'

'If God exists we are all victims,' he said, his voice raised. 'Look at you, huddled there. The meek shall inherit the earth. Well, you'll be first in line – you'll have it, it's yours. You'll last a day. You, your Bible-bashers, you'll last a week at the most without people like me to take charge.'

He left the living room by one door, angry, but rather calm. Helen left by the other, disappearing into the study and up the second stairs. He heard her feet soft on them.

★　★　★

331

In the afternoon he, Helen, the baby and Sara packed into the Mini and drove out along the icy roads, snow shovelled to the verges. Progress was slow and haphazard as the car slipped along the grooves of other tyres and tried to take several courses at once. They went to his father's grave, where they laid flowers and stood in a frozen breeze, a winter landscape without contrast. Helen, who had never known his father, began crying, and then wandered slowly from grave to grave reading dates and whispering into Henry's ear. She had hardly spoken to him since their fight. She was stiff with Sara, and he was struck by how Sara, in perverse response, warmed to her. She rubbed Helen's arm, commenting on the cold. Difficult for thin women, she said. Difficult to keep the chill away when you've no body fat. Despite herself he saw Helen smile, and then retreat again into a defensive gloom.

Then, at Sara's request, they went into the woods. Tucked up and quiet, Helen stayed in the car breastfeeding.

'I like to come here,' his mother said. 'The last bit of wood left for miles around – when I first came here it was all wood. Now it's all vegetables. Beetroot instead of trees.' She smiled wryly. 'Not so beautiful, hm.'

'It depends on your idea of beautiful,' he said.

'Mine is trees, not beetroot. I don't suppose I'm alone.'

As they walked she poured coffee from the flask

into the first gold-rimmed cup, handing it to him, then into the other. She tucked the flask away in her bag. Even under the trees the snow was thick enough to envelop their feet as they went.

'Your father visits me,' she said suddenly.

'Visits you?'

'Yes, comes to me. At night. He lies in bed beside me.'

'A ghost?'

'Something of the sort.'

'Can you touch him, is he *there*?'

Sara shrugged. 'It's hard to say, you have to be less literal about these things, Jacob.'

They walked on steadily, sipping their coffee.

'Does he say anything?'

'Asch, no.' She flicked the suggestion away. 'If we said anything we would only argue. We sleep, and when I wake up he is gone.'

Their feet creaked across the snow as they walked on, slowing unconsciously.

'Did you used to argue? I don't remember you ever arguing.'

'No, we never did, never, though we had this little war going on, silently of course.'

Not a little war, he thought. A huge war over whose thousands of years of history was the more relevant. A war too big for arguments.

The more he considered it, the more he found his parents' marriage singularly catastrophic. It had passed off wordless bitterness as peace, sacrifice as compromise; he for one had been convinced for years. He had chosen Helen – had he? – as someone with whom he could re-enact this quietude. It was a theory, at least, and it made him suddenly grateful for their argument; how he did *not* want to become his parents! He would not give up.

'Where does he go, I wonder,' he said. 'Father. When he leaves in the morning, where does he go to?'

From his mother, silence. Snow began to fall again. One flake, two flakes, a laid-back flurry. A gunshot sounded then and Sara jerked her free hand to her heart.

'Dreck!' she said. 'Good God. *Dreck!*'

She looked rapidly around her to see where the shot had come from. The air was confused with snow and completely quiet as if there had never been sound, as if it had never known sound at all. He, meanwhile, had spilt his coffee, not at the shock of the gunshot but at the speed and loose-ness of his mother's reaction – this from a woman usually so succinct and eloquent in her movements.

'Deer culling I expect,' he added, wiping the coffee on the sleeve of his coat.

'It scared me half to death.'

'Nothing scares you, you're never scared.'

'Untruth – untruth,' she muttered, motionless. 'I am very scared of being mistaken for a deer in the wood. But thank you all the same.'

He thought suddenly of a leaf, a leaf shape – he did not know why except that of course, images flash into the mind and out again, brain functions, nerves, strangenesses that are not there to be understood. He poured the remains of the coffee into the snow and put the mug in his pocket. Absently, he reached for his mother's hand but she withdrew from his touch.

'Look up,' she said.

Why, he wondered? Why look up? But he did. Perhaps Sara too had been thinking of this leaf? Often he had entertained the idea that they, he and his mother, thought the same things. If their brains were to be sliced in half like cabbages they would reveal the same patterns and layers. So he did not ask why, but just did as she said and expected a reason to follow.

Above was monochrome: perfectly white snow on black branches that jagged across a dark grey sky, a black bird passing through the scene. It was a photograph of the past, he in it. Snow fell on his face as if the photographic paper itself, old and pulpy, was disintegrating. There were no leaves, of course – it was winter. His brain flickered uncertainly.

He clutched the cup in his pocket, thinking that he ought to get back to Helen. It was incredibly cold and the baby would be unsettled by all this waiting. The handle of the cup – the precious cup that had once been Arnold's – snapped off in his fingers. *Shit*, he mumbled under his breath. *Shit*.

'I don't know where he goes when he leaves,' Sara said. 'I suppose he never really comes.'

They continued looking up towards the sky until the forest ran out, then they turned and walked back with longer, more hurried strides, their faces wet with snow.

Duly, Helen gave up.

'I've thought,' she said a few days later. 'I've thought and you're right. Let's give up. It's been seven months trying for Alice – for, I mean, a baby – and I think I was wrong. We're not meant to have another child, God doesn't want it.'

Her look was resilient; she held his gaze. She would give up on the specifics, the look said, but she would not give up on the general, the fundamental. God would not stop coming into it just because he had insulted her and her friends.

'So we'll stop trying,' she said. 'If it's to be, it's to be. My dreams are wrong. Forgive me.'

He let her fatalism go. The fanaticism. Once again the thing that most separated them was the thing in her that most impressed him – her ability to believe. No, not ability, her addiction to believing, her conviction, and the great power that sprang from it. So he agreed, and together they let their Conception Events go.

A month passed and another. The snow melted and small, tense buds appeared on the cherry tree. Another month passed. He was not prone to matching emotions with seasons; spring was not a time to be new and optimistic, it was spring in England because the face of the earth to which England clung was turning finally towards the sun, there was no emotion about it. It was a surprise to him then when he found himself harbouring hope that now that the freeze had gone and the leaves were opening and the birds were returning from Africa, Alice – not just any child, but Alice – would come. Then the hope turned to expectation, then, when summer came, the expectation turned to deep frustration, the frustration to desperation.

Helen seemed calm. She began volunteering at a hospice and came home daily inundated with gifts from dying people who thought their whole lives had been worthwhile if only because they had met her. Henry started crying again like a normal baby, crying and babbling and laughing. Eleanor had found a boyfriend and she stressed how in love she was; trade at The Sun Rises was increasing. Truly, the moors were a fantastic place to be in the summer, vast, warm and sewn through with flowers. Whenever he went to see Sara she was with Rook, and he was left to observe them dancing continual Strauss waltzes across Sara's orange carpet. Everybody but him, then, was at peace.

He wrote to Joy. He began telling her about The Big Death and the ghost of Elisabeth, elaborating until Elisabeth became potent to him. Perhaps Helen's dreams were not so unreasonable after all, if Sara could be receiving the ghost of her dead husband in her bed at night, and if he could lend himself so readily to these fairy stories, and if he could devote so much time to writing to a woman who was becoming less real by the day. And if Alice would not exit his plans.

And if the great humanitarian housing project he had crafted was turning out to look rather like any other housing project, with windows too small to make use of the sunlight and a budget shrinking faster than the dried-out peat. If what was so apparently real was failing, and what was so apparently false was thriving, then Helen's dreams did not look so irrational. And besides, without their social prophesies as to which film they should see or place they should visit, their weekends were certainly less interesting, he too often at The Sun Rises witnessing Eleanor's public love affair (doomed, he knew) and reaching back in drunkenness to old times there, times he had failed to repossess.

Then Joy wrote and told him about an argument she had had with her husband. *He hurled a lobster into the swimming pool*, she said. *So I hurled him in after it.* As if she had been told, in exact detail, his anguish over Alice and his conflict with Helen, she indulged in some advice. The French call the orgasm a *petite mort*, a little death. Her take on this was that the little death is necessary to life as well as pleasure – if a woman wants to have a baby a small part of herself has to die to make way. She can't be all life all the time.

Joy suggested that Helen had not had an orgasm for a long while, and that they would never conceive without it.

He was taken aback; he had not mentioned his impotence (this was how he regarded it on all levels) to Joy, and nor would he ever. What made her so knowing about him? Sometimes she talked as though she had fifty years of experience under her belt. And she was right, also, about Helen. When they had conceived Henry their relationship was new and pleasure had been everything, but this time they had wiped pleasure completely from their agenda. From this point onwards he would step back into this project; he reverted to his original stance on the dreams, weighing now the extent to which they had, with their fatalism, hoist him into a sexual lassitude and prevented a result. Alice, he suddenly thought, would be *his* child. Where Henry dismissed him Alice would crave him. By the time he reached the end of Joy's letter he was breathless. Knight E5 to F3, she concluded. He shifted her thus, and planned his next move.

Joy's next letter was a parcel. Helen picked it from the porch floor and gave it to him, asking if he knew what it was. He said no truthfully. Opening it in privacy he found it was a miniskirt, blue denim with red stitching and hopeless pockets. Joy had sent it for Helen, confirming that these were becoming fashionable in California. She had never met Helen but thought she would look vital in it, sexy and modern. There was also a pair of silk tights which Joy said were the new thing – where stockings were fiddly and uncomfortable and no good for miniskirts, tights were a second skin. He held them up by the waist and looked at their weird shrivelled form in some dismay, but then pictured them stretched over Joy's legs, over his wife's legs, and he wrapped them into a ball with a wry smile.

After a week – the minimum time needed, he guessed, without Helen associating the parcel with the gift – he asked Sara to look after the baby and took his wife to The Sun Rises. Helen was in good spirits, maybe she was pleased to see him happy again. They talked to Eleanor and her new partner most of the night and helped her now and again behind the bar.

'Eleanor is in love with you,' Helen whispered gently. 'Whatever pretence she makes with that man.'

He whispered back, stroking her neck, 'And I'm in love with you.'

When he got home he gave his wife the miniskirt and silk tights. He wondered what she would put in those pockets – poems on folded-up pieces of paper? A photograph of the baby? A photograph of him? A photograph of a man he did not recognise? She looked at the skirt quizzically, almost suspiciously. The hemline was a good few inches above the standard. He expected her to announce, I could never wear this, but she didn't. She just carried on looking, turning it in her hands.

Eventually he broke the silence. 'Put it on,' he said. 'I want to see it on.'

CHAPTER 12

There she is, there. In the garden. He has seen her before. He creeps to the window to watch her, filled with spy-like curiosity. There. Maybe she is Alice, but the light keeps blanching her features and makes it hard to tell. She moves through the light like a dolphin – so like Alice, but he cannot be sure, and is careful to rush to no outlandish conclusions. Be rational, Jacob, he thinks, and observe; do, at all costs, avoid being mad.

The child circles the sleeping dog, occasionally stooping to touch the creature's coat with her palm and to stare closely at the blackness of it. Then rising again to her trip-skip across the grass. The dog is untroubled, does not even wake or open her eyes for a solitary tolerant glance at her visitor; she just sleeps on with a peace that suggests she and the child have looped this loop many times. Between them is a thousand years of private solicitude. It makes sense now, if the child is Alice, because of course the dog would know Alice, there will have been years for these bonds to form.

He crouches at the French windows, toppling

the pile of stones, and lets his eyes follow the child. Her knees, too big for her it seems; her fingers splayed. Occasionally she lifts her fingers a few inches from her eyes and peers through them in experimentation for how the world looks as background. Just mere background for her fingers. Foreground, background.

He takes a stone in his hand and clutches it. One summer, the summer of 1966, they are all at the beach, the four of them: Helen, Alice, Henry and himself. The children insist on wearing their swimming costumes, but he and Helen give up the pretence of warmth and pull on their jackets. Alice pads silently across the rocks and crouches to peer into the eyes of a – thing – wet bear, legless thing. Seal, yes. Seal. *Always peering*, Helen says, *as if she can see what we can't.*

He approaches her. Be careful Alice, he says. Don't disturb her. (He has decided the thing, seal, is female by the slightly languorous side-tilt of her body, draped rather than ditched by the tide or sudden lethargy.) The seal's pitch, tar, wet-ink eyes are wide open. *Blat*, Alice observes. Black, he nods. Very black. Alice is beguiled by the eyes and puts her face within a finger's width of the seal's. The animal smell is overwhelming, even to him from this distance, and yet Alice seems not to notice it. He can see his child's reflection in the animal's eyes, like a flower growing in outer space. *Blat*, she repeats, *blat*. He takes her hand and leads her away.

The four of them sit where the stones begin to thin out and give way to sand, and he decides to explain something about existence, respect for other animals and objects, the growing sensation that an individual is an extremely small thing of small pursuits, that the world is sometimes background, sometimes foreground, depending on how big one feels, but inevitably – how to explain this to a child? – inevitably one is small whether one feels it or not. To learn to be small – perhaps this is important.

He drapes his arms over his knees, tries to think how to put it. They are fairly new thoughts, questing, humbling thoughts he has been having in the last two years since Alice was born. Alice provokes in him instincts that Henry did not. Religious? No, not that. Not even tinglings of awe and wonder. But something to do with equality, the equalising effect she has on him. Whereas he feels responsible for Henry, he suspects that he and Alice are responsible for each other – that, with her changeful eyes, she sees him truly; he sees her truly.

She staggers up to him now like a needy drunk and he straightens his legs and lifts her onto his lap. He is about to begin. *That seal, she is just one of millions and millions of animals, four of which are us, my darling* – he is about to explain, when Henry turns with a sudden *Jake?*, the tone that always precedes a question, and asks why the horizon is so straight.

It isn't straight, he replies, if you look properly you'll see it's curved.

344

Helen holds her hand out to Henry and says, Yes, Jake, but as you know, Henry's right, it appears straight.

Again Henry asks why. Because the earth is perfectly balanced, Helen tells him. She details the phenomenon with an example of their household scales, and Henry, who likes to help her cook, grasps it readily: the horizon is straight because the earth is balanced because it is God's earth and is in perfect harmony.

In celebration she cuddles Henry and they tickle each other. He watches his wife and son, deciding not to ruin their happiness with fact. Lifting Alice from him he stands. Come on, kids, he says, I'll show you about balance. Equality. Henry asks, what's equality? I'll show you, he answers. He gets them to find stones which they drop in his pockets. Henry's stone is small and almost pedantic in its fine speckles, where Alice's is too big for her to carry, so she stands calm and wordless until he comes to her aid. He drops a stone in each pocket, and tilts in Alice's direction, explains that her stone is bigger and heavier. (Like the kitchen scales, Helen winks to her momentarily confused son.)

The children work to balance him. A stone here, another there, a pebble, a few grains of sand. When he is upright they cheer. He smiles out over the boundless coast: equality, he says. He picks Alice up and stands quietly with her, both peering, peering earnestly out over the sea.

*   *   *

345

The memory, so arresting, is freshly encased in the child's motions. His gaze has not left her, and has sought out her lilac eyes until they, those fantastic eyes, turn purple with placid recognition. Suddenly the dog rushes awake and runs across the garden, and the child, unworried, continues trickling through the sunlight. A bright, slightly nervy day.

There is a sound which he recognises but cannot identify, something very familiar that makes him feel an action on his part is required. Pulling himself from the view of the garden he combs his hair with his fingers; perhaps he needs the toilet. He is not sure. Something, certainly, needs to be done.

A voice calls. 'Jake!'

He confronts both exits from the bedroom and is undecided about which to take and where they lead. At some point he finds himself halfway down the polished wooden stairs as if he is simply shrugged from one moment to another without his consent, and now in the study, now the living room, the woman is there, and a man he has never seen before.

'Look who I found at the door,' the woman says. 'Fergus.'

The man steps forward and takes his hand.

'Hello, Jake. Sorry to surprise you like this.'

'Of course it's fine.'

He smoothes his hand down his shirt before offering it out. He inspects the man – frazzled features, something very windswept and loose in even his small movements. He is wearing the matching clothes for work that everybody wears, that he remembers wearing himself, and has a bag over his shoulder and something of a schoolboy look about him. Large, excited eyes, hands that look cold. But no matter how he interrogates these pieces of evidence, no recognition comes.

'Are you well?' he asks the man, gesturing them towards the sofa.

'Yes, very.' The man casts an open look at him, a searching look that seems to expect to find something of great interest. 'But what about you?'

He gives the man what feels to him to be a charming smile, an emulation of some replete composure; maybe he should have affected this earlier in life. Now it is the ideal tool for digging himself out of utterly vacated silences such as this, when the right thing to say does not present itself. When nothing at all presents itself. The man has a dim rattle in his breath, a straight, narrow nose, broken blood vessels on his cheeks. He is out of shape like a man at the end of a long race.

'Anyway, I brought some books I thought you might like,' the man declares, whipping open his bag with fingers that behave with the same invisible speed as the wind. 'Just a moment, let me find them in here.'

'And how's your wife?' he says, watching the incredible fingers, wringing his hands in his lap.

The man holds his gaze in a way he has noticed

Henry doing, distrustfully, or surprised. 'She's great.'

'Very good. Then maybe you'd like coffee?'

Now the man beams, salvages his arms from the bag and reaches forward to grasp his shoulder. 'You know I would.'

The woman stands. 'So I'll go and make a coffee then. You'll be alright, Jake?'

Do be good, she means; don't be mad. And she leaves.

Some time is spent looking around the room.

'Do you like the house?' he asks eventually.

The man stands and looks around him keenly.

'I do, very much. Haven't you lived here for years?'

'No, no, I don't think so. We moved in recently.'

He gives a smile and the man returns it.

'We need to decorate. It's a mess,' he offers then, and the man comes back to the sofa and sits. Indeed, it is a mess; the stranger brings a light to the house, so that he can see what he had not noticed before. Objects on the floor, stacks of books and paper on the table and, what are they, the clothes that go on the end, so many of them it would be impossible now to match them into pairs. Things for the dog. The television activators, piles of shirts and jumpers by the iron.

'You seem –' the man begins, putting the books heavily on his lap, 'you seem well.'

'I am, I'm very well, there's so much fuss over it all.' He scratches his head. 'A lot of fuss over a bit of a car accident. I hit a dog. I haven't been the same since.'

The man looks at him strangely, then away. He opens one of the books and leafs quickly through until he finds a picture.

'Glass houses, Jake,' he says. 'I thought you might want to have a look.'

He does look, turning the pages over and over, one house after another: long crystalline sheets of glass hanging onto cliff edges or glittering in woods – they strike him as X-rays, with their contents visible, the furniture and people just small functioning parts of the building. Oddly medical and diagnostic, as if to say, this is a house; after thorough examining it seems certain that this is a real house. They seem obliquely frail and vulnerable under this pressure of scrutiny.

'You see this one,' the man says, 'built in the Forties, and this one – built about two years ago, and yet can you tell there's fifty years between them? Not at all. Glass and steel are timeless, didn't you always say it yourself?'

He nods, rubbing the silky pages with his thumb. The colours bleeding on the panes seem to him indescribably meaningless and beautiful; it was once his job, he perceives dimly, to do this sort of thing, but now he would not know where to start, how to get those colours just so; how do the colours get on the glass? The responsibility of it is too immense now to contemplate, it does not seem like the sort of task for a man, or at least not this man. Not this man.

Leaning over this book, his slippers on, in need of a piss, his pyjamas (he fears) still on under his clothes, his wedding ring tight on a finger that, along with the rest, has swollen with uselessness, he is overwhelmed by these charges of failure. Becoming anxious, he resorts to his winning smile, backing off from the book, eventually nudging it from his thighs and standing. He goes to the television and turns it on, immediately reassured by the sound and its gravity, the pull that allows his thoughts to settle. He sits cross-legged in front of it.

The man clears his throat and speaks over the sound.

'The truth is, Jake, things aren't the same without you. You brought a bit of idealism to the office. Nobody is *idealistic* any more, have you noticed that?'

He glances at the man over his shoulder, then languidly back. He sees a mouth moving, hears words cluster together like a series of shapes that promise tessellation, but which do not, no matter how one turns them.

The man breathes in, pauses, and raises his voice a little to compete with the television.

'At last we have an interesting project on our hands, though – we've been asked to build a visitor centre on the moors. Made primarily of glass, which is why I dug out all these books. And I came

350

to be thinking about all those plans you made way back for your own house – those designs, and how intricate they were. They were really *good.*'

He looks back at the man and suddenly sadness claims him, a roaring sadness almost indistinguishable from anger, envy, guilt, regret, and on its heels, an image from nowhere of his mother in some irreparable toothless state and Helen, Helen silhouetted by a tower of glass which veers away to a constantly escaping point in a bare sky.

The man now stands, comes to his side and sits. He spreads papers across the floor. 'These are copies of your drawings. We found them in your files when you retired. Look at them.'

The woman has reappeared and is dishing out coffee. Both look at him, and then the woman does something with the television and the noise cuts out. She too comes to the floor; the three of them lean over the papers.

'It's excellent, you see how there are different parts to the building?' The man traces his finger along a line of cubes. 'Each room was a glass box, and you linked each one to the other with a series of corridors, here.' The finger slips along parallel lines. It plots from cube to cube in a right angle. 'The idea was that you would excavate the peat, pour in concrete, and then embed the glass deep down into the foundations so that the house seemed to just rise from the ground.'

The strangeness of seeing this again; he remembers it now that he has it before him. Stretched across yellowing paper the design is elegant, and he enjoys the way the man's long finger scores the lines. In all of his memories, details about the house itself are absent. He smoothes his hand over the drawing and the man continues.

'At the end here you were going to put a playroom for the children – see this small room? The idea being that, with the house at right angles' – again he traces the shape – 'you would be able to see the playroom from the rest of the house. So you could be sure the children were safe.'

The woman shifts suddenly. 'I didn't bring sugar. Do you want sugar?'

'No, no. Without is fine.' The man nods, smiles, and goes back to the drawing. 'And this is an idea we want to adopt for the visitor centre – put a play area here which can be easily seen from everywhere in the building, because the council wants to attract families to the area. Get the idea of conservation going in young minds and have this idea' – he spreads his long nervous hands as if he is weighing something – 'that humans can live more see-through lives, and that our buildings don't need to interrupt nature. That's the theme.'

The man stops and takes a mouthful of coffee.

'Just one question, Jake.' He swallows loudly and taps the paper. 'What's this? This boat?'

The boat the man indicates is a small fine drawing in the empty area overlooked by the house, what would have been the garden. What is it? He has no recollection of drawing those careful besotted lines. They resemble a rack of ribs, a perfect skeleton.

The woman taps the paper. 'That's the boat we found in the peat when we were children. Do you remember, Jake?'

He nods; yes, or no, maybe.

'It lived for years rotting away up against the side of the Junk, and you wanted to get it preserved and have it sailing through the garden.'

'What happened to it?' the man asks.

Her face shrugs. 'I don't know.'

The three of them stare at the drawing, in hope that it might answer.

'That was good of Fergus to come and see you, Jake,' the woman says.

He pivots to see her at the door, her face flushed. Fergus?

'Do you remember Fergus being here?'

He regards her blankly and shakes his head. 'Was there a man here?'

'Yes.'

Her nod is tired and undecided as she gives herself up to the sofa.

'When?' he asks.

'Just now. He left two minutes ago.'

'He brought the map?'

'The drawings, yes. These are architectural drawings, Jake, not maps.'

Frowning, she looks around the room. Done something wrong, he thinks. Won't know what. Definitely done something.

'Did you clear away the coffee things?' she asks.

Relieved, he shakes his head. No, he did not clear anything away, he hasn't moved. For some time he has been sitting, staring at this paper, aware, more aware than he can remember being for a long time. He *does* remember the time they found the boat. And his body knows all those straight-backed hours in the study, and the smell of cooking pushing through from one end of the house to another, and the pleasure of complete absorption in the lines on the page.

'I haven't moved from this spot,' he says.

She leaves the room and returns quickly. 'The coffee cups aren't in the kitchen. Have you put them away?'

With some irritation she scrapes the hair from her face, and he thinks she looks like one of those frazzled housewives. Perhaps she should rest; he pats the floor as a gesture for her to join him.

'When we found the boat,' he says, 'me and Ellie, we had no idea what it was at first.' He looks up at the woman and steeples his hands. 'We used to dig graves in the peat and lie in them, and we were digging that day, that's why we found it. We used to lie there in those graves with the entire sky above. That sky. Have you ever seen anything so big?'

The woman kneels down beside him and rests

354

her arms on the spread of her belly. 'We used to play *golems*,' she nods. 'One of us would cover ourselves in mud, to become a golem, and pretend the other was the king whose orders had to be obeyed. Like, do a headstand! Run anticlockwise five times with no clothes on! And we had to write the word *emet* in mud on the golem's forehead.'

He swallows at the memory. He sees it; he and Eleanor running around into the setting sun, and in the window of the Junk the flames of the menorah flicking up their first light.

'*Emet* meant truth,' the woman says, 'so if you had *emet* on your forehead you had to tell the truth. About anything. You used to tell me that Sara had been queen of Austria and that she would have to go back there soon, with you. I used to tell you that my uncle was saving up rations to sell on the black market. And that I sometimes weed myself still even though I was fourteen. Cry for help. And that one day, even though I was four years older than you, we were going to get married.'

She puts a hand on his leg. 'And you always said you wouldn't marry me. So I told you I would settle for just living together instead, as if we were married.'

They sit in silence for a moment. He remembers scraping the earth from the boat bone by bone, finding the point of its hull, each strut of wood almost perfectly preserved.

'And then, when the game was over we used to

scrub out the letter *e* on the golem's forehead to make the word *met*, which was Hebrew for death. And we would dig a grave, the golem had to get in it and we shovelled peat back on top of them and count how long they could stay dead. We'd leave a foot or a hand uncovered, to give the signal. We used to call it the game of the missing *e*. That's how we found the boat.'

A long silence unravels between them that is saved by her standing and going to the other side of the room.

He absorbs himself in looking at the maps in front of him. Everything takes on a lucid sense: Ellie, the peat, the boat, childhood. Something in him rests. One day he would love to see Ellie again and sit at that piano while she sang and while Sara played the – thing, thing on the shoulder, and Rook the mouth organ.

He looks out of the window to see if the child is still there, and she is. There is suddenly the comfort of waiting – that if they wait, he and the child, probably somebody will come and collect them soon. He stands and goes to the window to where, on the other side, she plays quite heedless, and he pushes his hand against the pane and bangs, hoping to ask her who they are waiting for, and when they are likely to come, just roughly, just so that he might plan.

When the woman comes to his shoulder she makes him jump. He turns to see she is holding a tray of drinking things and spoons, wearing a sorry look on her face which does not in the least match his own peaceful mood.

'You put the coffee cups in the writing bureau, Jake. I knew I would find them somewhere.'

He goes back to the floor and the yellowed paper, sits, wonders why she can't share his peace.

'Who are you anyway?' he asks, irritated.

He spreads the paper flat and pushes down its dog-eared corners. The paper was once white, and now it is yellow, he thinks. Once flat, now creased. And there is the truth about life: once this, then that.

'You're gone, Jake. Gone,' the woman announces at length.

He pulls his legs crossed, grips his ankles and looks up at her.

'Going,' he corrects, and rubs fiercely at his leg, a patch of sore skin where all irritation and outrage now centres.

'To think I've waited for you for thirty years. I haven't even bothered to try to love anyone else. And now I've got you, and you're gone.'

He scowls. It is important: not gone, *going*. If he were simply gone the child would not be wasting her time with him; and besides, it is crucial to be clear about the mechanics of it, the increments, the balancing of the stones –

The train of thought loses its way, breaks up and scatters. 'In any case,' he states, 'we have to remain aware of the consolations.'

The woman picks at her nails and delivers up the same tired nod.

'The consolations,' she agrees.

He dips his head in shame. What has he done wrong? He closes his eyes against the waft of air as the woman leaves the room, as if she were never there.

STORY OF THE CURSE

The table was plainly set. A dinner, an announcement, Sara had said, but when they arrived at her house there was not the mood of announcement. The plates set out between the usual weekday cutlery were pattern-less and the wine glasses like the ones Eleanor used in the pub, too unimaginative for wine. At least there *were* wine glasses. He was feeling brimful with some almost belligerent optimism, and in the mood for celebration. Immediately he opened the cabinet and compared the wines – cherry, no, something white and sweet, no. He took an Italian red and put it in the middle of the table.

Helen wore her miniskirt. With elfish steps across the orange carpet she took Henry to the cot upstairs.

Strange creature that she was. The way she had formed this ambivalent bond with the skirt that caused her to wear it often around the house (it's so short, she marvelled, and you can see all my legs!) but disallowed her from wearing it in public (it's so short, she cringed, and you can see all my legs) – dear Helen. He had persuaded her that

Sara's house was not public, it was just a slightly more daring version of private, so she had put it on, getting into a thick blue sweater, humming self-consciously.

Now she reappeared in the living room, blinked, tucked her hair behind her ear, scratched her cheek, as if trying to make herself as one-hundred-percent pure *Helen* as possible, sat at the table where Rook was already smoking, passed her hand to his and said, 'Hello, forgive my legs.'

'Darling, I love your legs,' Rook insisted.

'They're new.'

'So I see.'

She flowered. They chatted about the passing of summertime and the first falling leaves on the cherry tree and their second autumn away from London. Rook was a vigilant listener as he turned corners of a napkin into birds which he flew in her direction, and which she gathered into an orderly flock on her side plate.

Dinner was served and they ate in good spirits: lamb shanks, boiled potatoes, vegetables. Plain and righteous food with sprinklings of salt and pepper, a little English mustard. He would not be churlish, he decided; would not comment on the lack of silver and cut glass, or on the unlit menorah, or on Sara's mild, aged presence, as if some substance had slipped from her.

'The announcement,' Sara said, once they were all settled with food and wine, 'is that – well, you might as well say it, Rook, hm?'

'The announcement,' Rook took up, 'is that I've managed to wrestle that piece of land for you.'

'The Junk? Wrestle from who?' he asked, setting his knife on the plate.

'Contacts,' Rook winked.

Helen's eyes widened a fraction. 'You know Mrs Crest?'

Rook seemed to think about this far deeper than the question merited. 'In a way.'

The table was drenched in yellow from the setting sun, charging up the cutlery, running across their hands. It scattered itself across Sara's dress and cleaned her of any possible sins or secrets; no point turning to her for clarity. Rook winked at him. He stared back and the entirety of his childhood flushed over him in a moment. Its frustrations and unanswered questions, Sara and Rook's collusion, the feeling that he was never getting the truth but should be grateful nevertheless, because the truth is not a right, it is a privilege at best and a burden at worst.

'It's time for our future, then,' he said, and reached for his wife's bare thigh.

'And are you still volunteering at the hospice, dear?' Sara asked Helen.

Dear. He was surprised to hear this sweet tone in his mother's voice.

'Yes, Sara, yes. It's – wonderful, fulfilling. To be with people in their last few days or weeks, it feels like my calling.'

Sara smiled and sank the prongs of her fork so slowly, so delicately into a potato, like a woman too beached in the middle of old age to have the gusto for eating.

'And also,' Helen went on. He saw her cross her legs under the table. 'I've become interested in – well, we have a man in the hospice who is – black.' She straightened. 'His daughter comes in to visit him and tells me about the terrible things that happen to blacks in this country. Do you all know? Are you aware?'

She lowered and lifted her gaze in one interrogative gesture, spearing a piece of carrot which she left balanced on the plate. 'They can't get work, they can't get houses. If you want to rent or buy a house you simply can't.'

A sympathetic murmur went around the table, even Rook had no acerbic quip to add. They ate on in thought for a few moments.

'I mean, these are the 1960s,' Helen added, cutting her food up as if preparing it for Henry. 'Have we learnt nothing?'

'Actually I read in the paper,' he said, topping up the empty glasses, 'that the blacks in London are being helped by the Jewish communities. Jewish people rent houses out to blacks and then, when the blacks have the money, they buy them.'

He smiled, and met a theatre of blank faces. Helen sat back from her food and put her hands on her hips.

'That's good,' she said. 'In fact, though, if

362

nobody minds me broaching the subject – I mean, you could argue that the whole problem with racism sprang from Jewish myths. It *has* been argued. I don't know if I agree, but let's not romanticise.'

He and Rook cocked their heads, Sara went on chewing.

'You know it, Sara, of course. The myth that Ham saw Noah drunk and naked, and in his shame Noah punished Ham by putting a curse on his son, Canaan. And the curse was for him to be smitten in his skin. Burnt, in other words, burnt and blackened – and from that the blacks were cursed.'

Sara raised her head and sighed. 'I think there is no agreement, dear, as to what that myth means.'

'All the same. Oh I know what horrors have happened, and I know it's very right, politically, to favour the Jews –'

'But it's never right to be blindly favourable to anything,' Sara added.

'Yes, precisely.'

'I agree, dear. Keep that vigilance in life and you won't come to harm.'

He stood and took his empty plate to the kitchen. His blood boiled. Not against his wife, no, he rather admired her courage, her relentless defence of fair play and good practice, her wish to work out who the unfortunate were and save them. But Rook, Sara? What world of neutrality had they slipped into? He looked to them for some rich-blooded darkness, red wine, human skin, the tiered glint of candles bashing out a statement of defiance, a lily in the hair, a gunshot to sunder the milky carriage of clouds: a dark counter-balance to his wife's whiteness, to bring his life into symmetry – a stone in this pocket, a stone in that. A perfection. A fucking joke! His history was dying.

'Do you remember that myth, Sara?' he said, striding back to the dinner table with a knife in his hand. 'What was it? A deer and lion living in a forest. What was the forest?'

'Dvei Ilai,' Sara returned.

He waved the knife in excitement, watching Helen slice a plum and wrangle the halves apart, noticing the juice run down her fingers.

'Dvei Ilai. A giant lion, a massive lion twenty feet wide. And the Roman Caesar wanted to find him and kill him, so he asked the rabbi to call the lion out of the forest. The rabbi said, no, not a good idea. The lion cannot be killed. But the Caesar was adamant so the rabbi did as he was asked. It was the big mistake of the Catholics to ignore the Jews. The lion came, roaring, and his roar crumbled all the walls of Rome.' He took his seat and poured more wine. 'Rome was destroyed.'

There had been streams of these stories when he was a child, myth upon myth, myth tangling with myth, myth becoming fact, fact becoming fiction. So many dark close nights of it. Jam, syrup, sugar, baked pastry, an intimate smell of religion come true.

'In a minute I'll go and get the deeds to the Junk, I've got them upstairs.' Rook raised his glass. 'Let's have a little toast to Mrs Crest.'

He ignored the old man and held his own glass firmly to the table. 'What's more,' he said, 'the lion's roar was so bone-breaking that all the Romans' teeth fell out.'

Sara put her hand to her mouth and pressed at her gums.

'I've made bread pudding,' she said. 'Will we all have some?'

'Memory,' Helen's voice fired from the darkness of the driver's seat.

He paused to consider. It was her tactic to make him talk – if she simply asked what he was thinking he would shrug, *nothing*, and mean it. Nothing. But if she asked him for a memory, in this place reminiscent of his whole life, surely something would come. It was a cheap trick, but it worked.

'House of the exaggerating soldier, just there,' he said.

They passed the dark outline of a derelict brick house.

'The soldier and his wife moved to London, I wonder what happened to them.'

He recalled tables of rich food, the eyes of the soldier and his wife glinting in the poor light, the candles, the wife's blonde custardy hair. Actually she had been an attractive woman, at least as he now remembered her; quite the counterpoise to Sara. Fair to Sara's darkness, tall to Sara's smallness. Of comparable beauty though, if it were possible to compare creatures from separate planets.

'Memory,' he fired.

She took in a breath. 'I'm in London, I'm about fifteen. I'm walking home and I see a man and woman in the ruins of a building, they are making love. They aren't completely naked, only from the waist down.'

She faced him for a moment, her hands tight on the wheel. She smiled.

'It was quite – comical – but, suddenly, I felt that place was human. That all the world was loving and human and there to belong in.'

He scratched briskly at his chin and smirked.

'So that's the reason.'

'Reason for what?'

'For you being so – forward. When we first met, when we were at the ruins in Stepney. When you dipped your hand down my trousers while I was merrily talking about, I don't know, buildings. When you did all that with the church looking on.'

'Yes,' she replied, 'I suppose so.'

He smiled at the thought.

'I decided that I couldn't leave London until I had done what that couple had done,' she continued, 'or done something similar. Until I had *used* part of the city for myself, used it like it was my playground.'

In a way, he understood. He too wanted to appropriate a place before leaving, just to affirm that it was indeed him leaving, and not him being expelled.

'I thought it was just your nature, back then, to do those sorts of things. Thought you were a little bit – ah – *loose.*'

She shrugged. 'Jake, I don't have a nature.'

'Of course you do.'

'Then tell me about it. Tell me a few words to describe it.'

He lit a cigarette and handed it to her, lit one for himself. She didn't decline, perhaps because her powers of negotiation were channelled into driving in the cave-like darkness, or because she was too intent on hearing his answer.

'Well, you're kind, generous, funny, compassionate –'

'Ah, see. Now you're describing what a woman is like when she can't think of any other more imaginative way to be. It's not anything as defined as a nature. It's a lack of ideas.'

'Helen –' He reached across and stroked her face. She drew on her cigarette and flicked his hand away.

'Let's go to the Junk,' she said.

'Now?'

'Now. Guide me there. I can't ever get my bearings in the dark.'

It was only two miles or so from where they were; as they went the car filled slowly with smoke. Helen sped up; he arched his neck back and stared at the ceiling of the car an inch or less from his nose, breathed out smoke and let it wash over his face. Things felt good – Helen smoking, Helen speeding, Helen arguing, Helen driving them off to a black patch of peat. The baby back at Sara's, there to collect tomorrow. A night alone. Land to build on.

They stopped where he indicated. There was the house, slumped, derelict, and behind it the solitary row of wind-bent birch.

Helen knocked the keys back and forth in the ignition with her finger. 'Let's go in.'

On the floor in the kitchen they sat cross-legged and took food from the knapsack – some sandwiches, some Battenberg cake, oranges, a flask of tea, mint julep for him at the bottom of a bottle. It was pitch dark and the damp foxy smell occupied all the senses. When his eyes adjusted he could see his wife's white legs, and he could make out the rest of her because she was blacker than the background. She pulled the edge of the picnic blanket over her knees. It was far too cold for the miniskirt she was wearing but she refused the offer of his coat. He tried to insist, because she wore the skirt for him as she did most things for him; all her suffering came via him. He had, he thought, been corrupting her from the day they met; *I do solemnly declare to corrupt you 'til death do us part.*

But she refused the coat three times, and he swallowed the fourth offer.

She took the clingfilm from the Battenberg cake and handed him some with a smile. As he dissected it she lit up a match and put it close to his hands.

'You're eating the yellow sections first,' she remarked.

'Yes. I don't like them.'

'So in that case you leave them till last.'

'No, you save the best till last.'

The match went out and he heard her shuffle and stand.

'It's fishy, all this business about Mrs Crest,' she said.

He nodded, though she couldn't have seen.

'Perhaps we shouldn't sign the deeds.'

'We *will* sign the deeds. I don't care where it's from. Once they're signed it's legal. Helen, it's ours.'

There was a pause.

'If we're going to live here, then, right here on this bit of peat, I want to, I don't know, run around all over the moors naked, to stamp my belonging.' She laughed.

'You could,' he suggested.

An intense darkness marked where she stood and he reached forward to where he calculated her ankle would be, stroked the bare skin.

As he touched her he felt an unexpected peace. There was no need to keep searching for something

369

else, no need to live here. He could throw the deeds back in Rook's face and tell him to fuck off. They already had a house. But then Helen crouched and put something in his hand, some clothing. He brought it to his face and smelt it: her top. It had the faint smell of her skin and the pleasant, faintest soap-sweetened sourness from her underarms, and when he looked up he could see her pale torso and the white of her bra.

'Why is it you always get what you want?' she said gently.

He put the rest of the cake on the floor, stubbed his cigarette out and began removing his shoes. He got out of his trousers, trying to keep his balance in the dark, kicking the trousers off his feet. The lame peace, the inertia of before, had now left him.

'Jake? Where are you?'

'We ought to mark our belonging here, shouldn't we, if there's three of us – if there's going to be four of us. That's an army, that's time to set territories.'

'Are you going outside?'

'Yes.' He lit a match and made his way to the door. 'Come with me.'

Out in the drab moonlight Helen removed her shoes. It was easier to see out here. The smells of sugar and steel competed in the air. The white limbs of the birch trees made him think of Joy, he could not help it, he did not want to help it. Long white limbs in the darkness, skeletal and spectral. His memory saw Joy's slender hand cut a square across the black: *here, see it?*, *Framed by the factory*. He longed for everything he did not yet have, he longed for himself even, as if he were chasing himself and never quite catching up.

With summer gone the night held little warmth or consolation. He ran. It was a peculiar feeling, to run nowhere for nothing, naked. But he couldn't have done it clothed, it would have felt too absurd, as if he were mad and being chased by phantoms. He ran and shouted nothing for no one. He gestured to Helen to follow him and then flung his arms up and began stamping his feet into the miry soil. In response to his lunacy Helen laughed and scampered in circles. *Freezing*, she giggled. *Bleeding freezing*.

'Ours!' he said. 'This is ours!'

'Ours!' she repeated.

He ran to the dyke by the road and bent to splash his face with water; the water was freezing and puckered his skin. Helen came up behind him and doubled in breathless laughter.

'You look ridiculous like that,' she said, 'with your great long body and your big feet and your testicles hanging down – like a savage!'

He snapped off a few flowers from the bank of the dyke and named them: 'Brooklime, Labrador tea – these used to be everywhere.'

Handing them to her he moved on again across the peat making figures of eight and shouting, 'This is ours!'

When they were cold to the point that no running could warm them, even though they had years more running in them, they retreated to the car, turned on the engine for heat, and then the radio for celebration: Irving Berlin. *I'm putting all my eggs in one basket,* they sang together. They climbed into the back seat. They were three times too big for the space, four times, they crowded themselves.

He held her down and pushed himself inside her, almost savage, as she had said – checking briefly to see that she was with him, that she was receptive, and then closing his eyes to block everything out. His head hit the car window with rousing violence. The birch limbs appeared to his vision in drunken intervals, maybe he had opened his eyes to see them, maybe he had only imagined them along with the flare of yellow, the lilac blink of a child not yet born, a miniskirt draped over the steering wheel, a gunshot, a leaf, a gunshot, some bizarre rememberings of the hammered silver samovar Sara used to display on the sideboard, appearing to him with erotic clarity as if the memory were extruded through the force of sex itself; a stray thought that he never let in of his grandparents in Dachau. Furious anger cancelled, with shameful ease, by overwhelming pleasure. Helen was shrieking, he clutched her hair and pushed deeper until her shrieks filled the car, filled the moors, made new waves on the sea.

*   *   *

'Memory,' she said.

'I have none.'

She indicated right and they pulled out onto the main road, heading away from the moors.

'Memory?' he asked.

'We're driving along a highway in America. We're listening to Buddy Holly. I'm pregnant – but I haven't told you yet. I will tell you, soon.'

He took a packet of mints from the dashboard and handed her one. The radio played: The Crystals, James Brown, Buddy Holly, and he was grateful for its intrusion into their marriage. He closed his eyes against the memory of his wife's shrieks, and against the slight awkwardness that now tied their tongues as they drove home.

'In fact I do have a memory,' he said at length, turning the mint around in his mouth. 'I'm ten, we have to get upstairs by climbing a ladder on the outside wall, it's late. We've had a dinner party with some neighbours and Sara and my father have had an argument, in public, about her being Jewish. She's saying that what she misses, really misses, is olives. You can't get olives in England. Then my father starts: he says she's *putting it on* – her religion, he meant – he starts mocking her. He hates Jewish food you see. She's broken some cardinal kosher rules – mixed meat and milk, eating pork, I don't know, my father thinks it's proof that the whole thing is just a show –'

He looked outside the car window and saw nothing but night.

'My father starts mocking her about manna, *Are you waiting for manna from heaven, do you think your God's going to save you or do you think, perhaps, that it's me going out to work that will save you?* My father takes some money from his pocket and waves it around. *This is manna, and it isn't from heaven!*

'Then Sara tells him, very coolly, that manner is in fact the way you are, your disposition – she used that word – and manners, with an *s*, is also the thing you observe when you are in company, and that it is the first thing any self-respecting Englishman should learn. Then she goes upstairs, leaving my father and the neighbours to themselves. I follow her, in case she's upset, but when I find her in the bedroom she is turning slowly in a kind of dance, twisting the praise ring. She looks so happy. I have this vision that my mother is utterly indestructible. And that she will protect me from anything.'

He then turned to Helen with a more resolute expression.

'And then the next day, the Second World War breaks out and after we hear the announcement Sara goes upstairs again. I want to see her do that dance, be that amazing, strong mother. But this time there she is in the bedroom completely nude. Completely. Her body isn't what I expect.'

He examined Helen's face for a reaction but saw only the quick flick of her eyes towards him and back towards the road.

374

'It's, I don't know, womanly. With clothes on she always seems so narrow and contained. But she isn't. She has a small pot belly, and her hair is loose all over her shoulders. So pretty, that's what I think, and *young*, and – vulnerable.'

Helen crunched her mint. 'Does she see you?'

'Yes. She tells me to go and fill the bath. When the war started there were no more stories about her childhood and Austria and the rest. She just gradually shed her skin and became – English. Her family died, so she thought she should die. And it was as if, Helen, that moment that I saw her naked and vulnerable was the moment where I grew up, and I didn't want to. I wasn't ready to.'

Helen put her hand on his knee.

'I think you were ready to.'

'And because I wasn't ready, I've spent my whole life missing what I left. And I'll spend the rest of my whole life doing the same.'

'No, darling. Don't say that. Everybody has a little something missing inside them, it's prudent, it's like keeping a spare room in the house for guests.' She opened the window for fresh air. 'And if there is a big thing missing, find what it is and replace it. *We* can replace it.'

His wife's words did not comfort him, though; they never did. The memory left him feeling that the urgent growing up of that day had involved transgressing a sacred boundary. The more he tried to rid his mind of the image of his naked mother the more it prevailed and sharpened, so that he could see the birthmark on Sara's hip, her thick pubic hair, that belly, like the most private of all things, laid bare to his scrutiny.

The white front of the Coach House flared in the headlights; they pulled up, stopped the car, gathered up the items of clothing that had not made their way back on – socks, Helen's bra, Helen's neck scarf, his leather belt. The car engine ticked as it cooled.

For the first time he was struck by the loveliness of their house as if he had been loaned Helen's eyes for long enough to see what she saw: the creamy walls, tall black-framed windows, the modest but clear announcement of its drive, the garden an all-consuming selfish green even in the darkness, the cherry tree burning yellow into another autumn.

'Jake,' Helen said.

He held back a few steps and watched her approach the back door. 'Yes?'

'Jake, I believe I'm pregnant.'

He looked at his wife. 'Since when?'

She smiled wryly. 'Fifteen minutes ago.'

Had it been any other person, he would have ridiculed the premature announcement, but Helen – Helen knew, he could tell.

'That hit the spot?'

She bit her lip. 'In more than one way.'

'It's Alice?'

'Yes,' she grinned, 'I'm sure of it.'

'Buddy Holly!' he said, his tones muted. He lifted

376

her and spun her around; her feet knocked a milk bottle at the back door and smashed it across the gravel.

His delight was genuine, kissing her, letting her go, hoping against hope that she was right in her inkling, brushing the broken glass aside with his foot. But when they switched on the kitchen light they saw that something was not right. A chair had been knocked over. The French doors were shattered.

'Shit,' he said. He ranged across the kitchen, to the hallway, up the stairs. Ornaments along the way were broken, nothing precious, but why break them? Why not either steal or leave them? He bartered with himself: if the money is still there under the bed it is alright. He paused a moment in Henry's room, seeing that it was apparently untouched. Music came from his and Helen's bedroom, the crackle of a record crawling around the turntable. If the money is still there, he wagered, all will be well.

He ducked through the secret door, lowered himself to his knees by the unmade double bed, noted the proximity of his knee to a piece of smashed china that had once been a statue of an angel – a rather fanciful thing, a gift from him to Helen that he trusted she would like precisely because he didn't. Fury filled him when he saw her diary torn up and scattered across the pile of laundry by the wardrobe. Confusion, relief, slight offence filled him when he registered also that the human-skin bible had been pulled from its shoe box in the wardrobe and thrown, intact, to the floor.

He screwed his face towards the darkness under the bed. The money, of course, was gone.

Helen perched on the sofa in her rayon skirt.

'Ginger, dear,' Sara said.

'Actually I don't like ginger.'

'Ah, so.'

Sara dwindled back to the kitchen and he followed her, reasoning lamely.

'They'll find who took it. There were fingerprints everywhere.'

He leaned against the counter and felt pressure on his bladder as the shot of water passed through the coffee. 'They'll find who it was.'

Sara prepared the mugs; not the gold-rimmed cups but some two-a-penny blue-and-white striped mugs that were bereft of saucers or the possibility of saucers.

'Jacob, dear, they will never find that money. The sooner you lose hope the better.'

He folded his arms and dug his fingers between his ribs, made a short laugh. It's only money, it's only money. So Helen had taken to assuring him. But, despite their haste to see the police off and get out of the house, get back to their child as if to make up for all they had failed to protect, she had taken the time to rid herself of the miniskirt and leave it in a pile like a curse. On their drive back to Sara's they had lamented at cross-purposes, Helen talking about changing locks and the prospect of rewriting what she had logged in her destroyed diaries, he persisting (so much that he began to irritate even himself) in questioning, why, *why did it happen*? She interrogating the future, he nursing the past. He suddenly becoming what he did not want to be; a dweller. A dweller on the done and dusted. A dweller in an old honeysuckled house, and condemned to it.

Helen went to bed; it was already two or three in the morning. He stayed up with Sara who seemed to have no tiredness, either that or no idea of the time. As she switched on her radio and sank back into the bentwood chair he wondered if it were really possible for a person to age in a week, to give up on even the remote idea of youth. She was vacant. The loss of the money had impacted on her enough to cause the faintest of shudders, and then had seemed to absent her mind. He would not be the one to remind her that it was her family, that money. All the blood and bones of it, the sum of the remains.

'Where is Rook?' he asked suddenly. 'Did he go home?'

'Yes,' Sara said, and feigned a yawn. 'Tomorrow he's going to America.'

He straightened. 'Why's that?'

'To see his granddaughter – I hear you've met her.' She smoothed her hands across the cushion on her lap. 'The poor girl got herself in trouble a few months ago; Rook wanted to go and help sort it out but she wouldn't let him. She went alone, stubborn girl. I like her. I pity her. It's easier in California – of course she had to go over the border still and keep it all quiet.'

She spoke as if it were all just a matter of course.

'Sara, do you mean what I think you mean?'

'Probably.'

He forced himself not to speak until he had thought precisely what to say. He poured himself a glass of wine, the sweet white stuff, the bottle already half empty.

'Over the border?'

'Mexico.'

He shuddered at the idea of Joy laid out somewhere hot and dark, somewhere with thick spicy air. He turned the vision away.

'Rook didn't say anything at dinner –'

'No, of course. He was quiet with thought. He has been worried, naturally.'

'But it's over? She's alright?'

'Oh, quite alright. But Rook wants to go and treat her and buy her things and make her happy. That girl's happiness is his meaning for life.'

Sara looked a little regretful at this. She tucked her large hands between her thighs.

'How long ago – the pregnancy?'

'Some months.'

He drank, wondering what *some months* meant.

'But she's getting married – isn't she? Joy? I think Rook mentioned.' He acted out ignorance with a shrug. 'So she could have – there was no need for any *sorting out.*'

'Ah, but she's certain the husband-to-be is not the – what is that word?'

'Father?'

'Culprit.'

He felt rather sick and dark.

'Then who?'

'Apparently she had something with a man here, in England, before she left. That's all she would tell Rook. Or at least,' Sara sighed, 'that's all Rook would tell me.'

He felt to be the embodiment of sin, some bedevilled creature polluting all he touched. Or he felt drunk. He thought of Alice gathering cell by cell upstairs; of Sara naked; of Helen's shriek; of Rook's wink; of a gunshot. Of a bible so bleakly bound that even criminals would not take it. In his mind a door opened, Alice walked through, it closed again, Alice was gone. She was not pleased with what she saw, so she left. Her life was no more than his hush-hush of a door opening and shutting.

'I was going to ask Rook to marry me this evening,' Sara said. 'That was to be the real announcement. After the other announcement.'

He tilted his head and watched her.

'But I lost courage. What a foolish idea it was.' She touched her teeth again as she had earlier that evening and lowered her gaze.

'What terrible fates got that girl pregnant and

sent him off to America? He's too old for this.' She stood and wandered to the mantelpiece as if it had asked her to come and listen to something it had to say.

'I want to go to the sea with him, this second,' she announced. 'Oh, I'm so tired of all this aloneness, every room I go in what do I find? Me. Ich, everywhere, ich ich. I was going to ask him to marry me. Maybe not now. The courage has left me now.'

CHAPTER 13

How else could Alice have entered life but with one eye on its exit? Conceived in the back of a car to a little death and infidel thoughts, she was never going to want to loiter in this world.

In that sperm travelling towards that egg (he can see it swimming, heavily laden with bad news) there was nothing but death and disappointment, and it was *his* doing. Alice was *his* child; it was always as though her mother didn't so much give birth to her as dispel her, not without love, but in recognition of the fact that Alice was uncomfortable with the level of goodness she found inside her mother's small, white, freckle-dusted body. And when dispelled she went straight to her source, her father, that was how it seemed at least.

When she was born everybody noticed how like her father she looked and how eerie that resemblance was, because it was not in the features, which were more like her mother's, but in the parts of the face that don't have a name. Or maybe not even there, but just in the moving interim between one expression and another. The closed eyes and open

383

eyes were her mother's, but the blinking eyes her father's. The smile was her mother's and the scowl too, but the graduation from one to the other, the little wilderness between states, was her father's through and through.

Every time he wakes up it is this wilderness that greets him, this no-man's-land, filled with his daughter's eyes and smiles on their way to an expression they never quite reach.

No matter what he attempts with the timeline, and no matter how he manoeuvres collapsing memories into stories that might get round to her, all that is left of Alice is three isolated flashes which, when they come, throw all other time out of bounds.

First, he is carrying Alice through the woods. There are gunshots: bang, they ricochet between the trees, lose their heart and stream onto the path in shreds of last sound. He covers Alice's ears (which, he thinks in wonder, are just like shells they found on the beach the week before she was born), and he takes the time to trace his fingers around their curves. Alice does not cry. Alice is three weeks old and not overly concerned by or interested in this world, not even the deer killing, not even the lattice of branches that bow down to her. Still, though, he covers her ears to spare her any concern that might come.

'When she's three,' he says, 'we'll harvest the cherries from the tree, but not till then. The laws of kashrut say to wait until the third year, and practice patience.'

Helen hugs Henry to her.

'The third year of the tree, Jake, not of Alice. Not all time begins with Alice. The tree's already ten, twenty years old. You've drunk its wine.'

'You think the birth of a tree is more important than the birth of a child?'

'We didn't do the same when Henry was born.'

'Because Henry was born before we even found the tree –'

'Anyway,' Helen intercepts, 'the law of kashrut, what point does it have?'

'It's about patience and –'

'Patience and virtue. Yes, yes. Since when did you care about those?' She smiles up at him.

'It's about observing rituals for their beauty. Why do we celebrate birthdays, or Christmas, or pancake day?'

She kisses Henry's head.

'I suppose. It just all seems so obscure, if you know what I mean.'

'And the Bible isn't?'

She smiles again, reaches over and touches Alice's nose with the tip of her finger.

'We can abstain from cherries for three years for the sake of beauty, and the sake of Alice,' he reasons.

'And what will we do for the sake of Henry?'

'Kashrut can be for Henry too, a belated kashrut. We can have it for both of them.'

'I suppose we can.'

He touches his daughter's nose in the same place. 'She's just as I imagined her.'

Helen puts her hands over Henry's ears against the gunshots.

'It's good that you love her so much,' she says.

It has snowed, and the prison is frozen like a monochrome photograph inside its fences. They make their way towards the entrance where the woman shows something to a guard and their bag is searched, and at that they are allowed along the corridor to the large, hot room. They take a seat at a table with a young man.

The man reaches his hands across the table and smiles. 'You need to get that coat off.'

Instinctively he hugs the coat to himself in refusal and shakes his head.

'I'll get us coffee,' the woman says.

'He always has tea when he's here. Strong and sugary.'

The young man smiles again and a sweetness passes over his face, a familiarity in the eyes also, in the small up-turn at their corners which seems to convey great curiosity in things.

'She won't leave me alone,' he says to the man when the woman has gone.

The man winks. 'Just as well.'

He observes the other people in the room, their hunched shoulders and anxious looks; all women. Not for the first time he wonders what he is doing here, thinking it is business perhaps, but then not able to say what business that would be, what he used to do here when he was younger and more important. He scratches around in the embers of a fire long gone out and, finding himself in that disconsolate clueless state that has become home, finally contents himself with turning the buttons on his coat one way and the other to see how far they will twist.

'I've done a painting,' the man says.

He smiles brightly. 'Oh? That's very nice. Painting. You've done a painting. On the banks of a river, very nice, very nice, well done you, that's good – good, good – that's –'

A hand on his arm stops the stutter of thought. 'It's for an exhibition of prisoners' paintings, called *Doing Time*. I may give it to you and Ellie when the exhibition's finished, if you want it. It's of four animals in a cage – a tiger, a dog, a cat and a bird. It's a sunny day at the zoo, and the animals are all watching each other. The question is, which will eat which first? Will the tiger eat the dog, will the dog eat the cat, will the cat eat the bird, will the bird fly away? It's called *A Matter of Time*.'

Out of the window he can see the reach of the manor house, which is eclipsed from view as the woman puts drinks on the table, and then returns to view when she sits. The bird will of course fly away, he decides, then loses the thought. He takes his cup of tea in his hands and stares at that view, disappearing into a thoughtless blankness. He can hear chatter around him and feels an increasing heat in his hands, as if they are on fire, insulating him against the snow that threads down outside.

When the man sinks his gaze to the table, just in that moment he is reminded of a time when Henry had fallen asleep at the kitchen table and he had picked him up and taken him to the bedroom, swaddling him in blankets, tucking them around his son's body, surprised at how small it was. Then he had sat on the edge of the bed for an hour or more watching, with a feeling of immense love and protectiveness, his son sleep.

The most vital thing is to protect one's children. There is no part of the soul or body that is complete without that guardianship, no part that is even alive. He feels the pressure of the sentiment on his cheeks, his shoulders, his eardrums, his bladder. Somewhere in the woods his son is running around shooting an imaginary enemy with an imaginary gun, and soon he will come home needing dinner. The table should be set in preparation; no time here to waste talking to strangers.

When he looks out restlessly through the window the sight of the manor house catches his eye again, dragged through time, exiled in the present moment.

'That's funny,' he says, bewildered, and the man and woman turn to him.

'What's funny?' The woman puts her hand on his thigh.

'That building was there yesterday, and the day before.'

The snow goes on weaving patterns before his eyes.

There is a gunshot. Bang! Henry shouts and his fingers form a gun. Alice wants to try walking but the snow is deeper than her, at least just here. She is now one and a half: how fast the time has gone! She windmills her legs and he clings to her while his wife and Henry follow behind. His wife sings. *Honey, and I've decided, love divided in two won't do.* Her voice carries out across Quail Woods in clean pleasant lines until it meets the moors.

'Henry, stay with me,' his wife says.

'Want to go to Jake.'

'Stay with me. Jake is looking after Alice.'

He waits for his wife and son to catch up. His wife is out of breath because of the snow and Henry's five-year-old weight on her hip, where Henry, in a needy mood, has insisted on being held; he kisses her cold cheek and then Henry's. Henry reaches out for him and he leans back; what can he do or say? He does not want to give his daughter over, and as the snow falls on them he holds her closer, pulling the yellow blanket around her. Joy's recent letters are in his pocket and brushing against his leg as he manoeuvres himself through the snow.

'*And they took their journey from Succoth, and encamped in Etham, on the edge of the wilderness,*' his wife announces. 'And they were happy to be encamped in their stone house, and not the glass house. And they found a cherry tree, and its branches were possibilities, possibilities within possibilities. Some possibilities were to become real, and some were to always remain just possible.'

He smiles at her, stoops and gathers up a snowball which he throws lightly at a tree. With some effort Helen holds Henry at the end of her reach and turns slowly in the snow, until his weight is too much. She sets him down on his own feet.

'And from them came two children, a boy and a girl, and their eyes were as the eyes of doves by the rivers of water, washed with milk –'

'– and fitly set,' he finishes. 'And the snow was milk and the sky was milk and their hearts and brains turned to milk.'

His wife scoops snow from a tree and throws it at him. They laugh, even Henry laughs. Alice chatters, *Jape, Jape*, like a bird, and a gunshot bounces out across the canopy of branches. It splices the possibilities into sometime and never. He thinks of all those things his life will not be, and wonders what he is without them.

(And as the snowballs fly in a three-way him-wife-son tangle they seem to break up and spill across the air until the air, the trees, the whole forest, are dripping with white milky liquid in which the only colour, just beyond them, is yellow, yellow dress, yellow foam, a pair of yellow shoes surfacing and submerging as the mother and child try to stay afloat.)

'Want to go to Jake,' Henry grizzles, as Helen hoists him up again to her hip. 'Go to Jake.'

'I'm with Alice at the moment, Hen.' His words come out as steam on the freezing air. 'Later you can come to me.'

His wife observes the now sleeping child on his shoulder, and she scratches her cheek and tightens her hold of Henry.

'It's good that you love her so much,' she says.

So then Alice is three, and his wife is walking barefooted along the path in her miniskirt, blotched in the green-and-yellow camouflage of the sunlight as it fights through from above. The overhang of trees sieves the light of its heat. Everywhere there are patches of yellow that force through from nowhere and give the effect of a dream. There is so much yellow that it works its way up his legs as he paddles through it and he feels like he is coming alive.

He is at his wife's side carrying Alice on his shoulders so that she can become a tree; she threads her fingers through his hair and chirps, *Jape, Jape*. Henry runs ahead and throws pine cones at targets on trees – a knot in the bark or a red cross painted to mark the tree as fit for felling. Most of the trees are marked.

He comments that woods are going to be cut down, and Helen replies that it is sad to lose the woods, their lovely woods where they like to come walking.

To lighten the mood he reminds his family that it's been three years since Alice was born, which means that their three years of kashrut is done. The day is gorgeous, the height of summer, and so he suggests that they go home and get up the ladder and pick cherries. They'll make, let's see, a pie.

Helen crouches and rummages in a bag; she pulls out some cake which she unwraps from its clingfilm and hands to them. *You're eating the yellow sections first*, she says as they tuck into the cake. Yes, he explains, because he doesn't like them. *So in that case you leave them till last*. No, he assures her, you save the best till last.

A series of gunshots rupture their debate. There is a war, or there has been a war, or – what? – he doesn't know now, reaching back into the memory is like putting his hand into a box blindfolded, knowing there are objects but not knowing quite what they are. War plays its part, but maybe it is just its steady tick that has never left him. Maybe just the tick of his own maudlin heart.

Henry points to the horizon through the trees and asks why the horizon is so straight. When Helen embarks on an elaborate explanation of God's aligned and unswerving nature, he steps in to tell his son it isn't straight, it just appears that way; but at that point Alice whispers in his ear, *Jape, I want to pick them*, and he loses interest in arguing about horizons.

Pick the cherries? he asks, and his daughter nods.

He kisses her cheek, of course, of course, whatever she wants she can have.

The only ripe cherries will be on the highest branches, Helen says tersely.

He stands in the middle of the path and closes his eyes to the next stream of gunshots. Helen turns her face up to the sound and shivers as though she wants to run from it all, that beat of darkness that seems to follow them around. When she looks back at him she eyes him curiously and tells him he looks just like a soldier, so serious, dressed in that military light.

He says he is trying to work out what's on the other side of that sound.

Peace, she answers. There's nothing quieter than the quiet after noise.

Jape, Alice whispers again to his ear. *I want to pick them.*

And then the next day, there is no Alice, and the cherry tree droops its branches in sympathy, or is it guilt.

The woman comes in to the room, waving her arms: Jake, you have put your clothes in the oven. Jake, you have fed Lucky five times today, she'll die if you don't stop it. Jake, you are wearing one shoe, one slipper; always wearing your coat, like you're about to escape at any minute, take it off. Jake, you are jostling about, do you need the loo? She looks like a madwoman, in and out like this with smoking clothes and dog bowls, getting red in the face as her voice rises.

'You stole my money,' he tells her coolly. 'It was under the bed.'

Then he is upset – she stole his money! He wrings his hands and frowns at a patch of carpet. And she stole the letters that man had been writing to him, the letters about the – thing – they are not in his pocket, he can't see them, and they were his licence, his goodness, what protected him. She stole his money, his letters!

'You stole everything!' he fumes.

'I didn't steal anything.'

'You stole my money!'

Then doors slam and silence encroaches, then the sound of tears, then a little while later a tray of food comes, which she lays on his lap. Her eyes are red.

'I have to have a break for a few days,' she says. 'I can't cope. There's a service I heard about and I'm going to see if I can use it – where you can go somewhere for two days while I stay here and have a bit of time alone – and you can have some time alone. Without me. In a nice place where you'll get looked after better than you do here.'

He looks at his hands gripping the edges of the tray.

'I don't want it.'

'It'll do us good – two days without each other.'

'I don't want to be without each other.'

'Just for two days. I need a rest, Jake. I think we both need a rest.'

'I don't want a rest without each other.'

'Just for two days.'

He transfers his grip from the tray to her arms and squeezes. A look of pain and anger passes across her face and she shakes her head: no, it means. Let go of me. He squeezes harder and she closes her eyes.

'Just for two days,' she says.

Again, he is faced with his old, frightened hands. I was a child once, he thinks with surprise. How criminal, how sadistic, how preposterous that I am not any more.

Outside the window, in all this cold weather, the little girl is gone. Snow falls like blossom.

STORY OF THE ESCAPE

'My father, Arnold, has a scar across each cheek. Here, and here.'

Sara's free hand – the hand that is not holding the gold-rimmed cup – touches one cheek then the other. 'Fencing scars, Jacob. From his days at the University of Vienna. Look, let me show you.'

She crouches under the shelter of a tree and dips her hands into her bag, allowing them to waft through the blackness before she pulls out a photograph.

'Here, my father.'

She presents the image to the freezing drizzle of the woods; she shows it to him, to the trees: here is where it all begins, and here you begin.

He takes one hand from the warmth of his pocket and holds the photograph with her. The baked potatoes that she gave him that morning, to keep his hands warm in his pockets, are only just beginning to lose their heat, and the drizzle is turning to snow.

Sara touches her father's cheeks, taps them gently as she taps the list of ingredients in a recipe, as if to say, yes then, that makes sense.

'Do you see them, the scars?'

Yes, he sees them, the silver glints along his cheekbones.

Across the treetops a gunshot rings, a deep pungent sound; he throws a pine cone at a target – a leaf in his path – and hits it square.

'The war is starting,' Sara says. 'And things will not be the same again.'

Her ring clinks against the china of the mug, and her spare hand reaches down to his coat and pulls up the hood. Then she tilts her head back.

'Look up, Jake, look up at the branches.'

And so he does, and they walk in this way, looking up at the breaks of light through the bare trees.

'Patterns within patterns within patterns.' She half smiles, half frowns. Their faces are wet with snow and he wipes his cheeks.

'My parents should get out of Austria,' she says. 'There's time, and it isn't safe there. All their friends are leaving. I've written to them and asked them to leave. They can come here, we have room.'

Of course, they don't have room, the lie is obvious and harmless, but the way his mother talks (each statement so mathematically assured) causes him to imagine the Junk somehow expanding to fit the need. Or that somehow these exotic tall people will bring their solid walls and high ceilings with them; their airy space, their time.

His mother crouches and pulls him gently to

crouch opposite her, her hands holding his arms. 'Jacob, at school – or anywhere – don't mention that I'm not English, if anybody asks. Nothing about the candles, huh?'

Though he nods, the words don't seem right from her lips. She has always argued with his father about her right to burn the candles, bake the little sugary triangles, fill their cramped kitchen with the coffee machine that gurgled its foreign language each morning.

'Don't be scared, no harm will come to us.' She kisses his cheek and the scent of lilies swarms him. 'It's just better to pretend you don't know anything. Sometimes it is better to be a fool, my dear. Where you are from, what is yours, what is home – sometimes these are not the point. The truth is not everything. You have to know when it is time to get away.'

A second, louder gunshot explodes in the distance and bounces through the branches above them.

'Dreck!' Sara stops and puts her hand to her chest. Coffee spills on the new dust of snow and melts the snow away. It is the gunshot at the start of a race, he thinks, and suddenly the woods are charged with the thought of escape. He and his mother look at one another with a slight excitement, a fever sketched giddily across their faces. The snowflakes are now fat and determined to settle, and he is impressed by how fast they turn the trees white. That letter his mother sent, he supposes, is shuttling across Europe on trains, a beat pulsing along the track like the beat now left in the air after the gunshot.

They fling away the dregs of coffee in their mugs and run for no reason but to run. They have a soft fight with the snow as it falls, the flakes so large now he could almost count the sides, and they begin laughing silly shrill giggles – both of them, he thinks (sure that he knows what his mother is thinking; their brains have the same folds and clefts and wiring) are thinking about Sara's parents doing the same, walking and then running across woods and countries with their yellow bands flickering, making a run for the sea. He looks forward to their arrival. He glances up at his mother's bright flushed face as they run and she looks more hopeful than the brilliant snow itself.

CHAPTER 14

The main thing he thinks now is that somehow he must get out.

A man leads him to his seat in the dinner hall and shows him his meal. He objects by shaking his head roughly. They did not used to sit like this at school, each person at their own chair with their own small table in their own world – instead they were in rows along benches, elbow to elbow, forming one long chain of interconnected worlds that nudged at each other, feet that tangled and rationed food that migrated from plate to plate in bouts of fighting and sharing. If it were like that now he would sit, eat and talk, but the place has the restless quiet of things lost and forgotten and it makes him anxious.

He spends his time getting up to look for his dog, then, after some wandering, sits, forgetting what it was he had got up to do. Then he gets up to look for his dog, and ends up out in a summer house in the thawing snow, smoking with a group of elderly people he does not know or care about, then returns inside to look for his dog.

He will not go to bed, he will not piss while being watched, he will not go for a walk, he will not drink his tea, and he will not sing songs or play games. There is a chink in the earth which he will have to head for in order to be funnelled out – a small port of exit – and so he will wait in the corridor for somebody to come for him, eventually to take him home.

'But you're going home in two days,' he is told by somebody who has no right to know more about him than he does. 'You're just here for a break, try to enjoy it.'

Not true, he has been here for weeks or months already, and can feel every one of the days dragging behind him, a load too heavy to pull. Abandoned! His wife has left him to rot, his mother too, his son. As a woman scrubs at his back in the bath he covers his crotch with his hand and bends his head downwards to hide his face from her. He tightens his body and refuses to move his arms from his body. If he had the words he would tell her what he thinks, but as it is he has a throat closed rigid with sentiments that have lost form. Eventually he is dragged from the bath by several hands, dried off and shovelled into a pair of pyjamas that he objects are not his. He is given a cup of tea that he refuses to drink, and then put into bed when not in any mind for sleep, and lies with an aching stomach and a need for the toilet. He is anxious that if he sleeps he will miss his lift home. The light goes out; he puzzles over where he is, where his mother is. He calls her name quietly in the dark – *Mama?*

When he finally sleeps he dreams that he is in the car with his wife on the moors and there are planes flying overhead; when the planes reach the steelworks they begin twirling and diving in spectacular formation, doing so for minutes until the twirling loses control and they pirouette down into the huge factory chimneys in yellow flames. He jumps out of the car and tries to catch the planes as they fall, one in this hand and one in that, and though he beseeches his wife to help she sits in the passenger seat nursing a child at her breast, her smile milky and cool and a song on her lips, and watches while the planes crash around him.

He dreams afterwards – or is it all the same dream? – that a woman with glossy black hair is in the back of the car whispering sharply to him with a polished Austrian accent, Wake up, I have left the man in the prison and he is dying there, wake up.

He does wake up, dumbfounded with fatigue and disorientation. A woman is at the side of his bed and gives him a glass of water and a tablet. The sheets are wet and cold. Ashamed of himself and too tired to fight he takes the tablet down with a gulp, sits blindly in a chair while she changes the bed, and feels a tiredness well in him as if he is clotting. She takes his hand and puts him back in bed, pulling the blankets up around his chin, and the next thing he knows they are still at his chin and his body has not moved, and it is morning.

Here, a perfect memory afloat in nothing. A blue peg with an elastic band wrapped tightly around it. Wait, it links back.

On the chair in the corner of the bathroom he presses his knees together and watches the peg spin past his vision. A woman bends over the bath and oars the water with her hand. This is not a bathroom he recognises, very large, white and clean, and the bath itself is as wide as a rowing boat and high sided so that, once the confused process of undressing is done and he has stepped into the water, he can barely see over the lip. He brings his long legs up to his body while the woman, humming, begins to lather soap over his back. In the water his skin is as white as a newborn's. The woman flannels up and down his arms, taking his hands one by one and cleaning the palms.

'So pale,' she says, 'compared to your lovely brown face. You haven't seen the sun for a while, Mr Jameson, hm?'

He turns his face up to the ceiling, peaceful and sleepy. The woman cups her hand under his knee and runs the cloth over his leg, then down under water to the ankle, then between the toes and the soles of his feet. Time moves forward at a stroll, his skin taking time to remember the cloth as it passes on to the next place, as if, patch by patch, it is waking up after a heavy sleep.

'We need to get you nice and clean for going home tonight,' she says, wringing the cloth with a quick strong tug. 'Can't have your wife thinking we haven't looked after you.'

She hangs the cloth over the taps and takes a bottle of something, pours it into her hand.

'Pop your head back for me, there we go.'

He is sitting cross-legged on the tiger skin, ten years old, and his mama is showing him how to turn the praise ring with the wrist, and she suddenly asks, Do you remember being born, Jacob?

He pushes his fingers through the tiger's fur and nods. They hear the tired creak of the front door opening.

Sara hoists him up from the tiger skin and says, Come on, Jacob, your father's coming home. She tucks the photograph of her parents in her dress and there ends the stories of warring Europe, Lucheni, the Big Death. She shoves the praise ring back in the tea chest. When his father comes into the room to see them standing quite innocently and Englishly, pale and upright, he rants at them anyway, just in case either has done anything. His father blows out the menorah, it clashes with his sense of identity. It is all about identity. All about What You Are, or What You Are Not. All about being something because you were born that way and about being *legitimate*. His mother lights it again. She uses firm words in a language nobody else in the house understands, dabs her dress to check for the photographs, and puts the kettle on without another word.

When they hear that evening that war has broken out, the three of them watch the scratched sound fizz through the speakers of the wireless, and he and his mother think (he knows what she thinks) that a device so strange, insectile, cannot be trusted with such huge news. She blows out the menorah candles and goes outside, up the ladder, and into her bedroom. His father mutters that if there is going to be a war he needs to get maps, and they need to start storing supplies, and they need to start working their land better. Excited about what will come, he wants to sit with his father and work out a plan, a strategy, but he feels he should check on his mother, so he follows her upstairs.

There, in her small damp room, she is naked, and the smart brown dress she had been wearing is folded on the bed, its row of four buttons picked out bright in the gaslight like four unspent coins. Because he can think of nothing else to do he stands and stares at her, and he weighs up whether he is a child or more than a child, whether they should be embarrassed, whether her surprising hips and small, smooth pot belly are those of a mother or a woman, whether therefore, to hug her or run away.

She doesn't even blink. 'Go and start filling your bath,' she says.

He goes back down the ladder, takes the tin bath from the shed, drags it across to the front door and into the kitchen. There is Eleanor, poor Eleanor in the kitchen in her purple and turquoise dress, come to say that her uncle has disappeared again and she is scared to be alone. His father is giving a lecture: they shouldn't leave you like this, it's preposterous, I'll have the police on to them – and Eleanor scuffs her foot at the stone floor in pleasure at his anger, because nobody ever takes the time to be angry on her behalf.

He meanwhile, is thinking of the birthmark he has just seen on his mother's hip, a faint leaf-shaped mesh of finely patterned sepia, like a scaled-down shadow of criss-crossing branches. His mother was born. She is not his, she is her own. If she is not his, he is not hers. If he is not hers, he is not a child and does not even exist. He doesn't want to simply hear the stories she tells, he wants to live in them, so that he might have been there from the beginning, from her birth, so that he is not left out.

When his mother comes back she is wearing a loose chequered dress and a shawl. She gives Eleanor a curt, kind hug and begins filling the pans with water to heat. His father goes out to talk to some friends about 'the future' (he will always remember this phrase, *the future*, wherein everything that was to come was already history) and to see what could be done about draining the land for crop-growing.

They get in the bath, he and Eleanor. His mother runs warm water over their heads and backs and lathers soap through their hair.

'You can stay here in Jacob's room,' she tells Eleanor. 'Until your uncle reappears.'

Eleanor nods and blinks the soap from her eyes. She has stayed with them many times for the same reason and they are used to sleeping top-to-toe in his bed. She has grown since last time he bathed with her. Her body is older than his and has become alien in its configuration of thick pink thighs, soft deep cut of flesh between her legs, rolling waist, awkward breasts obscured by a pair of clutching, self-conscious arms, fat hands, fat rosy feet. Sara sings to them as she washes their hair, *komm doch mein Mädel, komm her geschwind, dreh dich im Tanze mit mir, mein Kind* – and, having heard it all their lives, they sing along, rocking the water over the sides of the bath.

As they are getting dry he asks Sara to tell him the story of Lucheni again – this time he resolves to make himself Lucheni, to create himself where Sara began, to surface in the minutiae of her birth-mark – and so they travel through the European vistas in her words murdering and loving and ending and beginning, until she, finally, is born to the sounds, *oh peh kuh, kuh peh oh*, and the sight of a silver samovar.

'This is the first thing I ever saw,' she says. 'The first thing you see is precious, because it is also the last thing you see.' She towels them dry and boils milk for cocoa.

They ask for more stories, but Sara shakes her head. 'No, that's it. That's the last of them. You're too old for stories, there won't be any more stories.'

That night in bed he wonders about war and is angry in case the moors, in their wide blackness, absorb even this extraordinary event, and he decides, there and then, that whatever the war will or won't do, one day he will come back here as an adult and make a difference. But as soon as the thought is born it terrifies him, that there are no more stories, that there is a future in which this moment of childhood is lost. He hugs Eleanor's feet. He presses her toes into his cheek and closes his eyes.

All that night he reconsiders the question: do you remember being born? He doesn't know if he remembers or not; he doesn't know the difference between what you remember and what you think you remember, or worse still, what others remember for you. He doesn't know who he is. The boy who was not magnificent enough to lie on the tiger skin rug, 'All the way from India!' his father had said. 'Look at it, an English victory, get your scrawny white knees off it.' The boy who is trained to revere a curious praise ring and to learn, as if it were a game, the laws of kashrut. The boy who gets beaten by his father and pretends he knows nothing about kashrut. The boy who goes seeking Rook, and fights out his confusion in the peat until blood comes.

He doesn't know what legitimises him, so he decides that he can remember being born. He can remember opening his eyes for the first time and seeing the tiger stripes. He can remember being a baby; if he concentrates hard enough he is still a baby, he does not want to grow up and be free. His mind covers his mama's hips and belly with the brown dress, and ties her hair at her neck. He decides, yes, he can remember opening his eyes and seeing the tiger's eyes, he might as well remember being born and the sound of his own cry. It is, at least, a start.

She hums as she washes his hair. His head keeps falling forward, so she tucks her fingers firmly under his chin and holds it straight. She is talking to him, and though he barely hears or understands what she says, the sound of her voice alone, in the rise and fall of the story, is music to him.

Relationships sketch themselves out in his memory – wife, child, children, husband, parent – and form lines that are either snaking towards him or snaking away. And maybe they are not memories but inklings. He does not feel alone. Just the motion of the cloth over his skin and the peripheral voice skittering off the white walls prevents that. Of the relationships he is aware of, *mother* is the only one he can speak of, and though he cannot produce her name at this moment, he can see her, and then he can define himself: child. *Child.* He suddenly knows himself, not through fragments of memory or mirrors, but as a gut feeling, a seed deep in the stomach.

Life spreads ahead of him, choices he must one day make. They appear as planes on the horizon no bigger than flecks, but as they near and their drone is more insistent, his tiredness pushes them away and sends them spindling down into the peat. Somebody else can save them. He looks over the high rim of the bath, at the big unfamiliar bathroom. The palm of the mother's hand rests lightly on his forehead as she pours water over the crown of his head; he is not confused – she is not his mother, she does not have the clean cut of his mother's presence, but she brings with her the dense grounding feeling of somebody with whom he can be pale and wordless. The water washes past his ears, the only sound.

He sees again that peg painted blue with an elastic band wrapped around it. After all it links to nothing. Just a blue peg turning in a void. Just a strange, remembered peg.

STORY OF THE END OF THE WORLD

The sea washes up to his ankles. He steps back. When he looks up the beach there are no people, only stones, rocks and a flurry of leaves scudding across in the wind. Are they leaves, or are they birds? He reaches his arm out and snatches one from the air, inspects it to see it is a leaf, and puts it in his pocket.

Now there seem to be an infinity of leaves which he rushes up the beach to catch. But not an infinity, that is reckless, just a lot. How much is a lot? Is seven a lot? Running is easy even on the stones. The beach is made of pebbles here, stones there, rocks over there, and boulders beyond them, and the increase in size gives the impression that he is running into a reverse perspective, and that gives the impression that he is not really here, but he is. Of course he is here. If he keeps running he too will get bigger. The thought interests him, but does not grab him; maybe he wouldn't like to be bigger. Every now and again, as he pushes the leaves into his pockets, he looks back at the black bag he has left by the shore to check it is at a distance from the tide, then he progresses forward again until his pockets are full and the sky is cleared of leaves.

He returns to the bag and catches his breath. Then he squats and reaches his hands into its endlessness, where they disappear for so long that he wonders if he has lost them. Eventually he has to peer in. Hands? he calls quietly. Where are you? There in the bag's darkness he sees them large, paper-white and ageless. It is with surprise that he manages to take hold of the urn when his hands are so desperately cloudy, but he does, he clutches it either side and, holding it to his face, sees the breakage of his reflection in the hammered silver surface.

Maybe his hands unscrew the lid or maybe the spiralling wind does – in any case he drops the lid to the stones where it falls with an insolent clang as if announcing a song it will never again sing. He kicks it aside. Step by step, and holding the urn, he walks into the sea, up to his knees at first, stopping to see one lone leaf blow past and push its way out onto the horizon, then pressing his thighs into the water until he is up to his waist. He raises the urn, tips it, and shakes the ashes to the wind. As they leave the urn the ashes appear to stop momentarily and study their reflection in the silver, and then, without a second thought, they become smoke. Might as well have had her cremated after all, he thinks lightly. The smoke leaps out and up and disperses. Goodbye mother, he says. Mother, he thinks over and over as if it is the only word left to him. Up and down the shore the stones tremble the word back.

Waist deep in water, he looks once more up the beach and finds that where it was empty it is now populated by a handful of people who he can almost claim to recognise; they are all the original people. But as soon as he attempts to speak their names he feels fraudulent. It is more that he knows *of* them than knows them. On he goes into the sea, chest-deep, neck-deep, the salt slipping into his mouth through the absurd smile on his lips.

As he wades the last few inches he feels his hand getting wet and a voice fighting through the wind.

'Come on, Jake, we haven't got all day.'

The moment falls into view: the dog licking his hand, the woman taking the other, the flat bemused smile he offers, the one she offers back. Does he not have all day? What else does one have, he wonders, if not all day? He has no idea where he is, but he gets to his feet anyhow. Everywhere is perfectly dry all of a sudden. How strange, when it was all wet. Perhaps he is dead. Alive, dead, wet, dry, what difference? What reason to be anxious?

'What day is it, Jake?'

His hands come together; he is surprised to feel his fingers touch his face. He considers the words. They are foreign words. He offers a genuine smile, pleased to be here and to see her.

'Can you tell me the year?'

'Is that, by that do you mean, in the years before?'

'No, by that I mean, what is the year we're in now?'

'Ah. Yes, yes, yes, yes. The year is, and the years is, let me see, what was that? It must be about 1935 by now.'

'Do you know why you're here today, Jake?'

He raises his eyes to her and squeezes his hands tightly. 'I believe it has something to do with my hair.'

She nods. 'Your hair?'

'It falls out. What must we do to keep it?'

'I suppose we must let it go. What do you think?'

'I suppose that's the law.'

She closes the folder on her desk and pushes a glass of water his way.

'A kind of law,' she says. 'Yes.'

CHAPTER 15

The train cuts through a thickening suburbia. At points it congeals and the train, unable to press through, stops to unload. More people get on. He worries that it will not be able to progress with this new burden, tries, without even the expectation of success, to calculate the lost weight against the gained. Where the balance? Is balance to be hoped for? Is it not better that things gradually thin out?

Once off the train they get into a car; someone unknown drives them through part-known streets, and once in a while, rising from the slump of inexplicable stone, places spark with a dim, distant familiarity. He seeks out the bombed areas but can find none. Shifting within him, from limb to limb, is the sensation that he ought to *do* something, but as the buildings drift past he sees that there is nothing left to do.

Now there are other people, it feels like crowds, and a shabby brightness bearing the stench of animals. The metal arms frighten him as they turn, so he stands back and stares at them despite the mother's best efforts at encouraging him. *Come on, Jake, it's me, Ellie.* Finally she takes his hand and goes through with him. His breath is short from walking these few paces and from the close air, which seems too much for his lungs, but even with these irritations his mood is peaceful where it wasn't, and hasn't been for longer than he can say.

There is a man with them, who, he thinks, has just arrived, or maybe he has been here all day – has he? Has he seen him before?

'At some point I'd like to see the aquarium,' the man says. 'It has water from the Bay of Biscay –'

The woman says something in reply. He hears his name being said. Slowly he turns his head and blinks.

'Anywhere you want to go first, Jake?'

The ears are full of background noise, not unpleasant but rather as though the air itself is made of something knitted. Here has existed before, or no, perhaps here always existed, this moment has been long, or possibly short, but here is thick on his ears and eyes. Ahead of him is a patch of scrubbed dry grass and on it are the large, obvious creatures, they look like old men who have lost their jobs and taken to drink, the way they hang and loll and scratch. Macaques, he thinks, out of the blue. Just a word without meaning, a word he made up. He progresses along the fence, amused and intrigued. One sits in the hook of a tree and eyes him wearily, its arms folded. Dog? he wonders. No, it has arms, hands, look at the pale affectionate hands that it wraps around the thing.

He squints at them and creases his face in thought, the way they do. 'Interesting that they have the – fingernails,' he tries. 'For getting into it all.'

'It's a gorilla,' the woman says.

He frowns. He pushes his own nails into the palms of his hands and then smiles. The creatures' observation of him suggests that they doubt he exists but that, if they observed for long enough, they could make him exist just by looking, they could will him.

'Monkey,' she says.

Monkey goes. Monkey went. *Mankind's existence is utterly justified by this gift it will give to earth – the gift of sight – do you understand? Yes, understand. Yes. Do you? Yes.* The number of eyes staring at him is incalculable. Their scrawny arms and legs would appear to be strange servants of such large bodies. They are hairy old men, they are full of stories and little lies! He pushes against the fence to see if he might get to where they are, but the woman takes his hand and shuffles him on.

Past patches of dirt and low trees, along walkways lined with litter bins; sometimes, when he shifts his gaze from the ground, he is surprised to see animals behind wire, and feels that he wants to reach through to touch them. There are the black-and-white birds stiff in a ring of blue, some very still water that they cock their heads at as if to question its motives. There is a huge spinning wheel with the painted animals easing up and down to music.

Inside they sit at a table and the man brings drinks. It is a hot day of white sweating skies, and being in the shade is a relief. The man bends to a bag and takes out a thin book, which he opens on the table, pivoting it so that everybody can see what it says.

'This is the album we made when Helen died, just a few shots of her life. You spent hours looking at it, months, do you remember it?'

His eyes water with staring, but no recollection comes.

The man runs his finger over the first picture.

'Helen with her Bible group. Don't remember all their names – Hazel, somebody, somebody, is it Cathryn or Caroline or –' He shrugs and laughs fondly. 'All the women under the cherry tree praising God. And Helen with her blessed blanket.'

Helen. Does he know her? His mother perhaps? She looks like a mother in her kind curled pose, her dress and blue and white shoes and socks that give her the appearance of somebody who has stepped from a children's story, and her hands tender on the book. She looks like somebody he has met, but people tend to become too small eventually and slip through the fingers. Every person too slippery to keep. And it is a shame

418

because she has the trusting face of somebody who could make him better, but with the slipping, with the slipping she can do nothing for him.

The next image, a familiar path arched with trees and a woman with two children – one she is holding, the other is standing at her side. The one in her arms draws his attention, she has a terrible, almost frightening vacancy to her stare as if she is in pain, or not even that, as if she simply doesn't know what is what. Not confused. Blank.

'Me, Alice and Helen,' the man says.

The woman leans forward. 'I forgot all about Helen's miniskirt. That famous miniskirt.'

The man and woman laugh quietly at something and turn the page. Here is his mother, in that brown dress, standing in silhouette in front of the wraparound window of her living room. The four gold buttons at the neck beat back the darkness. Something of him remembers something of this. He gives the stubble on his cheek a lethargic rub and stares, just stares.

'Can't think why this one of Sara is here,' the man muses. He looks closer at the picture. 'Oh yes, it's the first colour picture Helen took – with the Polaroid – that's why.'

They move their attention to the facing page. A black-and-white picture of a tree. Pale mallow colour across the sky. A picture of a white house. The next, a colour picture of that same tree and a woman amongst its leaves, wearing a dress and nothing on the feet except a cross hatch of branch shadows and patterns. The next picture: the edge place, the place with the water and rocks. At the front of the scene there is a man and child watching an animal, the wet animals that never move, and the child is in that animal's eye.

'And this one,' the man says, pulling a photograph from the book. 'This one is here. Me, you and Helen by the aviary.'

He nods but does not understand what connection there is between those people and him, or that place and the place they now sit, or even what this place is where they now sit, or why they sit here, or when it will be time to go home – except that he does at last feel sure that when it is time to go home they will. The restlessness of recent times has abated. They bend deeper to the photographs, pages of forms and colours like debris from a car crash, like litter, or otherwise secrets found in demolished walls.

In this one there is a child in a white bed, and he recognises the open, empty features on their way somewhere, but perhaps lost. The child is grinning, but the grin still gives the impression of a journey not finished, or a lack of emotion, or something. Something. He cannot pinpoint what it is except to say his heart reaches to it. He wants to touch that smile, as he wanted to touch the animals, and he wants to take the series of tubes and machines from the bed so that she can be comfortable.

'Oh, dear Alice,' the woman says. 'She had been

in hospital for such a long time, look how tiny she is.'

'This was just a few days before she died.'

The two people are silent. They pick up their cups and drink without taking their eyes from the photograph.

Eventually, turning the page, the man straightens and puts his cup down. 'And these last two are just two I added.'

One shows a woman stepping off a bus, blonde and tall with a face that is all sunlight and no definition. Even in the vagueness of the shot she is beautiful, he sees it now, the kind of woman one would want to be associated with. The man tilts his face up from the picture, then he looks down again.

'Look, there's me.'

He points to an indefinable shadow on the bus behind the woman.

'It's the day I came back from university and Helen wanted a picture of me to see if it showed up my new *distinguished* intelligence. She got excited and took it a bit early and missed. So we got a picture of this random woman instead. I said it summed things up exactly. Put it in here anyway as a joke.'

He watches the man chase the memory down with a tripping laughter, as if needing something from it.

'And the others are of you, Jake. This is a newspaper clipping of you presenting your money to the council, to be sent to support the troops in the

Six Day War. A thousand pounds, your inheritance money from under the bed. Do you remember?' The man looks up. 'You became a local hero. And when everybody said it was God who helped win that war you used to object that it wasn't God who gave all his inheritance away, and that he always got too much credit for everything.'

The man smiles, then is serious. 'And it's true. He does.'

He picks up the last photograph and holds it to the light.

'And this one – this is you too, Jake. This is the day you took that flight over Quail Woods. That was only four years ago.'

The man in the photograph is wearing a thick coat and head thing with the ear pieces. He looks weathered, nervous, and excited in a calm, slow way. His eyes seem deep and black beneath the hat, stubble shadows the chin, the hand making a thumbs-up is reluctant, but still rather young and strong looking.

I remember this man, he thinks. I have seen him. It is the first thing he has been sure about for as long as he can recall. An unrefuted fact of life is packed away in that face, behind the expression of a man who looks like he has been winded. He doesn't remember the time itself of meeting the man, not even remotely, but he remembers the man. The eyes. The shifting gaze, looking out to what is far away.

★   ★   ★

This animal here, at a distance on a dry bank, tears into meat, an activity from which it flicks its eyes now and again while holding the meat in place. What is this? Is this a dog? His dog? Its colours warn. That space between the ears and the prick of the fur that is oilier and coarser than he had expected. He takes the woman's hand.

A sea of mesh. They walk inside the structure along a wooden path, surrounded by birds, the birds rising rare and frantic. It should be glass, he thinks, not mesh. This should be a sea of glass, a mountain of it, a fake glittering sky of it. It occurs to him: people build things. It comes as something of a revelation.

The man walks beside him and rubs his shoulder.

'You brought me here when I was a baby,' the man says. 'I almost remember it, or maybe it's just from the things Helen said. I don't know. I don't know if it really makes a difference. Did you ever bring Alice here?'

He turns slowly to face the man, awash, watered down. Alice? he means to say. Who is that? Vague memory of someone – but – but no, and he cannot ask because there are not the words.

The man turns away and rotates his thumbs around one another, then threads his fingers through the mesh. Something in that gesture of dejection reminds him of somebody. It is always this: something, somebody. Everything unspecific and free-floating.

One day he would like to build a thing like this for birds, but he would like to do it with glass. He wonders how it is done, and searches through an archive of other one-day thoughts and decides whether to guard them or dispose of them: at some point in his life, for example, he would like to marry, he would like to build something, he would like to have children. There is a clean slate and a run of events to be chosen or not. For the finest shard of time he believes that he has had his life and that it is over, and a panic grips him because he cannot remember it, not a thing, he has had it and lost it, or it has lost him. The fear isolates in a flash of yellow tearing up to the top of the glass mountain. Loss. But he must not consider it.

Nothing is lost, those choices are yet to be made. As they walk on he looks up at the mesh that knits paths above him and searches out the pattern, and the patterns in the patterns, and the patterns inside those, until he has to close his eyes to the logic and settle for the yellow on the inside of his vision, which sparks, then rapidly fades. He grips the hand that has found his, opens his eyes, and walks on.

ACKNOWLEDGEMENTS

Thanks to Anna and Dan, to all who helped with the research for this book, to my writing friends Anthea, Becky, Ian, Jason, Jenni, Karen and Pam, to my family, and lastly, mostly, to Rick, Terri and Dana.